# LOGICAL FANTASY:
## THE MANY WORLDS OF
## JOHN WYNDHAM

# LOGICAL FANTASY:
## THE MANY WORLDS OF
## JOHN WYNDHAM

—

*Edited by*
### DAVID DYTE

SUBTERRANEAN PRESS 2024

*Logical Fantasy: The Many Worlds of John Wyndham*
Copyright © 2024 by The Estate of John Wyndham.
All rights reserved.

Dust jacket illustration Copyright © 2024 by Bob Eggleton.
All rights reserved.

Interior design Copyright © 2024 by Desert Isle Design, LLC.
All rights reserved.

See pages 417-418 for individual story copyrights.

Edited by David Dyte

**First Edition**

**ISBN**
978-1-64524-143-0

Subterranean Press
PO Box 190106
Burton, MI 48519

**subterraneanpress.com**

Manufactured in the United States of America

# TABLE OF CONTENTS

—

Introduction *by Michael Marshall Smith* —— 7

The Lost Machine —— 13

Spheres of Hell —— 35

The Man from Beyond —— 63

Beyond the Screen —— 91

Child of Power —— 139

The Living Lies —— 171

The Eternal Eve —— 217

Pawley's Peepholes —— 243

The Wheel —— 267

Survival —— 275

Chinese Puzzle —— 303

Perforce to Dream —— 323

Never on Mars —— 339

Compassion Circuit —— 361

Brief to Counsel —— 373

Odd —— 377

The Asteroids, 2194 —— 387

A Stitch in Time —— 403

# INTRODUCTION
*by Michael Marshall Smith*

—

WHEN YOU THINK of Wyndham, it's the novels that inevitably spring to mind. *Day of the Triffids*, perhaps, or *The Midwich Cuckoos*—twice brought memorably to the screen as *The Village of the Damned*. Classic stories, of course, genre-defining and inspirational to generations of writers since.

There's a similarity to his near-contemporary Jack Finney, however (best-known for the seminal *The Bodysnatchers*, which by coincidence has also been filmed well on two occasions), in that much of Wyndham's most interesting ideas lie nestled in a body of short story work that winds its way through several genres. Genre is a hard call with Wyndham: even the two most famous novels might be seen as sitting in science fiction on the one hand, and horror on the other. Stephen King bluntly asserted that Wyndham was "the best writer of science fiction England has ever produced." David Mitchell gets much closer, however, when he claims Wyndham was "a true English visionary, a William Blake with a science doctorate."

Rationality married with imagination. "Logical fantasy," in fact. Christopher Priest added something important when he observed that Wyndham described "the odd rather than the fantastic, the disturbing rather than the horrific, the remarkable rather than the outrageous." Part of what helps Wyndham's fiction steer into deeper and more resonant territories than the merely fantastic, horrific or outrageous, is how grounded they are. How true they feel, emotionally, intellectually, and socially.

And how oddly modern.

―

THERE IS A beguiling variety in the stories in this collection, which are presented in chronological order of writing.

There are early stories like "The Lost Machine," and "Spheres of Hell". While these are jewels of 1930s sense-of-wonder SF, they're enriched by a writerly skill at entering the tale sideways, and through Wyndham always taking care to establish how the events would feel. Then come tales like "Beyond the Screen" and "Child of Power," which—while entirely satisfying in their own right—contain enough imaginative power to have been expanded into novels. In this they contrast nicely with "Brief to Counsel" or "Compassion Circuit," which each have one strong idea to convey, and come in low and hard to inject it into your mind with concision and force.

There are others like "Living Lies" or "The Eternal Eve" or "The Wheel" that enshrine a form of social commentary—using the prism of the future or other worlds to critique the ever-present. Wyndham is fundamentally concerned with humankind's constant battle with our own nature, as when he writes in "The Wheel:" "No discovery is good or evil until men make it so." At times this insight evolves into a concern with the overtly political. In "The Living Lies" a character observes: "It's an old, old game. Make the people distrust one another, keep them at loggerheads, prevent them from uniting for their rights, and you can rule"—an observation just as telling today, when the working classes in countries like the United Kingdom, and races all over the world, are encouraged toward fighting each other rather than noticing how they're all shackled within societal structures designed to work to their disadvantage.

Later in the story the character attempts to excuse a group's regrettable actions by saying, "They were savages at that moment. It's no good pretending they weren't. The thing to do is change the system that makes them that way." Again, a strikingly contemporary observation.

# INTRODUCTION

Wyndham had a varied life before he settled to being a full-time writer—featuring stints in the law, farming, advertising, then time in the army as a censor in the Ministry of Information and cipher operator in the Royal Corps of Signals, before joining the Normandy landings. He lived for many years in the Quaker-funded Penn Club in London, encountering a mix of socialists, pacifists and feminists that informed his writing for the rest of his life. He wasn't merely making things up for the fun of it. He had things to say. "The Eternal Eve," for example, presents a meditation on the role of women in society that's unusual for its time, especially from a male writer.

It contains beautiful throw-away phrases like, when discussing the attitude of two more worldly women to another's scholarship—"which they appeared to regard as a cleverly developed, though rather impractical, form of higher guesswork"—but also a clinical analysis of the actions of men, again put in the voice of a female character: "In a dump like this you've got to have a boss of some kind. A stuffed one was okay—with a government in back of him—but when the government's gone, and some guy's let out the rest of the stuffing then you just naturally find other guys getting big ideas. And the climate's likely to get kinda lively while they're deciding whose idea is the biggest."

Every post-apocalyptic television show of today, summed up neatly in a paragraph from seventy years ago.

The women are one of the most striking elements in Wyndham's tales. Almost without exception, if there's a female character then they'll be at the heart of the action, and often the most clear-sighted and richly drawn. Even in tales written during the pulp era he had no truck with the weak, decorative or ownable females of so much fiction of the time. His women were strong. They did things, and they meant them, and sometimes—as in "Survival"—they come from behind to overtake the men in dark or extraordinary ways.

In Wyndham's stories it's often the women who are the square-jawed heroes, and men who seem lost.

EACH OF THE tales in this volume contradicts Brian Aldiss's brisk dismissal of Wyndham's work as "cozy catastrophes." In truth the stories are never cozy, and instead often deeply unsettling. The resolution of a particular situation doesn't imply the world has been fixed too. Margaret Atwood noted that "The Midwich Cuckoos" could be interpreted as "a graphic metaphor for the fear of unwanted pregnancies," an issue which remains extremely volatile to this day. Wyndham had a knack for settling on the issues that truly matter. Moreover, his tales often have an intriguing little surprise to confront you with at the end. An ending isn't always the ending, much as with real life.

His cultural observations are similarly prescient. Consider this quote from "Pawley's Peepholes," written in 1951: "His definition of a fact is anything that gets printed in a newspaper—poor fellow. He doesn't mind a lot what subjects his facts cover so long as they're queer. I suspect that he once heard that the truth is never simple, and deduced from that that everything's not simple must be true." If you substitute "on the Internet" for "in the newspaper," doesn't that exactly nail a vast swathe of public attention right now, most especially the vocal and conspiracy-driven right?

This juxtaposes well with "Never on Mars," in which one character takes another to task for their rational rigidity: "'You've got a scientific theory,' he said. 'But me, I take things as they come—not as I think they should be.'"

You'll have to read the story to discover whose perspective wins. Wyndham was not a writer to bang only one kind of drum. He was a rational man, but didn't let rationality run away with him. His fantasies may have been logical, but never merely that.

—

IT'S ALL VERY well stories being intellectually satisfying, but with short fiction—all fiction, but perhaps especially shorts—they're no good, and there's no point to them, if they don't engage the heart and soul too. They need to sit with you afterwards, as if you have been through a genuine experience. Good fiction must touch the mind, the soul, and the heart. "Logical" simply means

# INTRODUCTION

"according to the best-known human reasoning." Unless you engage the truly human in the reader, the logic won't resonate.

Wyndham's stories achieve this, all of them. There's "Chinese Puzzle," in which a simple Welsh family is confronted with an unexpected parcel in the mail—an event which is built out with a determined rationality that's both undeniable and hilarious, politically wry and studded with insight into how real people act and feel. The same is true in "Perforce to Dream" and "The Asteroids, 2194," where affecting concerns of the soul are held up to view and left challengingly unresolved, as they should be. There are questions that have no answers, and often they're precisely the ones we should be asking ourselves.

—

FINALLY, THE STORIES all make sense. That's the remarkable thing. They're fundamentally plausible. They feel like they could happen—that they might, in fact, be happening right now.

You can't summon a sense of wonder simply by throwing ideas around. They have to fit with each other in a context that makes them feel real. Sometimes the sense is straightforward. At others it is curious, uncanny, just out of reach, compelling you to reach for it—as in "Odd" and "A Stitch in Time," two of my personal favorites in this collection: stories that dare to stand poised on the edge of rationality, trusting you'll feel the truth in them.

This means that Wyndham's fiction is not just still deeply relevant, but always will be. To capture the reader's mind you have to take their heart along for the ride. Through reading something fantastical and wondrous—that you believe nonetheless makes a kind of sense—you open the doors of your own perception. You see the world through a wider and more enriching lens.

That's the highest goal of all speculative fiction, and John Wyndham was very, very good at it.

Enjoy.

# THE LOST MACHINE

—

"**FATHER, HERE, QUICKLY.**" Joan's voice called down the long corridor. Dr. Falkner, who was writing, checked himself in mid-sentence at the sound of his daughter's urgency.

"Father," she called again.

"Coming," he shouted as he hastily levered himself out of his easy-chair.

"This way," he added for the benefit of his two companions.

Joan was standing at the open door of the laboratory.

"It's gone," she said.

"What do you mean?" he inquired brusquely as he brushed past her into the room. "Run away?"

"No, not that," Joan's dark curls fell forward as her head shook. "Look there."

He followed the line of her pointing finger to the corner of the room.

A pool of liquid metal was seeping into a widening circle. In the middle there rose an elongated, silvery mound which seemed to melt and run even as he looked. Speechlessly he watched the central mass flow out into the surrounding fluid, pushing the edges gradually farther and farther across the floor.

Then the mound was gone—nothing lay before him but a shapeless spread of glittering silver like a miniature lake of mercury.

For some moments the doctor seemed unable to speak. At length he recovered himself sufficiently to ask hoarsely:

"That—that was it?"

Joan nodded.

"It was recognizable when I first saw it," she said.

Angrily he turned upon her.

"How did it happen? Who did it?" he demanded.

"I don't know," the girl answered, her voice trembling a little as she spoke. "As soon as I got back to the house I came in here just to see that it was all right. It wasn't in the usual corner and as I looked around I caught sight of it over here—melting. I shouted for you as soon as I realized what was happening."

One of the doctor's companions stepped from the background.

"This," he inquired, "is—was the machine you were telling us about?"

There was a touch of a sneer in his voice as he put the question and indicated the quivering liquid with the toe of one shoe.

"Yes," the doctor admitted slowly. "That was it."

"And, therefore, you can offer no proof of the talk you were handing out to us?" added the other man.

"We've got film records," Joan began tentatively. "They're pretty good…"

The second man brushed her words aside.

"Oh yes," he asked sarcastically. "I've seen pictures of New York as it's going to look in a couple of hundred years, but that don't mean that anyone went there to take 'em. There's a whole lot of things that can be done with movies," he insinuated.

Joan flushed, but kept silent. The doctor paid no attention. His brief flash of anger had subsided to leave him gazing at the remains before him.

"Who can have done it?" he repeated half to himself.

His daughter hesitated for a moment before she suggested:

"I think—I think it must have done it itself."

"An accident? —I wonder," murmured the doctor.

"No—no, not quite that," she amended. "I think it was—lonely," the last word came out with a defiant rush.

There was a pause.

"Well, can you beat that?" said one of the others at last. "Lonely—a lonely machine: that's a good one. And I suppose you're trying to feed us that it committed suicide, Miss? Well, it wouldn't surprise me any; nothing would, after the story your father gave us."

He turned on his heel and added to his companion:

"Come on. I guess someone'll be turnin' this place into a sanitarium soon—we'd better not be here when it happens."

With a laugh the two went out, leaving father and daughter to stare helplessly at the residue of a vanished machine.

At length Joan sighed and moved away. As she raised her eyes, she became aware of a pile of paper on the corner of a bench. She did not remember how it came to be there and crossed with idle curiosity to examine it.

The doctor was aroused from his reverie by the note of excitement in her voice.

"Look here, Father," she called sharply.

"What's that?" he asked, catching sight of the wad of sheets in her hand.

As he came closer he could see that the top one was covered with strange characters.

"What on earth…?" he began.

Joan's voice was curt with his stupidity.

"Don't you see?" she cried. "It's written this for us."

The doctor brightened for a moment; then the expression of gloom returned to his face.

"But how can we…?"

"The thing wasn't a fool—it must have learned enough of our language to put a key in somewhere to all this weird stuff, even if it couldn't write the whole thing in English. Look, this might be it, it looks even queerer than the rest."

Several weeks of hard work followed for Joan in her efforts to decipher the curious document, but she held on with painstaking labour until she was able to lay the complete text before her father. That evening he picked up the pile of typed sheets and read steadily, without interruption, to the end…

## ARRIVAL

AS WE SLOWED to the end of our journey, Banuff began to show signs of excitement.

"Look," he called to me. "The third planet, at last."

I crossed to stand beside him and together we gazed down upon a stranger scene than any other fourth planet eyes have ever seen.

Though we were still high above the surface, there was plenty to cause us astonishment.

In place of our own homely red vegetation, we beheld a brilliant green. The whole land seemed to be covered with it. Anywhere it clung and thrived as though it needed no water. On the fourth planet, which the third planet men call Mars, the vegetation grows only in or around the canals, but here we could not even see any canals. The only sign of irrigation was one bright streak of water in the distance, twisting senselessly over the countryside—a symbolic warning of the incredible world we had reached.

Here and there our attention was attracted by outcroppings of various strange rocks amid all this green. Great masses of stone which sent up plumes of black smoke.

"The internal fires must be very near the surface of this world," Banuff said, looking doubtfully at the rising vapours.

"See in how many places the smoke breaks out. I should doubt whether it has been possible for animal life to evolve on such a planet. It is possible yet that the ground may be too hot for us—or rather for me."

There was a regret in his tone. The manner in which he voiced the last sentence stirred my sympathy. There are so many disadvantages in human construction which do not occur in us machines, and I knew that he was eager to obtain first-hand knowledge of the third planet.

For a long time we gazed in silent speculation at this queer, green world. At last Banuff broke the silence.

"I think we'll risk a landing there, Zat," he said, indicating a smooth, open space.

"You don't think it might be liquid," I suggested, "it looks curiously level."

"No," he replied, "I fancy it's a kind of close vegetation. Anyway, we can risk it."

A touch on the lever sent the machine sinking rapidly towards a green rectangle, so regular as to suggest the work of sentient creatures. On one of its sides lay a large stone outcrop, riddled with holes and smoking from the top like the rest, while on the other three sides, thick vegetation rose high and swayed in the wind.

"An atmosphere which can cause such commotion must be very dense," commenced Banuff.

"That rock is peculiarly regular," I said, "and the smoking points are evenly spaced. Do you suppose…"

The slight jar of our landing interrupted me.

"Get ready, Zat," Banuff ordered.

I was ready. I opened the inner door and stepped into the air-lock. Banuff would have to remain inside until I could find out whether it was possible for him to adjust. Men may have more power of originality than we, and they do possess a greater degree of adaptability than any other form of life, but their limitations are, nevertheless, severe. It might require a deal of ponderous apparatus to enable Banuff to withstand the conditions, but for me, a machine, adaptation was simple.

The density of the atmosphere made no difference save slightly to slow my movements. The temperature, within very wide limits, had no effect upon me.

"The gravity will be stronger," Banuff had warned me, "this is a much larger planet than ours."

It had been easy to prepare for that by the addition of a fourth pair of legs.

Now, as I walked out of the air-lock, I was glad of them; the pull of the planet was immense.

After a moment or so of minor adjustment, I passed around our machine to the window where Banuff stood, and held up the instruments for him to see. As he read the air-pressure meter, the gravity indicator and the gas proportion scale, he shook his head. He might slowly adapt himself partway to the conditions, but an immediate venture was out of the question.

It had been agreed between us that in such an event I should perform the exploration and specimen collecting while he examined the neighbourhood from the machine.

He waved his arm as a signal and, in response, I set off at a good pace for the surrounding green and brown growths. I looked back as I reached them to see our silvery craft floating slowly up into the air.

A second later, there came a stunning explosion; a wave of sound so strong in this thick atmosphere that it almost shattered my receiving diaphragm.

The cause of the disaster must always remain a mystery: I only know that when I looked up, the vessel was nowhere to be seen—only a rain of metal parts dropping to earth all about me.

Cries of alarm came from the large stone outcrop and simultaneously human figures appeared at the lowest of its many openings.

They began to run towards the wreck, but my speed was far greater than theirs. They can have made but half the distance while I completed it. As I flashed across, I could see them falter and stop with ludicrous expressions of dismay on their faces.

"Lord, did you see that?" cried one of them.

"What the devil was it?" called another.

"Looked like a coffin on legs," somebody said. "Moving some, too."

# FLIGHT

BANUFF LAY IN a ring of scattered debris.

Gently I raised him on my fore-rods. A very little examination showed that it was useless to attempt any assistance: he was too badly broken. He managed to smile faintly at me and then slid into unconsciousness.

I was sorry. Though Banuff was not of my own kind, yet he was of my own world and on the long trip I had grown to know him well. These humans are so fragile. Some little thing here or there breaks—they stop working and then, in a short time, they are decomposing. Had he been a machine, like myself, I could have mended him, replaced the broken parts and made him as good as new, but with these animal structures one is almost helpless.

I became aware, while I gazed at him, that the crowd of men and women had drawn closer and I began to suffer for the first time from what has been my most severe disability on the third planet—I could not communicate with them.

Their thoughts were understandable, for my sensitive plate was tuned to receive human mental waves, but I could not make myself understood.

My language was unintelligible to them, and their minds, either from lack of development or some other cause, were unreceptive to my thought-radiations.

As they approached, huddled into a group, I made an astonishing discovery—they were afraid of me.

Men afraid of a machine.

It was incomprehensible. Why should they be afraid? Surely man and machine are natural complements: they assist one another. For a moment I thought I must have misread their minds—it was possible that thoughts registered differently on this planet, but it was a possibility I soon dismissed.

There were only two reasons for this apprehension. The one, that they had never seen a machine or, the other, that third planet machines had pursued a line of development inimical to them.

I turned to show Banuff lying inert on my fore-rods. Then, slowly, so as not to alarm them, I approached. I laid him down softly on the ground near by and retired a short distance. Experience has taught me that men like their own broken forms to be dealt with by their own kind. Some stepped forward to examine him, the rest held their ground, their eyes fixed upon me.

Banuff's dark colouring appeared to excite them not a little. Their own skins were pallid from lack of ultra-violet rays in their dense atmosphere.

"Dead?" asked one.

"Quite dead," another one nodded. "Curious-looking fellow," he continued. "Can't place him ethnologically at all. Just look at the frontal formation of the skull—very odd. And the size of his ears, too, huge: the whole head is abnormally large."

"Never mind him now," one of the group broke in, "he'll keep. That's the thing that puzzles me," he went on, looking in my direction. "What the devil do you suppose it is?"

They all turned wondering faces towards me. I stood motionless and waited while they summed me up.

"About six feet long," ran the thoughts of one of them. "Two feet broad and two deep. White metal, might be—(his thought conveyed nothing to me). Four legs to a side, fixed about halfway up—jointed rather like a crab's, so are the arm-like things in front: but all metal. Wonder what the array of instruments and lenses on this end are? Anyhow, whatever kind of power is uses, it seems to have run down now…"

Hesitatingly he began to advance.

I tried a word of encouragement.

The whole group froze rigid.

"Did you hear that?" somebody whispered. "It—it spoke."

"Loudspeaker," replied the one who had been making an inventory of me. Suddenly his expression brightened.

"I've got it," he cried. "Remote control—a telephony and television machine worked by remote control."

So these people did know something of machinery, after all. He was far wrong in his guess, but in my relief I took a step forward.

An explosion roared: something thudded on my body case and whirred away. I saw that one of the men was pointing a hollow rod at me and I knew that he was about to make another explosion.

The first had done no injury but another might crack one of my lenses.

I turned and made top speed for the high, green vegetation. Two or three more bursts roared behind, but nothing touched me. The weapon was very primitive and grossly inaccurate.

## DISAPPOINTMENT

FOR A DAY and a night I continued on among the hard stemmed growths.

For the first time since my making, I was completely out of touch with human control, and my existence seemed meaningless. The humans have a curious force they call ambition. It drives them, and, through them, it drives us. This force which keeps them active, we lack. Perhaps, in time, we machines will acquire it. Something of the kind—self-preservation which is allied to it—must have made me leave the man with the explosive tube and taken me into the strange country. But it was not enough to give me an objective. I seemed to go on because—well, because my machinery was constructed to go on.

On the way I made some odd discoveries.

Every now and then my path would be crossed by a band of hard matter, serving no useful purpose which I could then understand. Once, too, I found two unending rods of iron fixed horizontally to the ground and stretching away into the distance on either side. At first I thought they might be a method of guarding the land beyond, but they presented no obstacle.

Also, I found that the frequent outcroppings of stone were not natural, but laboriously constructed. Obviously this primitive race, with insufficient caves to hold its growing numbers, had been driven to construct artificial caves. The puzzling smoke arose from their method of heating these dwellings with naked fire—so wasteful a system of generating heat that no flame had been seen on the fourth planet,[1] save in an accident, for thousands of years.

It was during the second day that I saw my first machine on this planet.

It stood at the side of one of the hard strips of land which had caused me so much wonder. The glitter of light upon its bright parts caught my lenses as I came through the bushes. My delight knew no bounds—at last I had found a being of my own kind. In my excitement I gave a call to attract its attention.

There was a flurry of movement round the far side and a human figure raised its head to look at me.

I was able to tell that she was a woman despite the strange coverings that the third planet humans put upon themselves. She stared at me, her eyes widening in surprise while I could feel the shock in her mind. A spanner dropped from her hand and then, in a flash, she was into the machine, slamming the door behind her. There came a frantic whirring as she pressed a knob, but it produced no other result.

Slowly I continued to advance and as I came, the agitation in her mind increased. I had no wish to alarm her—it would have been more peaceful had her thought waves ceased to bombard me—but I was determined to know this machine.

As I drew clear of the bushes, I obtained a full view of the thing for the first time and disappointment hit me like a blow. *The thing had wheels.* Not just necessary parts of its internal arrangements, but wheels actually in

---
[1] Mars.

contact with the ground. In a flash the explanation of all these hard streaks came to me. Unbelievable though it may seem, this thing could only follow a track specially built for it.

Later I found this was more or less true of all third planet[2] land machines, but my first discouragement was painful. The primitive barbarity of the thing saddened me more than any discovery I had yet made.

Forlornly, and with little hope, I spoke to it.

There was no answer.

It stood there dumbly inert upon its foolish wheels as though it were a part of the ground itself.

Walking closer, I began to examine with growing disgust its crude internal arrangements. Incredibly, I found that its only means of propulsion was by a series of jerks from frequent explosions. Moreover, it was so ludicrously unorganized that both driving engine and brakes could be applied at the same time.

Sadly, as I gazed at the ponderous parts within, I began to feel that I was indeed alone. Until this encounter, my hope of discovering an intelligent machine had not really died. But now I knew that such a thing could not exist in the same world with this monster.

One of my fore-rods brushed against a part of it with a rasping sound and there came a startled cry of alarm from within. I looked up to the glass front where the woman's face peered affrightedly. Her mind was in such a state of confusion that it was difficult to know her wants clearly.

She hoped that I would go away—no, she wished the car would start and carry her away—she wondered whether I were an animal, whether I even really existed. In a jumble of emotions she was afraid and at the same time was angry with herself for being afraid. At last I managed to grasp that the machine was *unable* to run. I turned to find the trouble.

As I laboured with the thing's horrible vitals, it became clear to me why men, such as I had met, showed fear of me. No wonder they feared machines when their own mechanisms were as inefficient and futile as this. What reliance

---

[2] The earth.

or trust could they place in a machine so erratic—so helpless that it could not even temporarily repair itself? It was not under its own control and only partially under theirs. Third planet men's attitude became understandable—commendable—if all their machines were as uncertain as this.

The alarm in the woman's mind yielded to amazement as she leaned forward and watched me work. She seemed to think me unreal, a kind of hallucination:

"I must be dreaming," she told herself. "That thing can't really be mending my car for me. It's impossible; some kind of horrid nightmare..."

There came a flash of panic at the thought of madness, but her mind soon rebalanced.

"I just don't understand it," she said firmly and then, as though that settled it, proceeded to wait with a growing calm.

At last I had finished. As I wiped the thing's coarse, but necessary oil from my fore-rods, I signalled her to push again on the black knob. The whirr this time was succeeded by a roar—never would I have believed that a machine could be so inefficient.

Through the pandemonium I received an impression of gratitude on my thought plate. Mingling traces of nervousness remained, but first stood gratitude.

Then she was gone. Down the hard strip I watched the disgusting machine dwindle away to a speck.

Then I turned back to the bushes and went slowly on my way. Sadly I thought of the far away, red fourth planet and knew that my fate was sealed. I could not build a means of return. I was lost—the only one of my kind upon this primitive world.

## THE BEASTS

THEY CAME UPON me as I crossed one of the smooth, green spaces so frequent on this world.

My thought-cells were puzzling over my condition. On the fourth planet I had felt interest or disinterest, inclination or the lack of it, but little more. Now

I had discovered reactions in myself which, had they lain in a human being, I should have called emotions. I was, for instance, lonely: I wanted the company of my own kind. Moreover, I had begun to experience excitement or, more particularly, apathy.

An apathetic machine!

I was considering whether this state was a development from the instinct of self-preservation, or whether it might not be due to the action of surrounding matter on my chemical cells, when I heard them coming.

First there was a drumming in my diaphragm, swelling gradually to a thunderous beat which shook the ground. Then I turned to see them charging down upon me.

Enormous beasts, extinct on my planet a million years, covered with hair and bearing spikes on their heads. Four-footed survivals of savagery battering across the land in unreasoning ferocity.

Only one course was possible since my escape was cut off by the windings of one of the imbecile-built canals. I folded my legs beneath me, crossed my fore-rods protectingly over my lenses and diaphragms, and waited.

They slowed as they drew close. Suspiciously they came up to me and snuffled around. One of them gave a rap to my side with his spiked head, another pawed my case with a hoofed foot. I let them continue: they did not seem to offer any immediate danger. Such primitive animals, I thought, would be incapable of sustaining interest and soon move off elsewhere.

But they did not. Snuffling and rooting continued all around me. At last I determined to try an experimental waving of my fore-rods. The result was alarming. They plunged and milled around, made strange bellowing noises and stamped their hooves, but they did not go away. Neither did they attack, though they snorted and pawed the more energetically.

In the distance I heard a man's voice; his thought reached me faintly.

"What the 'ell's worritin' them dam cattle, Bill?" he called.

"Dunno," came the reply of another. "Let's go an' 'ave a look."

The beasts gave way at the approach of the man and I could hear some of them thudding slowly away, though I did not, as yet, care to risk uncovering my lenses.

The men's voices drew quite near.

"'Strewth," said the first, "'ow did that get 'ere, Bill?"

"Search me," answered the other. "Wasn't 'ere 'arf an hour ago—that I'll swear. What is it, any'ow?"

"'Anged if I know. 'Ere, give us a 'and and we'll turn it over."

At this moment it seemed wise to make a movement; my balancers might be slow in adjusting to an inverted position.

There was a gasp, then:

"Bill," came an agitated whisper, "did you see that rod there at the end? It moved, blessed if it didn't."

"Go on," scoffed the other. "'Ow could a thing like that move? You'll be sayin' next that it…"

I unfolded my legs and turned to face them.

For a moment both stood rooted, horror on their faces, then, with one accord, they turned and fled towards a group of their buildings in the distance. I followed them slowly: it seemed as good a direction as any other.

The buildings, not all of stone, were arranged so as almost to enclose a square. As the men disappeared through an opening in one side, I could hear their voices raised in warnings and others demanding the reason for their excitement. I turned the corner in time to face a gaggling group of ten or twelve. Abruptly it broke as they ran to dark openings in search of safety. All, save one.

I halted and looked at this remaining one. He stared back, swaying a little as he stood, his eyes blinking in a vague uncertainty.

"What is it?" he exclaimed at last with a strange explosiveness, but as though talking to himself.

He was a sorely puzzled man. I found his mental processes difficult to follow. They were jumbled and erratic, hopping from this mind picture to that in uncontrolled jerks. But he was unafraid of me and I was glad of it. The first third planet man I had met who was not terror-ridden. Nevertheless, he seemed to doubt my reality.

"You fellowsh shee the shame s'I do?" he called deafeningly.

Muffled voices all around assured him that this was so.

"Thash all right, then," he observed with relief, and took a step forward.

I advanced slowly not to alarm him and we met in the middle of the yard. Laying a rough hand on my body-case he seemed to steady himself, then he patted me once or twice.

"Goo' ol' dog," he observed seriously. "Goo' ol' feller. Come 'long, then."

Looking over his shoulder to see that I followed and making strange whistling noises the while, he led the way to a building made of the hard, brown vegetable matter. At openings all about us scared faces watched our progress with incredulous amazement.

He opened the door and waved an uncertain hand in the direction of a pile of dried stalks which lay within.

"Goo' ol' dog," he repeated. "Lie down. There'sh a goo' dog."

In spite of the fact that I, a machine, was being mistaken for a primitive animal, I obeyed the suggestion—after all, he, at least, was not afraid.

He had a little difficulty with the door fastening as he went out.

## THE CIRCUS

THERE FOLLOWED ONE of those dark periods of quiet. The animal origin of human beings puts them under the disability of requiring frequent periods of recuperation and, since they cannot use the infra-red rays for sight, as we do, their rests take place at times when they are unable to see.

With the return of sunlight came a commotion outside the door. Expostulations were being levelled at one named Tom—he who had led me here the previous day.

"You ain't really goin' to let it out?" one voice was asking nervously.

"'Course I am. Why not?" Tom replied.

"The thing don't look right to me. I wouldn't touch it," said another.

"Scared, that's what you are," Tom suggested.

"P'raps I am—and p'raps you'd 've been scared last night if you 'adn't been so far gone."

"Well, it didn't do nothin' to me when I'd had a few," argued Tom, "so why should it now?"

His words were confident enough, but I could feel a trepidation in his mind.

"It's your own funeral," said the other. "Don't say afterwards that I didn't warn you."

I could hear the rest of them retire to what they considered a safe distance. Tom approached, making a show of courage with his words.

"Of course I'm goin' to let it out. What's more, I'm takin' it to a place I know of—it ought to be worth a bit."

"You'll never…"

"Oh, won't I?"

He rattled open the door and addressed me in a fierce voice which masked a threatening panic.

"Come on," he ordered, "out of it."

He almost turned to run as he saw me rise, but managed to master the impulse with an effort. Outwardly calm, he led the way to one of those machines which use the hard tracks, opened a rear door and pointed inside.

"In you get," he said.

I doubt if ever a man was more relieved and surprised than he, when I did so.

With a grin of triumph he turned around, gave a mocking sweep with his cap to the rest, and climbed into the front seat.

My last sight as we roared away was of a crowd of open-mouthed men.

The sun was high when we reached our destination. The limitations of the machine were such that we had been delayed more than once to replenish fuel and water before we stopped, at last, in front of large gates set in a wooden fence.

Over the top could be seen the upper parts of pieces of white cloth tightly stretched over poles and decorated by further pieces of coloured cloth flapping in the wind. I had by this time given up the attempt to guess the purposes of third planet constructions, such incredible things managed to exist on this primitive world that it was simpler to wait and find out.

From behind the fence a rhythmical braying noise persisted, then there came the sound of a man's voice shouting above the din:

"What do you want—main entrance is round the other side."

"Where's the boss?" called Tom. "I got something for him."

The doors opened to allow us to enter.

"Over there in his office," said the man, jerking a thumb over his shoulder.

As we approached I could see that the third planet mania for wheels had led them even to mount the 'office' thus.

Tom entered and reappeared shortly, accompanied by another man.

"There it is," he said, pointing to me, "and there ain't another like it nowhere. The only all-metal animal in the world—how'll that look on the posters?"

The other regarded me with no enthusiasm in his eyes and a deal of disbelief in his mind.

"That long box thing?" he inquired.

"Sure, 'that box thing.' Here, you," he added to me, "get out of it."

Both retreated a step as I advanced, the new man looked apprehensively at my fore-rods.

"You're sure it's safe?" he asked nervously.

"Safe?" said Tom. "'Course it's safe."

To prove it he came across and patted my case.

"I'm offering you the biggest noise in the show business. It's worth ten times what I'm asking for it—I tell you, there ain't another one in the world."

"Well, I ain't heard of another," admitted the showman grudgingly. "Where'd you get it?"

"Made it," said Tom blandly. "Spare time."

The man continued to regard me with little enthusiasm.

"Can it do anything?" he asked at last.

"Can it—?" began Tom indignantly. "Here you," he added, "fetch that lump of wood."

When I brought it, the other looked a little less doubtful.

"What's inside it?" he demanded.

"Secrets," said Tom shortly.

"Well, it's got to stop bein' a secret before I buy it. What sort of a fool do you take me for? Let's have a look at the thing's innards."

"No," said Tom, sending a nervous look sideways at me. "Either you take it or you leave it."

"Ho, so that's your little game, is it? I'm to be the sucker who buys the thing and then finds the kid inside, workin' it. It wouldn't surprise me to find that the police'd like to know about this."

"There ain't no kid inside," denied Tom, "it's just—just secret works. That's what it is."

"I'll believe you when I see."

Tom waited a moment before he answered.

"All right," he said desperately, "we'll get the blasted lid off of it... Here, hey, come back you."

The last was a shout to me but I gave it no notice. It was one thing to observe the curious ways of these humans, but it was quite a different matter to let them pry into my machinery. The clumsiness of such as Tom was capable of damaging my arrangements seriously.

"Stop it," bawled Tom, behind me.

A man in my path landed a futile blow on my body-case as I swept him aside. Before me was the biggest of all the cloth-covered erections.

"Here," I thought, "there will be plenty of room to hide."

I was wrong. Inside, in a circular space, stood a line of four-footed animals. They were unlike the others I had met in that they had no spikes on their heads and were of a much slenderer build, but they were just as primitive. All around, in tier upon tier of rings, sat hundreds of human beings.

Just a glimpse, I had, and then the animals saw me. They bolted in all directions and shouts of terror arose from the crowd.

I don't remember clearly what happened to me, but somewhere and somehow in the confusion which followed I found Tom in the act of starting his car. His first glance at me was one of pure alarm, then he seemed to think better of it.

"Get up," he snapped, "we've got to get clear of this somehow—and quick."

Although I could make far better speed than that preposterous machine, it seemed better to accompany him than to wander aimlessly.

## THE CRASH

SADLY, THAT NIGHT I gazed up at the red, fourth planet.

There rolled a world which I could understand, but here, all around me, was chaos, incredible, unreasoning madness.

With me, in the machine, sat three friends of Tom's whom he had picked up at the last town, and Tom himself who was steering the contraption. I shut my plate off from their thoughts and considered the day I had spent.

Once he was assured that we were free from pursuit, Tom had said to himself:

"Well, I guess that deserves a drink."

Then he stopped on a part of the hard strip which was bordered by a row of artificial caves.

Continually, as the day wore on, he led me past gaping crowds into places where every man held a glass of coloured liquid. Strange liquids they were, although men do not value water on the third planet. And each time he proudly showed me to his friends in these places, he came to believe more firmly that he had created me.

Towards sunset something seemed to go seriously wrong with his machinery. He leaned heavily upon me for support and his voice became as uncertain as his thoughts were jumbled.

"Anybody comin' my way?" he had inquired at last and at that invitation the other three men had joined us.

The machine seemed to have become as queer as the men. In the morning it had held a straight line, but now it swayed from side to side, sometimes as though it would leave the track. Each time it just avoided the edge, all four men would break off their continuous wailing sounds to laugh senselessly and loudly.

It was while I struggled to find some meaning in all this madness that the disaster occurred.

Another machine appeared ahead. Its lights showed its approach and ours must have been as plain. Then an astounding thing happened. Instead of avoiding one another as would two intelligent machines, the two lumbering masses charged blindly together. Truly this was an insane world.

There came a rending smash. Our machine toppled over on its side. The other left the hard strip, struck one of the growths at the side of the road and burst into naked flames.

None of the four men seemed more than a little dazed. As one of them scrambled free, he pointed to the blaze.

"Thass good bonfire," he said. "Jolly good bonfire. Wonder if anybody'sh inshide?"

They all reeled over to examine the wreck while I, forgotten, waited for the next imbecility to occur on this nightmare world.

"It'sh a girl," said Tom's voice.

One of the others nodded solemnly.

"I think you're right," he agreed with difficult dignity.

After an interval, there came the girl's voice.

"But what shall I do? I'm miles from home."

"'S'all righ'," said Tom. "Quite all righ'. You come along with me. Nishe fellow I am."

I could read the intention behind his words—so could the girl.

There was the sound of a scuffle.

"No, you don't, my beauty. No runnin' away. Dangeroush for li'l girlsh—'lone in the dark."

She started to scream, but a hand quickly stifled the sound.

I caught the upsurge of terror in her mind and at that moment I knew her.

The girl whose machine I had mended—who had been grateful.

In a flash I was among them. Three of the men started back in alarm, but not Tom. He was contemptuous of me because I had obeyed him. He lifted a heavy boot to send it crashing at my lens. Human movement is slow: before his leg had completed the back swing, I had caught it and whirled him away. The rest started futilely to close in on me.

I picked the girl up in my fore-rods and raced away into the darkness out of their sight.

## DISCOURAGEMENT

AT FIRST SHE was bewildered and not a little frightened, though our first meeting must have shown that I intended no harm.

Gently I placed her on top of my case-work and, holding her there with my fore-rods, set off in the direction of her journey. She was hurt, blood was pouring down her right arm.

We made the best speed my eight legs could take us. I was afraid lest from lack of blood her mind might go blank and fail to direct me. At length it did. Her mental vibrations had been growing fainter and fainter until they ceased altogether. But she had been thinking ahead of us, picturing the way we should go, and I had read her mind.

At last, confronted by a closed door she had shown me, I pushed it down and held her out on my fore-rods to her father.

"Joan...?" he said, and for the moment seemed unsurprised at me—the only third planet man who ever was. Not until he had dressed his daughter's wounds and roused her to consciousness did he even look at me again.

There is little more. They have been kind, those two. They have tried to comprehend, though they cannot. He once removed a piece of my casing—I allowed him to do so, for he was intelligent—but he did not understand. I could feel him mentally trying to classify my structure among electrically operated devices—the highest form of power known to him, but still too primitive.

This whole world is too primitive. It does not even know the metal of which I am made. I am a freak...a curiosity outside comprehension.

These men long to know how I was built; I can read in their minds that they want to copy me. There is hope for them: some day, perhaps, they will have real machines of their own... But not through my help will they build them, nothing of me shall go to the making of them.

...I know what it is to be an intelligent machine in a world of madness...

# THE LOST MACHINE

THE DOCTOR LOOKED up as he turned the last page.

"And so," he said, "it dissolved itself with my acids."

He walked slowly over to the window and gazed up to Mars, swimming serenely among a myriad stars.

"I wonder," he murmured, "I wonder."

He handed the typewritten sheets back to his daughter.

"Joan, my dear, I think it would be wisest to burn them. We have no desire to be certified."

Joan nodded.

"As you prefer, Father," she agreed.

The papers curled, flared and blackened on the coals—but Joan kept a copy.

# SPHERES OF HELL

—

THE PRINCE KHORDAH of Ghangistan was in a bitter mood. His council, seated cross-legged upon a semi-circle of cushions before him, had come to know too well that look of dissatisfaction. Of late it had seemed to dwell perpetually upon his dark features. The members of the council were aware of his words before he spoke, so often had they heard them.

"To all great nations" he observed, "might is right. Today we hear much talk of the rights of small nations—and to what does it amount? Nothing but so much dust in the wind to fill the eyes of those who would see."

He glowered upon his councillors. Each appeared occupied in an interested study of the mosaic floor; the beauty of its patterns was more soothing than the expression on the Prince's face. More than one grimy forefinger scratched in its owner's beard in order to give a misleading suggestion of thought.

The council was formed entirely of old men. Not that old men are always wise, but they do have the advantage of less fiery ambition, and, whether one is a Prince in Ghangistan, or a Big Shot in Chicago, too much ambition at court will prove embarrassing. The ambitions of most of the council rose little higher than a bountiful supply of food and drink and an occasional change of wives. The Prince continued to address unresponsive figures:

"What can we do? These English, and other foreigners, trifle with us. They do not so much as stir to consider our demands. We are treated like children—we, of Ghangistan, whose temples and palaces were weathered when these English hid in caves, whose ancestors reach back unbroken to the creation. We offer them war, and they laugh as one laughs at the ferocity of a cornered mouse. Here we must sit, impotent, while they pour over our country the froth and ferment of their way of life, in mockery of the wisdom of our sacred ancestors."

Again the Prince paused and looked questioningly about him. At the lack of response he shrugged his shoulders; some of the spirit seemed to go out of him, and he threw out his hands in token of helplessness.

"And we can do nothing. We have no big guns, no aeroplanes. We must sit by and watch our ancient race seduced from its gods, and hear the voice of wisdom drowned by the sounding emptiness of materialism."

He finished dejectedly. His anger had subsided beneath fatalism, and he brooded amid the respectful, if slightly bored silence of the council. One ancient looked up and studied the Prince. He allowed a decent interval to elapse before he inquired:

"Is it permitted to speak?"

The Prince regarded him with but little lifting of his despondency. "It is permitted to you, Haramin," he agreed.

The old man stroked his beard for some moments in placed reflection.

"It has seemed to me," he began with slow deliberateness, "that already we are more affected by the Westerners than we acknowledge. Even our methods of thought have become curiously coloured by their mental processes. We begin now to distort our pure wisdom to fit their strange conventions."

A murmur of protest ran round the council, but none dare give full voice to his indignation, for the old man was privileged.

"Explain the full meaning," commanded the Prince.

"It is well shown by an example, My Prince. See how these Westerners wage war. First they send a declaration to warn their enemies—is this not absurd? Then they use against that enemy a series of weapons similar to his own—which is plainly ridiculous. They have, in fact, rules for war—a conceit worthy only of children or imbeciles.

"We, in our wisdom, know better. We know that wars should be won or lost; not childishly prolonged until both sides give up for very weakness and weariness. And yet"—he paused and looked around him—"and yet we sit here lamenting our lack of weapons, lamenting that we cannot meet our oppressors on their own ground. It is a foolishness to consider the standards of the West in war."

The Prince Khordah frowned. The tone of the other's speech displeased him, but he was aware that some deeper thought had prompted it. He asked coldly:

"Is it necessary here, Haramin, to lurk like an old fox in a thicket of words?"

"I have a nephew, Prince, a man of great learning in the ways of the West, yet retaining the wisdom of his ancestors. He has a plan which should interest Your Highness."

The Prince leaned forward. At last they seemed to be getting somewhere.

"Where is this nephew, Haramin?"

"I have brought him to await Your Highness' summons."

The Prince struck a silver gong beside him. To the entering servant he said:

"The nephew of Haramin waits. Let him be brought before us."

## CHAPTER ONE

## THE MYSTERIOUS GROWTHS

RALPH WAITE'S FATHER beamed genially across the dinner-table.

"It's good to have you home again, my boy," he said. "How long do you think you can manage?"

Ralph, a lusty, fair-haired young man, turned towards him. "Only the week-end, I'm afraid, Dad."

Mrs. Waite looked up with a little wrinkle of concern and disappointment.

"Is that all, dear? Don't you think if you wrote nicely to them they might let you stay a little longer?"

Ralph checked a rising smile. "I don't think it would be much good writing nicely to Amalgamated Chemicals, Mother," he said gravely.

"I suppose you know best, dear, but—"

Mr. Waite broke in with some little excitement:

"I've got something to show you after dinner, Ralph. Quite the most remarkable thing in all my gardening experience."

His eyes were on his plate, so that he missed the look with which his wife favoured him.

"But, dear," she began, "Ralph will want to—"

Ralph checked her with a glance. Of course he wanted to go and see Dorothy. His real desire was to rush off at this very moment, but he knew his father's enthusiasm for his hobby. The old man would be sadly disappointed if he could not impress his son with his latest horticultural triumph. After all, Ralph reflected, the old boy got little enough pleasure, pushed away in this little Cornish town for the rest of his life.

"What is it?" he asked.

Mr. Waite chuckled. "You'll see, my boy. All in good time; all in good time."

The town of St. Brian lies not far from the south coast of Cornwall. A swift river, the Bod, flows through it on its way to join the English Channel at a point where it is almost the Atlantic Ocean. To the north one can see those strange, dazzling white cones which are the refuse of the clay pits, and from the higher points it is possible to trace the course of the Bod right down to the sea in the south.

The houses are mostly built of grey stone, their roofs clamped down upon them lest they should be whirled off by the gales which in winter sweep in from the Atlantic. In sheltered spots, where they are able to take advantage of kindly climate, flowers and plants thrive, as was excellently testified by Mr. Waite's garden.

Dinner concluded, he led the way importantly across a stretch of smooth lawn to the thick hedge masking the far corner of his ground. As they reached a gap he paused, and with something of the manner of a showman, waved his son forward.

"There, my boy," he said proudly. "Just take a look at that!"

Ralph, as he stepped forward to the hedge, was fully prepared to be impressed, but at the sight which met him, the nicely turned phrases he had thought up for the other's gratification fled away. He stared speechlessly for a moment, then:

"What on earth's that?" he demanded.

"Ah, I thought it'd surprise you. Fine growth, what?"

# SPHERES OF HELL

"But—what *is* the thing?" persisted Ralph, gazing in horrified fascination.

"Well," Mr. Waite admitted doubtfully, "I don't think it's been named yet—sort of experiment they got me to try out. A new form of marrow or something of the sort, I gather. Wait a minute, and I'll get the letter…"

—

HE BUSTLED ACROSS the lawn while his son turned to regard the 'fine growth' with renewed interest. Experiment or not, he decided that it was quite one of the most unwholesome looking plants he had ever seen. Roughly spherical, it reminded him mostly of a pumpkin with a diameter every bit of two feet.

But it was not so much the size which was responsible for his surprise as the colour. It lay before him, clammily glistening in the evening sunlight, a ball of blotchy, virulent yellow. The ground all round it was bare, and it lay on one side attached to the earth only by a poor, twisted wisp of a stalk, as foolishly disproportionate as a pig's tail.

"Must be a good weight, a thing that size," he muttered to himself. With some distaste, he inserted his hand beneath it, and then stared at the thing in blank surprise. It weighed possibly a pound.

He was still staring at it when Mr. Waite returned with a paper fluttering in his hand.

"Here you are. That, and the instructions for growing, are all I know about it."

Ralph took the typewritten letter. It was headed 'Slowitt & Co.,' and underneath in smaller type was added: 'Agents for Experimental Growers Company.'

Dear Sir [he read], in the course of our experimental work we have succeeded in evolving a new form of vegetable. We have the greatest hopes that this extremely prolific plant will successfully adapt itself to a great range of climatic conditions. In so far as we have been able to reproduce the various conditions in our laboratories, the results leave nothing to be desired, and we now feel that the time has come to put the plant to test in the actual climates it will have to face.

Our agents, in pursuance of our instructions to find persons likely to be interested in this development, forwarded us your name as that of a consistently successful exhibitor at a number of fruit and vegetable shows, and as one who takes an interest in the scientific side of horticulture. We have, therefore, great pleasure in asking you if you would consider assisting us in the introduction of this new form..."

Ralph read far enough to enable him to grasp essentials.

"This is all very well, Dad," he remarked. "But what on earth's the good of the thing? It must be hollow; have you felt its weight?"

"Oh, that's all right. It says in the growing instructions, which they sent with the seeds, that one must not be surprised at the extraordinary lightness. I gather that when it is full-grown it begins to solidify or harden. Though it is a queer looking thing, I'll admit, and so were the seeds."

He fished in his pocket and found an object which he handed over.

"I kept this one out of curiosity. You see, they've enclosed it—or, rather, several of them—in a kind of capsule. The instructions were emphatic that the capsule must not be opened in any circumstances."

"Then how—?"

"You just bury the whole thing and water it very plentifully; I suppose that dissolves the capsule and lets the thing begin to grow. It certainly shows a fine turn of speed. You'd never guess how long it is since I planted this chap." He stirred the yellow ball with his toe.

Ralph did not attempt the guess. "How long?" he inquired.

"Three days," said his father with pride. "Only three days to reach that size! Of course, I'm not sure how long it will be before it's any use, but it's started very well, and—"

But Mr. Waite's intended lecture was frustrated. His wife's voice tactfully summoned him to the house.

"Don't tell anyone about this, yet, my boy. I promised to keep it quiet till the thing should be full-grown," he said as he hurried across the lawn.

Ralph thankfully departed on his intended visit. Later, he was unable to remember whether it was curiosity or absence of mind which caused the one remaining seed capsule to find its way into his pocket; he only knew that it was lucky he had kept it.

―

DOROTHY FORBES HAD expected Ralph earlier. She had even employed sundry of her waiting moments in inventing such reproaches as might be becoming in a lady slightly neglected. It was a pleasant mental exercise, but little more; Ralph's method of greeting did not allow of the interview being placed on a dignified basis.

Instead of venting displeasure, she smoothed her frock, shook back her fair hair, wondered for a moment why one should blush quite so warmly, and suggested that there was a swing seat in the garden.

The swing seat was such a success that it was quite half an hour before an object on the other side of the garden caught Ralph's eye and caused him to sit up, staring. Just visible over the top of a cucumber frame was a curved section of a familiar yellow surface.

"Good Lord!" he said.

"What?" asked Dorothy. Following his line of sight, she added: "Oh, that's one of Daddy's secrets—you're not supposed to see it."

"Well, now I have seen it, what about a closer view?"

"I suppose it doesn't really matter, but don't tell him you've seen it."

A few seconds sufficed to settle any lingering doubt. The plant behind the frame was identical with that in his father's garden, though possibly a few inches smaller.

"That's queer," Ralph murmured.

Dorothy nodded, though she misapplied the remark.

"I think it's horrid. I told Daddy I'm sure it's unhealthy, but he only laughed at me. Somehow I hate the thing. There's such a nasty, poisonous look about that yellow."

"He's keeping it secret?"

"Yes; he's very jealous about it. He says it will make him famous one day."

Ralph nodded. This made it queerer still. He considered for a moment. Two people, each thinking himself unique, were growing this most unprepossessing vegetable.

"What about a little walk?" he suggested. Dorothy, with slight surprise at the sudden change of subject, assented.

It was a wandering stroll, apparently aimless. Nevertheless, it took them close to a number of back gardens. Altogether, they counted over twenty of the strange yellow balls.

CHAPTER TWO

## THE RASH

WHEN RALPH RETURNED home to London, it was obvious that in a very short time there would be no more concealment of the strange growths. They were swelling to prodigious sizes with a swiftness which was rendering secrecy impossible. Already two peppery gentlemen who had considered themselves favoured experimenters had discovered one another's rivalry and were indulging in wordy unpleasantness.

It could not be long before all twenty, and other yet undiscovered growers, would hear about it and join in the indignation. Dorothy's next letter, therefore, did not astonish him when it announced that the cats were out of the bag and the gardeners of the town of St. Brian were in full cry for one another's blood.

"When our fathers discovered that they were rivals," she wrote, "it was bad enough. But now there are more than a score of them tearing their hair and threatening legal proceedings. It isn't only in St. Brian, either. We've heard reports that hundreds of gardeners both in Cornwall and west Devon are growing the things.

"Ours is so big, too. It's over four feet in diameter now, and looks more evil than ever. I'm beginning to feel a bit afraid of it; I know that sounds silly, but it's the truth. I told Daddy the other day that there was something wicked about it and that I was sure it was never meant to grow in England, but he only laughed and said neither were potatoes. All the same, I think the balls are beastly things. I hear that some boys cut the stalk of one near Newquay and rolled it down the cliffs so that it burst. I'd like to do the same with ours, only I hate the idea of touching the thing—ugh!"

The earlier part of the letter caused Ralph some quiet smiles. He knew very well the temperament of the amateur gardener, with all its jealousies and enthusiasms, and the prospect of the warfare which must now be disturbing the community could give the unprejudiced onlooker no little amusement. But he grew more serious as he recalled the sickening appearance of those growths when they were only two feet in diameter; already they had swelled to four…

Unreasoning as Dorothy's dislike of them might be, he found himself able to understand it and to sympathise with it. He was worried by the feeling, for he preferred reason to prejudice.

Nevertheless the matter was gradually slipping into the back of his mind until it was recalled a few days later by a paragraph tucked away at the foot of a newspaper column:

> "Several cases are reported from Newquay, the well-known Cornish holiday resort, of an outbreak of rash which is puzzling the local doctors. It is thought that the condition may be consequent upon prolonged or injudicious exposure of the skin while sunbathing."

For a moment he was puzzled to know when he had lately thought of Newquay; then he remembered that it was near there that the yellow ball had been pushed over the cliffs.

—

DOROTHY'S NEXT LETTER informed him that a state of excitement was prevailing all over the West Country. The inhabitants, it appeared, had split into two schools of thought on the subject of the yellow balls.

The growers and their friends were noisily upholding their rights to grow what they liked on their own land, while the opposition, without apparent grounds for the statement, proclaimed that the things were unhealthy. They shared, Dorothy surmised, her revulsion against them. Some days before a minor riot of protest had taken place in Bodmin. In the course of it, three balls had been slashed open.

After he had finished the letter, Ralph turned to his newspaper and found information which brought wrinkles of speculation to his forehead.

The cases of rash at Newquay had become serious. One of the victims had died, and the others were in a precarious condition. It was, according to the correspondent, impossible to state definitely that the rash was the cause of death, but he evidently had more than suspicions.

Then followed the information that the same mysterious rash had made its appearance at Bodmin, coupled with an assurance that it could not, in the later cases, be in any way attributed to sunbathing.

Thoughtfully, Ralph withdrew his father's seed capsule from his pocket and regarded it.

"I may be a fool. It's probably just a coincidence, but it's worth investigating," he told himself.

Before he sought his own office, he called in at the laboratory of a friend who worked in the bio-chemical department of Amalgamated Chemicals, Ltd.

Two days passed before he heard any result of the examination of the capsule. Then Arnold Jordan, the bio-chemist, entered his office just as he was finishing off for the day.

"You've tackled it?" asked Ralph.

Arnold nodded.

"Yes, I've tackled it. And I'm not sure whether I owe you a dinner for putting me on to it, or whether you owe me a dinner for putting in the devil of a lot of work. On the whole, I approve of the latter."

"Oh, all right. You look as if some good food wouldn't do you any harm. Come on!"

It was not until the end of the dinner, over the coffee and cigarettes, that Arnold consented to discuss his conclusions. Then he began with an expostulation.

"I do think, old man, you might have given me a bit more warning about that beastly stuff you brought along."

"Well, I told you I had an idea it was pretty noxious," Ralph pointed out. "But, after all, the reason I brought it at all was that I didn't know much about it."

"Where did you get it?" asked Arnold curiously.

His manner shed its slight banter, and a look of seriousness crept into his eyes, as Ralph explained.

"Good God! You don't mean to say these things are being grown! What for?"

"Food—what else does one grow vegetables for?"

"But this is a fungus."

"I thought it looked that way, but quite a lot of fungi are edible when they're cooked."

Arnold failed to reply for some seconds; he seemed not to have heard and was staring fixedly into space. When he turned back Ralph was startled by the expression on his face.

"Do you know anything about fungi?"

"No," replied Ralph promptly.

"Well, I'll be short about it, but I'll try to show you what this business means. First of all, there are two types of fungi. Either a fungus is a saprophyte and lives upon decaying matter, or else it is a parasite, in which case it exists upon living matter. As far as the saprophytes are concerned—well, you've eaten a good many in your time as mushrooms or cheese, or a hundred other ways; but the parasites are not so numerous—the kind which most frequently afflicts human beings is ringworm.

"Now this particular bit of evil which you kindly handed to me is neither one nor other of these forms; it is both. That is to say that it flourishes equally well on decay, or on living flesh. Do you see what I'm getting at?"

Ralph began to see.

"This thing," Arnold continued, "is not only a parasite, but a more vicious parasite than any known. All these growths you have told me of must be scotched—utterly wiped out and obliterated before they can become ripe. Once allowed to burst and scatter their spores—" He spread his hands expressively.

Ralph regarded him nervously. "You're sure of this?"

Arnold nodded. "Of the danger I am certain. About the plant itself I'm very puzzled. Obviously the spores were enclosed in a soluble capsule so that they might be planted and brought to fruit in safety.

"If your information is correct, the whole thing seems to be deliberate, and on a large scale. It is not merely a case of scattering a few spores to grow haphazard, but immense trouble has been taken to induce people to cultivate the fungi so that millions of spores will be spread."

He paused, and added: "It's up to us to try to stop this thing, old man. Somebody must, or it's God help thousands of miserable people!"

Ralph was silent. He remembered the mysterious rash at Newquay, and the similar outbreak at Bodmin. He recalled, too, the sight of that slimy, yellow ball in his father's garden, and his face was pale as he looked at the other.

"We're too late," he said. "It's begun."

## CHAPTER THREE

## THE DANGER INCREASES

"STUFF!" SAID MAJOR Forbes, with some violence. "Stuff and nonsense! You ought to have known better, young man, than to come to me with an old wive's tale like that."

Ralph gave up his attempt to convince the old man. After Arnold's warning of the previous evening, he had caught the earliest possible train for the West Country and travelled all night. There had not been any time to lose. So far as he knew, the enormous puff-balls might burst of their own accord at any hour, quite apart from the danger of one of them receiving an accidental puncture and spreading its spores about the neighbourhood.

He had arrived, tired and anxious, to be greeted by both his own and Dorothy's father with complete disbelief. In vain he put the cases of rash forward as evidence and quoted Arnold's warning. It was useless. Each, at the back of his mind, seemed determined that this was some deep ruse by rival growers to get him out of the way; and, even if the thing was a fungus, what man worth his salt was going to be scared by a mere puff-ball, however big?

"No," Major Forbes repeated firmly. "You say that your mother and my daughter are willing to leave—of course they are. Women are always wanting to run up to London for some fal-lal or other. Take 'em along with you; the change'll do 'em good. But don't come bothering me!"

And there was a similar interview with his own father. Mrs. Waite attempted to smooth over her husband's irritation.

"Now, don't worry your father any more, dear. You must see that he doesn't want to come. I should like to go to London for a week or so, but don't bother him. I should have to go soon, in any case, to do a little shopping."

"But you don't understand, Mother. This is really serious—it's dangerous. These things he is growing are rank poison!"

Mrs. Waite looked a little distressed.

"Do you really think so, dear? I mean, it seems so unlikely—and the people who sent them don't seem to think so. They definitely said they were vegetables."

"Never mind what they said. Take it from me—or, rather, from Arnold, who is an expert—that these things are deadly and must be destroyed."

"Eh? What's that?" Mr. Waite chimed in. "Destroyed? I'd like to see anyone attempt to destroy my specimen. I'd show him what's what! There's still a law in the land."

"You'll promise me, won't you, John, not to eat any of it while I am away?" Mrs. Waite spoke as though her presence should nullify the plant's poisonous quality. Her husband ungraciously conceded the point.

"All right," he said gruffly. "I'll promise you that much—though I repeat that I think the whole thing is a scare."

"Well if you won't come, I can't make you," said Ralph, "but I do beg of you—"

Again he went over the details of Arnold's warning, only to succeed in thinning his father's temper and his own. At last he turned back to Mrs. Waite.

"This is a waste of time. You'd better pack your things and get ready, Mother."

"You mean now, dear?"

"Yes. At once."

"Oh, but I couldn't possibly be ready before tomorrow. There are such a lot of things which just have to be finished off."

Ralph went around again to see Dorothy.

"We'll have to wait until tomorrow," he told her. "I can't make them believe there's any danger in delay."

"Well, one day won't make much difference," she suggested.

"It might. I want to get you both out of here as soon as possible. Any moment it may be too late."

"We'll be right away this time tomorrow. Now let's talk about something else."

"I can't think of anything else. I've heard Arnold on the subject, and you haven't. Let's go out and have a look at the brutes."

―

"HULLO," SAID ARNOLD, entering Ralph's office. "Where the devil have you been for the last two days?"

"Down in Cornwall; trying to make my people clear out."

"Did you?"

"Got Dorothy and my mother up here. Neither of the fathers would shift—stubborn old fools! What have you been up to?"

Arnold disregarded the question. "You've done all you could?"

"Of course I have—short of kidnapping the old blighters."

Arnold looked grave.

"I'm afraid the news is rather serious," he began. "The morning after our chat I went round to see a fellow I know at the Ministry of Health, and they welcomed me there with open arms. This thing is a good many times bigger than we thought it was. The authorities have been minimising—didn't want to ruin the holiday traffic, or some rot like that. They told me that there have been hundreds of cases of the rash and several dozen deaths. Not only that, but soon after the dead have been buried those yellow puff-balls start growing from the graves.

# SPHERES OF HELL

"Their experts were as sure as I was that this form of fungus has never been heard of before, and most of us are pretty certain that somebody has been up to some rather ugly cross-breeding, with malice aforethought. They issued orders yesterday that no more of the things were to be planted, but that was useless; already round the centres where the things have burst, the place is littered with the balls."

"Growing already?"

"Thousands of them, around Newquay and Bodmin and several other places. And nobody dare touch them."

"But aren't they doing anything—destroying them?"

"How?"

"Can't they—can't they spray them with acids, or something? Do you realise that the first lot hasn't reached its natural bursting point yet? All this second crop is the result of accidental breakage. God knows what will happen if they are allowed to burst."

"Nobody seems to know how to tackle the situation. But they're not lying down; they see the danger all right, and they're going after it day and night. You can see yourself that the problem is how to destroy the balls without liberating the spores."

"There must be some way..."

"Oh, they'll find a way, but it's got to be drastic and well organised. The thing they're most anxious about at present is that there shall be no panic. You know what people are like when they lose their heads. If they go wild and start smashing the things wholesale, there'll be hell to pay. You can take it from me that the departments concerned are already making things hum behind the scenes."

"Meanwhile, the first crop of balls must be pretty nearly ripe..."

---

RALPH SEARCHED THE lounge of the hotel where his mother and Dorothy were staying. He eventually found Mrs. Waite occupying a comfortable arm-chair in a secluded corner. He greeted her, and seated himself beside her.

"Where's Dorothy?" he asked a few minutes later. "Getting ready?"

"Ready?" repeated Mrs. Waite inquiringly.

"We arranged to go out and dance this evening."

"Oh, dear me, of course. Then you didn't hear from her—she said she would telephone."

"She didn't. What was it about?"

"Well, she won't be able to go out tonight. You see, she's gone down to Cornwall."

"She's what?" shouted Ralph, in a voice which echoed across the lounge.

"Yes, dear, she said she felt she must go to Cornwall," Mrs. Waite repeated placidly.

"But why didn't you stop her? Surely you realise the danger? Good God, she may have caught the rash—she may die of it!"

Mrs. Waite looked a little shocked.

"Well, dear, I did tell her that I didn't think you would like it. But she seemed so anxious about her father—such a nice trait in a young girl, I always think—that I didn't feel it was right to interfere."

Ralph made no reply. His mother, glancing at him, saw that his face was drawn into tight creases. There was an expression in his eyes which hurt her. For the first time she began to appreciate that there was real fear behind his actions and talk of the last few days. Futilely she started to talk when she should have kept silent.

"Of course, this may not be so very dangerous after all. I expect it's just another of these scares. Things will be all right in the end, and we shall all have a good laugh at our fears. Don't you worry, dear; I expect—good gracious!"

Ralph was roused out of his thoughts to see what had caused her exclamation of surprise. He looked up to find himself facing his father and Major Forbes. An hour ago he would have been pleased to see them and cheered by the thought that the whole party was reunited; but now his greeting was cold.

Major Forbes looked around him.

"And where is Dorothy?" he asked.

Ralph answered him bitterly.

"She's gone to save you," he said.

## CHAPTER FOUR

## FIGHTING THE MENACE

"YES, MY BOY," said Mr. Waite, "we certainly owe our escape to you. You seemed so positive about the danger that I did a bit of investigating; poked about a bit among the local officials.

"It was old Inspector Roberts who gave me the tip—he's always considered himself in my debt over that matter of his boy. 'Mr. Waite,' he said, 'I ought not to tell you; in fact, I'm breaking orders by doing so, but if you take my advice you'll get out of the district just as soon as you can.'"

"Yes, it was a straight tip, by gad!" agreed the Major. "I managed to hear a few things about the country round about—pretty bad. Some fool started a panic in Launceston. Half the town was out with sticks and stones and knives, smashing all the yellow balls they could find.

"A man told me the ground was white with spores, as if there had been a snowstorm. Some of the growers tried to interfere, and there was something like a battle. Pretty much the same thing seems to have happened in Tavistock and other places in west Devon."

Ralph looked up.

"Spores or riots," he said, "I'm going down by the midnight train to get Dorothy out of that. What's the time now?"

The Major snorted.

"Don't be a fool, young man! The girl's all right. She'll be back any moment now, I'll warrant. They're not allowing anyone to enter the area now, so she'll *have* to come back. Your father and I came out on one of the last trains allowed through."

"What's the time?" Ralph demanded again.

"Twenty to ten," said the Major, "and I repeat that you are wasting your time if you go down there."

"The news," Mr. Waite said suddenly. "There's sure to be something about all this." He called a waiter and asked for the radio to be switched on. A few moments later they were listening to the calm, familiar voice of the London announcer.

The general weather report was unencouraging and the voice went on to add:

"Gale warning. The Meteorological Office issued the following warning to shipping at twenty hours, Greenwich Mean Time. Strong westerly winds, rising to gale force, may be expected on all the Irish coast. English coast west of a line from Southampton to Newcastle, and English Channel."

Ralph glanced at his father, who caught his eye, but sent a warning glance in the direction of his mother. Both of them grasped the implication. Thousands of light, yellow balls attached merely by skimpy stalks—and a gale rising…

The announcer began on the news:

"We are asked by the Ministry of Transport to broadcast the following. Suspension of service. All train services between Exeter and points west thereof have been temporarily suspended. Further details will be announced tomorrow."

The Major looked at Ralph triumphantly.

"I told you so! They're isolating the whole district. There's no point in your going down. We shall have Dorothy back here in no time."

But Ralph was unconvinced. Dorothy had set out to get to her home, and he had a horrid fear that she would do it if it were humanly possible. The Major did not seem to know his own daughter's tenacity of purpose. Ralph stood up with determination.

"I'm going down there *now*. There are still cars, even if they have stopped the trains."

---

THUMP…THUMP…THUMP…WENT RALPH'S MALLET. It was three days since he had left London, and now he was engaged in driving stakes into the hard soil of Dartmoor.

A message earlier in the day had informed him that no news had been received of Dorothy. There could be no doubt that she had been trapped in the isolated area and was now—if she had succeeded in reaching St. Brian—still forty or fifty miles to the west of him. He reflected angrily on the events which had landed him at his present occupation.

# SPHERES OF HELL

He had rushed from the hotel in search of Arnold. Before midnight he had borrowed the other's car and was running down Piccadilly, in company with the taxis of homeward-bound theatre-goers. The traffic grew faster and sparser as he passed through sprawling suburbs. He looked forward to showing a good turn of speed on the Great West Road. But when he reached it the volume of traffic had undeniably increased once more.

Long lines of trucks, not too punctilious about keeping to the side of the road, stretched before him. A constant flow of private cars against him, unprecedented for the time of night, made it a difficult business to overtake the trucks. Ralph cursed the obstruction of the lumbering line and noticed for the first time that they were not commercial vans, but were painted khaki or grey, with Army markings on their sides. He swore again. A piece of foul luck to get mixed up in Army manoeuvres; but perhaps they would drop off at Aldershot. They did not. They held on the road to the west and, to his exasperation, were augmented by hundreds more.

"Anybody would think," he muttered to himself, "that there was a war on. The whole blooming Army seems to be going my way!"

To add to his troubles, the wind was rising, bringing with it sharp flurries of rain. Instead of making a dash through the night as he had intended, his speed was reduced to a crawl. Only infrequently did the traffic against him allow him to cut past a few of the lumbering shapes ahead. It was full daylight long before he reached Exeter, and he passed through the narrow streets of the old city still escorted by the Army wagons.

Two miles beyond, the road was blocked by a barricade. Sentries with fixed bayonets were assisting the police to turn back all private cars. The representatives of both forces were equally unmoved by his offers of money or his loss of temper.

"It's no good makin' a fuss, young feller," advised a police sergeant. "If I'd been taking money today, I could have made my fortune and retired on it. You get back 'ome now!"

There had been nothing for it but to turn his car round and drive sullenly back to Exeter. There he munched a necessary, though unappreciated, meal, while he decided on the next move.

"No private cars along 'ere," the policeman had said. But the trucks were going through—those same damned trucks which had hindered him all night. Hundreds of them. They were passed without question, and, moreover, without a search. It ought to be possible to jump one and stow away…

---

AFTER A NUMBER of uncomfortable miles the truck stopped. The tail board was lowered.

"'Ere, you, come along out of it," demanded a voice. A hand fastened firmly on to Ralph's collar and dragged him painfully from his hiding place amid wooden stakes and rolls of barbed wire. He landed among a group of men under the command of a sergeant. The latter came close to him, his pointed moustache adding ferocity to his expression as he shouted:

"What the —— blazes do you think you were doing in that —— lorry? You come along 'ere with me."

The officer to whom he was taken had heard him out and then regarded him seriously.

"I like your spirit," he said, "but just listen to me a minute. You seem to know something of the situation, but you're tackling it the wrong way. It's no good going over there." He waved his hand to the west. "You couldn't do a damned thing if you got through, except make yourself another victim.

"Your girl doesn't want you to die. You know, if you give it a moment's thought, that she'd be far prouder of you for helping to fight this stuff and beat it; for helping to blot the damned growths out and make thousands of people safe."

"But she's—!"

"And don't you realise that from the body of every man who dies out there, more of the yellow balls grow? If you go out there, you'll not only be helpless, but you'll be giving your body to feed them. No, my lad, your job is to help us fight against the menace. This is a state of emergency, and we need all the help we can get. What about it?"

Ralph at length consented, though with not too good a grace. He knew the officer was right. It was his job to fight, not to throw away his life, but… He did not quite trust himself. Sometime the urge to find Dorothy might prove too strong for him...

His working partner's voice broke in on his thoughts. "What d'yer say to a cigarette, mate?"

Ralph delivered a final blow to the stake they were fixing, and agreed. To right and left of them across the moorland hills stretched the long line of posts. Here and there, parties of men who had completed their sections were already beginning to weave an impenetrable net of barbed wire around the stakes. Behind, on the roadway, was a never-ending line of trucks loaded with more wire and yet more stakes, while closer, between themselves and the road, a sweating army of men laboured to dig a broad trench.

Ralph was amazed at the organisation which in two or three days had enabled the authorities to be well on the way to barricading off a whole corner of the country. At the same time he was puzzled; the purpose of the wire was obvious, but he failed to understand the reason for the broad, shallow trench. Nor was his partner, Bill 'Awkins, as he called himself, able to explain its use. But he was ready to concede that the authorities knew what they were about, and were not wasting any time.

"Yus," he remarked, "they're quick on the job, they are. Why, a few nights ago there was a gale warning—p'raps you 'eard it?"

Ralph nodded.

"Well, the minute they knew that, they changed their plans like a flash. This 'ere line was to 'ave been miles farther forward; they'd even begun to get the supplies up there when the order for retreat came. You see, the wind in these parts is pretty near always from the west; that's what's got 'em scared—the idea of this stuff being swept right across the country. If it's true what they say about some feller a-startin' it on purpose, then 'e picked a likely place.

"'Owever, the wind didn't come to much, after all. Most of them yeller balls just rolled a bit, and then got stuck in the valleys and 'ollows and suchlike—blamed lucky it was, too."

"Then all this," said Ralph, indicating the defences, "is in case a real storm comes along?"

"That'll be about the idea," Bill agreed.

They smoked for a while in silence. From time to time a great plane would roar across the moor, carrying food supplies to be dropped to the isolated; and, once, a large caterpillar tractor came swaying and plunging past them, bound for the west. Bill grinned as he caught sight of the men aboard it and the instruments they held.

"What are they?" asked Ralph. "Looks like a squad of divers going on duty."

"Asbestos suits and masks," the other explained. "And they're carrying flame-throwers. Those'll give the blinkin' things a bit of a toasting!"

## CHAPTER FIVE

# THE ATTACK ON THE WIND

SOME SIX NIGHTS later, Ralph sat with a group in the stable which was their billet. One man was holding forth pessimistically.

"I supposed they're doing a bit of good with all this flame-throwing and whatnot, but it ain't getting 'em far. It's the plant underneath that they want to get at, not just the yellow balls. They're only the fruit—you don't kill an apple-tree by knocking off the apples. Fungi have a sort of web of stuff spreading all through the ground around them; that's the life of the things, and that's what they—"

There came a thunderous knocking on the door and a stentorian call to turn out.

"Wind's rising," said the sergeant. "You all know your jobs. Get to 'em, and look slippy!"

The wind swept in from the Atlantic at gale force. The first few puffs stirred the yellow balls and rolled them a little at the ends of their skimpy stalks. Later followed a gust which twisted them so that the stalks snapped and they were free to roll where the wind urged. As the pressure grew to a steady blast, it swept up a mass of the light balls and carried them bounding across the countryside, an army of vegetable invaders launching their attack to capture the land and destroy human beings.

The wind of a week before had moved only the balls in the most exposed positions, but this time, none but the youngest and least developed had the

# SPHERES OF HELL

strength in their stalks to resist the air which tore at them. Every now and then a splashing flurry of white would spring from the hurtling, bouncing horde as the tough, yellow skin of one was ripped by some sharp spike or the corner of a roof. Then the great spores themselves were caught up by the wind and carried on faster as an advance guard of the yellow army.

The gale seemed to display a diabolical zest for this new game. It increased its force to drive the balls yet more furiously. Hedges, ditches and trees failed to check the headlong charge. Even rivers proved no obstacle; with the wind behind, the balls sailed across in their thousands, bobbing and jerking on the rough surface.

They were thrust relentlessly down the narrow streets of the little towns, jostling and jamming against the corners of the buildings until the houses were hidden in a cloud of swirling spores, and the surviving balls tore loose to follow bowling in the wake of their fellows.

This time, the wind did not desert them. Many lodged in sheltered hollows, but they served merely to fill them up and make a path over which the rest could travel. The wave of invaders climbed the slopes and swept up and out on to the moor, where, unobstructed, they gathered speed to charge yet more swiftly upon the defenders.

There was a line of fire across the country. Ralph had soon learned the purpose of the broad trench. Filled now with blazing oil and wood, it formed a rampart of flame.

"Here they come," cried the look-out, clinging to a swaying perch high above.

Soon all could see the few whirling balls which seemed to lead the way, and the turgid mass of yellow pressing close behind the outrunners.

They held their breaths...

The first balls hurled themselves to destruction upon a *cheval-de-frise*, a hedge of bristling spikes which slit and tore their skins and set free the spores to go scudding on into the flames. But they came too thick and fast. In many places they piled up solid against the sharp fence, forming ramps for those behind to come racing over the top and fall among the meshes of barbed wire.

Every now and then a ball seemed to leap as though it possessed motive power within itself. Missing the wire, it would bowl across no-man's-land to a final explosion in the flaming ditch, its burning spores shooting aloft like the discharge of a monstrous firework.

"My God!" muttered the man next to Ralph. "If this wind doesn't drop soon, we'll be done. Look at that!"

'That' was one of several balls which, miraculously escaping all traps prepared for it, had leaped past them into the darkness behind.

"They'll catch it in the nets back there and burn it when the wind drops," Ralph replied with a confidence which he scarcely felt. "The thing that worries me is that the fires may die down—we can't get near to fuel them from the lee side here."

But, as luck had it, the fires outlasted the wind.

—

"MEN," BEGAN THE officer in charge, the next morning, "it was a pretty near thing last night, and we have to thank providence that we successfully withstood it. But we can't afford to waste time. We've got to get to work at once. There may be another wind any time, and that mass of stuff choking the spikes must be cleared before it comes. I want every man who has experience of flame-throwers to step forward."

Ralph, in company with many others, stepped out. He had no knowledge of flame-throwers, but it was the only way he could acquire an asbestos suit and get out into the danger area. For more than a week he had stifled his anxiety to know Dorothy's fate, and now he could bear it no longer.

As he struggled into the heavy covering which would not only insulate him from fire, but also withstand the deadly spores, he turned over his plan. Perhaps such a simple getaway was unworthy of the name of a plan. Roughly, it consisted in placing himself among the foremost of those who would be clearing the ground with their fire-sprays, and working gradually ahead until the thickly scattered balls should give him concealment from the rest of the party. All he had to do then was to walk off to the west.

The only risk, once he was away, was that one of the food-carrying planes might spot him. But the chance was remote, and it was unlikely that a lone straggler would be considered worthy of investigation.

The scheme worked as he had expected. No hue and cry was raised after him as he wormed away. In a very little while he stood alone at the threshold of the stricken district.

As far as he could see in three directions, the land was dotted with the yellow balls, poised ominously where the wind had left them, and seeming to wait for the next gale to pick them up and send them swirling onward to more victims. Surrounded by the evilly glittering skins, he shuddered for a moment before his determination reasserted itself.

He drew a deep breath through his mask, threw back his head and strode on, a lone, grey figure, the only moving object in a scene of desolation.

In the first village he found a motor-cycle with its tank half-full, and for six miles it shattered the silence of the moor as he drove it, zigzagging to avoid the growths which littered the road. Then came a sharp valley so choked with balls that he must leave the motor-cycle, throw away the heavy flame-thrower and climb across the balls themselves.

On several occasions one burst beneath his weight and he dropped some feet in a flurry of spores which threatened to choke his breathing mask until he could wipe them away. Then, laboriously, he must pick himself up and struggle on, while streams of sweat soaked his clothing beneath the clumsy suit. Once he almost turned back to pick up the flame-thrower with the idea of burning his way through the mass, but he remembered that its cylinder was already half discharged. Desperately he battled, until at last his feet found the bracken and heather of the farther hill-side.

---

AFTERWARDS, HE COULD recall little of that journey. He became uncertain even of the number of days which passed as he tramped on and scrambled through one choked valley after another.

Only odd incidents startled him now and then out of a stupid weariness: the little town on the moor where men and women lay dead in the streets while the fungus preyed on them, and the windows of the houses were full of yellow balls which mercifully hid the rooms...the voice of a madman chanting hymns in a barricaded hut; hymns which turned to cursing blasphemies as he heard Ralph's step outside...the things which had been men, and which he was forced to move when thirst tortured him to find a drink in a dead inn...

But somehow, with dulled senses, he strove on through the nightmare while with every mile he covered, the fear of what he might find at his goal increased.

He felt that he was almost home when he crossed the River Tamar which separates Devon from Cornwall. The bridge was choked with the fungus. Upstream was wedged a solid mass of yellow, but below it the river raced, bearing an occasional serenely floating ball which would later meet its fate before the fire boats in Plymouth Sound.

At last, St. Brian. The balls were fewer here. The wind had carried most of them away. His own home. Farther on, Dorothy's home—blank, locked... deserted?

He broke a window to enter, and wandered about the empty rooms. No trace of fungus inside the house. No trace, either, of Dorothy. Perhaps she was upstairs. He was weak and hungry. Every step of the climb was an effort.

At the door of her room he hesitated. Would she be there; the yellow balls growing from her, feeding upon her still body? He opened the door; anything was better now than uncertainty. No one on the bed—no one in the room at all. He began to laugh hysterically. Dorothy had fooled the balls. They hadn't got her. She was alive, he was sure now—alive in spite of those damned balls. He fell on the bed, half-laughing, half-crying.

Suddenly he stopped. A sound outside. Voices? Painfully he crawled across to look out of the window. A group of people was coming up the road. People he knew. They were wearing ordinary clothes, and among them was Dorothy—Dorothy!

He tore off his mask and tried to shout to them. Funny; his voice wouldn't work, somehow. Never mind. Dorothy had fooled the yellow balls. That was damned funny. He was laughing again as he sank to the floor.

"YES, DEAR, I'M real," said Dorothy, at the bedside.

"But—but how—?"

"When I got here I found that Daddy had gone. The only thing was for me to go, too. Several of us went down the river in a boat and rowed along nearly to Land's End. Right in the toe of Cornwall we were beyond the balls, and to windward of them. Then, when it was safe—"

"Safe?"

"Yes, dear. It's safe now. The balls are just like an ordinary fungus now—they don't attack living things any more. Then we came home and found you here."

"But—"

"Not now. You mustn't talk any more, dear. You've been very ill, you know."

Ralph acquiesced. He went to sleep peacefully, her hand in his and a smile on his face.

## ENVOI

THE PRINCE KHORDAH of Ghangistan regarded the nephew of Haramin, bent low before him.

"Your plan has failed," he said.

The nephew of Haramin nodded dumbly.

"But," continued the Prince, "it has cost that accursed country more than did ever our wars—and we have lost nothing. Tell me, why did it fail?"

"Your Highness, the stock did not breed true. After two or so generations it was no longer a parasite, but had reverted to a common, saprophytic fungus."

"Which, however, it will take them many years to suppress?"

"Many years," the other repeated hopefully.

The Prince Khordah spent a few moments in contemplation.

"We are not displeased," he said at length. "Doubtless the first arrow did not kill a lion. There are other means, nephew of Haramin?"

The bent figure heaved a sigh of relief.

"There are other means," he agreed.

# THE MAN FROM BEYOND

—

ONE OF THE greatest sights in Takon[1] these days was the exhibition of discoveries made in the Valley of Dur. In the building erected especially to house them Takonians and visitors from other cities crowded through the corridors, peering into the barred or glass-fronted cages, observing the contents with awe, interest or amusement according to their natures.

The crowd was formed for the most part of those persons who flock to any unusual sight, providing it is free or cheap. Their eyes dwelt upon the exhibits. Their minds were ready to marvel and be superficially impressed. But they had come to be amused and they faintly resented the efforts of the guides to stir their intelligent interest. One or two, perhaps, studied the cases with real appreciation.

But if the adults were superficial the same could not be said of the children. Every day saw teachers bringing their classes for a practical demonstration of the planet's prehistoric condition. Even now Magon, a biology teacher in one of Takon's leading schools, was having difficulty restraining his twenty pupils for the arrival of a guide. He had marshalled them beside the entrance and, to keep them from straying, was talking of the Valley of Dur.

"The condition of the Valley was purely fortuitous and it is unique here upon Venus," he said. "Nothing remotely resembling it has been found, and

---
[1] All Venusian terms are rendered in their closest English equivalents.

it is the opinion of the experts that nothing like it exists anywhere else. This exhibition you are going to see is neither a museum nor a zoo, yet it is both."

His pupils only half attended. They were fidgeting, casting expectant glances down the row of cage fronts, craning to see over one another's backs, the more excitable among them occasionally rising on their hind legs for a better view. The passing Takonian citizens regarded their youthful enthusiasm with a mild amusement. Magon smoothed back the silver fur on his head with one hand and continued to talk.

"The creatures you will see belong to all ages of our world. Some are so old that they roamed Venus long before our race appeared. Others are more recent, contemporaries of those ancestors of ours who, in a terrible world, were for ever scuttling to cover as fast as their six legs would carry them."

"*Six* legs, sir?" asked a surprised voice.

Some of the youths in the group sniggered but Magon explained considerately.

"Yes, Sadul, six legs. Did you not know that our remote ancestors used all six of their limbs to get them along? It took them many thousands of years to turn themselves into quadrupeds but until they did that no progress was possible. The forelimbs could not develop such sensitive hands as ours until they were carried clear of the ground."

"Our ancestors were animals, sir?"

"Well—er—something very much like that." Magon lowered his voice in order that the ears of passing citizens might not be offended. "But once they got their forelegs off the ground, released from the necessity of carrying their weight, the great change began. We were on the upward climb—and since then we've never stopped climbing."

He looked around the circle of eager-eyed, silver-furred faces about him. His eyes dwelt a moment on the slender tentacles which had developed from stubby toes on the forefeet. There was something magical in evolution, something glorious in the fact that he and his race were the crown of progress.

It was a very wonderful thing to have done, to have changed from shaggy six-footed beasts to creatures who stood proudly upon four, the whole front part of the body raised to the perpendicular to support heads which looked out proudly and unashamed at the world.

Admittedly several of his class appeared to have neglected their coats in a way which was scarcely a credit to the race—their silver fur was muddied and rumpled—but then boys will be boys. No doubt they would trim and brush better as they grew older.

"The Valley of Dur—" he began again but at that moment the guide arrived.

"The party from the school, sir?"

"Yes."

"This way, please. Do they understand about the Valley, sir?" he added.

"Most of them," Magon admitted. "But it might be as well—"

"Certainly."

The guide broke into a high-speed recitation which he had evidently made many times before.

"The Valley of Dur may be called a unique phenomenon. At some remote date in the planet's history certain internal gases combined in a way yet imperfectly understood and issued forth through cracks in the crust at this place, and this place only.

"The mixture had two properties. It not only anaesthetized but it also preserved indefinitely. The result was to produce a form of suspended animation. Everything that was in the Valley of Dur has remained as it was when the gas first broke out. Everything which has entered the Valley since has remained there imperishably. There is no apparent limit to the length of time that this preservation may continue.

"Among the ancients this place was regarded with superstitious fear and though in more recent times many attempts have been made to explore it none were successful until a year ago when a mask which could withstand the gas was at last devised.

"It was then discovered that the animals and plants in the Valley were not petrified as had hitherto been believed but could, by means of certain treatment, be revived. Such are the specimens you are about to see—the flora and fauna of a million years ago—yet alive today."

He paused opposite the first cage.

"Here we have a glimpse of the carboniferous era—the tree ferns and giant mosses thriving in a specially prepared atmosphere, continuing the lives which were suspended when Venus was young. We hope to be able to grow more specimens from the spores of these. And here," he passed to the next case, "we see the beginning of one of Nature's most graceful experiments—the earliest form of flower."

His audience stared in dutiful attention at the large white blossoms which confronted them. They were not very interesting. Fauna has a far greater appeal to the adolescent than flora. A mighty roar caused the building to tremble. Eyes were switched from the magnolia-like blossoms to glance up the passage in anticipatory excitement.

Attention to the guide became even more perfunctory. Only Magon, to the exasperation of the pupils, thought it fit to ask a few questions. At last, however, the preliminary botanical cases were left behind and they came to the first of the cages.

Behind the bars a reptilian creature, which might have been described as a biped, had its tail not played so great a part in supporting it, was hurrying tirelessly and without purpose to and fro, glaring at as much of the world as it could from intense small eyes. Every now and then it would throw back its head and utter a kind of strangled shriek.

It was an unattractive creature covered with a grey-green hide, very smooth. Its contours were almost streamlined but managed to appear clumsy. In it, as in so many of the earlier forms, one seemed to feel that Nature was getting her hand in for the real job.

She had already learned to model after a crude fashion when she made this running dinosaur but her sense of proportion was not good and she lacked the deftness necessary to produce the finer bits of modelling which she later achieved. She could not, one felt, even had she wanted, have then produced fur or feathers to clothe the creature's nakedness.

"This," said the guide, waving a proprietary hand, "is what we call *Struthiomimus,* one of the running dinosaurs capable of travelling at high speed, which it does for purposes of defence, not attack, being a vegetarian."

There was a slight pause while his listeners sorted out the involved sentence. "You mean that it runs away?" asked a voice.

"Yes."

They all looked a little disappointed, a trifle contemptuous of the unfortunate *Struthiomimus*. They wanted stronger meat. They longed to see—(behind bars)—those ancient monsters which had been lords of the world, whose rumbling bellows had sent *Struthiomimus* and the rest scuttling for cover. The guide continued in his own good time.

"The next is a fine specimen of *Hesperornis,* the toothed bird. This creature, filling a place between the *Archeopteryx* and the modern bird, is particularly interesting."

But the class did not agree. As they filed slowly on past cage after cage it was noticeable that their own opinions and that of the guide seldom coincided. The more majestic and terrifying reptiles he dismissed with a curt, "These are of little interest, being sterile branches of the main stem of evolution— Nature's failures."

They came at length to a small cage, occupied by a solitary curious creature which stood erect upon two legs though it appeared to be designed to use four.

"This," said the guide, "is one of our most puzzling finds. We have not yet been able to classify it into any known category. There has been such a rush that the specialists have not as yet had time to accord it the attention it deserves. Obviously, it comes from an advanced date, for it bears some fur, though this is localized in patches, notably on the head and face.

"It is particularly adept upon two feet, which points to a long line of development. And yet, for all we know of it, the creature might have occurred fully developed and without any evolution—though of course you will realize that such a thing could not possibly happen.

"Among the other odd facts which our preliminary observation has revealed is that, although its teeth are indisputably those of a herbivore, it has carnivorous tastes—altogether a most puzzling creature. We hope to find others before the examination of the Valley is ended."

The creature raised its head and looked at them from sullen eyes. Its mouth opened but instead of the expected bellow there came from it a stream of clattering gibberish which it accompanied with curious motions of its forelimbs.

The interest of some of the class was at last aroused. Here was a real mystery about which the experts could as yet claim to know little more than themselves.

The young Sadul, for instance, was far more intrigued by it than he had been by those monsters with the poly-syllabic names. He drew closer to the bars, observing it intently.

The creature's eyes met his own and held them. More queer jabber issued from its mouth. It advanced to the front of the cage, coming quite near to him. Sadul held his ground—it did not look dangerous. With one foot it smoothed the soil of the floor, then squatted down to scrabble in the dirt.

"What's it doing?" asked someone.

"Probably scratching for something to eat," suggested another.

Sadul continued to watch with interest. When the guide moved the party on he contrived to remain behind unnoticed. He was untroubled by the presence of other spectators, since most of them had gravitated to watch the larger reptiles feed.

After a while the creature rose to its feet again and extended one paw towards the ground. It had scrawled a series of queer lines in the dust. They made neither pattern nor picture. They did not seem to mean anything. Yet there was something regular about them.

Sadul looked blankly at them and then back to the fact of the creature. It made a quick movement towards the scrawls. Sadul continued to stare blankly. It advanced, smoothed out the ground once more with its foot and began to scrabble again. Sadul wondered whether or not he should move on. He ought, he knew, to have kept together with the rest. Magon might be nasty about it. Well, he'd stay just long enough to see what the creature was doing this time.

It stood back and pointed again. Sadul was amazed. In the dirt was a drawing of a Takonian such as himself. The creature was pointing first to himself and then back to the drawing.

Sadul grew excited. He had made a discovery? What was this creature which could draw? He had never heard of such a thing. His first impulse was to run after the rest and tell them. But he hesitated and curiosity got the better of him.

Rather doubtfully, he opened the bag at his side and drew out his writing tablet and stylus. The creature excitedly thrust both paws through the bars for them and sat down, scratching experimentally with the wrong end of the stylus. Sadul corrected it, then leaned close to the bars, watching over its shoulder.

First the creature made a round mark in the middle of the tablet, then it pointed up. Sadul looked up at the ceiling, but quite failed to see anything remarkable there. The creature shook its head impatiently. About the mark it drew a circle with a small spot on the circumference—outside that another circle with a similar spot, then a third. Still Sadul could see no meaning.

Beside the spot on the second circle the creature drew a small sketch of a Takonian. Beside the spot on the third, a creature, itself. Sadul followed intently. It was trying very hard to convey something but for the life of him he could not see what it was. Again a paw pointed up at the light globe, then the forelimbs were held wide apart.

The light—an enormous light!

Suddenly Sadul got it—the sun—the sun and the planets! He nearly choked with excitement. Reaching between the bars, he grabbed his tablet and ran off up the corridor in search of his party. The man in the cage watched him go and as Sadul's shouts diminished in the distance he smiled his first smile for a very long time.

---

GOIN, THE LECTURER in phonetics, wandered into the study of his friend Dagul, the anthropologist in the University of Takon. Dagul, who was getting on in years as the grizzling of his silver fur testified, looked up with a frown of irritation at the interruption. It faded at the sight of Goin.

"Sorry," he apologized. "I think I'm a bit overworked. This Dur business gives such masses of material that I can't leave it alone."

"If you're too busy—?"

"No, no. Come along in. Glad to throw it off for a time."

They crossed to a low divan where they squatted, folding four legs beneath them.

Dagul offered refreshment.

"Well, did you get this Earth creature's story?" he asked.

Goin produced a packet of thin tablets from a satchel.

"Yes, we got it—in the end. I've had all my assistants and brightest students working on it but it's not been easy even so. They seem to have been further advanced in physical science than we are. That made parts of it only roughly translatable but I think you'll be able to follow it. A pretty sort of villain this Gratz makes himself out to be—and he's not much ashamed of it."

"You can't be a good villain if you are ashamed."

"I suppose not but it's made me think. Earth seems to have been a rotten planet."

"Worse than Venus?" asked Dagul bitterly.

Goin hesitated. "Yes, I think so, according to his account—but probably that's only because it was further developed. We're going the same way—graft, vested interests, private traders without morals, politicians without conscience. I thought they only existed here, but they had them on Earth—the whole stinking circus. Maybe they had them on Mars too if we only knew."

"I wonder?" Dagul sat for some moments in contemplation. "You mean that Earth was just an exaggerated form of the mess we're in?"

"Exactly. Makes you wonder if life isn't a disease after all—a kind of corruption which attacks dying planets, growing more and more vicious in the higher forms. And as for intelligence—"

"Intelligence," said Dagul, "is a complete snare and delusion. I came to that conclusion long ago. Without it you are wiped out—with it you wipe out one another, eventually yourself."

Goin grinned. Dagul's hobby-horses were much-ridden steeds.

"The instinct of self-protection—" he began.

"—is another delusion as far as the race is concerned," Dagul finished for him. "Individuals may protect themselves but it is characteristic of an intelligent race to try continually by bigger and better methods to wipe itself out. Speaking dispassionately I should say that it's a very good thing, too. Of all the wasteful, destructive, pointless…"

Goin let him have his say. Experience told him that it was useless to attempt to stem the flood. At length came a pause and he thrust forward his packet of tablets.

"Here's the story. I'm afraid it will encourage your pessimism. The man, Gratz, is a self-confessed murderer for one thing."

"Why should he confess?"

"It's all there. Says he wants to warn us against Earth."

Dagul smiled slightly. "Then you've not told him?"

"No, not yet."

Dagul reached for the topmost tablet and began to read.

## THE EARTHMAN'S STORY

I, MORGAN GRATZ of the planet Earth, am writing this as a warning to the inhabitants of Venus. Have nothing to do with Earth if you can help it—but if you must, be careful. Above all I warn you to have no dealings with the two greatest companies of Earth.

If you do, you will come to hate Earth and her people as I do—you will come to think of her, as I do, as the plague spot of the universe. Sooner or later, emissaries will come—representatives of either Metallic Industries or International Chemicals will attempt to open negotiations. Do not listen to them.

However honeyed their words or smooth their phrases distrust them, for they will be liars and the servants of liars. If you do trust them you will live to regret it and your children will regret it and curse you. Read this and see how they treated me, Morgan Gratz.

My story is best started from the moment when I was shown into the Directors' Room in the huge building which houses the executive of Metallic Industries. The secretary closed the tall double doors behind me and announced my name.

"Gratz, sir."

Nine men seated about a glass-topped table turned their eyes upon me simultaneously but I kept my gaze on the chairman who topped the long table.

"Good morning, Mr. Drakin," I said.

"Morning, Gratz. You have not met our other directors, I believe."

I looked along the row of faces. Several I recognized from photographs in the illustrated papers. Others I was able to identify, for I had heard them described and knew that they would be present. There is no mystery about the directors of Metallic Industries Incorporated.

Among them are several of the world's richest men and to be mounted upon such pinnacles of wealth means continual exposure to the floodlights of publicity. Not only was I familiar with their appearances but in common with most I was fairly conversant with their histories. I made no comment, so the chairman continued.

"I have received your reports, Gratz, and I am pleased to say that they are model documents—clear and concise—a little too clear, I must own, for my peace of mind. In fact, I confess to apprehension and, in my opinion, the time has come for decisive measures. However, before I suggest the steps to be taken I would like you to repeat the gist of your reports for the benefit of my fellow-directors."

I had come prepared for this request and was able to reply without hesitation.

"When it first became known to Mr. Drakin that International Chemicals proposed to build a ship for the navigation of space, he approached me and put forward certain propositions. I, as an employee of International Chemicals, being concerned in the work in question, was to keep him posted and to hand on as much information, technical and otherwise, as I could collect without arousing suspicion.

"Moreover, I was to find out the purpose for which International Chemicals intended to use her. I have carried out the first part of my orders to the chairman's satisfaction but it is only in the last week that I have been able to discover her destination."

I paused. There was a stir among the listeners. Several leaned forward with increased interest.

"Well," demanded a thin, predatory-faced man on the chairman's right, "what is it?"

"The intention of the company," I said, "is to send their ship, which they call the *Nuntia,* to Venus."

They stared at me. Save for Drakin, to whom this was not news, they appeared dumbfounded. The cadaverous-looking man was the first to find his voice.

# THE MAN FROM BEYOND

"Nonsense!" he cried. "Preposterous! Never heard of such a thing. What proof have you of this ridiculous statement?"

I looked at him coldly.

"I have no proof. A spy rarely has. You must take my word for it."

"Absurd. Fantastic nonsense. You stand there and seriously expect us to believe on your own, unsupported statement, that I.C. intends to send this machine to Venus? The moon would be unlikely enough. Either they have been fooling you or you must be raving mad. I never heard such rubbish. Venus, indeed!"

I regarded the man. I liked neither his face nor his manners.

"Mr. Ball sees fit to challenge my report," I said. "This, gentlemen, will scarcely surprise you, for you must know as well as I that Mr. Ball has been completely impervious to all new ideas for the past forty years."

The emaciated Mr. Ball goggled while several of the others hid smiles. It was rarely that his millions did not extract sycophancy, but I was in a strong position.

"Insolence," he spluttered at last. "Damned insolence, Mr. Chairman. I demand that this man—"

"Mr. Ball," interrupted the other coldly, "you will please to control yourself. The fact that Gratz is here at all is a sign not only that I believe him but what I consider his news seriously to concern us all."

"Nonsense. If you are going to believe every fairy story that a paid spy—"

"Mr. Ball, I must ask you to leave the conduct of this matter to me. You knew, as we all did, that I.C. was building this ship and you knew that it was intended for space-travel. Why should you disbelieve the report of its destination? I must insist that you control yourself."

Mr. Ball subsided, muttering indefinite threats. The chairman turned back to me. "And the purpose of this expedition?"

I was only able to suggest that it was to establish claims over territories as sources of supplies. He nodded and turned to address the rest.

"You see, gentlemen, what this will mean? It is scarcely necessary to remind you that I.C. are our greatest rivals, our only considerable rivals. The overlapping of interests is inevitable. Metals and chemicals obviously cannot be expected to keep apart. They are interdependent. It cannot be anything but a fight for survival between the two companies.

"At present we are evenly balanced in the matter of raw materials—and probably shall be for years to come. But—and this is the important point—if their ship makes this trip successfully what will be the results?

"First, of course, they will annex the richest territories on the planet with their raw materials, and later import these materials to Earth. Mind you, this will not take place at once—but make no mistake, it will come, sooner or later, as inevitably as tomorrow.

"Once the trip has been successfully made the inventors will not rest until they have found a way of carrying freight between the two worlds at economic rates. It may take them ten years to do it, it may take them a century, but sooner or later, do it they will.

"And that, gentlemen, will mean the end of Metallic Industries."

There was a pause during which no one spoke. Drakin looked around to see the effect of his words.

"Gratz has told me," he continued, "that I.C. is convinced their ship is capable of the journey. Is that not so?"

"It is," I confirmed. "They have complete faith in her and so have I."

Old John Ball's voice rose again. "If this is not nonsense why have we let it go on? Why has I.C. been allowed to build this vessel without interference? What is the good of having a man there who does nothing to hinder the work?" He glared at me.

"You mean?" inquired Drakin.

"I mean that this man has been excellently placed to work sabotage. Why has there been none? It should be simple enough to cause an "accidental" explosion."

"Very simple," agreed Drakin. "So simple that I.C. would jump to it at once. Even if there were a genuine accident they would suspect that we had a hand in it. Then we should have our hands full with an expensive vendetta. Furthermore I.C. would recommence building with additional precautions and it is possible that we might not have a man on the inside.

"I take it that we are all agreed that the *Nuntia* must fail—but it must not be a suspicious failure. The *Nuntia* must sail. It is up to us to see that she does not return.

"Gratz has been offered a position aboard her but has not as yet returned a definite answer. My suggestion is that he should accept the offer with the object of seeing that the *Nuntia* is lost. The details I can leave to him."

Drakin went on to elaborate his plan. Directly the *Nuntia* had left, Metallic Industries would begin work on a space-flyer of their own. As soon as possible she would follow Venus. Meanwhile I, having settled the *Nuntia,* would await her arrival.

In the unlikely event of the planet being found inhabited I was to get on good terms with the natives and endeavour to influence them against I.C. When the second ship arrived I was to be taken off and brought back to Earth while a party of M.I. men remained to survey and annex territory. On my return I would be sufficiently rewarded to make me rich for life.

"You will be doing a great work for us," he concluded, "and we do not forget our servants." He looked me straight in the eye as he said it. "Will you do it?"

I hesitated. "I would like a day or so to think it over."

"Of course. That is only natural. But there is not a great deal of time to spare—will you let me have your answer by this time tomorrow? It will give us a chance to make other arrangements in case you refuse."

"Yes, sir. That will do."

With that I left them. As to their further deliberations I can only guess. And my guesses are bitter.

Beyond an idea that it would appear better not to be too eager, I had no reason for putting off my answer. Already I had determined to go—and to wreck the *Nuntia*. I had waited many years to get in a blow at I.C., and now was my chance.

Ever since the death of my parents I had set my mind on injuring them. Not only had they killed my father by their negligence in the matter of unshielded rays but they had stolen his inventions and robbed him by prolonged litigation.

Enough, you say, to make a man swear revenge. But it was not all. I had to see my mother die in poverty when a few hundred dollars would have saved her life—and all our dollars had gone in fighting I.C.

After that I changed my name, got a job with I.C. and worked—hard. Mine was not going to be a paltry revenge. I was going to work up until I was in a responsible position, one from which my blows could really hurt them.

I had allied myself with Metallic Industries because this was their biggest rival and now I was given a chance to wreck the ship to which they had pinned such faith. I could have done that alone but it would have meant exile for the rest of my life. Now M.I. had smoothed the way by offering me passage home.

Yes, I was going to do it. The *Nuntia* should make one trip and no more.

But I'd like to know just what it was they decided in the Board Room after I left.

## MURDERS IN SPACE

THE *NUNTIA* WAS two weeks in space but nobody was very happy about it.

In those two weeks the party of nine on board had been reduced to seven and the reduction had not had a good effect upon our morale. As far as I could tell there was no tangible suspicion afoot—just a feeling that all was not well.

Among the hands it was rumoured that Hammer and Drafte had gone crazy before they killed themselves. But why had they gone crazy? That was what worried the rest. Was it something to do with conditions in space—some subtle, unsuspected emanation? Would we all go crazy?

When you are cut off from your kind you get strange fancies. Imagination gets overheated and you become too credulous. That is what used to happen to sailors on their long voyages in the old windjammers. They began to attribute the deaths to uncanny malign influences in a way which would never have occurred to them on Earth. It gave me some amusement at the time.

First had been Dale Hammer, the second navigator. Young, a bit wild at home, perhaps, but brilliant at his job, he was proud and overjoyed that he had been chosen for this voyage. He had gone off duty in a cheerful frame of mind.

A few hours later he had been found dead in his bunk with a bottle of tablets by his side: one had to take something to ensure sleep out here. Everyone agreed that it was understandable, though tragic, that he had taken an overdose by mistake.

It was after Ross Drafte's disappearance that the superstitions began to cluster. He was an odd man with an expression which was frequently taciturn and eyes in which burned feverish enthusiasms. A failure might have driven him desperate but under the circumstances, he had everything to live for.

He was the designer of the *Nuntia* and she, the dream of his life, was endorsing his every expectation. When we returned to make public the story of our voyage his would be the name to be glorified through millions of radios, his the face which would stare from hundreds of newspapers—the conqueror of gravitation. And he had disappeared.

The air-pressure graph showed a slight dip at one point and Drafte was no more.

I saw no trace of suspicion. No one had even looked askance at me nor, so far as I knew, at anyone else. No one had the least inkling that any one man aboard the ship could tell them exactly how those two men had died. There was just the conviction that something queer was afoot.

And now it was time for another.

Ward Govern, the chief engineer, was in the chartroom, talking with Captain Tanner. The rest were busy elsewhere. I slipped into Govern's cabin unobserved. His pistol I found in the drawer where he always kept it and I slipped it into my pocket. Then I crossed to the other wall and opened the ventilator which communicated with the passage. Finally, after carefully assuring myself that no one was in sight, I left, closing the door behind me.

I had not long to wait. In less than a quarter of an hour I heard the clatter of a pair of magnetic shoes on the steel floor and the engineer passed cheerfully by on his way to turn in. The general air of misgiving had had less effect upon him than upon anyone else. I heard the door slam behind him. I allowed him a few moments before I moved as quietly to the ventilator as my magnetic soles would allow.

I could see him quite easily. He had removed his shoes and was sitting at a small wall desk, entering the day's events in his diary. I thrust the muzzle of the pistol just within the slot of the ventilator and with the other hand began to make slight scratching noises. It was essential that he should come close to me. There must be a burn or at least powder marks.

The persistent scratching began to worry him. He glanced up in a puzzled fashion and held his head on one side, listening. I went on scratching. He decided to investigate and released the clips which held his weightless body to the chair. Without bothering to put on the magnetic shoes, he pushed himself away from the wall and came floating towards the ventilator. I let him get quite close before I fired.

There was a clatter of running feet mingling with cries of alarm. I dropped the pistol inside my shirt and jumped around the corner, reaching the cabin door just ahead of a pair who came from the other direction. We flung it open and I dashed in. Govern's body under the impetus of the shot had floated back into the middle of the room. It looked uncanny, lying asprawl in mid-air.

"Quick," I yelled, "fetch the Captain."

One of them pelted to the door. I managed to keep my body between the other and the corpse while I closed the dead fingers around the pistol. A few seconds later everybody had collected about the doorway and the Captain had to push them aside to get in.

He examined the body. It was not a pleasant sight. The blood had not yet ceased to flow from the wound in the head but it did not drip as it would on Earth. Instead it had spurted forth to form into red spheres, which floated freely close beside the corpse. There was no doubt that the shot had been fired at close range. The Captain looked at the outflung hand which gripped the automatic.

"What happened?"

No one seemed to know.

"Who found him?"

"I was here first, sir," I said. "Just before the others."

"Anyone with you when you heard the shot?"

"No, sir. I was just walking along the passage—"

"That's right, sir. We met Gratz running 'round the corner." Somebody supported me.

"You didn't see anyone else about?"

"No, sir."

"And was it possible, do you think, for anybody to have gotten out of the room unseen between the time of the shot and your arrival?"

"Quite impossible, sir. He would have been bound to walk straight into me or the others—even if there had been time for him to get out of the room."

"Very well. Please help me with this." He turned to the other four who were still lingering in a group near the door. "You men get back to work now."

Two began to move off but the other pair, Willis and Trail, both mechanics, held their ground.

"Didn't you hear me? Get along there."

Still they hesitated. Then Willis stepped forward and the Captain's unbelieving ears heard his demand that the *Nuntia* be turned back.

"You don't know what you're saying, man!"

"I do, sir, and so does Trail. There's something queer about it all. It's not natural for men to kill themselves like this. Perhaps we'll be next. When we signed up we knew we'd have dangers we could see but didn't reckon with something that makes you go mad and kill yourself. We don't like it—and we ain't going on. Turn the ship back."

"Don't be a pair of fools. You ought to know that we can't turn back. What do you think this is—a rowboat? What's the matter with you?"

The two faces in front of him were set in lines of stolid determination. Willis spoke again.

"We've had enough and that's flat. It was bad enough when two had gone but now it's three. Who's going to be the next? That's what I want to know."

"That's what we all want to know," said the Captain meaningly. "Why are you so anxious to have the ship turned back?"

"Because it's wrong—unlucky. We don't want to go crazy even if you do. If you don't turn her back we will."

"So that's the way it blows, is it? Who's paying you for this?"

Willis and Trail remained uncomprehending.

"You heard me," he roared. "Who's behind you? Who's out to wreck this trip?"

Willis shook his head. "Nobody's behind us. We just want to get out of this before we go crazy too," he repeated.

"Went crazy, eh?" said the Captain with a sneer. "Well maybe they did and then again, maybe they didn't—and if they didn't I've got a pretty good idea what happened to them." He paused. "So you think you'll scare me into turning back, do you? Well, by the stars, you won't, you bilge rats. Get back to your work. I'll deal with you later."

But neither Willis nor Trail had any intention of going back. They came on. Trail was swinging a threatening spanner. I snatched the pistol from the corpse's hands and got him in the forehead. It was a lucky shot. Willis tried to stop. I got him, too.

The Captain turned and saw me handling the pistol. The suddenness of the thing had taken him by surprise. I could see that he didn't know whether to thank me or to blame me for so summary an execution of justice. There was no doubt that the pair had mutinied and that Trail, at least, had meant murder. Strong and Danver, the two men in the doorway, stared speechlessly. Nine men had sailed in the *Nuntia*—four now remained.

For the time the Captain said nothing. We waited, looking at the two bodies still swaying eerily, anchored to the floor by their magnetic shoes. At last the Captain broke the silence.

"It's going to be hard work for four men," he said. "But if each of us pulls his weight we may win through yet. To the two of you all the engine room work will fall. Gratz, do you know anything of three-dimensional navigation?"

"Very little, sir."

"Well, you'll have to learn—and quickly."

After the business of disposing the bodies through the airlock was finished, he led me to the navigation room. Half to himself, I heard him murmur, "I wonder which it was? Trail, I should guess. He's the type."

"Beg your pardon, sir?"

"I was wondering which of those two was the murderer."

"Murderer, sir?"

"Murderer, Gratz. I said and I mean it. Surely you didn't think those deaths were natural?"

"They seemed natural."

"They were well enough managed but there was too much coincidence. Somebody was out to wreck this trip and kill us all."

"I don't see—"

"Think, man, think," he interrupted. "Suppose the secret of the *Nuntia* got out in spite of all our care? There are plenty of people who would want her to fail."

I flatter myself that I managed my surprise rather well.

"Metallic Industries, you mean?"

"Yes, and others. No one knows what may be the outcome of this voyage. There are a lot of people who find the world very comfortable as it is and would like to keep it so. Suppose they had planted one of those men aboard?"

I shook my head doubtfully. "It wouldn't do. It'd be suicide. One man couldn't get this ship back to Earth."

"Nevertheless I'm convinced that either Willis or Trail was planted here to stop us from succeeding."

The idea that both the men were genuinely scared and wanted only to get back to Earth had never struck him. I saw no reason to let it.

"Anyway," he added, "we've settled with the murdering swine now—at the cost of three good honest men."

He took some charts from a drawer. "Now come along, Gratz. We must get to work on this navigation. Who knows but that all our lives may soon depend on you."

"Who indeed, sir," I agreed.

## STEALING THE SHIP

ANOTHER FORTNIGHT PASSED before the *Nuntia* at last dipped her nose into the clouds which had always made the nature of Venus' surface a matter for surmise. By circling the planet several times, Captain Tanner contrived to reduce our headlong hurtling to a manageable speed.

After I had taken a sample of the atmosphere—(which proved almost identical with that of Earth)—I took my place close beside him, gaining a knowledge of how the ship must be handled in the air. When the clouds closed in on our windows to obscure the universe we were traveling at a little more than two hundred miles an hour. Despite our extended wings we required the additional support of vertical rockets.

The Captain dropped cautiously upon a long slant. This, he told me, would be the most nerve-racking part of the entire trip. There was no telling how far the undersides of the clouds were from the planet's surface. He could depend on nothing but luck to keep the ship clear of mountains which might lurk unseen in our path.

He sat tensely at the control board, peering into the baffling mist, ready at a moment's notice to change his course although we both knew that the sight of an obstacle would mean that it was too late. The few minutes we spent in the clouds seemed interminable.

My senses drew so taut that it seemed they must snap. And then, when I felt that I could not stand it a moment longer, the vapours thinned, dropped behind and we swept down at last upon a Venusian landscape.

Only it was not a landscape, for in every direction stretched the sea—a grey, miserable waste. Even our relief could not make the scene anything but dreary. Heavy rain drove across the view in thick rods, slashing at the windows and pitting the troubled water.

Lead-grey clouds, heavy with unshed moisture, seemed to press down like great, gorged sponges which would wipe everything clean. Nowhere was there a darkling line to suggest land. The featureless horizon which we saw dimly through the rain was a watery circle.

The Captain levelled out and continued straight ahead at a height of a few hundred feet above the surface. There was nothing for it but to go on and hope that we should strike land of some kind. For hours we did, and for the difference it made to the scene we might have been stationary. It was just a matter of luck.

Unknowingly, we must have taken a line on which the open sea lay straight before us for thousands of miles. The rain, the vastness of the ocean and the reaction from our journey combined to drive us into depression. Was Venus, we began to ask ourselves, nothing but a sphere of water and clouds?

At last I caught a glimpse of a dark speck away to starboard. With visibility so low I could not be certain what it was. We had all but passed it before I drew the Captain's attention. Without hesitating he swerved towards it and we both fixed our eyes on it and anxiously watched it grow.

As we drew closer it proved to be a hill of no great size, rising from an island of some five or six square miles. It was not such a spot as one would have chosen for a first landing but he decided to make it. We were all thoroughly tired of our cramped quarters. A few days of rest and exercise in the open air would put new heart in us.

It would be absurd for an Earthman to describe Venus to Venusians but there are differences between your district of Takon and the island where we landed which I find very puzzling. Moreover, the conditions which I found elsewhere also differ from those which abide here. I know nothing about the latitude of these places but it seems that they must be far removed from here to be so unalike.

For instance, our island was permanently blanketed beneath thick clouds. One never saw the sun at all, but for all that the heat was intense and the rain, which seldom ceased, was warm. Here in Takon, on the other hand, you have a climate not unlike that of our temperate regions—occasional clouds, occasional rain, warmth that is not too oppressive.

When I look round and observe your plants and trees I find it hard to believe that they can exist on the same planet with the queer jumble of growths we found on the island. I know nothing of botany, so I can only tell you that I was struck by the quantities of ferns and palms and the almost entire absence of hardwood trees.

Two days were occupied in minor repairs and necessary adjustments, varied by occasional explorations. These were not pleasure trips, for the rain fell without ceasing, but they served to give us some much-needed exercise and to improve our spirits.

On the third day the Captain proposed an expedition to the top of the central hill and we agreed to accompany him. We were all armed, for though the only animals we had seen were small timid creatures which scuttled from our approach, there was no telling what we might encounter in the deeper forest which lay between the hill and the beach where *Nuntia* rested.

We assembled shortly after dawn, almost in a state of nudity. Since the heat rendered heavy waterproofs intolerable we had decided that the less we wore the better. It would be hard enough work carrying heavy rifles and rucksacks of supplies in such a climate.

The Captain shepherded us out into the steady rain, pushed the outer door to behind us and we began our tramp up the beach. We had all but crossed the foreshore scrub which bordered the forest proper when I stopped abruptly.

"What is it?" asked the Captain.

"Ammunition," I told him. "I put it aside, ready to pack, and forgot to put it in."

"Are you sure?"

I hauled the rucksack off my back and looked through the contents. There was no sign of the packet of cartridges he had given me. In order to travel light we had only a few rounds each. I could not expect the others to share theirs with me in the circumstances. There was only one thing to be done.

"I'll go back for them. It will only take a few seconds," I said.

The Captain grudgingly agreed. He disliked inefficiency but could not afford to weaken his party by taking a member of it unarmed into possible dangers. I hurried back to the ship, stumbling along through the sand and shingle. As I pulled open the air-lock door I glanced back. The three, I could dimly see, had reached the edge of the forest and were standing under such shelter as they could find, watching me.

I jumped inside and threw down my rifle and rucksack with a clatter. First I rushed for the engines and turned on the fuel taps, then I went forward to the navigation room. Hurriedly I set the controls as I had been shown and pulled over the ignition switch.

With my fingers above the first bunch of firing keys, I looked once more out of the windows. The Captain was pounding across the beach, followed by the others. How he had guessed that there was anything wrong I cannot say. Perhaps his glasses enabled him to see that I was in the control room. Anyway, he meant business.

He passed out of my line of sight and a moment later I pressed the firing keys. The *Nuntia* trembled, lurched and began to slither forward across the sand. I saw the other two wave despairing arms. It was impossible to tell whether the Captain had managed to scramble aboard or not.

# THE MAN FROM BEYOND

I turned the rising ship towards the sea. Again I looked back, just in time to see the others running towards a form which lay huddled on the sand. Close beside it they stopped and looked up. They shook wild, impotent fists in the direction of my retreating *Nuntia*.

## THE MYSTERIOUS VALLEY

AFTER A FEW hours I began to grow seriously worried. There must be other land on this planet but I had seen none as yet. I began to have a nasty feeling that it would end with the *Nuntia* dropping into the sea, condemning me to eventual death by starvation should I survive the fall.

She was not intended to be run single-handed. In order to economize weight many operations which could easily have been automatic were left to manual control on the assumption that there would always be one or more men on engine room duty. The fuel-pressure gauge was dangerously low, but the controls required constant attention, preventing me from getting aft to start the pressure pumps.

I toyed with the idea of fixing the controls while I made a dash to the engine room and back but since it was impossible to find a satisfactory method of holding them the project had to be abandoned. The only thing I could do was to hold on and hope land would show up before it was too late.

In the nick of time it did—a rockbound inhospitable-looking coast but one which for all its ruggedness was fringed to the very edges of the harsh cliffs with a close-pressed growth of jungle. There was no shore such as we had used for a landing ground on the island.

The water swirled and frothed about the cliff-bottom as the great breakers dashed themselves with a kind of ponderous futility against the mighty retaining wall. No landing there. Above, the jungle stretched back to the horizon, an undulating, unbroken plain of tree tops.

Somewhere there I would have to land, but where?

A few miles in from the coast the *Nuntia* settled it for me. The engines stopped with a splutter. I did not attempt to land her. I jumped for one of the spring acceleration hammocks and trusted that it would stand the shock.

I came out of that rather well. When I examined the wrecked *Nuntia*, her wings torn off, her nose crumpled like tinfoil, her smooth body now gaping in many places from the force of the impact, I marvelled that anyone could sustain only a few bruises—acquired when the hammock mountings had weakened to breaking point—as I did.

There was one thing certain in a very problematical future—the *Nuntia*'s flying days were done. I had carried out Metallic Industries' instructions to the full and the telescopes of I.C. would nightly be searching the skies for a ship which would never return.

Despite my predicament (or perhaps because I had not fully appreciated it as yet) I was full of a savage joy. I had struck the first of my vengeful blows at the men who had caused my family such misery. The only shadows across my satisfaction was that they could not know that it was I, not Fate, who was against them.

It would be tedious to tell in detail of my activities during the next few weeks. There is nothing surprising about them. My efforts to make the *Nuntia* habitable—my defences against the larger animals—my cautious hunting expeditions—my search for edible greenstuffs—were such as any man would have made. They were makeshift and temporary.

I did only enough to assure myself of moderate comfort until the Metallic Industries ship should arrive to take me off. So for six months by the *Nuntia*'s chronometers I idled and loafed and though it may sometimes have crossed my mind that Venus was not altogether a desirable piece of real estate, yet it was in a detached impersonal way that I regarded my surroundings.

It would be a wonderful topic of conversation when I got home. That "when I got home" coloured all my thoughts. It was the constant barrier which stood between me and the life about me. This planet might surround me but it could not touch me as long as the barrier remained in place.

At the end of six months I began to feel that my exile was nearly up. The M.I. ship would be finished by now and ready to follow the *Nuntia*'s lead. I waited almost a month longer, seeing her in my mind's eye falling through space towards me. Then it was time for my signal.

I had arranged the main searchlight so that it would point vertically upwards to stab its beam into the low clouds and now I began to switch it on every night as soon the darkness came, leaving its glare until near dawn. For the first few nights I scarcely slept, so certain was I that the ship must be cruising close by in search of me.

I used to lie awake, watching the dismal sky for the flash of her rockets, straining my ears for their thunder. But this stage did not last long. I consoled myself very reasonably that it might take too much searching to find me. But all day too I was alert, with smoke rockets ready to be fired the moment I should hear her.

After four months more my batteries gave out. It is surprising that they lasted so long. As the voltage dropped, so did my hopes. The jungle seemed to creep closer, making ominous bulges in my barrier of detachment.

For a number of nights after the filaments had glowed their last I sat up through the hours of darkness, firing occasional distress rockets in forlorn faith. It was when they were gone that I sensed what had occurred. Why I did not think of it before, I cannot tell. But the truth came to me in a flash—Metallic Industries had duped me just as International Chemicals had duped my father.

They had not built—never intended to build—a spaceship. Why should they, once I.C. had lost theirs? That, I grew convinced, was the decision which had been taken in the Board Room after my withdrawal. They had never intended that I should return.

I could see now that they would have found it not only expensive but dangerous. There would be not only my reward to be paid but I might blackmail them. In every way it would be more convenient that I should do my work and disappear. And what better method of disappearance could there be than loss upon another planet?

Those are the methods of Earth—that is the honour of great companies as you will know to your cost should you have dealings with them. They'll use you, then break you.

I must have been nearly crazy for some days after that realization. My fury with my betrayers, my disgust with my own gullibility, the appalling sense of loneliness and above all the eternal drumming of that almost ceaseless rain combined to drive me into a frenzy which stopped only on the brink of suicide.

But in the end the adaptability of my race asserted itself. I began to hunt and live off the land about me. I struggled through two bouts of fever and successfully sustained a period of semi-starvation when my food was finished and game was short.

For company I had only a pair of six-legged, silver-furred creatures, which I had trained. I found them one day, deserted in a kind of large nest and dying with hunger. Taking them back with me to the *Nuntia* I fed them and found them friendly little things. As they grew larger they began to display remarkable intelligence. Later I christened them Mickey and Minnie—after certain classic film stars at home—and they soon got to know their names.

And now I come to the last and most curious episode, which I confess I do not yet understand. It occurred several years after *Nuntia*'s landing. A foraging expedition upon which Mickey and Minnie accompanied me as usual had taken us into country completely unknown to me. A scarcity of game and a determination not to return empty-handed had caused me to push on farther than usual.

At last, at the entrance to a valley, Mickey and Minnie stopped. Nothing I could do would induce them to go on. Moreover they tried to hold me back, clutching at my legs with their forepaws. The valley looked a likely place for game and I shook them off impatiently. They watched me as I went, making little whining noises of protest, but they did not attempt to follow.

For the first quarter mile I saw nothing unusual. Then I had a nasty shock. Farther on an enormous head reared above the trees, looking directly at me. It was unlike anything I had ever seen before but thoughts of giant reptiles jumped to my mind.

Tyrannosaurus must have had a head not unlike that. I was puzzled as well as scared. Venus could not be still in the age of the giant reptiles. I could not have lived here all this time without seeing something of them before.

The head did not move—there was no sound. As my first flood of panic abated it was clear that the animal had not seen me. The valley seemed utterly silent, for I had grown so used to the sounds of rain that my ears scarcely registered them. At two hundred yards I came within sight of the great head again and decided to risk a shot.

I aimed at the right eye and fired.

Nothing happened—the echoes thundered from side to side; nothing else moved. It was uncanny, unnerving. I snatched up my glasses. Yes, I had scored a bull's-eye, but… Queer. I decided that I didn't like the valley a bit, but I made myself go on.

There was a curious odour in the air, not unpleasant yet a little sickly. Close to the monster I stopped. He had not budged an inch. Suddenly, behind him, I caught a glimpse of another reptile—smaller, more lizard-like but with teeth and claws that made me sweat.

I dropped on one knee and raised the rifle. I began to feel an odd swimming sensation inside my head. The world seemed to be tilting about me. My rifle barrel wavered. I could not see clearly. I felt myself begin to fall. I seemed to be falling a long, long way…

When I awoke it was to see the bars of a cage.

---

DAGUL STOPPED READING. He knew the rest. "How long ago, do you think?" he asked.

Goin shrugged his shoulders.

"Heaven knows. A very long time, that's all we can be sure of. The continual clouds—and did you notice that he claims to have tamed two of our primitive ancestors? Millions of years."

"And he warns us against Earth." Dagul smiled. "It will be a shock for the poor creature. The last of his race—though not, to judge by his own account, a very worthy race. When are you going to tell him?"

"He's bound to find out soon, so I thought I'd do it this evening. I've got permission to take him up to the observatory."

"Would you mind if I came too?"

"Of course not."

Gratz was stumbling among unfamiliar syllables as the three climbed the hill to the Observatory of Takon, doing his best to drive home his warnings of the perfidy of Earth and the ways of great companies. He was relieved when both the Takonians assured him that no negotiations were likely to take place.

"Why have we come here?" he asked when they were in the building and the assistant, in obedience to Goin's orders, was adjusting the large telescope.

"We want to show you your planet," said Dagul.

There was some preliminary difficulty due to differences between the Takonian and the human eye but before long he was studying a huge shining disc. A moment later he turned back to the others with a slight smile.

"There's some mistake. This is our moon."

"No. It is Earth," Goin assured him.

Gratz looked back at the scarred pitted surface of the planet. For a long time he gazed in silence. It was like the moon and yet—despite the craters, despite the desolation, there was a familiar suggestion of the linked Americas, stretching from pole to pole—a bulge which might have been the West African coast. Gratz gazed in silence for a great while. At last he turned away.

"How long?" he asked.

"Some millions of years."

"I don't understand. It was only the other day—"

Goin started to explain but Gratz heard none of it. Like a man dreaming he walked out of the building. He was seeing again the Earth as she had been—a place of beauty, beautiful in spite of all that man had made her suffer. And now she was dead, a celestial cinder.

Close by the edge of the cliff which held the observatory high above Takon he paused. He looked out across an alien city in an alien world towards a white point that glittered in the heavens. The Earth which had borne him was dead. Long and silently he gazed.

Then, deliberately, with a step that did not falter, he walked over the cliff's edge.

# BEYOND THE SCREEN

---

### CHAPTER I

### A DEMONSTRATION

MAJOR-GENERAL STALHAM FINISHED the kidneys and bacon and got down to the toast and marmalade. His nephew watched him patiently from the other side of the table.

"More coffee, Uncle?" he suggested.

The Major-General hauled in his faculties from a long distance.

"Er—yes, thank you. Wish I could get coffee like this at home. No good. I've tried. No idea." He drank and lapsed into silence again until the meal was finished. Then, with the first cigarette of the day between his lips, he became more sociable.

"Where's your friend?" he inquired.

"Judson?" answered Martin. "Oh, he's outside, fiddling with his contraption, I fancy."

The Major-General gave a half smile.

"So you really think there's something in it?"

"That's for you to say, sir."

The soldier nodded, and got up from the table.

"May as well go out to the lawn and see if he's ready now," he said, leading the way.

When they arrived Judson was bending attentively over a trapezoid black box mounted upon four well-splayed legs. From beneath the box two cables emerged to curl away over the grass like thick black worms, in the direction of the stables. About ten yards further lay a mysterious pile of broken bricks, pieces of wood, and odds and ends of metal, grotesquely out of place on the carpet-like lawn.

Judson straightened up as they approached. He was a tall, thin man of thirty of the type which always looks slightly untidy in limbs and clothes despite its most careful efforts at control. In his case the effect was enhanced by thick fair hair which nothing could keep in permanent subjection. Both his long thin face and his pale blue eyes showed a trace of anxiety as he raised them; it was possible that the War Office man might resent being forced to watch a demonstration under such conditions. But his expression cleared when he saw that the other was genial and interested.

"How about it? Ready for us?" the Major-General inquired.

"Yes, sir. It's ready now."

"Good. Where'd you want us to stand? What sort of range has this death ray of yours got?"

Judson looked hurt.

"It's not a death ray, sir. It's an annihilating screen. This particular machine has a range of a hundred feet over an angle of ninety degrees and is directed vertically upward. If you imagine a large fan, a hundred feet in length and extended to a quarter circle, balanced on its point on this box, that will give you an idea of its field of influence. Actually this is a kind of toy model. It is just as effective as the big one within its range, but the range is small."

The soldier looked curiously at the box. There was not much to see externally save a switch or two. He noticed a slot, six inches by perhaps half an inch, in the top casing; within was a gleam of glass.

"And the thickness of this 'fan'? The fore and aft spread, so to speak?" he inquired.

"Very little, sir. It is projected at the thickness of half an inch. My tests have shown an increase of about 1/64th of an inch at a hundred feet."

"You mean it has absolutely no influence beyond that half-inch-thick quarter circle?"

"I have discovered none yet, sir. All the same, it is advisable to stand well clear while it is on. I mean, if one were to make a careless movement—"

"Yes, yes, of course. Where do you want us to stand?"

—

BY JUDSON'S ADVICE they moved ten yards or so toward the house; the side opposite from himself and his pile of rubbish. Judson nodded.

"That's it. Now please don't come any nearer until I have shut off the machine again."

"All right, my boy. We're not fools," said the soldier, testily.

"Sorry, sir. But it really is dangerous though it looks innocent. Here goes, then."

He walked back a few steps, holding a switch attached to a cable. At the full extent of the cable he pressed the switch and dropped it on the grass. A red bulb lighted on top of the box.

"It's on now," he said.

Major-General Stalham felt disappointed. He had not known what to expect, but he was aware that he had counted on some visible or audible manifestation. There was nothing save the red light and the young man's claim the machine was 'on.'

Judson walked back to his pile of rubbish and picked up a stone. He faced them across the machine, and drew back his arm.

"Catch," he shouted, flinging the stone toward them.

The soldier instinctively put out his hands to receive it, but the stone did not arrive.

Halfway on its journey, exactly over the machine, it vanished.

Judson chuckled.

"Try again," he said, and lobbed over half a brick. It sailed through the air, but at the top of its curve it just ceased to be.

The general grunted and stared. "Stone," said Judson, and threw a flint out of existence. He followed it up with a piece of wood and then metal in the form of an iron bar.

The soldier blinked. He had a hazy suspicion that he was being fooled by some kind of conjuring trick. Had he been able to see the emanations from the machine, or if the objects had disappeared with a flash or bang it would have been less outrageous. Somehow the very neatness and cleanness of the operation encouraged his suspicion.

He and Martin, carefully keeping their distance, walked round to the side to observe the effect from there. It was even more odd to follow the parabola of a flying tin can and see it uncompleted because the can had winked out of existence.

Judson switched off the machine and tossed half a brick over it; it fell with a thud. He switched it on once more; a similar half brick never fell.

"This is remarkable," said the general, though even his cautious nature felt that the words were a trifle inadequate.

Martin left his side and hurried into the house. He was back in a few minutes carrying a twelve-bore and a box of cartridges.

"Here you are," he said, handing them over.

A piece of notepaper was pinned to a pair of steps set up on one side of the machine; General Stalham took up a position on the other. He let the paper have the choke barrel and blew the middle out of it. Judson set up another piece of paper and waited until he had reloaded.

"Now try again," he said, as he pressed the switch.

The general let it have left and then right. He lowered the gun, and stared incredulously at the unharmed paper.

"Wait a minute," he called, and hurriedly reloaded.

Again he fired both barrels in quick succession; still there was no mark on the paper. An expression of real awe came over his face. His voice was uncertain as he spoke.

"My God, Judson, what have you found?"

## CHAPTER II

# THE POWER OF THE ANNIHILATOR

"YOU TWO REMEMBER one another, don't you?" said Judson, casually.

Martin found himself shaking hands with a serene young woman in whom it was difficult to recognise the schoolgirl Sheilah Judson of a few years ago.

It was ten days since the demonstration to his uncle, but a rush of business had intervened, making it impossible for him to call at Judson's house until now.

Sheilah was thanking him for helping her brother.

"It wasn't much," he told her. "Juddy really had the whole scheme cut and dried; all I had to do was to be a yes-man. Considering what he had to show, the whole thing was a foregone conclusion. What I want to know is how yesterday's demonstration went. Sorry I couldn't be there, but I had to go over to Paris."

"I think it shook 'em a bit," Judson admitted.

Sheilah laughed. "You know him, Martin, most of his swans are geese. Shook them, indeed! I should say so. I've never seen a body of men so dumbfounded and knocked endways as they were when it had finished. I doubt whether they're really believing in their own senses yet. Tell him about it, Tommy."

Judson, fishing in the cupboard for beer bottles, landed his catch, and turned round.

"Sheilah's right," he admitted. "I wish you'd been there to see. They sent an army lorry and a squad of men. We loaded the big thousand-yard brute aboard and the little one too, in case of accidents. I mean, the big one had never been tried out properly—it's not the kind of thing you can fool about with in the back yard.

"We followed in style in a staff car to the site of the demonstration; a particularly desolate stretch of the Plain, a few miles beyond the camp. The exact position of the machine and its danger area were marked out, and power lines had been run there ready for us.

"It didn't take long to open the cases and get the bigger machine assembled. And after we'd connected up to the mains there was nothing to do but hang about and wait for the nobs to arrive. They turned up in a whole covey of staff cars about eleven-thirty.

"Your respected uncle was well in evidence, as jumpy as a flea on a hot plate. I don't know quite what the old boy had been telling them, but he was as nervous as hell lest the whole thing should be a flop—it must have been a good yarn to have got the demonstration arranged so soon. The rest weren't much excited. They drifted up and sniffed round the machine as if it had a bad smell—they might have been more impressed if I'd painted it khaki.

"The show was timed to begin at twelve. About a quarter to they started telephoning to clear the course, running up danger flags, sounding bugles and all the rest of it. At twelve a lesser officer announced to a greater officer that all was clear—it had been perfectly clear for a couple of miles each way all the morning, but now it was technically clear. Then—oh, I forgot to tell you there'd been one or two lorries, a small field gun and some other things drafted up in the course of the morning; they were parked at a respectful distance. Well, then the big noise—he was a Field Marshal, and that speaks well for your uncle's pull, told me to go ahead.

"He and his satellites moved off a bit, so I tagged along too, trailing the switch cable behind me. When they came to anchor I pressed the switch, and the red warning light went on. The bigger machine sets up a semi-circular screen, covering the whole hundred and eighty degrees from side to side.

"'Well, what are you waiting for?' the old boy said, shortly.

"'Nothing, sir,' I said, nicely and politely. 'The screen's up; it's for your men to test the resistance of the field.' And I explained to him that the game was to get anything past the machine within a thousand yards to either side, but not to go for the machine itself as it wasn't protected at present. He just grunted and gave some orders.

"Out on the left six men marched up out to a line about twenty yards from the screen. Their timing was perfect. Six pins were drawn, six arms swung over, and six little black bombs sailed away."

Judson chuckled.

"I wish you could have seen the staff's faces when the bombs vanished—the look of relief on your uncle's face was nearly as good. The rest of them stared after the bombs, then they stared at me, and then again at the place where the bombs should have burst. There was a faint thudding noise far away in the distance if you listened for it, but no sign of an explosion. The Field Marshal pulled himself together and ordered another bomb shy. Of course that lot vanished too. Some of the staff began to look at me pretty queerly.

"Well, there's no need to go into all the details. They went through a whole armoury of weapons. They put machine guns on it with ordinary and tracer bullets, they pumped shells at it, tried flame throwers and all sorts. Some young fool even wanted to drive a tank at it; I was arguing with him when the accident occurred.

"There was a shout somewhere, and I turned round to see people pointing to the right. A man was sawing away at the mouth of a bolting horse which was carrying him hell for leather at the screen. Everybody yelled at him to jump clear. I was a hundred yards from the switch then for we'd had to move back when the field gun got to work. I sprinted my best for it, but I was no more than halfway there when the horse and rider ran clean into the screen and vanished. I reached the switch and turned it off. Then I walked back.

"I arrived in a funny sort of silence. It was as if they had only just realised what the screen meant. The man who had suggested the tank idea looked particularly sick. The rest kept glancing over the plain as if they expected the horseman to reappear suddenly somewhere. We all walked down to the spot where he had disappeared. The hoof-marks were plain up to the screen line—there they stopped dead.

"The old Field Marshal turned and looked at me. He stood quite a time without speaking. Then he said:

"'God forgive you, boy, for what you may have begun.'

"He turned away and went slowly back to his car. He didn't seem to see us or anything about him."

Judson paused. In a different tone he added: "Well, then it was all over. We packed up and came home."

"And now?" Martin asked.

"Today I've been down at the War Office, talking for hours. It looks as if I shall be having a busy time for a bit. Curious men," he added, reflectively, "they tested it yesterday with most things short of big guns—we shall be floating it on a raft and testing out big naval guns against it next week, by the way—but what really impressed them, you know, was that man on the horse. It got 'em; meant more than all the rest. Nice, simple-minded fellows."

"I can understand that," Martin said. "But, tell me Juddy, what actually does happen? I mean, I can understand that there may be a form of radiation that shakes things to bits—a kind of disintegrating wavelength—but it ought to vary with different substances, and there ought to be some kind of residue even if it's only dust in the air. Or I could understand one that would incinerate immediately, but there again there ought to be a residue—certainly of metal—and there ought to be the dickens of a detonation in the case of explosives touching it. As far as I can see it's against nature and science and everything else for things to cease to exist when they hit your screen. The most that can happen to them is that they are changed into something else: a gas, for instance. What actually does happen?"

Judson lifted his face out of his tankard, and shook his head.

"That's where you've got me, old boy. And that's a point the War Office people have been hammering at half the day. They can't believe, though I've told them till I'm blue in the face, that I don't know."

"You don't know!"

"Exactly. I have got hold of a force, but I don't know what that force is. It's another manifestation of the power of electricity. Radio is one, X-ray is another, and heaven knows how many others are waiting to be discovered. All I have found out—and to be frank it was half by accident—is that if you do certain things with an electric current you produce this result."

"Do you mean to say you've no idea what happens to, say, a brick when you chuck it into the screen?"

"I do," he admitted, "though we don't know a great deal yet, we're learning by degrees. For instance, Sheilah noticed on one of the early trials that it acts as a windshield. And there are funny things about sound. We've established that sound does not pass through it, but round it. That wasn't surprising when we knew it stopped air. But what is odd is the result if you throw a noise at it, so to speak. We set an alarm clock ringing and heaved it into the screen. It, of course, disappeared at once, but the ringing didn't. I went as close to the screen as I dare, and I could still hear it faintly buzzing. A most uncanny sensation first time. And the hand grenades and shells also; there was that faint, far away thudding noise although they had vanished.

"As far as solids are concerned," Judson explained, "we don't know a lot, but we can show you a few specimens." He led the way into his study, and picked up a piece of stick from a pile of objects in one corner.

"That," he explained, "was once an old broom. Sheilah pushed the head of it into the screen, goodness knows what happened to that, but there is what was left in her hand."

Martin examined the stick. The end which had touched the screen was a bushy mass of splayed out fibres.

"It was queer," Sheilah told him. "The whole stick sort of shuddered in my hands; I could feel little tremors running up and down it, but it didn't seem to twist or pull in any way."

There were other examples: an iron rod twisted off, a glass rod curiously fractured. Martin inspected them all with interest.

"It's very odd indeed," he said. "You mean to say that you thrust a rod into the screen, that the end of it disappears at once, that the end of it does not protrude on the other side of the screen—and yet it is not severed immediately?"

"Exactly. Sometimes—with the iron bar, for instance—it takes two or three seconds to part. But if you find that odd, look at this."

He handed over a small branch from an oak. A few withered leaves still clung to it. The thick end showed a bunch of wrenched fibres similar to those on the broomstick.

"We found it on the lawn one day when we were clearing up after an experiment," he added.

Martin looked at it. It was quite unremarkable.

"Well," he said, "it looks as if you had set the machine up too close to a tree, and lopped it off."

"It does," Judson agreed. "But the trouble is, old boy, that we haven't an oak tree here, and there isn't one anywhere near that either of us knows of."

## CHAPTER III

## A WEAPON OF DEFENCE

MARTIN BECAME A not infrequent visitor at the Judsons' during the next eighteen months, but he saw little of Judson himself. Judson, in fact, seemed to see very little of his home. Much of his time was spent traveling, and the intervals mostly in his study. Sheilah was worried about him.

"They're working him to death," she told Martin. "When he's here he works until three or four in the morning and when he's away he's being rushed here and there all the time. He can't stand that kind of thing too long. Besides, the organisation and business side isn't really his kind of work."

Martin agreed. The few glimpses he had had of Judson were enough to show that. There were new lines on his face and signs of strain round his eyes; he fidgeted incessantly and was short-tempered with his sister and with everyone else.

"It'll end in a breakdown," she said unhappily. "Lots of people have told him so, but he won't take any notice."

"I know," Martin told her. "I hear from my uncle that he's so edgy that he's becoming impossible to work with. But the trouble is that they're all in a hurry, and they can't get on without him. He keeps too much in his own hands, and won't let go. Why on earth doesn't he depute more and take it easier?"

"I'm not sure. I think he wants to keep all the control he can because at the bottom of everything he's a bit afraid. You know what the old Field Marshal said to him, well, he still makes fun of that—makes fun of it too often for a man with an easy mind. I may be wrong, Martin, but I've an idea that he thinks he can stop it if it doesn't seem to be working out as he expects."

"But that's ridiculous. He'd never have a chance now."

"You'd think so, but I don't know. He may be keeping some essential part of the machine a secret."

"But would they take it on such terms, do you think?"

"They wouldn't like it, but he makes the terms. Tommy can be remarkably stubborn, you know."

Whether Sheilah was right or not about the cause it was clear that Judson could not keep on at his present pitch indefinitely. On her behalf Martin tried to reason with him. Judson put it aside.

"You don't understand, old boy. The work's got to be done, and done damn quick. There's no time to lay off."

"But you've been working madly for over a year now. Surely there's someone else who can give you a breather for a bit," Martin protested.

"Not now, not yet. It ought to slack off in a few months, then I'll see. We're working against time, and we've got to beat it. Now, if you don't mind, old boy, there's some work I must get on with…"

—

THE SCHEME DEVELOPED with remarkably little publicity. Large metal boxes in stands set in concrete began to appear here and there. There was one on top of London University tower, one on Bush House, others on Westminster Cathedral, on a chimney of Battersea Power Station, on a tower of the Alexandra Palace, and on one of the remaining towers of the old Crystal Palace. There was said to be one even on the top of the cross of Saint Paul's. It was generally understood that the boxes contained air raid alarms of some kind though there were varied opinions on how they would work.

Other things less obvious than the metal boxes appeared. There were two telephone boxes on the most exposed parts of Hampstead Heath and another at Highgate which had locked doors and permanent "out of order" notices on them. There were several objects which looked like transformers to be found here and there upon high ground both in Surrey and Middlesex. Also on Surrey hilltops there appeared some new summer-house-like huts reputed to be lookout shelters for fire-wardens. Out Dagenham way were to be found occasional oddly positioned structures bearing an entirely superficial and quite exasperating likeness to public lavatories. Down near Bromley several small water towers arose; only the local authorities knew that they contained no water—and they were at a loss to know what they did contain.

Nor was this outbreak of decidedly minor architecture confined to the London area. Manchester, Birmingham, Liverpool, Leeds, Glasgow, Edinburgh were a few of the many cities and towns it invaded. Certain seaports learned to their surprise that the landmarks which had served them perfectly well for several generations were inadequate and that it was urgently necessary for them to have new and more solid landmarks; as the Government unexpectedly undertook to defray the entire cost, they had them. Comment was sparse. True, certain of the unusable telephone boxes came in for scathing remarks in letters to local papers, but nobody can tell merely from its external appearance whether a transformer or a fusebox is unusable or not, and there is a natural reticence on the subject of being taken in by a dummy public lavatory.

If it was suspected that numbers of heavy cases leaving England for Singapore, Aden, Hong Kong and other strategically important spots did not in fact all contain pianos or agricultural tractors, no one mentioned it. There was activity in the naval dockyards and at the naval bases. New, strange bulges appeared at the foretops of His Majesty's ships of war. There was no disguising them. Foreign agents learned by subtle questions that the British had discovered and were employing a new tap-proof method of wireless communication. Their various governments thereupon started to spend much time and money in the attempt to tap the untappable, not to say non-existent, system, and to disbelieve all normal radio messages.

―

THE SUMMER PASSED. The Roman Empire continued to rebuild itself in a series of sabre-rattling crises. The Reich made public references to fertile and foreign lands which were the natural heritage of Wotan's children. The words of democracy, heartened by the voice of freedom from across the water, grew a little more dependable. The Balkans took heart and stiffened slightly. There was a faint stirring in the east; a suggestive clink from the hammer and sickle. The sensation that the curtain was about to go up grew more acute.

The Rome-Berlin axis, though still slightly out of true, held together. An inconsiderable island off the Estonian coast was acquired by the Reich in conditions which resembled a forced sale. The Scandinavians looked on uneasily.

# BEYOND THE SCREEN

Late in October came a rising in Algeria, trouble in South West Africa, and renewed demands for colonies. Then, while anxious efforts were being made to localise the trouble on the north African coast, an Italian troopship and its escort vanished without trace on its way from Sicily to Tripoli. Threats, accusations and counter accusations flew wildly. In Government buildings in all parts of the world men nodded as they read. "Here it comes," they said, with a half sigh of relief from the tension that it was over.

There was no declaration of war; it was not expected that there would be. The value of surprise had grown too high to be thrown away lightly. It was acknowledged that the one who could first strike a crippling blow was half way to winning. For three or four days vituperation erupted from the presses; then came action.

At ten o'clock on the night of November the fifth trusted members of the Nazi Party engaged themselves in long, and sometimes not very important, foreign telephone calls. It came about that all lines from Germany were in use. The scheme was admirably calculated to stop any news getting out of the country, save one in particular—that the first batch of Germans so anxious to greet their friends abroad all wished to do so at exactly ten o'clock G.M.T., not a minute before and not a minute after. This curious occurrence taken in conjunction with the knowledge that the Belgian wires were also humming with business deals or friendly greetings in German, and that there was unusual pressure on the Italian service also, was warning enough.

The general public knew nothing. There was no dimming of lights, no alarming notice from the radio; superficially all remained normal.

---

IN AN OFFICE in Whitehall a group of experts hurriedly summoned together sat in front of a large scale map of southwest England which covered the whole of one wall. There was little talking. Judson, fidgeting and lighting one cigarette from another continuously, looked ill to the point of collapse. There was sweat on his forehead, and the cigarette trembled in his fingers as he raised it. The old Field Marshal muttered to his aide to get the fellow a drink quickly.

On the tables were maps of smaller scale. Below the wall map an officer sat at a keyboard which suggested a calculating machine. At the back of the room were two operators with private exchanges. They called out telephone messages as they received them.

"British merchant vessel *Ellen Kate*, ten miles off Ostende, reports large fleet of planes without lights passed over her in westerly direction, 11:32 p.m."

"Mail plane, Amsterdam to Croydon, reports large number of planes without lights at great height heading west. Latitude, 51.56 north. Longitude, 2.55 east. 11:36 p.m."

"H.M. Destroyer *Nous* reports considerable number of planes, estimate impossible, proceeding west; 12 to 14 thousand feet, without lights. Latitude, 51.50 north. Longitude, 2.30 east. 11:40 p.m."

An orderly entered the room silently and handed a sheet of paper to the Field Marshal. He read it, and passed it on to the Marshal of the Air. The message ran: "H.M.S. *Unappeasable* reports large fleet of planes left Sicily. Passed south over Licata 11:30 p.m." The Marshal of the Air looked up, his lips silently forming the word "Malta." The Field Marshal nodded. Both turned their attention back to the maps and the telephonists. Messages were still coming in:

"Swedish liner, *Varmland*, Gothenburg to New York, reports fleet of unlighted planes to the south of her, apparently headed west. Latitude, 51.60 north. Longitude, 2 degrees east. 11:45 p.m."

"U.S.S.R. merchant vessel *Turksib*, London to Leningrad, reports large number of planes passing north of her, heading west. Latitude, 51.71 north. Longitude, 1.90 east. 11:48 p.m."

An officer looked up swiftly.

"They've split, sir."

"Warn Harwich."

"Harwich on the line, sir. They've heard. They're passing on warning to Leicester, Birmingham and Manchester. Hull on the line, sir. They're warning Leeds and Sheffield. North Foreland calling, sir. The detectors there have picked them up. They're passing north of the coast, following the estuary. They estimate five or six hundred planes."

A pause followed, then:

"Shoeburyness calling. They think the fleet's divided again. Chatham calling. They say they will proceed independently according to plan."

"Stand by," ordered the Field Marshal abruptly. The man beside the map stiffened and poised his hands over the keyboard.

"Horizontal screens, sections D and E," directed the old man.

The operator pressed two keys. The districts east of London, both north and south of the river glowed faintly on the wall map.

"Tillbury reports they are overhead," intoned the telephonist.

"Alignment Seven," snapped the Field Marshal.

The operator's hands rattled over the keys. A string of lights broke out on the map. They ran in a curve from Brentwood, through Romford, Ilford, Woolwich, and Sidcup to Eynsford. A row of bright points which meant that the Judson Annihilator had come into action in earnest for the first time.

There was dead silence in the room for perhaps three minutes, then:

"Add Alignment Twelve," said the steady voice.

Again a string of lights starting at Brentwood sprang out on the map, but this time it ran by way of East Horndon, Orsett, Tilbury, Rochester, Kingsdown.

In that irregular glowing circle there was contained to the best belief of everyone in the room every attacking plane of the southern division save the few handled by Chatham.

Someone opened a window. Above the regular murmur of traffic there was another sound; the far away drone of hundreds of engines. Most of the men in the room crowded closer to the window and held their breath to listen the better.

"It's getting less," said someone. "By God, it's getting less."

Judson got up unsteadily. He looked round the room with a rather foolish smile.

"Well, it's the end for some of you chaps," he said, quickly. "Better start looking for new jobs tomorrow." He began to laugh and sway on his feet.

His neighbour caught him as he fell.

"The fellow's tight," he said. "I'm not surprised. I'd be tight myself if I'd done half what he's done."

NOVEMBER THE SIXTH dawned in London a clear, sunny day. Suburban trains decanted their regular thousands, offices and shops opened, trade went on as usual. Yet for all the appearance of normality there was a tenuous, indefinable sense of something in the wind. Fleet Street, which was buzzing with rumours, found little substantial enough to print. The later editions carried an official government regret for any disturbance its surprise aerial manoeuvres might have caused to residents in east London and certain other parts of the country. Contenting itself with that, Whitehall sat back and awaited developments, happily picturing the consternation in Berlin and Rome.

And consternation there was. Even a totalitarian state cannot hope to hush up indefinitely the complete disappearance of a large part of its air force and most of its best flyers. Agents estimated that in all, bombers and fighters to the number of a thousand or twelve hundred had set out upon the greatest raid in history. They had kept touch by radio until the English coast was reached—after that there had been silence. The cones of the home plane detectors remained turned skyward to catch the first sound of the return. Radio operators waited throughout the night for news, and in the dawn they were still waiting.

Official accounts written beforehand were set up in type and held ready; press time came and the accounts remained unused. London and all the other cities of England were untouched; even from the lips of their Embassy and consular staffs Berlin could scarcely believe it. Weary groundstaffs still waited ready on the flying fields. The underground hangars remained forlorn. Radio men still called desperately into the unresponsive ether.

Rumours of disaster started to creep out from the flying fields and the newspaper offices. Those who had heard the fleet set out began to talk. The fiasco could not be kept quiet; the friends and relatives of the missing men could not all be quieted; there were too many of them. Gradually the tale got around of a new Armada which had never returned.

Similarly in Italy. A fleet estimated at about seven hundred planes had set out to blow Malta to bits. Malta still lay unperturbed in the kindly sunshine—but the planes; il Duce's pride which were to 'darken the sky with their wings'; where were they?

No one seemed to know; no one *did* know.

A near panic spread through the army councils of the world.

England professed an inability to understand the situation. She had a number of planes up practicing on the night of the fifth; all had landed safely. But she understood that several German and Italian planes, also practicing, had disappeared. She offered help in the search, if informed of the localities of the disappearances.

Totalitarian speeches reached masterly heights of face-saving, but the planes were gone and the pick of the flyers with them. A new force must be trained, but—and here lay the real root of apprehension—for what? To vanish from the face of the earth like the rest?

## CHAPTER IV
## STRANGE OCCURRENCES

IT WAS FOUR months later that Martin met the Judsons on their return from Cornwall. Letters from Sheilah had told him that her brother was making a good recovery from the strain of overwork, and they had not exaggerated. Judson was looking better than he had at any time since the demonstration of the machine to Major-General Stalham. Martin's interest, however, was chiefly in Sheilah. In that time he had seen her only on two of her brief visits to London; hurried, unsatisfactory meetings which had to be worked in between appointments—no fit occasions to find out whether she had made up her mind yet.

Things had been in that stage a long time now. She liked him, oh yes, she liked him; she was fond of him. But marriage, well, that was different. Oh, yes, she'd sooner marry him than anyone else she knew; but she wasn't sure that she wanted to marry at all—not at present. She didn't know; she couldn't make up her mind. A most uncomfortable and not very flattering state of affairs, Martin felt. A different type of man would, he knew, have forced the issue long ago; but he avoided that, aware that though failure would make him miserable, success would leave him uneasy. He preferred a voluntary answer, whichever it might be, to one sprung by shock tactics.

Judson was talkative, rambling from one subject to another. He inquired after Martin's uncle.

"How is the old boy? Haven't seen him since the great day. Haven't seen any of them, as a matter of fact. No loss to either side. I don't like them, and they despise me."

"Despise you?" Martin echoed, surprisedly.

"Well, it's partly that and partly disapproval. For one thing it has now dawned on them that the annihilator has upset the entire military apple-cart, and for another they feel that there's something ungentlemanly about it as a weapon. They've put up with me because they've had to, but they don't want to have more to do with me than they must. To your professional soldier war is a game, a kind of super chess—civilians like you and me who look on it as a mess to be cleared up as soon as possible are gate-crashers and boors."

Martin understood, and agreed:

"I know. We've a number in the family. But what about you, Juddy? What are you going to do now it's over?"

"Me. Oh, now I can get on with useful and sensible applications of the annihilator. There are all sorts of things one might do with it. It will be useful for rubbish disposal, for instance—just tip the stuff onto a screen, and it vanishes. No more dumps, no more hideous slag heaps. It may be possible to use it for smoke disposal so that we shall have decent, clean cities. I don't know, there are plenty of possibilities, but the first thing is to learn more about it; make it reasonably safe to handle; work out positive controls, find an insulator if possible, and all that kind of thing. We're going to get down to that as soon as we can get the stuff together."

"We," Martin noticed. That meant that Sheilah would be helping.

It did. Sheilah admitted it unhappily. A long conversation with her settled nothing new; it criss-crossed back and forth over the same old ground, and got nowhere. She ended miserably: "It's no good, Martin. I've got to be sure, and I'm not absolutely sure. And that makes it unfair for you. Martin, why don't you find someone else? You deserve someone else, Martin—a nice sensible girl who can make up her own mind, and make you happy."

"There isn't anyone else," Martin said.

■

JUDSON TOOK A roomy house in Surrey. It stood in forty acres of wall-encircled grounds a few miles from Dorking, on the lower slopes of the hills overlooking the country to the south. Workmen were busy on it for some weeks and when he and his sister moved into it at the end of April it had become part dwelling house and part experimental workshops and laboratories. An electric alarm fence had been run around inside the boundary wall. Two assistants lived in the house, and two burly individuals who seemed to have no well-defined duties occupied the erstwhile coachman's quarters. The ex-policeman who dwelt with his wife in the gatehouse gave all visitors severe scrutiny, and unless their names were in his list telephoned to the house before admitting them. Martin on his first visit had the sensation that he lived in a state of invisible siege.

"It's all rather irritating and melodramatic," Sheilah confessed, "but we hadn't any choice in the matter. It was a case of putting up with what the War Office calls 'adequate protection of official secrets' or doing no work on it at all."

Judson had overcome some technical difficulties and produced an annihilator throwing a quarter circle of ten feet radius. It had led to some interesting discoveries. One was that for annihilation it was necessary for the object to pass through the screen either by its own motion or by movement of the screen itself.

They took the ten-foot projector into the garden which was still untidy from the neglect of years. In front of a dreary looking laurel bush Judson set the machine low on the ground. He tilted the projection slot upward, and brought the invisible screen down to horizontal. The bush vanished from the top downward until only a ragged stump remained.

"As I tilted it the bush passed through the plane of the screen," he said. "But—" he searched around and found a half dead tree. "Watch this," he added.

The machine was set up again, this time the slot was horizontal, pointed directly at the trunk.

He switched on, tapped the machine lightly, and switched off again. The tree, with a tired, slow motion, leaned over and fell in a crackle of its rotten branches. Martin stared at the stump.

"If you were to measure it you would find that a slice approximately half an inch thick has been taken out of the trunk," Judson told him. "The work's not quite as neat as a saw, but it ought to revolutionise the lumber industry."

"Or quarry work," Martin suggested. "Or canal digging and drainage work."

Judson hesitated at that. He frowned.

"You'd think so," he agreed, "but that's one of the things I'm up against. There's something funny about that, something fundamental about it I can't make out yet."

"You mean you can't make solid earth disappear," Martin smiled. "Well, there's something consoling about that. But if a brick—why not earth?"

"Exactly. Why not? But I'll show you."

A few moments later he and Martin bent over a patch which had been swept by the annihilator's rays. In theory there should have been a short ditch ten feet deep. There was not even a depression. Martin prodded his fingers into the soil.

"It's real enough," he said, amazedly.

A few minutes ago the space in front of them had been a patch of barren earth with a covering of last year's beech leaves. Now, along the line where the screen had passed, and nowhere else, was a covering of coarse grass.

"If it had been the other way around—" he said, feebly.

"Quite," Judson agreed. "But it isn't."

Later Martin mentioned the phenomenon to Sheilah. She nodded without surprise.

"I know, there've been several things like that. Did you hear about my birds?"

Martin shook his head.

"That happened about ten days ago. I was working in the lab with the small machine when I suddenly found two swallows flying wildly around the room. They couldn't have flown in just then because it happened that all the windows were closed. And it doesn't seem likely that they'd been there all the time without my knowing because I'd been working for an hour and a half before they began fluttering about. They just came from nowhere.

"But that wasn't nasty, like the thing that happened some months ago near London. They were trying out one of the defence machines when something plopped down close to the projector. When they went up to it they found it was a man's hand hacked off at the wrist. It was still warm when they picked it up, but it belonged to nobody who was there.

"There's some explanation, of course," she added, "some angle to the thing which neither Tommy nor I nor anyone else has any idea of yet. But we don't seem to be getting much nearer the answer."

Martin left later with plenty to think about and a feeling that there was an element of danger which none of their elaborate precautions covered. He had a sensation that Judson and Sheilah were not unlike people walking too close to the edge of a cliff in a thick fog. It was no light uneasiness, it would not be dismissed, and remained as a background to all his conscious thoughts. Next Sunday, he determined, he would have it out with Sheilah and try once more to get her away from it all. But that left time for a lot to happen.

———

ON FRIDAY EVENING as Martin entered his club, intending to dine, the porter handed him a telephone message.

*Mr. Judson urgently wishes you to ring him as soon as possible.*

Five minutes later he heard Judson's voice.

"Thank the Lord," it said. "I've been trying to get you all day. Martin, it's about Sheilah. She's disappeared."

Martin put out a hand to steady himself. He felt as if he had had a physical blow. At the back of his mind a voice was gabbling—'It's happened. This is what you were afraid of. That damned machine has killed her.' He took a grip of himself. His voice was curiously flat as he said, "I'll be there in an hour or so."

It was a few minutes under the hour when he stopped his car with a splatter of gravel in front of the house. Judson himself opened the door and led him straight to the lounge.

"What's happened?" Martin asked.

Judson poured some whisky into a tumbler and handed it over.

"Drink this. I'll tell you. It happened about twelve o'clock this morning. I was upstairs working out some results. Sheilah was on the front lawn. She'd got a one hundred and eighty degree projector there and was trying out some smoke experiments. All at once I heard her scream. I thought she'd hurt herself somehow, and rushed to the window.

"She was down there on the lawn, and there was a man there too—a big fellow with a beard and ragged clothes. He's got a hold of Sheilah by the wrist, and she was fighting like a demon. She screamed again; I shouted and the man looked up. I just caught a glimpse of his face as I turned to bolt downstairs for all I was worth.

"It can't have taken more than a few seconds, but when I came out both Sheilah and the man had gone. Just as I arrived the two guards came pelting around the corner of the house. They were at the back somewhere when she screamed, and they'd seen nobody as they ran to the front. One of the assistants turned up a moment later. He'd seen the struggle from the workshop window, but like me he'd missed the end of it.

"The alarm fence hadn't been touched, so it was clear they hadn't got out of the grounds yet. We split into couples and searched the place. We didn't find a trace of Sheilah or of the man. The lodgekeeper swore that the gate had not been open since half-past eleven. We know the alarm fence was in perfect order because we tested it. One of the guards suggested that the man might have climbed a tree and swung over the fence that way—it's not likely because there are plenty of alarm wires about connected with the fence, besides that didn't explain Sheilah's disappearance.

"We put the local police on to it at once. They've pulled in one or two tramps, but not the man we wanted. And so far they've found no trace of Sheilah.

"Whitehall's been on the phone cursing and swearing. They've got men watching the boats and the airports. I tell you, Martin, it's a hell of a business. There's no saying what they might do to her."

"They?" Martin said.

"Yes, the people who've got hold of her. Don't you see what it means? They'll think she can give them the secret of the annihilator, and there's nothing they'll stop at to get it."

"But can she?"

"No. I wish to heaven she could. She's worked with it a lot, as you know, but I've never told her the basis of the construction—I thought it would be safer for her not to know. My God, what a fool thing to do! If she could tell them, that'd be that. But if they think she's just holding out on them... There's damn little chivalry in the espionage business. Oh, Lord, what the hell can we do about it?"

Martin sat silent. His reasoning power was swamped for the present. Instead of thinking, he was looking at a series of fearsome mental images which he tried and failed to suppress.

When, some hours later, they went upstairs, the idea of sleep was impossible; even to rest in a chair, intolerable. For more than two hours he paced back and forth across the room smoking furiously. At length he found himself methodically laying out each aspect of the affair, considering it and weighing the probabilities.

There was only one way out of the grounds which would leave no trace—Judson's screen. What way into the grounds would leave no trace? Was that also Judson's screen?

There had been the birds, the severed hand, and, still longer ago, the inexplicable oak branch...

Surely the answer was that the annihilator did not annihilate. But what did it do?

With that question still in his mind Martin dropped on the bed and surprisingly fell asleep.

---

THE BIRDS WOKE him. It was still early, soon after six. He crossed the room and looked out on the new late spring day. The shadows still slanted, and the lines thrown by the tree trunks barred the lawn below him. In the middle of the open space he noticed the projector Sheilah had been using yesterday. It had been switched off, of course, but no one had remembered to put it away. He stood motionless for five full minutes, staring at it; then with his mind made up he turned and left the room cautiously.

The machine was in order. He had been half afraid lest the lead to the mains might have been disconnected, but the red warning light flashed on as he pressed the switch. To make certain he scrambled his handkerchief into a ball and threw it into the invisible screen. It vanished.

Martin stepped back a few steps and braced himself. Somewhere behind him a window opened. Judson's voice called in alarm:

"No. Martin. Stop it, you damned fool!"

Martin clenched his fists, put his head down, and ran full tilt at the annihilator's screen!

## CHAPTER V

## AN AMAZING NEW WORLD

SOMETHING TRIPPED HIM. He fell forward with a queer twisting, wrenching sensation, and met the ground with a thud which winded him. He struggled, gasping, to a sitting position. Not until then did he realise that he was no longer on the lawn.

The first thing to catch his eyes was the handkerchief he had thrown through the screen. It lay beside him on a tuft of wiry grass. He stared at it a moment and then lifted his gaze.

He sat in an open space, a kind of gap in a hillside wood. Trees closed in his view on three sides, but in front the ground was clearer, encumbered only by shrubs and sprawling brakes of bramble. The slight downward slope enabled him to see over them into the distance beyond. The valley in the foreground was a sea of tree tops; featureless save where some slight rise suggested a frozen green wave. Behind it, bounding the scene, rose a ridge of smoothly rounded hills. He gazed instantly at them, following the contours; there was no doubt about it, however unfamiliar the immediate surroundings, they remained the same line of Downs which one could see from Judson's lawn.

He turned around to look again at the trees near him. They grew haphazard, unthinned and with little room to develop. Unrestrained ivy climbed to throttle them, and many of the trunks it had killed leaned on their still-living neighbours for support. Among the boles was a choked undergrowth whence protruded occasional broken limbs of trunks slowly rotting in the tangle below.

Behind him the edge of the wood was only a few yards away. Nothing appeared to intervene between him and it. Thoughtfully, he reached for his handkerchief; he crumpled it and threw it toward the undergrowth. Five feet from his hand it whisked out of existence. A moment later it re-appeared, materialising from nowhere, to flutter down beside him. He got to his feet. As he straightened, another white object flew close past his head. He retrieved it; a piece of paper wrapped around a stone. On it was a hurried scribble in Judson's hand:

"*What's happened? Where are you?*"

Martin found a pencil in his pocket. He turned the paper over and considered his answer. He looked again at the line of the Downs. They told unmistakably where he was, but— He shook his head, and wrote simply:

"*Am all right. Will try to find Sheilah. Screen invisible from this side. On no account move it. Keep it going till we come back.*"

He rewrapped the stone and threw it back. Leaving his handkerchief to mark the spot, he went to the trees and returned with an armful of rotten branches. He broke them into smaller pieces and laid them carefully in a double row leading to the invisible screen. The thought that one had only to run up the path they marked to be projected back into the familiar everyday world gave considerable comfort.

So far he had acted in a dreamlike, half automatic way, forcing himself to believe in the reality of the surroundings.

A little distance away a laurel bush lay on its side. The leaves were turning brown, and the stem was badly mangled. He recalled Judson's demonstration the previous week-end. Not far from it lay a curious wooden disc. He remembered Judson saying that a half inch slice of the dead tree had been removed—well, here it was. But where was it—and where was he?

He stood still, listening. There was no sound but the rustle of the leaves in the light breeze, the song of small birds close at hand, and far away the call of a cuckoo. It was disturbing. In every place he had known save on the tops of high mountains there had been at least distant reminders of human presence; the sound of a car, the distant rattle of a train, the whistle of an engine, something to give assurance that one was not alone. Here, there was a sense of desolation.

He began a search of the open space. The result was disappointing until he drew toward the western edge, but there he came upon the faint suggestion of a track winding close to the fringe of the woods. It was not well trodden and showed little sign of recent use, but that it had been made by human feet was indisputable.

He looked carefully around once more to fix the aspect of this place in his memory before he left.

Soon he was in the wood traveling circuitously though with little difficulty southward.

At the bottom of the hill he crossed a stream by means of a fallen tree, and picked up the track again on the further bank with some difficulty. He consciously realised for the first time that whatever else might have changed, the season of the year remained about the same. It was an unwelcome thought for he was growing uncomfortably conscious of his hunger. He began to regret that he had not thought of asking Judson to throw food though the screen.

A short stretch of unexpected uphill led on to a sandy ridge where the deciduous trees gave way to pines. Among them was a pile of rubbish, grass and weed grown, but showing the ends of squared stones in places. He climbed to the top to get his bearings. To the north the wooded hillside was broken in several places by patches of grass, but he was unable to identify for certain the one which he had found himself. In the other directions stretched a plain of swaying tree tops without a landmark; not a spire, nor a chimney, nor a power pylon showed above them. Far away to the east there was a smudge of smoke, save for that nothing but the hills, the sky, and the trees—unending trees.

He descended to the path again and followed it doggedly. At the foot of the ridge a better used path joined it from the right, and the two bore eastward as one giving him hope that it must lead to a habitation of some kind before long. Down on the level the ground was moister and the increased lushness of the bushes shut him in, limiting his visibility to two or three yards in each direction. The discovery of the first clearing, therefore, took him completely by surprise. One moment he was imprisoned in the trees; the next he stood looking over an open space of five or six acres.

He stopped in astonishment for the rectangular patch had not only been cleared, but tilled and planted. Rows of pale shoots which as a townsman he could not identify were already thrusting upward. He looked to right and left, half expecting to see bent figures at work, but there was no one in sight. Nevertheless, it was with rising hope that he went on, following the line which the path took straight across the field.

Halfway to the other side he stopped, staring down at the impression of a woman's heel...

Its owner, he noticed as he went on, was not the last who had used the path. In many places the marks had been wholly or partly obliterated by shapeless impressions such as a soft slipper might make. Once, a little to the side of the main beat he found the print of a man's boot with a plain sole and nailed heel. It made him curious, for he could find no repetition of it, and was irritably aware that to a man of experience the signs might read as plainly as a direction book.

His eyes were on the print and he was unaware that there was any other living person near until a voice spoke suddenly close behind him.

He started violently and spun around. Ten feet away stood a young man in a soiled and much worn grey uniform who held in a steady, capable hand a large automatic pistol. Martin raised his hands instinctively though he had not understood the other's words. The man spoke again. Martin shook his head:

"Can you speak English?" he asked.

"Enough," said the other. "You will stand still," he added.

He stepped closer. The muzzle of the pistol pressed against Martin's solar plexus as its owner patted pockets and armpits experimentally. Satisfied that Martin was unarmed, he withdrew a pace.

"How are you here?" he demanded.

Martin thought quickly.

"I don't know. Something funny has happened. I was walking in a garden—then I suddenly found myself in the woods up there. I don't understand it. But," he added more aggressively, "I don't see that that gives you any right to threaten me with a pistol. What's going on? Who are you?"

He was doubtful whether the other understood much of what he had said, but it seemed the right line to take. The man was impassive, he showed neither belief nor disbelief. After a few moments' consideration:

"You come with me," he decided, and waved his pistol to indicate that Martin should turn around. "You keep to the path. Not to run."

"But, look here—" Martin began, more for the form of the thing than for any other purpose.

"You come," said the man with the pistol, briefly.

## CHAPTER VI
## INCREDIBLE DISCOVERIES

THE LANGUAGE DIFFICULTY was a barrier. In the two miles of woods and occasional oases of cultivation which followed the man spoke only to give directions where the path branched once or twice. Martin marched obediently, acutely conscious of the pistol behind him, pondering what its presence and that of its owner implied.

They arrived at their destination almost without warning. The trees ended abruptly as usual. A few scrawny looking cows of no recognisable breed and some sheep of equally miscellaneous descent grazed on a meadow of rough grass. A small stream which crossed the place north to south was bridged by a few trunks crudely squared and set together. Close to the further bank clustered a village of wattle-walled, thatched huts.

They crossed the bridge, passed between two of the insecure looking buildings, and came out on an open space. The inescapable first impression of the place was its smell. Each of the encircling hut dwellers appeared to dispose of his refuse by flinging it just outside the door so that the whole place was fringed with heaps of reeking, rotting matter. Opposite some of the doors and in front of the main exits and entrances the filth had been shovelled aside to leave a free path, and as these gauntlets were used swarms of gorging flies rose on either hand.

The few men and women who were to be seen were vastly outnumbered by the children who played in the dust or crawled adventurously over the heaps of filth. The smallest of these were naked, but the older ones and every adult in sight wore garments of coarsely woven, undyed and, it would appear, unwashed wool. On their feet were cross-laced pieces of soft leather. The men were bearded more or less unkemptly, the lank hair of the women was mostly worn long and in plaits. None took more than passing notice of Martin and his captor. Martin, in spite of the pistol, stopped, and then looked at the other in amazement. The man wrinkled his nose and shook his head.

"Swine. We teach them," he said, disgustedly.

They turned to the left. Further up the bank of the stream and well clear of the village they drew near a log-built house which if not luxurious, was a great improvement on anything the village had shown. At the rear, a clumsy, undershot water wheel turned slowly. On a small, roofed verandah in front, two men in uniforms similar to his captor's were sitting in comfortable, crude chairs. The only other article of furniture present was a machine gun mounted on a block of wood.

The man with Martin shifted his pistol to his left hand and raised his right. "Heil Hitler!" he said.

The other two, one verging on middle age, and the other little more than a boy, rose and responded though their attention was on Martin. The new arrival reported rapidly in German, then all four entered the house.

The main room was lit dimly by two windows. There was no glass in them and they could be closed only by shutters of clay-filled basket work. Three or four chairs and a table ingeniously constructed from roughly trimmed wood were set on the naked earth floor. The rear wall was in shadow but he could make out a large wooden pulley which turned continuously, and the slow movement of the water wheel beyond made a background of incessant creaks and groans.

The senior man pulled a chair up to the table. He produced a notebook, opened it carefully, and fixed Martin with a direct gaze.

"Your name, occupation, nationality and place of birth?" he said in fluent, but throaty English.

"Just wait a minute," Martin objected. "I want to know what's happened first. Everything's crazy. A few hours ago I was walking in an ordinary English garden. Now the whole world's gone topsy-turvy. Miles of forest, no people, no houses—except an incredible stinking hut village—and you. I want to know what's happened. Am I mad? You must explain."

The man at the table shook his head.

"I am not here to explain. You are an enemy subject, and our prisoner. Your name?"

"Enemy subject! What do you mean? There's no war."

---

HE WAS AWARE that they were all looking at him intently, seeming not to believe him. He went on:

"I tell you. I was in London yesterday. There's no war in Europe—and no immediate sign of it. There's trouble in the East, and the Red Army is advancing in Brazil, but there isn't war in Europe. It's ridiculous to say that I am an enemy subject."

"You were in London yesterday?" his questioner asked, slowly.

"Certainly I was." Martin put his hand in his pocket and pulled out some letters. "Here you are, look at them, look at the postmarks and see the date."

The man took the letters. All three bent over them and exchanged remarks. The leader looked up again.

"These may be genuine, but they do not prove there is no war. Letters are delivered even in wartime."

"But I tell you—"

"War began on the fifth of November," the other interrupted, dogmatically. "If, as you say, there is no war, when was peace made?"

"But war didn't begin then. It—"

"On the fifth of November Germany sent an aerial fleet to bomb London. If you are trying to tell me that England and France failed to reply with military action, then I do not believe you."

"But London was not attacked," Martin protested. He affected to think back. "I remember that there was some international excitement somewhere about then. It was said that Germany had lost a great number of planes on

# BEYOND THE SCREEN

manoeuvres, and Italy too, as it happened, but the papers were never quite clear as to how many or what actually happened to them. However, it is quite certain there is no war."

The three Germans looked at one another. They were a trifle less confident. The leader turned back to Martin.

"Do you know how many planes were lost in these 'manoeuvres'?" he asked.

"No," Martin admitted, "though according to the rumours it was a considerable number. The whole thing seemed to be kept as quiet as possible."

"I see," said the other, thoughtfully.

After a moment or two of frowning contemplation he rose and crossed to the back wall, near the turning pulley. He did something there and began to talk rapidly in German. It took Martin some seconds to realise that the dark corner held a small wireless transmitter. After a short conversation he returned.

"I have orders that you are to be sent to headquarters for examination. As it is late today for starting, you will leave tomorrow at dawn."

It was an unpleasant suggestion. Martin had no wish to go to headquarters, wherever that might be. His object was to stay in the neighbourhood and search for Sheilah. But the subject of the girl was not easily broached. If he were to let it be known that he was searching for her his captors would immediately and rightly assume that his presence was not accidental. Once that became apparent and they would do their best to find out how much he did know. The situation was out of hand at present, and he could see no satisfactory means of dealing with it. He shrugged his shoulders with a fatalistic acceptance.

"Then may I have some food?" he asked. "I've eaten nothing today."

The meal produced for him was of salted meat, served in a wooden dish, a bowl of chopped root vegetables, a few slabs of hard, dark bread, a little butter and some cheese. A woman, evidently from the hut village, made it ready for him. He watched her curiously as she came and went between the table and an adjoining room.

Like the others he had seen she was not attractive to the eye. Her single, clumsy garment of undyed wool bore marks of long wear, and the only attempts to relieve its pure utilitarianism were crudely stencilled or blocked designs in a dark brown pigment at hem and neck. Her only ornament was a necklace woven of copper wire. The skin of her arms, legs and face was brown from exposure, and her hair ill cared for. But despite the superficial neglect there was no slovenliness in her movements. They were quick and deft. With surprise he realised that she was much younger than he had thought at first. The shapeless dress had misled him, but as she stood where the light touched her face he could see that she was little more than a girl. He saw, too, a pair of alert, intelligent brown eyes with an expression, as they met his own, which was partly curiosity, and partly something he was at a loss to determine.

The leader of the Germans and the one who had brought him had gone out together, leaving the third and youngest member of their party on guard. He looked about twenty-four or twenty-five, and a not ill-disposed young man. He was healthy and well developed without being burly, with a look of straight-forward honesty in his blue eyes. Though the fair hair was a trifle ragged in its trimming, the shave not perfect and the uniform over well-worn, his manners suggested that the defects were due to necessity rather than carelessness. He politely informed Martin that for lack of table implements one had to make shift with a pocket knife, and inquired whether he minded smoke during the meal. Upon Martin's reassurance he deftly rolled some brown shavings into a leaf and lit them. An odour of autumn bonfires drifted through the room. Martin hastily offered a cigarette from his own case; it was accepted with gratitude.

Neither spoke again until the meal was finished. Martin, feeling the better for it, lit a cigarette himself and set his elbows on the table. He looked thoughtfully at the other. The young German sat comfortably in one of the crude chairs. A large pistol holster at his belt was well in evidence, but his expression was not unfriendly, and there was a slight twinkle in the blue eyes as they met his own.

"Well, you're a cool customer," he said, and only a faint trace of accent told that it was not an Englishman speaking.

"Bluff," Martin assured him. "In reality I'm an extremely bewildered customer, but there's nothing to be gained by my registering bewilderment. However,

I'd be very grateful if you would explain just what's going on. For quite a long time I thought it was a nightmare, but I don't seem to be able to wake up."

"It is a nightmare," said the other. "We've lived in it for six months."

"This place," Martin said, waving an arm to include both immediate surroundings and far horizons, "where is it? It is unfamiliar, and yet it is not; I could swear that I know that line of hills to the south."

"Probably you do. They are the Forest Ridges, and beyond them, a little to the west, the South Downs."

Martin shook his head.

"That only makes the nightmare more nightmarish. We can't both be having the same hallucination. What's happened? What sort of unknown England is this? How can a countryside change in a flash from a well-populated farming and residential area to a land of forests and squalid settlements?"

"I don't know," the German admitted. "There are several theories, but—well, most of us just try to accept what's happened and make the best of it."

"But that's what I want to know: what *has* happened?"

The other hesitated a moment, then:

"I don't see why I shouldn't tell you as much as we know. After all, you're in the same mess—you'll have to live with us and like us... Can you spare me another cigarette, or are you treasuring them? You won't be able to get any more, you know."

"Go ahead!" Martin told him, offering his open case.

"Our squadron," the German pilot began, "joined the main fleet soon after ten o'clock on the evening of November the fifth. Everything had been planned with precision. Just after ten we caught the first faint distant humming of the fleet. They were traveling fast. The noise grew quickly from a murmur to a throbbing, drumming sound which beat down upon us in waves. The whole world seemed to tremble with the noise of engines: never before had the sky been so full of sound. To hear it grow was exciting. One felt a surge of pride, a sense of overwhelming power at being part of such an irresistible force.

"As we flew on, other squadrons joined us. Sometimes they came in to the flanks; at others, when we passed directly over their aerodromes, we could see them slide along the ground as they took off to climb after us.

"There was little radio communication, but as we approached the frontier, Franz, my observer, called to me that orders were for the whole fleet to extinguish navigation lights. The moon was up, giving a clear light. Our line stretched out many miles to my right. There were planes ahead of me, and planes strung out for miles behind: so great a number that as one looked across them there was a sense that we were stationary while the world revolved below.

"Before long we caught sight of the sea. It shone as brightly as the moon it was reflecting. Occasionally we thought we could make out ships like tiny dark specks on the spangled surface.

"Three quarters of the way across the order came to divide. The right wing altered course, and half the fleet fell away, bound for the industrial cities of the Midlands and North. The rest of us held on for the Thames estuary which would guide us up to London.

"The coast when it came into sight amazed us. We had expected that at least a late warning of our coming would reach England before we could hope to arrive. But it appeared that the English are indeed sometimes as casual as they would like others to believe. The coast towns were fully lighted; the lighthouses and lightships flashing as usual.

"We were dead on our course, and as we made the estuary we could see the glow of London painting the whole sky a dingy red in front of us. Before long we could see the massed millions of lights and signs which caused it. There was criminal negligence somewhere in the English service. Clearly no news had come through about us for not a district had dimmed. More amazing still, not a single British plane had climbed to intercept us.

"Franz called to me in a worried voice. He did not like it. Failing any other information, he said, the sound detectors on the coast must have picked us up long ago, but not one gun had opened fire. He had a superstitious feeling that it was too easy.

"Six bombers with their fighters were detached to attack Chatham. We went on. London lay open to us. The bombers would be at work now long before enemy planes could reach anything like our height. I did not feel as Franz did. The glittering, careless arrogance of the city just ahead angered me so that I regretted that I was not handling bombs.

"We began to extend for action, and it was then that the incredible thing happened. My machine seemed to wrench and twist in a quite unfamiliar way. For a moment I thought that a wing had collapsed. It had not, but something had gone very wrong with the engine. It slowed suddenly, with a horrible grinding noise; the plane shuddered all through with the jarring, then the whole thing seized solid. Simultaneously there was a shout from Franz in my earphones.

"'It's gone,' he cried. '*Herr Gott!* It's all gone.'

"I looked down. He was right. Every one of the millions of lights had vanished. All was black save for the gleam of the moonlight on the curling river. It was uncanny, a blackout beyond belief. Not a glare from a railway engine, not a flash from trams or electric trains, no lights of moving cars or of craft on the river, no glow from factory chimneys.

"'No bridges,' shouted Franz.

"He was right about that, too. There was not a single bridge over the pale Thames. Even the river itself looked different from the map I had memorized that afternoon. The turns were not the same, and there seemed to be lakes alongside it where no lakes should be.

"I glanced hurriedly around. A large number of planes seemingly in the same helpless state as ourselves was dropping down. I saw three falling in flames. Another, with a collapsed wing, fell past us and disappeared, twisting and turning beneath. Some had already hit the ground, their cargoes of bombs exploding with tremendous concussions. But still up above us was a mighty throbbing of engines telling that not all the fleet had been overtaken by the same fate.

"I turned my attention to making the best landing I could.

"We were lucky, Franz and I. I made a pancake. The soft ground tore off our undercarriage. The plane stood on her nose for a second, and then fell back. We had a nasty shaking, and I took a bump to my head. The next thing I remember was Franz offering me a flask.

"'Pretty good work,' he was saying.

"After a drink we lit cigarettes. We could still hear the sound of motors up above, but it was faint now, and as we listened it gradually died away. I felt forlorn as silence closed in on us, and so, I think, did Franz. And what a silence! It was as if the whole world were dead.

"Here and there was a glow of burning wreckage. Out on our right came a sudden new burst of flame. As we sat we could see the fire run across the fabric of a plane and take hold; for some seconds the frame glowed in ghostly outline before it collapsed.

"Franz and I looked at one another. We knew what that meant. Orders were to destroy one's machine if forced down in enemy country. Nevertheless, we hesitated. We felt that there was something here that our orders had not reckoned with: we both felt it. A sense that the catastrophe was in some way uncanny. I looked questioningly at Franz; he shook his head.

"'Let's get ready, but wait until they come,' he suggested. 'We can fire it at the last moment.'

"Franz looked to the radio in the hope it might still be unbroken. As far as one could tell from inspection it seemed to have survived, but the aerials had been carried away, and it took him some time to rig up a makeshift. When he had done it and connected up his earphones he looked at me with a grin of satisfaction.

"'They're calling,' he said. 'We are not to destroy our plane, but are to report, and await further signals.'

"In the morning the radio got busy again. The senior officer from each plane was to report personally to the Air Commodore if possible. But with every machine there must remain at least one man capable of destroying it if necessary and of tending to any injured. The Commodore's position would be indicated by a smoke signal.

"Five minutes later a thin column of greasy black smoke rose to the southeast of us. I made ready to go. Franz looked dubiously at the ice-rimmed pools among the tussocks.

"'Sooner you than me,' he said. 'Go carefully. It's the kind of ground that can swallow a man.'

"More than a hundred of us came to that meeting, and a more bewildered lot of men never gathered. But even that pitch of consternation was raised by the return of a party of scouts. They had been sent to the hilltop with glasses and instruments. They showed us on a map the position their reckonings gave. They were unanimous in their figures, but more bewildered than we, for the point they had determined lay only a few seconds west of the

Greenwich Meridian, almost on the Kent-Surrey border. Where the swamp and marsh stretched out toward the northern hills should have lain the city of London.

"One man who knew London well went further. He claimed that a hill upon which their glasses had shown a cluster of huts among the trees stood in the exact geographical position of Ludgate Hill, and that a green mound further west and close beside the river was identical with the position of Westminster Abbey. Furthermore, observations taken with a range finder had supported him completely.

"The radio experts managed to get into touch with the part of the fleet which had not been forced down. It seems that after the sudden blackout about a third of our machines remained in the air unharmed. They did not understand what had happened to the rest of us, and were thrown into confusion. They lost their bearings, for though they could see the Thames, they could not identify any of the reaches. We gathered that there had been not only confusion, but a near panic. It was not clear who took command, but someone had ordered a retreat.

"On the way back they dropped many of their bombs in the sea to lighten the machines. They saw no ship's lights. The Belgian coast was in complete darkness, and—most worrying of all—their radio could not make contact with their bases. The ether was dead save for communications between themselves.

"They crossed an utterly blacked out Belgium, flying entirely on their instruments. They crossed the Meuse still without answer from their bases. Beyond the frontier they found Germany as black as Belgium had been—incredibly and deathly black. In spite of desperate messages, not a landing field was lit. Orders went out for the survivors of squadrons to make for their own aerodromes. The main part of the fleet headed on toward Cologne.

"They found the Rhine familiarly turning and twisting northward—but Cologne they did not find. Then petrol began to run short, and the last order was: 'Every man for himself.'

"Now they were in a worse state than we were. Most of the men had taken to parachutes and were scattered over a large area without means of communication. They believed that almost all their planes were total wrecks. The bomber in touch with us had been lucky. It was resting in the treetops two or three miles from Cologne—but where Cologne should have been there was nothing but dense forest."

## CHAPTER VII

## UNEXPECTED AID

THE GERMAN PILOT went on to tell Martin of the days and weeks which followed, which resulted in this camp. Of how out of the early welter of speculation it was Ernst Gröner who emerged with the greatest following. He was a physicist of considerable standing, and unsubstantiated though his theories were, they did recognise all the known facts.

Gröner, basing his view on the conception of extra-dimensional time, held that it was no less possible theoretically to project an object into free-time than into free-space.

They had, he maintained, flown into something which had jerked them into another groove of time, or another part of the same groove.

As an explanation of the fact that some of the planes had suffered and others not, he suggested that the instrument causing the jerk was some kind of active field, and that those which had encountered the field head-on had survived partly or entirely unharmed, while others, touching it obliquely and remaining for an appreciable period half in and half out of its influence, had suffered since the revolutions of the two time phases, though similar, did not exactly coincide[1].

---

[1] Just as the expression "free-space" is inaccurate since a body situated in space must of necessity be held there by certain forces, so the expression "free-time" is inaccurate, or only relatively accurate. There would be stresses at work which for lack of a better word can be called time-gravitational attractions. If a rocket is shot into space at random it must either fall upon some sun or planet, or settle into an orbit determined by their pull; it would not be free. Similarly an object projected into space-time would not be free; it would gravitate to a certain point determined by the conditions of its projection. The mental image of time as progress along a line from a beginning to an end, such as lay in most people's minds, is a misconception and a barrier to a better understanding of its nature.

As a rough, though admittedly faulty analogy, instance the state of a gramophone which has been suddenly jolted. The machine still plays, the record is the same, the needle is still in

That, Martin's informant admitted, was about as far as he had been able to follow Gröner's theory. The mathematical backing of his arguments, though it impressed those who knew about such things, had conveyed little to him.

Martin listened without comment. He had to be careful not to give himself away while at the back of his mind he was wondering how Judson would take the theory. It could explain a number of puzzling points. The notion of the slightly dissimilar rotation of the two time phases, for instance, offered a tenable explanation of the odd way in which the sticks held in the screen had been broken off. That sounds were faintly audible through it might be due to air passing through in pulsations and thus transmitting the sound.

"And the natives?" Martin asked. "How do they take all this?"

"Oh, they don't like it at present, of course. You could hardly expect them to. So far we've been taking all the time, and we've not been able to give them any of the benefits of civilisation in return yet. But they're a peaceful lot on the whole, and don't give much trouble."

Martin underwent a sudden change of mood. The utter impossibility of the situation came over him with a rush, swamping his acceptance entirely. He frowned.

"But this gets more fantastic than ever—I mean, it just can't be so. This is England, and I have no alternative to offer to the time theory. But if you are going to make these changes and build up a civilisation there'll be something left to show for it; some signs of your influence are bound to remain."

"Of course. If not, why should we do it?"

"But they can't, they don't. Archaeologists would have found at least traces of them."

The young man looked puzzled, then his face cleared. He laughed.

"Do you mean to say that you've been thinking that these dirty, hut-dwelling savages are your ancestors?"

"But isn't that what you've been telling me?" said Martin, perplexedly.

"Heavens no, man. They're your descendants."

---

the sound track—but it is in a different part of the track.—Author.

—

LOOKING UP, MARTIN saw that the girl who had brought the food was standing some six feet behind the opposite chair. How long she had been there, listening, he could not tell. She caught his eye, laid a finger on her lips, and nodded at the back of the unconscious German. Martin, glancing back quickly, saw that his momentary inattention had gone unnoticed. He made idle talk.

Out of the corner of his eye he was watching the girl. Not a sound betrayed her, but she was drawing closer to the man. In her hand she held a square of rough cloth. When she was directly behind him she paused and lifted the cloth. Martin edged forward on his chair, and sat ready.

The cloth fell over his head. Martin was round the table in a flash. His left hand grabbed the hand which went to the pistol holster. His right shot up to the man's jaw. There was weight behind it, and the other fell limply back in his chair. The girl backed half frightened across the room and beckoned him urgently. He delayed only long enough to take the pistol before he followed.

She led the way through the inner room, scrambled through its glassless window, and dropped crouched onto the grass beneath. When he had joined her she raised her head and looked cautiously about, then, with a tug at his sleeve, she slipped away to the left and down the bank of the stream. Martin followed without hesitation, and bending low to keep beneath the level of the banks trudged against the current behind her.

They kept to the stream for two hundred yards or more, until they were well screened by the woods, and then they climbed out on the further bank. Still the girl said nothing, but beckoned him on. After thrusting through a few yards of bushes they came upon a narrow footpath. She stopped and pointed along the path to the north and the hills behind. Then, still without a word, she turned and went back swiftly by the way they had come.

Martin stood without moving for some moments. The whole affair had bewildered him by its suddenness and unexpectedness. What reason could she have for rescuing him, a stranger, from people who were, after all, more kin to him than she was? Yet her manner showed that she knew what she was about: lacking any other advice he could do no better than to follow hers. He started toward the hills.

A quarter of a mile further on a movement to one side of the path caught his eye. He levelled his pistol at the bushes.

"Come out of that," he ordered.

"You needn't shoot me, Martin," said Sheilah, as she stepped on to the path.

### CHAPTER VIII

## SHEILAH'S STORY

"WE SHALL HAVE to stop somewhere till it gets light," Sheilah said.

Little as he liked the idea, Martin had to assent. The light was failing fast: beneath the trees it was already so dark that the way was hard to see. They must be, he reckoned, about half-way up the hillside by now, though hemmed in by the trees it was little better than a guess.

The plan was to make for the hilltop first and then make west. When they were above the space where the annihilator stood they would turn downhill again and come to it from the north. It was a longer way round, but the certainty that the pursuit would have set out along the lower path as soon as Martin's escape was discovered forced them to take it.

They left the track reluctantly at a point where the trees were thinner. In a few moments they were safe from the chance sight of anyone using it, and Martin was breaking off small branches to make a couch.

"And now," he said, sitting down beside her, "perhaps you'll be kind enough to explain just what's happened—and how you come to be capering about in that fancy dress."

Sheilah looked down at her clothes. There was still light enough to show the clumsy, smock-like dress of unbleached wool and the crude, soft leather sandals on her feet.

"It's not becoming, is it?" she said. "But it couldn't be helped."

"Explain," demanded Martin. "This affair's gone all wrong. I set out as a rescue party of one after you; and end up by owing my own rescue to you. It's all thoroughly untraditional."

Sheilah chuckled.

"All right, but I expect you've guessed all the first part. How that great bearded brute suddenly appeared while I was experimenting, and dragged me through the screen after him?"

"Yes, I supposed that was about what had happened," Martin admitted.

"Well, the next thing I knew, I was sprawling on the grass. He'd fallen too, but he was still holding my wrist. After half a minute or so he got up and dragged me up with him. He stood staring at me in a puzzled way as if he didn't quite know what to do next. His mind evidently worked slowly, but mine was going quickly.

"I looked over his shoulder as if I could see someone coming, and he fell for it right away. As he turned his head I bent and bit his arm and wrenched my hand away. Then I turned and ran toward where I knew the screen must be. The yard or two's start I had should have been enough; it could not be much more than that from where we had fallen. In a few steps I should have come back on our own lawn, but I ran twice as far as I expected, and nothing happened.

"I stopped helplessly and let the man catch me, for I guessed why it was. Somebody had heard me call, and the first thing he had done when he got to the lawn was to turn the projector off and destroy my chance of getting back.

"The bearded man was more careful after that. He kept hold of my wrist until we were well in the woods, and then he made me walk in front. We went quite slowly. He seemed to be dawdling on purpose: in fact, he was.

"After we had gone some miles and crossed a cultivated field he deliberately turned off the path and waited there till it got dark. Before we went on he tied my wrists together, put his finger on his lips, and pressed the point of a very sharp arrow against my back. We came into the village quietly and got to one of the huts not far from the bridge, without meeting anyone.

"It was a filthy hovel and the smell of the whole place was nauseating. He lit a few sticks in the fireplace to give us some light, then he made me sit down on a dirty pile of straw, and fastened my ankles together with a coarse cord.

After that he freed my hands and gave me something to eat: it was nasty stuff, but I was hungry, and I ate it.

"I found that I was less afraid of him now. Whatever he intended to do, he showed no signs of being ill-disposed towards me. Evidently he had some plan which involved keeping me hidden, and I tried to find out what it was.

"When I talked he listened with a puzzled expression. And I was as perplexed by his reply, for in amongst it I heard a few intelligible English words though they were twisted by an unfamiliar pronunciation. It wasn't easy to get meanings across, but we managed to make a few things clear to one another. I understood, for instance, that I was not to show myself outside the hut or it would in some way be the worse for me—though just what would happen was not at all clear. But I could not discover what he intended to do, nor who he and his people were.

"After an hour or so he seemed to get tired of trying to talk. He tied my wrists together again, and with a final warning against being seen or heard, he left me. No more than two or three minutes after he had gone out a girl slipped in.

"She was the girl who helped you this afternoon. She stood in the middle of the beaten earth floor looking down at me with interest, but without surprise—which suggested that our arrival in the village had not been so secret after all. We faced one another for a while, then she began to speak carefully and, to my astonishment, in German.

"We talked for perhaps two hours. Many of the things I wanted to know she couldn't tell me, but she did explain a great deal which had been perplexing me. And I learned something about her.

"She was the wife, according to tribal custom, of the man who had brought me there. This hut had been her home until four months before when the three Germans had come. She could not tell me where they had come from, but by this time I had a pretty good idea. Not long after their arrival the leader had noticed her and suggested a change of domicile. Apparently without hesitation or scruples she had gone to the German, leaving her husband to shift for himself. She had, she said, never thought much of him, anyway.

"There was very little fuss about it. Whatever the village people think of the Germans' intrusion, they are awed by them and too much afraid of their weapons to object actively to anything they may decide to do. They gave a demonstration of pistol practice soon after they came, and that was enough to make even an outraged husband think twice before starting trouble. So the girl continued to live peacefully with the leader.

"But that did not prevent her from keeping a prudent eye on her ex-husband's behaviour. She had no idea what was in his mind concerning me, but she meant to find out. For the present she warned me against trying to escape. It was unlikely that I would succeed in getting clear of the village unseen, and if I did I should be unable to find my way through the forests in the dark. With that, she left me, promising to come again the next day.

"The bearded man returned not long after she had gone. He barely glanced at me. After throwing some wood on the fire, he lay down on a pile of straw on the other side of the room and went to sleep.

"The next morning—this morning, that is—he got up early, gave me a bowl of a kind of porridge, ate some himself, and then went out. And that's the last I saw of him.

"It was after noon when the girl came at last. She said she had been delayed by the arrival of a new man whom the rest called an Englander. There wasn't much difficulty in recognising you from her description.

"She had brought me this dress and sandals like her own so that I could at a distance pass as one of the villagers, and the only hesitation I felt about changing into them was on account of their being so very secondhand. It didn't take me long to do it, and then she was ready for us to leave—but I wasn't, quite.

"'Look here,' I told her in German, 'I'm as anxious as you are to get rid of me, but this Englander is a friend of mine. If I go, he goes too. You've got to get him away somehow, or you don't get rid of me.'

"Apparently it never crossed her mind that the German might, if offered the choice, prefer her company to mine. She had taken the opposite view flatteringly for granted, just as her ex-husband had.

"She looked distressed.

"'It will be difficult,' she said.

"'All the same, it's got to be done,' I told her. 'If you don't bring him to me, I shall come back.'

"And—well, it took her some time, but she did it. I don't know how, but you do, so it's your turn to do the talking for a bit," Sheilah ended.

—

IT WAS MORE than an hour after sunrise when they reached the smooth grass near the top of the hill. They climbed no more since there would be a risk of exposing themselves on the skyline. Instead, they turned west, keeping along the flank of the hill, a little above tree level.

It was easy going over the open ground; a light breeze was in their faces and an early morning freshness put a better complexion on the world.

"Did the Germans tell you their tale of how this state of things came to be?" Sheilah asked.

"No," Martin admitted.

"Well, the girl told me. It's the story of the devil-birds who lived in the land beyond the sunrise. It seems that the devil-birds' lands were also overcrowded. The devil-birds had built nests on top of one another as the men had built their huts, but they reached the sky and couldn't go any further. They began to want to build and to lay their eggs in the lands this side of the sunrise. But the men said 'no.' They wanted all the land to grow food on for themselves and their children, and that the devil-birds would be shot if they came.

"But the devil-birds went on complaining about overcrowding and at the same time laying more eggs and hatching out more families until their land could not support them. Then they came across the sunrise. They came in flocks so huge that they filled the sky, and they roared with anger so that the whole world trembled. They spat fire onto the land below. So mighty were their droppings that the earth staggered as they fell and the piles of huts were shaken down. A vapour arose from the droppings so terrible that all who breathed it died at once. They scattered poison into the sky, and the sky poisoned the earth.

"Then the devil-birds went back, but the poison stayed. It was in the air, in the water, in the food. The skins of men and women who took the poison came out in black patches. They went mad, and died in agony—and the next day all their friends and families showed the black patches, and the braver ones killed themselves because they had seen what was going to happen. People died by the thousands, by the millions.

"Only a few small islands went untouched by the plague: places where the prevailing wind was off the sea, keeping the poisoned air away. The people on the islands shut themselves off from the mainland and from one another, and waited.

"Some of the smaller islands could not support their inhabitants, but any men who could be found brave enough to go to the mainland did not return. So the islands communities grew less, though they hung on.

"The legend says that it was several generations before at last a man returned to tell them that it was possible to live on the mainland again. Probably that's an exaggeration, but it implies a long time, and there were pitifully few of them left. Anyway, it shows you what I mean by the survivors of a civilisation."

"Gas, disease-bombs, air-borne bacilli," said Martin.

"Yes, a plague, started deliberately, and then getting out of control—probably by an unexpected mutation—so that it spread everywhere, wiping out its creators as well as their enemies."

"Could it? It seems impossible. It may have been some local affliction greatly exaggerated—I mean, think of the tales of the flood. After all, it's only a legend."

"Only a legend," she agreed, "but it's a remarkable legend for a simple people to have invented. Have you a better means for accounting for all of this?" She waved an arm to include the whole wilderness of forest.

They walked on for a time in silence.

"Then Juddy's annihilator did not—will not—stop war," Martin said.

"No. It's just another new weapon to be counteracted," Sheilah said.

"And the people in the village—I wonder if they will grow up just to destroy themselves in the end?"

"Who can say? Their minds may develop differently; they may lack suicidal will to war. They may consider the fighter a dishonourable man and a bad citizen. They may, unlike us, see their danger before it is too late."

"But you don't sound very hopeful."

"Hopeful! Why should I be hopeful? Hasn't civilisation after civilisation climbed up and then fallen down the sink of war? I thought that in helping

Tommy I was doing something which might help to change all that—now I know it wasn't. It makes me feel that the whole stock is tainted." She turned to look up into his face. "I will marry you, Martin, if you still want me. But I don't think I want to bring children into this kind of world."

---

SHEILAH STOPPED. AND pointed across the valley.

"This is far enough. You see those two hill crests exactly in line. That's how they look from the hill behind the house."

"There should be a path," Martin said.

She nodded. "I remember. It ran up the west edge. Let's look a bit further."

They found a track emerging from the tree belt a hundred yards further on. It was little used, but there was no other, so they took it.

The track wound to take advantage of open ground, and they passed cautiously down the sides of two spaces similar to, but smaller than the one they sought. At the edge of the third Martin stopped. He could see the head and shoulders of a man who stood in the open. Sheilah touched his sleeve.

"It's the man who caught me."

He nodded. The man had known where to come. There was not much to be feared from him alone; the question was, had he brought the Germans with him?

The projector, he remembered, was not far from the top end of the open ground. To make a way through the trees to the left would bring them nearer to it and also give a better view of the whole place.

The going was bad. Brambles and thorn bushes tore their clothes and faces. After a yard or two Sheilah's legs were lacerated and bleeding, and her hair was continually tangling in small branches. In spite of their care Martin felt that a herd of cattle could scarcely have made more noise. After twenty-five or thirty yards of zig-zagging to avoid the worst thickets he led the way downhill with still more caution. Sheilah kept close behind. Progress was slow and painful. At last he reached a point where it was possible to look out between the leaves.

He could see the double track of dead branches he had laid to mark the path to the screen; the screen itself should now be between him and them if Judson had obeyed instructions and kept it up—a bare thirty feet from the top fringe of the bushes. The bearded man was also visible.

Martin turned his head slowly to whisper directions to Sheilah. She rose on tiptoe to see the ground beyond, and as she moved a branch went off like a cracker under her foot. The effect on the bearded man was immediate. He waved an arm at someone out of sight further down the hill, and started toward their hiding place.

There was nothing for it but to make a dash. Martin flung himself through the last few yards of bushes. The oncoming man threw something which whizzed past his head; there was a thud just behind him. He fired wildly, and saw the man stop. He glanced back to see Sheilah lying where the missile had felled her.

As he picked her up he caught sight of the three Germans racing up the hill toward him, beyond the screen. Holding Sheilah, he ran headlong down the hill in their direction. He saw them come to a stop, looking puzzled. Then the sun seemed suddenly to leap higher in the sky. There was the same strange twisting fall that he had felt before. Trees and sky whirled before his eyes—and he dropped on a smooth lawn.

Martin scrambled to his feet, and staggered. There came one last message from the world beyond the screen: a bullet whistled past him, ricocheted from an iron seat, and broke a window in the house behind.

He reached swiftly for the switch. The red light winked out. The screen was down.

He picked Sheilah up in his arms, and walked to meet the men who were running from the house.

# CHILD OF POWER

—

### CHAPTER ONE

### OF MICE AND MEN

IT WAS ONE of those evenings more often imagined than granted in the Lake District. The stir in the air scarcely ruffled the water and it was warm enough to enjoy sitting out on the terrace after sunset. Peace had crept gradually over the valley to settle down finally with the closing of the public bar. The peak of the mountain opposite was still silhouetted against the lingering afterglow, lights occasionally wandered across its black base and the sound of a car engine came over the lake to us no louder than the buzz of a bumble bee. One sat and drank beer and smoked and chatted.

We were a chance-met group, such as any pub in the district might have held that night. A business man and his son from somewhere in Lancashire, two American college boys energetically seeing England from bicycles bought within an hour of their arrival at Southampton, a tall man in whose speech was a faint suggestion of the north Midlands, his wife, and Joan and myself. The four others in the place, two young men and young women whose notion of a holiday seemed to consist of dissipating the maximum of ergs in the minimum of time, had already left us in order that no mountain might put them to shame on the morrow.

Conversationally, we had rambled quite a way. We had considered the inhabitants and character of the neighbourhood, thence we had somehow arrived at the Spanish question and settled that, which had entailed our decision that certain social reforms were vitally necessary all over the world, and this in its turn had led us to speculation on the future in general and the future of man in particular. One of the Americans was touched into eloquence on the subject.

"It's such a darned muddle in most people's minds," he said. "They know that nothing is really static, it's all got to change, but along with that they're convinced that modern man is God's last word—and yet that's contradicted again because if they were as convinced of it as they think they are they'd do something to straighten out the system and make it a decent world for this climax of evolution to live in—to settle down in permanently."

"As it is," put in his companion, "they just tinker away at it a bit because instinct rather than reason tells them that it's a waste of time to make the perfect social set-up for our kind of man when he may be superseded by another kind who won't be satisfied with that set-up at all."

—

"WHAT DO YOU mean by another kind of man?" asked the Lancashire man from behind his pipe. "What other kind can there be?"

"What about a type with a super brain?" suggested his son. "Something like 'The Hampdenshire Wonder' that Beresford wrote about, or Stapledon's 'Odd John.' Didn't you read those books?"

"No, I didn't," his father said, bluntly. "I've something better to do with my time than readin' tales about fancies and freaks."

"It's only the form," said his son. "What they're suggesting is that the next step will be a great brain development."

"Oh, aye. Chaps wi' big 'eads, and suchlike. I don't believe it."

"That's not the only possibility," put in Joan, beside me. "I think the next step will be psychic. Perhaps telepathy, or a kind of clairvoyance that can really be used; or perhaps they'll be able to see things that we can't see now—as some people say animals can."

"Sounds retrogressive to me," the first American told her. "I'd say most of those things did exist in man, and do in animals to a certain extent now, but that they've atrophied with the development of the brain. No, I guess brain development's the way to go. Though in a way I'd say you're right about seeing things. Eyes are still improving. Maybe they'll be able to see the infra-red or the ultra-violet, and p'raps some emanations we know nothing about. But I think the brain and the reasoning faculties will gradually develop beyond anything we can conceive at present."

"Why gradually?" asked his friend. "There doesn't seem to have been much change in the last five thousand years. Why not at a jump?—that's the way with mutations."

"Maybe, but how do you think a sudden mutation is going to survive bone-heads like us? We'd probably put it out of the way out of kindness, or lock it up in an asylum and not let it breed. I can see us defending ourselves mighty toughly against any mutations."

"And very right, too," said the Lancashire man. "'Oo wants to breed freaks or mutilations or whatever they are? Put 'em out of their misery, be 'umane, I say."

"But they wouldn't be freaks, Father. If they were the natural next step in development, they'd be normal."

"If they 'ad big 'eads and thought different from other people they'd be freaks. A big 'ead's a freak, same as a bearded woman. I've seen 'em at Blackpool. A man's the same as the rest of us or 'e's a freak. Stands to reason."

―

THE TALL MAN from the Midlands spoke out of the darkness to the Americans.

"I think you're right about the jump, but what sort of a jump's it going to be? That's the question. It can't be too big a physical change at one step. We, just like the wild animals, hate a variation from our norm, and I agree we'd be pretty sure to suppress it for a humane or for any other reason which happened to suit us. No, we must have survived to reach this stage by taking a series of small and not very obvious jumps in safety."

"But small jumps would mean pretty frequent jumps, or we'd never have had time to get from the amoeba to here," said one of the Americans. "Now, if there's been a jump worth a nickel in the last five thousand years I've not heard of it. That's surely a long time to stay put. Maybe we have come to the end or maybe nobody's noticed it when it happened."

"Or," said the tall man, "maybe it's just about to happen." He puffed at his cigarette so that it glowed and lit up his face. One had a feeling from his tone that he was not just speaking at random. The American asked:

"You've an idea what it might be?"

"*Might* be—well, yes. But, mind you, I'm laying no claim to prophecy. As far as I go is to say that I have seen a variation from the normal which does not seem to be due to any of those glandular upsets which commonly cause freaks. It is, to the best of my knowledge, unique, but, of course, there may be others. If there are, I see no reason why they should not survive and stabilise the new type."

"Which is?" prompted the American.

"An additional sense. A sixth sense." There was a slightly disappointed pause.

"Well, I don't know that there's much in that," said the Lancashire man. "Means knowing things as nobody told you, and you 'aven't read. There's a word for it—oh, aye, intuition, that's it. Young lady I once knew 'ad it. She went into the fortune reading business. Didn't do so bad, either."

"That's not what I mean," the tall man told him a trifle shortly. "I'm not talking about a mixture of guesswork, humbug and adding two and two. I mean a real sense, with organs of perception as real as your eyes and your ears and your nose and your tongue."

"I don't see as you need any more. They're enough, aren't they?"

The rest ignored him.

"Organs for the perception of what?" asked the elder American curiously.

The tall man did not reply at once. He turned up the end of his cigarette and regarded it for a moment.

"All right," he said. "I'll tell you about it. But I warn you that all the names and places will be faked. If there is any chance of following the business up, I want to do it myself."

## CHAPTER TWO
# THE STRANGE CASE OF TED FILLER

THE TALL MAN paused again as though seeking an opening.

"It's an odd little story, and to explain to you how I come to know so much about it, I shall have to reveal that I practice medicine. That's a thing I keep quiet as a rule when I am away from home. It alters people's attitude if they know it and shuts one off from them almost as much as if one were a clergyman.

"However, that is my profession and for twenty years, until, in fact, two years ago when I moved south, I practised in Irkwell in Derbyshire. It's a place which is typical of the kind of semi-industrialised village you find round there. Most of the men are employed in the quarries or the mills, a few work lead in the pits where there's any left to work. The women work in the mills, too, until they marry and start having more children than they want. The place is partly cottages of local stone but mostly rows of shoddy cottages put up in the last century when the mills came. In general, it's a kind of semi-rural slum. Not the kind of place you'd expect to produce any advance on modern humanity—and yet there's no doubt in my mind that young Ted Filler was something more than an ordinary freak.

"His mother, Ada, regarded his arrival more as an act of God than a personal achievement until she found out that he was a boy. It was a discovery which had the result of infusing more interest into the family life. Her three previous contributions had all been girls, and this, and the deaths of the two younger in infancy, had helped to give her an attitude of discouraged fatalism about the whole business. But with Ted's birth she seemed to make a fresh start and he began his independent existence enviably protected by first child devotion and fourth child experience.

"Not that he appeared to be in the least in need of special treatment. He was a healthy, well-formed child whose yells when he was washed were encouragingly lusty. I did not detect the least sign of abnormality in him, nor do I think would anyone else have done so. I was able with complete honesty to assure his father and mother that they had a remarkably fine son—and that wasn't too common in my Irkwell practice.

"Nevertheless, when I called on Mrs. Filler again I found satisfaction somewhat diluted.

"''E worries us, 'e does,' she said. 'Not but what 'e ain't a dear little chap and me proud of 'im,' she added, in the manner of one anxious not to appear ungrateful. 'But 'e ain't like the others was. 'E's that difficult to get to sleep, you'd never believe. And then sometimes when you've got 'im to sleep 'e'll wake up all of a sudden and look at you just like 'e's 'ad the fright of 'is little life, then 'e'll begin to 'owl. Ee, an' 'e does 'owl. Fair frightened me and Jim first time 'e done it. We thought 'e wasn't never going to stop. An 'e didn't, not till 'e was fair wore out—and so was we. I'd like you to 'ave a look at 'im, Doctor, if you will. I don't feel easy about him, an' that's a fact.'

"I gave the child a careful examination. From what I knew of Ada Filler I was fairly certain she wasn't one to get worked up unnecessarily, though of course you can never be sure. The baby was lying in its cot, blue eyes wide open, but quite quiet and peaceful. There didn't seem to be a thing as it shouldn't be and I said so.

"'I'm glad to 'ear that,' said his mother. 'Still—I don't know. 'E'll lie quiet that way for hours when you'd think 'e'd be asleep, then all of a sudden, for no reason, off 'e'll go like a 'ooter. An' nowt as I can do'll stop 'im.'

"Well, there wasn't anything really to worry about. Some children are like that; they take one look at the world and hate it on sight and you can't blame them much in a place like Irkwell, but in the end they learn to put up with it, like the rest of us. Nevertheless, young Ted Filler seemed to be taking his time about settling down. Whenever I looked in during the next few weeks it was the same tale. Once or twice I heard him howling. It was a remarkable achievement. I didn't wonder that his parents were looking worn and that the rest of the street was behaving pretty offensively to them.

"''E don't sleep enough, not near enough,' his father assured me. ''T'ain't natural. 'T'ain't fair on a man as 'as to work, either.'

"All I could tell them was that I'd stake my reputation there was nothing wrong with the child and that he would soon outgrow it.

# CHILD OF POWER

"IT WAS TWO months later that something occurred which might have given me an early clue to the whole thing had I had the wit to perceive it as a clue.

"I had called at the Fillers' cottage about something to do with their daughter, Doreen, I think, and naturally inquired after the baby.

"'Oh, I found out what to do with 'im,' his mother said.

"She showed me. The heir of the Fillers was sleeping peacefully and with an expression of blissful satisfaction. His bed was made up in an ordinary galvanised iron bath with a handle each end. He could have passed for an Italian cherub or a patent food advertisement.

"'Sleeps pretty near all the time now. Makin' up for it, like,' she said.

"'How did you do it?' I asked.

"She explained that it had happened by accident a week or two before. She had been ironing when Ted started one of his howls. She had fetched him down to the kitchen because, even if you couldn't stop him, you could keep an eye on him, but no sooner had she got him downstairs than the insurance man had called.

"The baby had to be put somewhere while she got the money and paid the man and the handiest place for the moment was on top of the clean linen stacked in one of the tin baths. When she came back from the door he had not only stopped crying but was fast asleep, so she left him there as long as possible. The next time he yelled she did the same again, and with the same result. It seemed to work every time.

"'So now I makes 'is bed in there regular,' she added. 'Seems queer, but it suits 'im. Good as gold, 'e is, in there. Won't sleep nowhere else.'

"I didn't take much notice at the time. A preference for sleeping in a tin bath just seemed one of those odd infantile idiosyncrasies which the wise accept and use gratefully.

"Well, time went on. I used to look in at the Fillers' occasionally, so I saw young Ted from time to time. I didn't take a great interest in him for he was a healthy enough baby. I gathered that he persisted in his odd preference for sleeping in a tin bath, but beyond that he seemed undistinguished. And yet, when I came to think it over afterwards, there was another incident which might have given me a hint.

"On that occasion he was lying in a dilapidated perambulator outside the back door. He did not show that he noticed me. His eyes were wide open, gazing far away, but he was not quite silent; he seemed to be humming a little tune. As I bent over him I could swear I caught that theme from the New World Symphony. You know how it goes."

The doctor broke off and hummed a few bars.

"That was what it seemed. Hummed by a child one year old. I was curious enough to ask Mrs. Filler whether she had heard it on the wireless and learned that the family taste fancied variety, sports news and cinema organs almost exclusively. I remember thinking that even if the child had happened to hear a version on a cinema organ he showed astonishing tonal memory, and then for one reason or another I forgot the incident until later. Probably, I very reasonably told myself that I had made just a foolish mistake.

"I must have seen the child several times during the next two or three years, but I admit I've no recollection of doing so, for, as I said, he was too healthy to be really interesting, though I wish now I'd kept an eye on him. It was not until his boy was over four that Jim Filler came to see me one Monday evening and gave me an interest in the boy which I'm never likely to lose.

"Jim had cleaned up and polished off the quarry dust for the occasion. He seemed a bit uncertain of himself.

"'I don't want to waste your time, Doctor,' he said, 'but I would be grateful if you'd come, casual-like, and 'ave a look at our Ted sometime when me and the missus is there.'

"'What's wrong with him?' I said.

"Jim fiddled his cap in his hands.

"'I don't know as there's owt wrong with 'im, exactly,' he said. 'It's—it's, well, 'e's a bit queer, some'ow, in a manner o' speakin'. It's got me and the missus fair worried an' all. She don't know as I've come 'ere. So if you could drop in kind of accidental like, you know—?'

"'But what's wrong with him?' I asked again. 'Do you think he's backward; not up to the rest, or something like that?'

"'Nay, t'lad's bright enough that way. 'Taint nothin' o' that kind. Fact, some ways 'e's a bit too bright, that's a funny thing. 'E don't often talk like a nipper and many's the time I've 'eard 'im use words what I'm sure 'e ain't never 'eard from me and the missus. Understands what's said to 'im, too, better than any kid I know.'

"I asked a few more questions, but Jim seemed to be holding back for some reason or other. If it had been another man I might have been short with him, but I knew Jim. His type is the incarnation of stubborn commonsense. In the end I got rid of him by promising to go round the next evening, though I didn't expect to find much amiss."

CHAPTER THREE

## THE BOY WHO SAW SOUND

"EVIDENTLY JIM FILLER had changed his mind and told his wife that I was coming, for she didn't seem surprised to see me. In honour of the occasion they took me into the front room, an apartment with a curious stage-set appearance, but I stopped Ada Filler as she was putting a match to the fire and suggested that we all went to the kitchen. We'd all feel more natural and less Sunday-best in there, as well as warmer.

"Even so, it wasn't easy to begin. Neither of them was anxious to come out plainly with the trouble. We had to exchange a number of ineffective sentences before Jim cut through it and became his usual forthright self again. He put on a dogged expression.

"'I know it'll sound daft, Doctor, but it's God's truth. Me and the missus's ready to swear to that, so if you'll 'ear me right through—?'

"'Go ahead and tell me. I'll ask questions afterwards,' I assured him.

"'Well, this is 'ow it was. Saturday tea time we was all in 'ere waitin' for news on t'wireless so as I could check my coupons—' he began.

"It certainly was an odd tale that Jim had to tell.

"Mrs. Filler had been setting the table, while her husband and the two children waited for their tea. Jim had copies of his pool entries and a pencil ready to check them. At six o'clock he switched on to Droitwich. It meant that they'd have to listen to the weather forecast and a lot of political talk before the important stuff came along, but you could never be sure how long it would take to get the sports bulletin and it wasn't worth risking missing any of it. Well, he switched on all right and the dial lit up, but nothing came out of the speaker. He pressed the switch on and off a bit and looked at the outside connections. They were right enough.

"'Eeh-h-h, there's summat wrong wi' t' bastard, there is, an' all,' he decided.

"He turned the set round and took off the back. It looked all right, at least there was nothing obviously adrift. He scratched his head. It's not as easy to trace trouble in a modern mains set as it was in the old battery days. The insides look alarmingly efficient.

"It was then that young Ted took an interest.

"'What's oop with it, Dad?' he asked, coming closer.

"''Ow should I know?' inquired Jim, with irritation.

"Well, it was then that the strange thing happened. Jim said that young Ted had looked at him 'sort of surprised like,' then the child had pushed in between him and the set. He didn't look inside it, Jim said; he put his head down at it as if he were going to butt it, then he lifted his face again and looked at his father.

"'It's in there. That's where it stops,' he said and pointed to a black object in the cabinet.

"'It were a transformer,' Jim said. 'An' 'e were right, too. Chap 'ad a look at it yesterday and one of the windin's was gone.'

—

"LATER, JIM HAD remembered another 'funny thing.'

"Several weeks previously he had been taking his son for a Sunday walk. They were on the Derby road where the grid lines run almost alongside when young Ted looked up at a pylon for no reason and said suddenly, 'It's stopped.'

"Jim couldn't make out what he was talking about and probably didn't care much, but he remembered that on the way back young Ted, equally without reason, had said, 'It's going again, now.'

"It wasn't until he got back that he learned there had been a breakdown somewhere which had put the grid out of action for half an hour or so.

"But he only recalled that afterwards. At the moment, he was chiefly concerned over the prospect of missing his football news.

"'Now I'll 'ave to go and buy t'Football Special, when t'papers come in,' he groused.

"Young Ted had made no immediate reply to that. He had sat silent for a while looking rather puzzled, then with the air of one who had considered the subject unsatisfactorily from all angles he said:

"'Why, Dad?'

"'Why, what?' asked Jim, whose mind had gone on.

"'Why'll you 'ave to get a paper?'

"'Because,' explained Jim, patiently, 'because we can't 'ave t'bloody wireless, that's why.'

"There was a pause while young Ted took this in.

"'D'you mean you can't 'ear what the man's sayin'?' he inquired.

"'Course that's what I mean. 'Ow d'you think any of us is goin' to 'ear owt now t'set's busted? You shut up, and eat your tea.'

"There was another pause.

"'I can,' said young Ted thoughtfully.

"'You can what?'

"''Ear what 'e's sayin'.'

"Jim transferred his gaze from his tripe to his son. He looked at him hard for some moments without speaking. He didn't want to turn on the lad for lying if it was only some childish make-believe game.

"'Well, tell us what t'chap is sayin' then,' he invited.

"Young Ted did. 'Brentford, one,' he said. 'Stoke City, nought. Derby County, nought. Birmingham, one. Everton, two…'

"'An' 'e were right,' Jim went on, leaning forward. 'I know 'e were right. I checked 'em up on my list as 'e said 'em, an' then I went out an' got t'paper to make sure. 'E were dead right, every time.'

"Ada Filler went on as he stopped.

"'I never 'eard of nothin' like it. It don't seem natural. Do you think it's dangerous, Doctor?'

"I looked at them, feeling pretty puzzled. There was no doubt they believed what they said. Jim was in dead earnest and a bit worried. Ada was more worried; she showed all that maternal solicitude which so oddly hopes that its child will be outstanding while being absolutely normal, distinguished while being indistinguishable.

"I was at a loss for a reply. In my mind I was searching for a set of circumstances which could possibly produce the appearance of what they believed to have happened, and I could not find one at the moment. There floated into my mind the memory of the child's curious humming as it lay in its perambulator, over three years ago now. Curiosity prompted me to ask.

"'Is Ted fond of music?'

"'Well, 'e can't play anything,' Mrs. Filler said. 'It's early days for that, ain't it? But 'e's often 'ummin' things, all sorts of tunes I never 'eard of.'

"Jim was looking at me.

"'You don't believe it, Doctor? Not that 'e was really 'earin' the wireless without a set, I mean?'

"'Well, it takes a bit of swallowing you know, Jim. Would you believe it if you were in my position? There must be some explanation.'

"'Oh, there's that, all right, but it'll be a queer one, not a trick one. I'll get t'lad down 'ere and you'll see.'

—

"HE LEFT THE room. We heard him clatter upstairs and then down again. He came in carrying young Ted in his arms and put him down in a chair. The little boy sat there, sleepy and perhaps a trifle pale, though he looked well enough otherwise.

"'Now, Ted, lad, tell t'doctor what's on t'National now.'

"'Ain't it mended?' said Ted, eyeing the wireless set on the dresser.

"'Aye, it's all right. But you just tell 'im what's on t'National.'

"Young Ted appeared to think for a moment, then:

"'Music,' he said. 'Loud music.'

"''Ow does it go?' his father persisted.

"Ted began to hum a part of a march quite recognisably one of Sousa's, I think.

"'That's right, lad. Now you keep on 'ummin',' said Jim, and switched on the radio set.

"Nobody spoke while the set warmed up. The only sound was Ted humming his march with a fine martial air. Jim leaned over and turned the volume control. A march came flooding out of the speaker. It was the same tune exactly on the beat and in pitch with Ted's humming.

"I couldn't think of anything to say. I just sat staring at the child. Jim turned the volume control right down to nothing and reset the dial.

"'What's on Regional?' he asked his son.

"'People clappin',' said young Ted with the briefest pause. 'Now there's two men talking.'

"'Sayin' what?'

"'Good evening, cads,' said young Ted, in a travestied drawl.

"Jim turned the knob. The weary-toned wit of the Western Brothers pervaded the room.

"'What else?' Jim asked, damping out again.

"'Lots of things. A man shouting very loud over there.' Ted pointed to a corner of the room. He lapsed into a gabble which sounded like a vocal cartoon of German.

"'Try Berlin,' I suggested to Jim.

"'That's 'im,' said young Ted, between the bolts of impassioned rhetoric which leapt out at us.

"Jim gave it a few moments and then switched off.

"'Well, there it is, Doctor,' he said.

"There, indeed, it was, unmistakably. And I was supposed to make something of it.

"I looked at the boy. He was not paying attention to us. There was an abstracted expression on his face, not vacant in the least, but preoccupied. As his father said:

"''Tain't no wonder 'e seems dreamy-like sometimes if 'e's got that goin' on in 'is head all the while.'

"'Ted,' I asked him, 'do you hear that all the time?'

"He came out of his abstraction and looked at me.

"'Aye,' he said, 'when it's going.'

"It occurred to me then for the first time that I had been thinking of him—and that he had behaved—as if he were quite twice his age or more.

"'Does it worry you?'

"'No,' he said, a bit uncertainly, ''cept at night, and when it's so loud I 'ave to look at it.'

"He always used that queer hybrid of expression. He talked about 'quiet' and 'loud' and yet coupled them with 'looking.'

"'At night?' I asked.

"'Aye, it's loud then.'

"'Always puts a tin box over 'is 'ead at nights, 'e does,' his mother put in. 'I've tried to stop 'im time and again. Doesn't seem natural, not to sleep with yer 'ead in a tin box, it doesn't. But 'e would 'ave it, and it does keep 'im quiet. 'Course, I didn't know about this 'ere. 'E just said it were noises and music, and I thought it were fancies.'

"I remembered the tin bath of his babyhood.

"'Does the box stop it?' I asked him.

"'Middlin',' said young Ted.

"'Maybe,' I said cautiously, 'we could stop it altogether at nights somehow. Would you like that?'

"'Aye.'

"'Well, come here and let me have a look at you.'

"His mother stretched out her hand and brought him over under the light.

"As I've told you there was nothing at all unusual about his appearance, it was just that of any normal little boy. With the story of the tin and the memory of Jim's description of him as he bent at the wireless set, I put my hands on his head and began to feel the structure. It wasn't long before I came on something decidedly unusual.

"On either side of the vault of the skull, about two inches above the temples, I found a round, soft spot about the size of a halfpenny. Hair grew on the spots as thickly as on the rest of the skull, but there was certainly no bone beneath, and the spots were situated with exact symmetry. The child winced involuntarily as my fingers touched them.

"'Does that hurt?' I asked him.

"His 'no' sounded a little doubtful.

"I told him to close his eyes and then touched the lids with the tips of my fingers. It brought exactly the same wincing reaction. I was aware of a curiously excited feeling growing inside me. I had never heard of anything at all like this. It was unique. I parted the hair over the soft spots and looked closely. The skin was continuous and unbroken. There was nothing to see. Again I cautiously explored the spots with my fingers. The child did not like it. He dodged and broke away from me.

"I was aware of his parents looking at me expectantly, but I kept my eyes on young Ted. I was trying to control my own excitement. I think an astronomer who has found a new planet or an explorer who has discovered a new continent must have felt rather as I felt then. Unable to believe his own luck and busily cramming his imagination down with reason; seeking for a hold on the hard facts and their implications.

"I had an automatic desire to keep the child as unaware as possible of his singularity and an instinctive impulse to belittle its importance for his parents' benefit. The motives for that impulse were, I confess, mixed. In fact, I've never really been able to sort them out honestly yet. There was a professional desire not to be sensational, undoubtedly a jealous wish to keep the thing to myself for the time being until I could learn more about it, and probably a lot of others.

---

"HIS MOTHER TOOK the child upstairs again and I waited for her to come back before I said anything, then I was deliberately matter of fact.

"'It's unusual, most unusual,' I told them, 'but it's certainly not anything to be frightened about. It's an extra sensitivity which, I confess, I don't altogether understand at present, but we shall undoubtedly learn more about that from talking to him and watching him, now that we know what to look for. I'd like you to observe very closely all he does or says with reference to electricity and let me know in as much detail as you can. His general health appears to be perfectly good, but if you like I'll go over him thoroughly tomorrow.

"'One thing strikes me, and that is that perhaps he's not getting enough sleep, or not sleeping soundly when he does. We may be able to get over that by giving him a better shield than a tin box. About the rest of it, his being so forward for his age in the way he speaks and understands questions, and that kind of thing—I don't think you need worry either. It's rather soon to be definite about anything yet, but it does seem likely that if he has had this kind of thing going on all the time the constant stimulation may have forced his brain to develop abnormally fast. He doesn't laugh much, does he?'

"'No, 'e's a solemn one.'

"'Well, you know, I'd say at a guess that his brain's pretty tired. You see, it gets no rest from this, night or day, except perhaps when he's sleeping—we can't tell that for certain until we know more about it—and that's bound to tire him. Besides, although it must stimulate in one way, yet in another it deadens because it gives his mind no chance to develop along its own lines. We shall have to find a way of altering that. It may not be very difficult.

"'I'm very glad you called me in now because, though of course we don't know how he actually feels it, it's difficult to believe that it isn't putting a considerable strain on him, and the sooner we can relieve the strain to some extent, the easier he will find things.

"'There's nothing to worry about. I'll come round tomorrow, as I said, and perhaps I shall be able to explain more about it.'

"I left them puzzled, though considerably, if vaguely, reassured. But I myself went home with my mind revolving unrestrainedly around the most astounding discovery. The boy had a sixth sense, something I had never heard, read or dreamed of. But from that moment I had not a vestige of doubt that young Ted was—the word seemed to coin itself—electro-sentient."

## CHAPTER FOUR
## STRANGE NEW WORLD

THE TALL MAN paused. His face became suddenly visible in the darkness as he lit another cigarette.

"It must be difficult for a non-medical man to appreciate all that meant to me," he went on. "There were so many sides to it. The sheerly professional interest, the fact oneself and no other had the opportunity to study it, the evolutionary aspect and the question of whether such a thing would become stabilized, the developments which would ensue if it did, as well as the work to be done in determining its capacities, limitations and nature.

"Some people would say, I've no doubt, that I should, in the interests of science, have announced the discovery—and so I shall one day—but you can judge the playing up and sensationalism which would have swamped us and made quiet, normal observation impossible. Imagine what would happen when the newspapers got it—it would be worse than that silly Quins business and make scientific study even more difficult than it is with them. I thought, and I still think, that the way to learn about young Ted was to study him in his natural setting and not in a three-ring circus of advertisers and publicity men. So I laid myself out to play the whole thing down and keep it as quiet as possible.

"It wasn't as difficult as you might think to work that. Ada Filler was anxious to co-operate; her fear lest the neighbours should think there was anything 'queer' about him was a great help. Jim wasn't awkward either. If he had been unemployed it would have been different, but he had a decent job and enough sense to see that, although there might be a bit of money in it, once the thing was known young Ted would become of public interest and virtually pass out of his parents' control.

"''Ave to 'appen one day, I s'pose,' was his opinion, 'but the later the better, both for 'im and 'is mother, I say.'

"More of a problem was young Ted himself. The most likely source of leakage was a child's natural desire to show off before other children. Luckily, when he did try it later, chance so arranged things that he was unconvincing and merely gained a discouraging reputation among his friends as a liar. That didn't matter, nearly all children boast and expect it of others, sometimes they believe one another, more often and without resentment, they don't.

"The first necessity seemed to me to give him a more efficient means of shielding himself from electrical influences than the one he had discovered. It was clear from his behaviour that his sense organs were always open to them, as one's ears are to sound, but with much more troublesome results. For the purpose I cut a strip of copper foil, padded it on one side and covered the other with brown cotton, with the idea that he might wear it as a kind of broad fillet. Experimentally there was a wire lead from it with a clip at the end, for it appeared likely that the screen might work better if it were earthed.

"I took the contraption round the following evening and let him try it on. The results were as good as I hoped; with an earth connection the radio influence was almost entirely screened off. It acted, one might say, as the eyelid of his new sense.

"Later, I developed a variation on it for daytime use. The fillet was hidden under a cap, and wires running down inside his clothes were attached to metal tips on his boots. This, he found, had considerable damping effect; if he could put his feet on a wet surface the screening was almost complete. The device became particularly useful later when he went to school. I supplied a certificate stating that, owing to a sensitive condition of the skull, it would be necessary for him to wear a cap indoors; but for this, I think he would have found concentration against the distractions which poured in on him difficult, if not impossible.

---

"WHEN I SET myself to learn what I could about young Ted's sensory experiences I very soon found myself engaged on a harder task than I had bargained for. Imagine yourself born blind and trying to understand the power of sight, or born deaf and being told about sound and music, and you'll begin to see something of what I was up against. Add the fact that your only source of information is an infant—extremely precocious in speech and understanding, it is true, but with an infant's wandering interest—and that no words exist to express his sensations except in terms of other senses, and progress is understandably slow.

"Nevertheless, I made some headway and began to form some hazy conceptions of the world his sixth sense showed him. It seemed to me that the new organs were somehow interconnected with the centres of vision and hearing, not like smell and taste, but more after the fashion of touch and hearing—you know how you can both feel and hear a deep note.

"For instance, he did not care to go very near the high-tension pylons. He complained sometimes that they were 'too loud' and sometimes that they were 'too bright.' The perception itself seemed to partake of the nature of both. There was no occlusory device, so that, like his ears, the new organs were always on duty, yet, like eyes, they were capable of a kind of focus.

"The analogy which gradually built itself up in my mind was something like this. Imagine a man standing on a hilltop. Around him in every direction—and he can see in every direction at once—is a vivid, almost glaring, landscape. He can focus on any detail of the landscape and see it clearly amid the rest whenever he likes, but focused or not, he cannot help looking, for his eyes are fixed open.

"Or sometimes I would think of a man surrounded by all the intentional and unintentional instruments of noise; the sound waves beat at him incessantly, but he can pick out certain instruments if he tries. That, however, is a poorer analogy, for the boy's 'electro-sentient' organs had a much greater power of discrimination than the human ear has.

"I'm afraid I can only convey poorly what I very dimly perceived myself, but I hope you can catch the idea to some extent. One was so hampered by lack of words and the looseness of meaning in those that had to be used. One continually ran up against things like this. It was clear enough that whatever Ted's system of reception of radio, his cognition made it intelligible to him as music and speech just as our auditory system does for us, but if one took him close to a transmitter, as I did experimentally, he complained that the broadcasting was 'too bright.'

"'You mean too loud,' I suggested.

"But no. He wouldn't have that at all. For him it was 'too bright.'

—

"I DON'T WANT to bore you with technicalities and detailed accounts of my findings. That sort of thing is for the experts; I've got volumes of notes at home which I shall publish one day for them to scratch their heads over. More patience went into those than I have ever put into anything. I had to grasp each little hint and be ready to return to it later as the boy grew, for it was no good trying to force description and explanation before he was sufficiently developed to understand what I asked him. That sort of treatment produces, as I expect you know from experience, only a defiant sulkiness.

"Very often it was no good putting a question flatly. One had to set the scene and observe results. For instance, I had discovered that for him telegraph wires were alive, 'lighted' he called it, with their electric messages. But it was no good putting the general question which occurred to me as a natural corollary: 'Can you overhear telephone conversations?' He had probably never noticed whether he could or not—try asking the average child about overtones or the composition of a shade of colour. One had to take him close to a telephone wire and inquire the result. Actually the result was positive. He could 'overhear' up to a distance of ten feet or so from the wires though he found it 'faint.'

"There were plenty of other discoveries. He knew at once whether an electric wire was 'live' or not. The current he seemed to perceive perhaps as a fluid stemmed by the gap in the circuit. The radiation from cars with magnetos worried him, coil ignition bothered him only a little. He could judge voltages in wires with astonishing accuracy up to about 500 volts. Above that he found them all 'bright.'

"He had a high sensitivity, too, to static electricity, so much so that in certain weather nothing could induce him to brush or comb his hair, and, perhaps as a side issue of this, he showed a power of weather prediction some degrees more accurate than his elders'."

# CHAPTER FIVE
## VOICES OF THE VOID

"BY THE TIME young Ted was ten and a half Jim had come to accept his son's powers as a permanent quality and not, as he had half suspected before, something which would be outgrown with childhood. He began to make plans for him. More impressed, perhaps, by the means of Ted's first self-revelation than by any of its subsequent manifestations Jim had ambitions to get him into the best wireless shop in Irkwell when he should leave school at fourteen.

"'That's the thing,' he said. 'Just let 'em try 'im once, that's all. Why 'e can tell where any set's wrong in a jiffy—and put it right, too. There's good money in a wireless shop, if a man knows the job, which most of 'em don't, seemingly. The lad ought to do well—maybe get a better job in one of the big places in Derby in a year or two.'

"He looked disappointed when I shook my head.

"'What's wrong wi' that?' he demanded.

"'Not good enough, Jim,' I told him. 'What he ought to have if it can be managed is a real training. He'd just be wasting his time in a shop.'

"'What, a college trainin' like? Seems to me like that's more like wastin' 'is time than t'other. If t'lad can do a job and 's a chance, let 'im do it, I say. There's plenty o' chaps full of book learnin' an' unemployed with it.'

"'Ted wouldn't be,' I said. 'You don't realise it, Jim. This gift makes him something altogether exceptional. There's no telling where it may lead. Have you ever seen him examine a wireless valve? The contempt he has for it! He looks at it as you or I might look at a car without springs. I took him to a hospital once to show him the apparatus; he looked at all the radiography stuff and the rest of the electrical set-up the same way.

"'You see, Jim, all our most advanced electrical appliances seem quite primitive to him. Before long he'll begin to improve them. I tell you, Jim, I'm as certain of it as I ever was of anything in my life that he's going to revolutionise our conceptions and use of electricity. Once he gets going we're going to learn more in a few years than we've learned in the hundred and fifty since

Volta made his battery. I can't see, no one can see, what changes he may bring about. Not just here, Jim, not just in England, but all over the world. It's going to be tremendous, I know it. And it's up to us to see that he has the best start we can give him.'

"I think now that I made a tactical error in putting it to him like that. It might have been better if I had taken his own ideas for Ted and worked him up to broader views by degrees. Sprung on him like that, it just didn't register properly. In his own mind he probably put it down as a crazy idea. A suggestion that the boy might become locally important would have carried more weight. He shook his head.

"'Tha knows there's no money to send our Ted to college, Doctor.'

"'Not much difficulty in raising it for a boy like him,' I said.

"'What, borrow on the chance of 'is payin' it back when 'e 'ad a job? 'Oo's goin' to lend like that—'e might never 'ave a job, there's plenty as 'asn't; then what?'

"'No fear of that.'

"'You can say so, but you can't be sure. I don't like it. I've always paid my way and owed nobody owt. It'd be a fine thing if I was to borrow for the lad and leave 'im to find t'money to pay back. Might take 'im years. 'Amperin' not 'elpin', that'd be. No, 'e shall 'ave the best I can give 'im, but what I can't, 'e shan't 'ave; and that's flat.'

"And flat it remained. No amount of reasoning or argument did anything but confirm him in what to his eyes was the decent, self-respecting course. When at last I was forced to recognise the hopelessness of converting him I tried to tell myself that in the long run it would make little difference—a bit more slogging, more time wasted in beginning, but the same later on—yet at the back of my mind I knew that wasn't the whole thing.

---

"YOUNG TED DEVELOPED well, with all his father's sturdiness, a good share of the local commonsense outlook, and an amiable enough disposition. He held his place easily at school, not, I think because his brain was anything but

# CHILD OF POWER

average, but because it was still in advance, though to a less extent, of his years. He got on well enough with the others and was frequently to be seen roving the town as a member of a gang of his own age or playing with them in the Irkwell Urban District Gardens. One was glad that, superficially, his interests seemed quite dully normal.

"In his eleventh and twelfth years, when I had feared he might want to forsake my company entirely for that of his gang, I still managed to see quite a lot of him—largely because he liked to come out in my car, I fancy—and it was when he was nearly twelve that I got a hint of something which bowled my imagination over.

"We were out late. My car had run a big-end up on the moors miles from anywhere. We had reached a main road and at last succeeded in getting a lift part of the way home, but we were left with five miles to cover and only our feet to carry us. It was a fine summer night and about as warm as it ever is on top of the hills. We had been going for some twenty minutes when Ted took off his cap and with it the copper shield which he wore concealed in the lining.

"'It's stopped,' he said.

"I knew without asking that he meant that the B.B.C. middle and long-wave stations had closed down, and most of the powerful foreigners, too.

"'After midnight, then,' I said.

"'Aye.'

"We trudged on without speaking for a while. I knew that he was ranging about that queer electrical landscape of his, aware of things I should never know. And never had I been so—well, so jealous, I suppose it was, of his power as I was at that moment. Just then I felt that I would have given anything that could be asked of me just for a glimpse of the world through his sixth sense—just a glimpse, no matter how brief, so that I could begin to understand.

"He was at ease now. He complained these days that when the big stations were on, they were too loud so that they 'dazzled' him unless he wore a shield, just as he complained that electric sparks hurt him like a very loud noise 'only brighter-like.' I knew that was so for I had seen him wincing painfully on account of a quite distant thunderstorm. I found myself suddenly and irrationally angry with him for having this extra world open to him and being unable to convey it to me.

"It was he who broke the silence and with it my unreasonable mood. He raised his hand and pointed upwards.

"'What's out there, Doctor?'

"I looked into the star scattered blue-black sky.

"'Space,' I said. 'Emptiness, or nearly, with little suns and planets floating about in it.'

"'Aye, Mr. Pauley learned me that at school. But he didn't say owt about what goes on out there.'

"'Goes on?'

"'Aye, goes on. 'E said as they was worlds, maybe like this, some of 'em, but nowt about t' chaps as lives on 'em, and what they do there.'

"'He couldn't very well. You see, we don't even know that anyone does. Some people think that there may be life in some forms where conditions allow it, but others, the majority, think it unlikely.'

"'They're daft.'

"'Which of them?'

"'The ones as don't think so.'

"I looked at him. His head was thrown back and his upturned face shone dimly white in the starlight. A rush of excitement, almost physically painful, made my heart thump.

"It was hard to make my voice anything like normal as I asked:

"'Why?' and hung on his answer.

"'Why! Because if it ain't chaps like us doin' things out there, 'oo is it?'

"I did not dare to respond for a moment. From long experience I knew that at any display of excitement he took refuge in suspicious self-protection. Young Ted couldn't be driven, only led cautiously.

"'It wouldn't be God, would it?' he suggested hopefully.

"I told him I considered it unlikely.

"'What is it? Voices?' I added, as if out of a mild interest.

"'No. It's like—oh, like colours or notes.'

"'Music?'

"'No, and 'tain't like any of the ordinary things, either. I'd know as it were different even if it weren't a long way away like it is.'

"It took some time as usual to discover what he was meaning, but I had the impression at last that it was a thing happening at the far limits of his extra sense. As one cannot see stars in daylight, so he could perceive this disturbance only when the more powerful stations were off the air. It was something, it seemed, which happened in three tones. Tones of what? Something which was neither sound nor colour. They occurred in some deliberately arranged sequence—he was emphatic that they could not be accidental—yet they did not exactly repeat. They were faint and far away. He knew, knew without doubt, that they meant something, yet he couldn't tell what it was.

"'Like a chap gabbin' foreign,' he tried, 'you know as it means summat, but you don't know what. Like that, only different,' he added with fair lucidity. 'And as different from accidental influences as 'singin' from a motor 'orn.'

"It left me more confused than usual. At one time I would think he implied someone signalling in a three-tone code, analogous perhaps to the dots and dashes of Morse. At another, that it was a system of communication which his intelligence could not grasp, in much the same way that we cannot grasp insects' methods of communication.

"But of one thing I went home that night quite certain. Here was such a possibility as I had never suspected. Beside it, all my earlier discoveries which had seemed so important, became trifling. Contact, perhaps some day communication, with the planets!"

## CHAPTER SIX
## THE GIFT OF AGES

"I THOUGHT OVER it all the next day with a great desire to do nothing precipitate. A wrong move now, I felt, might have tremendous effects.

"But the main result was that my earlier conviction grew clearer and clearer as a necessity. Young Ted must have a good education—the best we could get for him. The job of making sense of those signals, if it were possible at all, was not going to be easy.

"To use a metaphor over again, he was in the position of a man who hears dots and dashes, realises they are rational, but has never heard of Morse and is ignorant of the language used—perhaps Ted would be up against a worse problem; a quite unsimilar, incomprehensible type of intelligence behind signs.

"A puzzle like that is going to take all the intelligence and knowledge that can be brought to bear on it. For Ted to attempt it without all the resources one could give him would be inviting discouragement and failure. It needed a mind trained to patience and the scientific approach, perceptive and yet plodding, a mind with tenacity of purpose.

"Perhaps you can't give a mind those characteristics, but at least you can give it the chance to acquire them, and hope for the best. It was a chance I determined that young Ted in some way must have.

"With my own mind fully made up I went to see Jim Filler next evening.

"I intended to press again for Ted's education, but not to bring out my new reason for its necessity save as a last resource. For now our positions were curiously reversed from those of eight years ago; then it was he who was afraid I would not believe him, now I was pretty certain of being unable to convince him of the further development.

"It had been an uncertain kind of day, and there were dark clouds piling up on the horizon and a thundery feeling in the air when I arrived. Jim was working in his garden, but he stuck his fork into the ground when he saw me and led the way into the cottage.

"It wasn't difficult for him to guess what I'd come about. He was pretty used to my tackling him on the education issue by this time, though we never got any further, but this time the opening was easier than usual. It was, in fact, volunteered.

"'I've been thinkin' it over about our Ted,' he said, 'an' I don't know as it'll do 'im any 'arm to learn a bit, even if it don't do 'im no good.'

"'Good,' I said, feeling a bit taken aback at the complete *volte face*. 'I was going to mention it.'

"'Y' don't say,' he answered drily.

"'I'm glad, very glad indeed,' I went on, 'I'm sure you'll never regret it, nor Ted either. Well, now we'll have to go into the matter of raising the money.'

"He shook his head.

"'No, we won't. I said as 'ow I wasn't borrowin' for 'im, and I ain't.'

"'But—well, it's going to cost a bit, you know,' I told him.

"'I know. I've been into all that.'

"I waited. Jim's sort takes its own time.

"''E'll earn it 'imself. Maybe it'll take 'im a year or two, but then 'e'll be able to go to college an' pay 'is own way.'

"'How?'

"Jim chuckled.

"'Way you never thought of. Mr. Pauley's notion, an' a good one, too.'

—

"I HAD KNOWN that it must come; it was surprising that I had had the field to myself for so long, yet I felt a hot resentment.

"'Pauley, where does he come in?' I asked, though I knew on the moment exactly where he came in. It was inevitable that someone should find out about young Ted soon, and who likelier than his schoolmaster.

"'Same way as thaself. 'E came 'ere sayin' same as you, as 'ow our Ted ought to go to college. So I tells 'im just t'same as I tells you. Aye, an' I tells 'im it's no good 'im tryin' to change my mind, seein' as you been tryin' to for t'best part of two years, and not done it. So 'e goes off. Next day 'e's back. 'E's been thinkin', 'e 'as. 'E says why not let our Ted go on t'Alls and make a bit o' money 'imself?'

"'The Music Halls?'

"'Aye. 'E says a friend of 'is could get Ted on as 'The 'Uman Wireless Set.' Might make five quid a week and more.'

"I thought of the plans I had made for the boy, a good school and then Cambridge if it could be managed—and now, 'T'Alls!'

"'Jim,' I said earnestly. 'You can't do this. He can't afford it, man, he's too important. He can't afford to spend the most impressionable years of his life in Music Halls, it'd be the ruin of him. How could he settle down to learn after that kind of life? And he must learn, he's got to study, as hard as he can, he must.'

"Jim removed his pipe and looked hard at me.

"''Oo says 'e must? 'E's my own lad, isn't 'e? I got a right to do what I think best for 'im, ain't I?'

"'But you don't understand, Jim, this is important, tremendously important. It may mean a major turning point in history, Jim, pivoting on him. It's like a sacred trust, we must do our best to prepare him for it.'

"I told him of my new discovery about Ted. I put my case for all I was worth—and I might as well have shouted at the hills. I could see his face harden into the all-too-familiar lines of obstinacy as I talked. He could not, would not, see, even if he believed. The stupendousness of the possibilities, contact with life beyond the Earth, perhaps knowledge from older, wiser worlds, the coming of a stage when man gropes out from the universe beyond, the importance to science, to mankind itself; all this was wasted, blunted against his conviction that it wasn't 'right to borrow on t'lad's future.'

"Because I felt so deeply, and partly because the coming storm made the air sultry and fretted the nerves, I lost my temper with him. But it would take more than words and threatening thunder to move Jim. Cloddish, without imagination, the embodiment of all the stupidities that clutter and clog the world, he seemed to me then.

"He wouldn't get excited, he refused to argue, he just sat there behind his unassailable rectitude, beating me off with flat negatives. No lash I used could sting him out of his quiet, narrow assurance. He just waited patiently for me to finish. I did that suddenly, for I felt that in another minute I should punch his silly face if only to make him come alive.

"'I'm going to see Pauley,' I told him, 'and I hope to Heaven that he at least has enough brains to see that this mustn't be allowed to happen. God, to waste the gift of the ages in a Music Hall!'

# CHILD OF POWER

"I FLUNG OUT of the place and across the pavement to my car. I was going to see the schoolmaster right away; perhaps he would believe easily, perhaps he would need convincing, but either way I could not believe that he would fail to see that Ted was going to deserve the best education possible. We might be able to raise the money as a gift, though I had my doubts whether Jim would accept it now. But somehow or other we must ensure Ted's—not only Ted's; the whole world's—chance.

"And then a rumble of thunder made me pause with my hand on the door handle. I looked up, suddenly aware that the sky was full of ominous black clouds; they looked fantastically heavy with an evil, almost green light in their caverns.

"That was why I did not rush off to see Pauley then; afterwards it wasn't necessary...

"The threat of the thunder brought young Ted vividly into my mind. I knew how storms worried him, I knew, too, that he was not at home. I hesitated. After my exit I could scarcely go back and ask where he was; besides, Jim could hardly fail in the circumstances to misconstrue my motive, which was, in fact, merely a desire to be sure that the boy was as well protected as possible against an electrical upset. Instead, I turned from the car and spoke to the woman who stood in the doorway of the next cottage studying the sky resentfully.

"'Young Ted Filler?' she said. 'Aye, 'e's along t'canal with our Rosie. Fair soaked they'll be, the pair of 'em.'

"I remembered Rosie; she was one of those children who get themselves remembered. She was suspected, and not without reason, of being concerned in any bit of trouble for streets around.

"Even now I don't quite know why I changed my mind and went to look for young Ted instead of for Pauley, but I did.

"The canal ends in Irkwell so there was only one way to go. A few minutes later I stopped the car on a hump-backed bridge just as the first big drops of rain began to fall. From there I had a view of the towpath for half a mile each way, but I didn't need it. The path was deserted save for two small figures a hundred yards or so away; any others who may have been there had wisely left to seek shelter.

"The children were scuffling on the cinders a yard or two from the water's edge, much too occupied to pay attention to me, the coming storm, or anything else but their own quarrel. Rosie was no silent scrapper; her yells of protest were forceful even at that distance. Perhaps that was not to be wondered at. It must be painful to have an opponent take a good grip of one's hair, even if one does manage to get in a hack or two on his shins. I leaned out of the car and shouted at the little brutes.

"'Ted,' I called, 'stop it and come here.'

"Surprised, he looked round. The victim seized her chance to pull free. Quick as a flash she snatched his cap off, flung it into the water, and tore off down the towpath with screams of derision.

"Ted clapped both hands to his head, as if in pain.

"'Come here,' I shouted, getting out of the car.

"He heard me, for he turned and began to run with his hands still pressed to his head.

"I started off the bridge to get down to him, then I saw him stagger and stop. In the same split second came a vivid flash right above us and a crash of thunder like the end of the world. The rain fell as if a cloud had ripped right open. When I reached the towpath young Ted was lying there, pathetically asprawl and soaked through already."

He paused.

"That's all," he said, "that was the silly end of it."

—

WE LOOKED OUT over the dark lake in silence for a while.

"He was dead?" asked one of the Americans at last.

"No, he wasn't dead. But the thing that made him different was dead. That terrific discharge of lightning had finished his sixth sense for good. In that new sense he had gone as blind as a man without eyes, as deaf as one with split eardrums. He came round again, an ordinary little Irkwell urchin, with a raging headache. Now, he's a quarryman like his father.

"Some day perhaps he'll do something silly and I shall be able to have a look at his brain—if his pigheaded relatives allow it. But there's pretty cold comfort in that when one thinks of the possibilities which were snuffed out in a second."

No one spoke again for some minutes. Then there was a movement in the darkness from the Lancashire man's direction.

"Aye, it were a rum do," he said, "but 'e'll be 'appier that way, you know. Freaks ain't 'appy. Now, there was one as I once talked to at Blackpool. 'E wasn't 'appy, 'e said…"

# THE LIVING LIES

—

I

**F**IVE LITTLE GREEN girls wrangled on the sidewalk; the central disputants held, one the legs, and the other the arms, of a large doll.

"You said I could have her to-day," yelled Legs, bitterly.

"No, I didn't. You had her yesterday," screamed Arms. "I want her."

"You said I could," Legs persisted doggedly.

"She's mine. You let her go." Arms tugged violently. The doll's stitches strained, but it held together. "Will you let *go*?" howled the one who held the arms.

On the last word she tugged with all her weight. The suffering doll's arms tore off. The child, still holding them, staggered back and fell into the roadway. Her shriek, as a wheel crushed her, was drowned in the screams of her four little friends.

Leonie Ward, her hands on the wheel, her foot hard down on the brake, did not scream. Something seemed to take her by the throat, she felt her heart turn over inside her and her face went sickly pale. For an instant everything appeared to stop, held in a ghastly tableau. The people transfixed in the street, the car hanging on its gyroscopes, Leonie frozen in the driving seat; the only sound an unforgettable scream.

A woman flung herself into the road and dragged the child's crushed body from between the wheels. For a moment she clasped it, then she looked up. The girl, half-stunned, had not moved from the wheel; she shivered as their eyes met. The woman's face and the hands were as green as those of the child she held; it made her hatred and anguish the more horribly terrifying. Without lowering her burning eyes, crouched with the dead child pressed against her, she began to scream threats and curses.

There was a crowd around the car now, a ring of green-faced men and women rapidly pressing closer. Still Leonie sat unmoving, unable to think or act, but feeling the growing hostility of the crowd.

Two burly men in uniform came shouldering their way through the press. They made a strange contrast with the others, for their faces beneath their padded hats and their hands, already clutching batons in readiness for trouble, were a brilliant magenta in colour. They worked close to the cream car and began pushing the people back.

"Now then, get along. Move along there."

One of them went to the mother of the child. Not unkindly he laid a hand on her shoulder. She shook it off, sprang to her feet and spat at him.

"Don't you touch me, you filthy Red."

There was a murmur in the green-faced crowd. The woman seemed to forget him for a moment. She leaped towards the car and clawed at Leonie through the open window.

"You murderess. I'll kill you for that."

A uniformed arm came over her shoulder and pulled her away. She turned and raked at the man's red face with her nails. He put up a hand to save his eyes.

"Bloody Green bitch," he muttered, fending her off.

"D'you hear that?" she shrieked. "D'you hear what he called me?"

The crowd had. Someone put an arm around the red man's throat and dragged him backwards. Half a dozen green-faced men and women leapt upon him; simultaneously his companion went down in a whirl of crashing fists. From one of the fallen policemen came a scream of shuddering agony. It brought Leonie suddenly alive again. In terror she struck at the green arms reaching in to seize her, desperately she sought to restart the engine. With panic in her veins she did not care if she cut down a dozen of the Green people if she could only thrust clear of the mob. But even as the engine came to life she felt the car rise and sway, and knew that they had lifted the driving wheel clear off the ground.

# THE LIVING LIES

A green hand caught her wrist and wrenched it off the wheel, she was dragged half out of the window. Her shoulder socket hurt like fire; she felt her arm being torn off like the doll's. A row of gloating green faces awaited her. Then the whole car tilted beneath her and a curtain of black fell over everything.

—

SHE WAS LYING on her back, looking up at a white ceiling. There was a moment before it all came back, then, fearfully, she turned her head. Close beside her she saw a face that was not green, magenta or black, but the pink and white of her own race. She burst into tears of relief, aware through them of a hand which patted her shoulder and a voice which tried to soothe her, but unable to stop the storm of weeping.

"I'm sorry," she said at last, as it subsided. "I'm sorry to be such a fool."

"Nonsense," a voice told her. "Best thing you could have done. Now drink this. No, don't try to move. I'll hold it."

A hand raised her head slightly. Another held a glass to her lips. The spirit stung her throat, but it worked like an elixir. In a few minutes she began to feel like an utterly new person.

She turned and studied the man beside her. Later middle aged, fifty-five, perhaps sixty, she judged. His hair was mostly grey, and surmounted a finely shaped, ascetic type of face. The eyes were grey, too, and kindly, with fine webs of little wrinkles at the corners; the mouth was firm, but without hardness.

"What happened? Where am I? Who are you?" she asked, almost in one sentence.

The man smiled.

"My name is Francis Clouster and this is my house. A friend of mine brought you here."

"But how did I get out of that crowd?"

"He'll be able to tell you that better than I can. I'll call him." He went to the door and opened it. "Jimmy," he said, "the lady would like to see you."

Leonie recoiled involuntarily at the sight of the man who came in. She had expected a man of her own kind. The newcomer was green as a grass lawn. The two men either did not notice or affected not to notice her movement.

"This is Jimmy Craven," the older man introduced, "Miss…?"

"Leonie Ward," Leonie told them.

"Miss Ward would like to hear what happened, Jimmy," said the older.

"I happened to be there when the accident took place," the Green man said. "It was quite obvious to anyone who saw it that no driver could have avoided it. You were as quick on the brake as anyone could possibly be. No blame whatever can be attached to you. But most of the people who were in the crowd didn't actually see it happen. Even so, it might have passed off quietly but for that Red policeman.

"Just as your car went over, a squad of Red police turned up. Green police might have smoothed things over, but that mob was just right for trouble with Reds, they'd killed two already, and they went bald headed for this lot. In the mix-up I saw that half-crazy woman making for you. Your left arm was jammed under the car so that you couldn't have fought her off, even if you'd been conscious. So I chased her off, managed to get your arm free, and carried you out of the mess. If anybody noticed they probably thought you were an injured Green, because I'd put a rug over you."

Leonie was watching him as he talked, deciding that he was personable and, but for his colouring, might have been handsome. Possibly in the eyes of another Green he actually was so.

She thanked him as he stopped. He shook his head.

"It was common justice. The accident was in no way your fault. That woman was crazy enough to have killed you, or defaced you for life. If you don't mind my saying so, it was extremely rash of you to come here alone at all. And in the circumstances you are lucky to have got off as lightly as you have done."

"I don't feel as if I had got off exactly lightly."

"You've been pretty well bruised," put in Clouster, "but your main injuries are a compound fracture of the left forearm and a badly strained right shoulder."

"I wonder the shoulder wasn't dislocated; it felt like it. But, tell me, why shouldn't I have come here alone?"

"I should have thought that was obvious enough."

"Do you mean I might have been attacked even if there had not been an accident?"

# THE LIVING LIES

"I do."

"But why?"

Her host and the Green man looked at one another.

"Weren't you warned against it?" Clouster asked.

"Oh, yes, they did say something. But they used to tell me to be careful of all sorts of places on Earth and nothing ever happened."

"Venus," said Clouster, "is not Earth. Do you mean you've only just come here?"

"Well, I've only just come back—about a month ago—they sent me to be educated on Earth. I was very young when I left."

"I see. Well, I'm afraid you're going to find that a lot of things you can take for granted on Earth are very different on Venus. There is not the problem there of the Reds, the Blacks, the Whites of our kind, and the Greens of Jimmy's."

"There are Black men on Earth."

"So there are, but they have learned to co-operate with Whites and Yellows."

"They must be very different from our Blacks," the Green man put in, bitterly. "All ours want to do is rule."

He looked up and caught the older man's expression.

"Yes, I know that's not what you like to hear, Francis, but, hell, it's true."

"And the Greens?" inquired Clouster.

"They want justice and permission to live in peace: is that too much?"

"That's just what the Blacks tell me."

"Oh, well, if you believe them—"

"Why not try believing them a bit, Jimmy? After all, what's the difference beyond the colour of our skins?"

The Green man rose.

"Sorry. If you're going to preach, Francis, I'm leaving. Goodbye, Miss Ward. I'm glad to have been able to help you."

Francis Clouster looked at the door as it shut.

"And there," he said, turning back to Leonie. "There you have the state of Venus in a nutshell."

"Tell me some more about it," Leonie said.

"All right. But hadn't you better send some message to your family first? I'm afraid it won't be possible for them to fetch you to-night. There's too much trouble round here, but you ought to let them know. I'll bring you the telephone."

Leonie spoke into the instrument while he held it. It roused in her the feeling, always latent, that in coming back to Venus she had gone back a few centuries. Telephones, because radio wouldn't work on Venus, but it wasn't only the lack of radio...

---

MR. MATTINGTON WARD returned to the dinner table.

"It was Leonie," he explained to his guests. "She's over in Chellan. Bit knocked about in a Green and Red riot, I'm afraid. Tells me not to worry, but to come over and fetch her in the morning when the neighbourhood's quietened down a bit. She's right, too. Police say there's quite a bit of trouble down there."

The most important of his guests looked at him hard. Wilfred Baisham, head of the Venus Mineral Products Consolidation, had not only a dominating position, but an authoritative personality.

"Chellan?" he said. "What the devil was your daughter doing in Chellan?"

"Taking a short cut, I understand." Mr. Ward, if he resented his guest's tone, did not show it.

"But Chellan!"

"I've warned her, of course, but I suppose she didn't really appreciate it. I don't suppose it's too easy for her to grasp at first."

Mr. Baisham said, weightily:

"I don't approve of the practice of sending Venus-born children to Earth for education. It gives them false standards. How can they be expected to have a proper appreciation of our system when they are educated in another. It just gives them subversive ideas which they have to unlearn before or after they get into trouble."

Mr. Ward made no reply. Indeed, at the back of his mind, he agreed with his guest. He would have preferred to have Leonie educated at home and would have done so but for the promise he had made to her mother. He had kept that promise in spite of a feeling that he was alienating his child and a fear that she might not be able to feel at home on Venus any more than her Earthborn mother had done.

"Who's looking after her?" Mr. Baisham inquired.

"Some people called Clouster, I gather."

"Oh, yes, I know. Idealists, type that might have been missionaries on Earth at one time. They do some kind of social work in Chellan. They'll look after her all right." He smiled at a thought. "Funny, isn't it, these people who give their lives to spreading brotherly love among Greens, Reds and Blacks. You'd think it would dawn on them that if people have to be told to love one another all the time there must be some pretty good reason why they don't. But it doesn't seem to. Well, it's probably a good thing; it'll teach your daughter to keep clear of Chellan and such places in future."

Again Mr. Ward found himself in agreement. Leonie had given him no details of her injuries so that his impression was that she had had a scare—there was nothing like a touch of that kind of wind up to show a girl the necessity for conventions and taboos.

---

"NOW TELL ME about Venus," Leonie directed. "Nobody has, except for what I learned at school. It's all so usual to everyone here that they don't bother to explain any of it. Now and then they say 'Don't,' that's all. Now, like the geography books: 'The inhabitants of Venus are of four types…'"

"…the Whites, the Greens, the Reds and the Blacks," he took her up. "But I quarrel with your word 'types.' They are all the same type—only their skins are different colours."

"They wouldn't thank you for that from what I've heard."

He nodded. "They wouldn't; that's the tragedy."

He went on to describe the Venusian social state, speaking not as a White, but as one who had tried to consider himself as one of all the four classes. As for the Whites, their position was simple, they were of Earth stock on both sides and some of them actually Earth born. They dominated socially, industrially, commercially: they were, in fact, the undisputed ruling class, they despised the coloured peoples, and the one common sentiment of the three colours was dislike, tempered by fear, of the Whites.

Leonie nodded. "Something like all the little nations on Earth before the Revolution led up to the Great Union," she suggested.

"Very like, in some ways," Francis Clouster agreed, "but even more tragic here. On Earth there were physical differences as well as different languages to overcome. Here the language is the same, the physical structure is identical. They differ in nothing but their skins—and they do not, they refuse to, know it. My wife and I know it. We have lived among Greens, Reds and Blacks; we have friends of each colour whom we trust, but who would hate one another at sight if we were to allow them to meet. You saw just now how an intelligent Green reacts when one mentions a Black."

"But he saved me—a White."

"Certainly. You are a girl and very good looking. The dislike of the colours for the Whites is different from their dislike of one another, it is based on envy, not contempt. That makes a lot of difference, you see. I don't want to be uncharitable, but it wouldn't surprise me to hear that Jimmy is rather fancying himself for having rescued a White girl."

He went on to talk of the three colours and the hatred they held for one another. How the Reds believed that the Blacks were dirty and dishonest, and the Greens were vicious and sly to a man: how the Greens and Blacks considered the Reds to be bullies and braggarts, frequently unstable in the small amount of brain they possessed. How the children of all three groups grew up in their homes and in their separate schools, hearing these things from their earliest years and believing them.

"There's a parallel for that, too, in Earth history," Leonie observed. "There was teaching like that against Jews."

"Certainly. There are plenty of parallels. Too many. But the good one is yet to come." He sat silent a minute, lost in thought.

"You mean like the Great Union?"

He nodded. "There was a day on Earth when the people revolted. They refused any longer to be thrown into slaughter of and by people of whom they knew nothing, for the profit of people who exploited them. They rose against it, one, another, and another, to throw out their rulers and rule themselves. And so came the Great Union. Government of the People, by the People, for the People, over the whole Earth. How long will Venus have to wait for that?"

"You are a revolutionary?"

He looked at her steadily. "Yes, I suppose I am that. A revolutionist with no party to lead," he smiled wryly. "Quite harmless to the Whites and their authorities, I assure you. If I were to collect a following of Greens, the Blacks and Reds would unite to crush us: if I collected Reds the Blacks and Greens would combine. We should slaughter one another while the Whites went on living comfortably, untroubled."

"But how did this happen? Who are these coloured peoples, where did they come from, and why do they hate one another so much?"

"That is not clear. They are said to be descendants of the first Earthmen who came to Venus long ago and mated with the natives. The theory is that the natives died out from contact with civilisation as some races died on Earth, but not before the ancestors of our present Blacks, Reds and Greens were fairly numerous."

"What else could it be?"

"Exactly. What else?"

Leonie had opened her mouth to speak again when the door suddenly swung wide. A young man, green as her rescuer had been, strode in without noticing her as she lay on the day-bed.

"Hullo, Dad, is Mother a..." he broke off suddenly as he caught sight of her. There was a moment's silence.

"Is Mother Clouster about, Francis?" he asked, in an uncertain tone.

## II

LEONIE RETURNED HOME to spend her convalescence in her father's house on a slight rise overlooking the city of Tallor. The period coincided with that nostalgic depression which afflicts all but a few of the newly arrived or newly returned on Venus. Leonie felt it the more since the best antidote of exercise was barred for her.

The garden was planted in pathetic imitation of gardens on Earth, with plants and flowers specially imported, yet in spite of sunlight lamps and prepared soil the blooms were pallid versions of those which grew naturally in Earthly gardens. They were unnatural, too, in losing their seasons, so that here, at the end of the Venus winter, Leonie discovered spring and autumn flowers struggling into bloom together. From the terrace where she spent most of her time she could make out the suburbs, Chellan where the Greens lived, Barro the Red quarter, Tingan which was almost entirely Blacks.

And in each she could see the big blocks of factories and warehouses where the people worked. North lay the cleared and cultivated country where they grew either indigenous crops or species bred by careful crossing with strains from Earth. West, where the ground was lower and waterlogged rose the thick wall of swamp forest cut by the broad channel to the sea. South lay more forest, it looked weakly and unhealthy to her eyes because of the paleness of its green, but, nevertheless, it was formed in reality of sturdy Venusian trees quite different from the soft growths of the swamp forest.

Venus knows no horizon line. All the way round the scene grew hazy at the edges, disappearing in the haze which thickened imperceptibly into the clouds. Sometimes above the southern forest she saw the clouds glow red as if a sunset tried to struggle through them; there was a distant, trembling roar and one knew that a rocket ship had arrived or taken off from the great port clearing twenty miles beyond the city.

It was the haze and ever hanging clouds which depressed the Earth-accustomed. Never to see the sun, never to have a clear view, never to see a sharp cut shadow on the ground; despite the fact that the light was good its perpetual diffusion made them feel that they were living in a kind of monotony of twilight.

Everybody assured Leonie that this was to be expected; that all newcomers felt a lowering of spirit at first, and that it would pass, but she found it hard to believe. She was aware of a growing dislike for the planet, for its inhabitants, and for the kind of life which lay before her. She did not care for the standards of her father's friends. She found in them a self-satisfied, almost callous, strain which was continually shocking her Earth-trained mind. The narrowness of their interests bored her and the lavishness of their style of living troubled her.

In Milota, their residential district of Tallor, no luxury that money could buy went unbought. Down in the coloured districts there was poverty and struggle without end, men and women living in warrens which must surely be as bad as those of Earth before the Great Union. Even Rome at its greatest, Leonie felt, could scarcely have shown greater discrepancies, yet it left Milota undisturbed. Beyond the occasional distribution of a little condescending charity Milota maintained its amusements and pursuits as though the people whose labour supported it did not exist.

It was the dull weeks of her convalescence which made her give more attention to those things than she otherwise might have spared; which made her feel strongly the sense of being a stranger among strangers, and set her clinging grimly to anything which made Earth seem closer. Much of her time was spent with a little recorder in her lap through which she dictated endless letter-reels of her impressions to her distant friends. Whenever a mail rocket came in she fell upon the reels addressed to her and hurried away to a distant corner where she could listen to the little voices coming out of the machine, with her eyes closed, pretending that Venus did not exist. It was no way to cure Earth-sickness, but she did not wish to be cured. For the same reason she burnt herself painfully with her sunlamp, over-using it for fear she might under-use it and grow pale like a true Venus dweller.

There was little company for her during the long days and seldom, except in the evenings, anyone to talk to but the Magenta-Red house servants. From them she learned much to substantiate the things she had heard from Francis Clouster down in Chellan. The mention of a Black or a Green to any of them brought a curl of the lip which, off duty, would undoubtedly have been a sneer. The Reds, she discovered, considered themselves the aristocrats of the coloured peoples, ranking a little below the Whites themselves. It was later she learned directly the Greens' opinion of the Reds—that not only were they bullies as Clouster had said, but that they were toadies and sycophants of the Whites, who chose them for house-servants and bribed them into meanness. It was impossible to get past those things, in every direction these barriers of colour cropped up—and every worth-while position was reserved for the Whites.

In those eight weeks was thoroughly planted and set an idea which was never uprooted—that the basis of Venusian society was a state of hatred and spite.

By the time she was recovered enough to drive the new car with which her father had replaced the smashed one, spring had come and the vegetation, never slow of growth, was bursting upward and outward with a furious energy almost alarming to a stranger. It was a season when hours of work in the factories had to be cut, and Leonie went out with parties of other Whites to watch the released workers fighting the encroaching forest back from the city's outskirts and keeping it off the cultivated lands with hatchets and flame throwers.

There were expeditions to the flower groves. She took part in them but they disappointed her. Venusian flowers were almost all simple and primitive, not unlike magnolias, lovely to touch, making the air heavy and sweet with their scent, but appealing little to the eye. All the way they went they passed gangs of Greens or Blacks and sometimes Reds, hacking and burning back the vegetation which threatened to choke the roads.

There was another expedition which took her down to the sea. That was somewhat disappointing, too. The sea when reached looked much as the sea does anywhere else on a dull day, and you couldn't do anything with it when you got there: you couldn't go out on a small boat, because one good snap from one of the saurians and it would be the end of you and the boat; and you couldn't bathe because the water had swarmed with tiny sharp-toothed fish who would attack in thousands and have all the flesh off your bones in a few minutes. Even a picnic meal was a fidgety business; one of the party had to act sentry all the time for fear something or other dangerously nasty would come crawling out of the sea. There were occasional longer jaunts by plane to other cities which neither in themselves nor their inhabitants were noticeably different from Tallor.

Leonie began to find the first strangeness wearing off. Her eyes became accustomed to the softer colourings and she began to perceive delicacy of shading where before she had dismissed a view as merely "grey." The scarcely recognised sense of claustrophobia caused by the hazy blanketing of all horizons began to wear off. But she refused to believe that she liked Venus any more. The furthest she would go was to admit now that it might be just tolerable, whereas before she had not believed even that.

One of the first things she had done when she was able to get about was to join a society of Whites which promoted charitable and philanthropic intentions towards the less fortunately coloured. It took her one meeting to discover that it existed chiefly to enhance the self-esteem of its own members, and three to resign, somewhat curtly, her association with it. Inquiries revealed another society, but one which existed, it seemed, solely to rival the first. It took her some little time to get on to the track of one which appeared to have more serious intentions than social ambitions, and it was Francis Clouster who told her of its existence.

She had visited him several times—taking precautions suitable for the district—partly to thank him and his wife, Marion, for their care, but even more because they were the only people she knew who seemed to share in any way her own feelings on the injustices of Venusian life.

She pleased him by her opinion of the societies she had already investigated.

"Rubbishy," he agreed. "The real effect of charitable societies like that is to bolster up the very conditions which make them necessary."

"But there must be others who are seriously interested?"

He looked at her thoughtfully.

"You might try the Pan-Venus Club, perhaps."

"Do you belong?"

"I did. I—er—fell out with them. It might be wiser not to tell them you know me."

"Why did you fall out?"

He shrugged. "Difference of views." Changing the subject, he asked:

"Do you really still feel as you did, even after living all this time up at Milota?"

"More, I think. I look at the people there, and I remember what happened down here. I can still see that policeman's horror as he went down, I can still hear him scream as those savages killed him with their bare hands. It's not the kind of thing one forgets. It meant that there's something dreadfully, tragically wrong underneath. You can't build up a decent world with that kind of beastliness in the foundations."

"'Savages' isn't very kind to my friends the Greens."

"I know, but it's true. They were savages at that moment. It's no good pretending they weren't. The thing to do is change the system which makes them savages."

"So easy to say."

"Yes. I begin to understand what you were telling me more now. But it can be done. If it could be done on Earth, and it was, it can most certainly be done on Venus."

"It will be—one day."

She looked at him, wondering at his tone.

"You told me you were a revolutionary."

"I am, but I am not a firebrand. You don't know these people yet. Still at the back of your mind you feel that you only have to say loudly enough, 'Unite and this World is Yours' for them to perceive its truth. I know that that is not the way of it. First you've got to make these people *want* to rescue themselves. You talk to a bunch of, say, Greens on the wage rate—which is disgustingly insufficient. And what do you find their greatest interest is? To raise it, you would say. Well, you'd be wrong. Their real pressing anxiety is lest the Reds or the Blacks get more. That's the kind of thing you're up against."

"But if you show them…"

"They don't want to be shown, they don't want reason. They're too fond of their discontents. Doesn't that discourage you?"

"Why should you want to discourage me?"

"I don't. But nor do I want to see you run headlong into trouble—dangerous trouble. If you want to go on, do so by all means, but do it with your eyes open. Know what you are handling, and you may light a lamp on the road to freedom: ignore the human factor and you may be fuel for reaction."

Francis and Marion Clouster saw her off together as she left. There was a frown on the woman's face as the car drove off.

"What do you think?" she asked as they went back indoors.

Francis fingered his chin.

"Good stuff, but it's early to judge. Plenty of them came here from Earth feeling just like that. What are they now? Hostesses in the big Milota houses. Crown opinion too strong for them. Still, we shall see, we shall see."

"I hear she's seeing a lot of young David Sherrick."

Francis looked at her in surprise.

"Really, the things you manage to hear, shut away down here."

"That might be interesting, don't you think?"

"It might—and then again it might be just another couple of young marrieds in a new house on Milota."

## III

"THAT GIRL OF yours settling down all right?" inquired Wilfred Baisham, depositing the ash of his cigar with careful delicacy.

"So-so," said Mr. Ward. "Takes time, of course. But she's young. They all have these half-baked, socialistic ideas when they're young, but they grow out of them."

"Half-baked?" inquired Mr. Baisham, with a lift of his eyebrows. "What about the Great Union?"

"Yes, of course. But it can't happen here."

"Comforting theory. All Milota says that. Don't you ever have less comfortable moments when it occurs to you that it might very easily happen here?"

Mr. Ward looked up, startled and uncertain.

"You don't mean that?"

"I decidedly do."

"But our order of society is perfectly stable."

"My good Ward, there never was an order of society yet which did not have to protect itself against disintegration—not just now and then, but continuously. Any form of society is, after all, a method of training Nature, but Nature never sleeps, and never gives in. Just a little too much of this 'it can't happen here' stuff and one day—Pouf! And you and I, your mills and my mines—where are we?"

"But I had no idea of this, Baisham, what are we doing about it?"

"Oh, about the same as usual. Just seeing that it doesn't take place."

Mattington Ward reached for another cigar and lit it.

"Confound you, Baisham, for a moment you scared me."

"If your Leonie had her way it would happen here, from what they tell me."

"She's hardly more than a child, you know. It's just these notions she picked up on Earth, she'll forget them. But I must say I see more and more clearly that it was a mistake ever to send her. She wouldn't have had all this readjustment to go through if she'd stayed here."

"You're right. The less contact between us and Earth except in the way of trade, the better."

"Anyway, Leonie's got another interest that's soon going to put paid to all that," said her father. "Dr. Sherrick."

"Young David Sherrick! Well, I'm glad to hear that. Nothing like a little affair of that kind for knocking that sort of nonsense out of their heads."

"I'm hoping it'll be more than an affair."

"Good. Fine young couple. By the way, I hear she goes down Chellan way to see that queer fish Clouster sometimes. See that she goes somewhere else on Wednesday."

"Why?"

"Going to be trouble. Greens and Blacks. Only don't tell anyone I told you."

—

DR. SHERRICK CAME down the hospital steps to see a familiar car balanced patiently on its gyroscopes before the entrance. He went up to it.

"Hullo, Leonie. What are you doing here?"

"Waiting to take you for a run I hope. Get in."

He opened the door and slid in beside her. The car tilted slightly and then readjusted itself.

"But I thought you were at the Pan-Venus Club?" he said, as they started.

"I should have been, but they've chucked me out—or at least asked me to resign. Same thing."

David grunted.

"You're not surprised?" she inquired.

"Not much."

They rode for a mile or two in silence.

"What did you say?" he asked. "I mean, to make them chuck you out."

"I told them they were dabblers. That if they really believed all the stuff they talk about the equality of man it would not be a club just for Whites, but for all colours—and with equal standing for all members. I said they were trying to square their consciences by talking and not doing—and seemed to be succeeding pretty well, to no one's profit. I asked them to give me one *practical* way in which they had tried to lower the colour hatred. And—oh well, quite a lot more."

"That makes me even less surprised. What did you expect them to do? Cheer?"

"I didn't care. I just wanted to jolt them a bit."

"Well, I gather you did that."

Leonie stopped the car.

"David, they made me so *angry*. Even *they* don't really care how these wretched people go on quarrelling and killing one another in their slums. Does anyone care?"

"Aren't you doing them an injustice? I think if you talked to them separately you'd find they genuinely care, but they're stuck. They don't know what to do."

"If they are, they've been stuck all their lives."

"They've learnt some of the things not to do. For instance, I'm willing to bet that one thing you wanted them to do was preach to all three coloured peoples that they are the same under their skins?"

"Yes, I did say something like that. In fact, I offered to do it."

"Well, there's quite enough reason for asking you to resign. They know better than that. When will you understand, Leonie, that each of the three colours considers itself superior to the others? A Black man is actually *proud* of being black because he thinks it shows he has none of the nasty characteristics he imputes to the Reds and Greens."

"But…"

"Leonie, dear, there isn't any but to that. It's a fact."

"It's also a fact that there's no racial difference. There must be some way of telling them that."

"Telling, but not convincing. Listen, Leonie, I'll tell you a story. I had a friend called Dick. We went through all our medical training together and qualified about the same time. Both of us felt, knew in our hearts, that this is a rotten system and that something ought to be done to clear it up. He, I suppose, felt more badly about it than I did, anyway, saw it more simply—he was more like you, and I was more like your Pan-Venus people.

"After we passed out he went and set up a practice among the Reds in Barro. He wasn't popular, the practice began to fall off the moment he took it over, but he was a damned good man at his job, so he managed to keep going although they didn't like him. And he knew well enough *why* they didn't like him—it was because they knew that he refused to agree with them when they ran down Greens and Blacks. But he thought he could get over that. His idea was that if he went on doctoring and doing the best he could for them they'd gradually come round to paying some attention to what he said.

"My own belief is that they wouldn't. The furthest they would have gone was to admit that he knew his particular job, but was quite obviously crazy in certain directions, notably on that racial question. Patience would have taken them that far, but unfortunately he hadn't much gift of patience. Things went too slowly for him and he decided to speed them up.

"He did it at a public health meeting. The hall was packed with Reds, and what must Dick do but get up and tell them that not only were they every bit as good as the Whites, which they didn't mind, but that the Greens and Blacks were every bit as good as the Whites, too. It was brave, but it was madness. They went for him like tigers, of course."

"What happened?" Leonie asked.

David Sherrick looked at his hands, avoiding her eyes.

"Nobody ever told the exact details, but the next day most of his clothing was found at the foot of a tree on the edge of the swamp forest. It was ripped to pieces and bloodstained. There were some ropes loosely tied round the tree, marks which showed that saurians had been there—and a few human bones, that was all…"

Neither spoke for a few minutes. It was David who went on.

"There have been other things like that. Everyone has heard of them, can you blame the Pan-Venus people for being careful? And if the Reds hadn't dealt with Dick the Whites would have."

"The Whites?"

"Well, the Government—it's the same thing. He'd be in prison now for incitement to break the peace, subversive activities or something of the kind.

"You see, Leonie, I've already lost one friend, my best friend, through this and I've no wish to see what happened to Dick Clouster happen to you."

Leonie was brought up short by the name.

"Clouster? Was he related to Francis Clouster who lives down in Chellan?"

"Yes, he was his son, only son."

Leonie opened her mouth to speak, and then thought better of it. There was a pause which she broke.

"But, David, something must be done. You think that, don't you?"

"I probably think it even more strongly than you do, Leonie. As a doctor I come into contact with its actual results. In hospital we're never without cases who've been beaten up for no reason but their colour. And when there's a big row we're rushed off our feet with the wounded. It's stupid and cruel, it causes endless suffering—you know how easily any cut gets infected here—it wastes our time when we might be doing really important work. God knows there are plenty of fevers to be tackled yet. Of course, something must be done, and we ought to do it. Damn it, it was the doctors who made it possible to colonise Venus at all by conquering rheumatism. But for that no one could have stood this climate, now it's up to us to make it worth living in. But how? I wouldn't mind using my life on it, but I'm hanged if I'm going to waste my life on it as Dick did. Listen, I'll tell you another story.

"Three days ago they brought a Green woman in. She was dreadfully hurt. Heaven knows why she was still alive, but she was. There was nothing we could do for her but give her some dope. And I'll tell you why it happened. You know, don't you, that it's about the equivalent of suicide for any woman on Venus to have a child anywhere but in a hospital?"

"Streptococcus infection?"

"Exactly. But sometimes by accident it does happen. Well, it had happened to this woman. When her husband saw that the baby was white, he went crazy. He killed the child, went for his wife with a knife and then ran out into the street and killed the first White he saw, just to show what he thought of us."

"Because the baby was white? What would he have done if it had been red?" said Leonie.

David looked at her oddly.

"It…" he began, then checked himself. "And that's not an isolated instance by any means. It's a thing which is deliberately built up in their schools and their homes."

"Deliberately."

"I said deliberately."

Leonie frowned.

"I don't think I understand. Isn't it mostly a prejudice handed on in the families?"

"It is. But who stands to gain from that prejudice? Who rules and owns Venus?"

"The Whites, I suppose."

"Exactly. The people living in luxury on Milota—and all the Milotas in the other cities. Don't you see? It's an old, old game. Make the people distrust one another, keep them at loggerheads, prevent them from uniting for their rights and you can rule. Let them combine and you're sunk. Your precious societies on Milota like to patronise, but they don't want Reds, Greens and Blacks to combine, that'd be the end of the Whites' rule—and they know it."

Leonie was silent, trying to grasp this new aspect. Hitherto she had believed at the back of her mind that her friends on Milota were merely apathetic and selfish, that they recognised the shamefulness of affairs but did not bother to bestir themselves to mend it. It required reorientation to see them as deliberate partisans. She found it difficult. And yet, why not? Wars on Earth had been engineered and countless people slaughtered for ends no more noble—indeed there were some who claimed that was almost invariably the motive. But—her own father and his friends intentionally keeping the coloured peoples at enmity for their own profit? That was more than she could take in. Her feelings rejected it in spite of her reason.

"I can't believe it."

"Haven't they tried to laugh you out of it, argue you out of it? Have they lost any opportunity of impressing on you that liberty, equality and fraternity may work on Earth, but it won't do so here? Have they given you any encouragement whatever?"

Leonie turned and gazed miserably at him. She shook her head. It was perfectly true, every word. They had been tolerant sometimes as one might to a child, never more than that. She began to see it now. Milota and its rule would be swept away in a moment if the people rose and took their rights. David was watching her intently. He saw her take the shock, waver a moment in divided loyalties, then a hardening light in her eyes, a firmer line to her lips.

"There is," she said slowly. "There is a kind of absolute right. The right of any human being to freedom and equality of opportunity. And there is an absolute wrong; to enslave, and to incite to murder."

David Sherrick sighed.

"I was afraid of that. The other way would have been so much easier for you, Leonie, dear. And yet I'm glad, so glad. You're one of the real people, Leonie."

He looked at her seriously. Her eyes dropped and she turned her head away.

"No, no, darling, don't cry," he said.

She clung to him for a few moments.

"David. I'm sorry. I—I feel as if I had lost something—something very precious."

"You have, dear, but that had to be. You had come to the point where something had to be lost—either your illusions, or your principles."

There was a silence, neither of them spoke for some minutes. Then David slipped his arm away from her. He looked straight before him. His tone was hard as he spoke.

"Leonie dear, I'm going to shock you, I'm afraid. But I must. I am going to put myself in your hands because I trust you, because I know that you are the most genuine person I have ever met. And because I love you for it, Leonie, I am going to break a solemn oath..."

"David..."

"I am, because it is an oath which should never have been asked or given, there should have been no need for it." For one last moment he hesitated on the brink, then he plunged.

"You asked what would have happened if the Green woman's baby had been red."

"Yes."

"Well, it couldn't have been. That's all."

"I don't understand. If it could be white..."

"Leonie, all the babies are white. Red, Black, Green women: they all have white babies. Don't you see?"

---

NOBODY KNEW HOW nor quite when it had begun, David told her. It must have been back in the early days of colonisation when men were struggling for a foothold on Venus. In those days life had been a horribly uncertain business. Exploration had been dangerous, uncounted hundreds of men had gone out from the settlements so laboriously established and had never returned. The saurians had not learned from experience to avoid the high land and keep to the water and the marshes. Scientific acclimatisation had not yet been developed, so that the heat and humidity were a burden to everyone. The mortality rate was appalling. Fevers, infections in wounds, and, worst of all, rheumatic afflictions carried men and women off in such numbers that at one time the idea of permanent colonisation was all but abandoned.

They were times of chaos and uncertainty when even the least adventurous had no more than a slippery hold on life. It was then that someone's ingenuity managed to establish it. It could never have been done on Earth, but on Venus where a woman must give birth to her child in the hospital or face certain death, it was somehow accomplished.

# THE LIVING LIES

But if the how and the when were uncertain, the why was plain. Colonisation began away back in the heyday of international finance in the days before the Great Union when groups of interests lived comfortably out of the profits which came from pitting one section of the Earth's population against another. It was a technique developed over centuries, seldom failing, and yet unperceived for generations by the mind of the common man. The days of profit from victory of one's own side had long gone by. To the big interest it mattered little any longer which side won; their concern was now two-fold, to sift wealth out of the waste of war, and to see that neither side emerged from a conflict dangerously strong. They were upheld, as it were, by a balance of forces ingeniously held in equilibrium; in peace the scales tilted slowly back and forth, in war there was a hurried throwing of weights into this pan and then that to prevent either coming down with a crashing victory. It was good while it lasted, and it had lasted a long time, but of late there had been signs that the central pivot was about to crack as the movements which were to culminate in the Great Union gathered force.

It was a system which had been developed out of the natural conditions of Earth and it had suited the select dwellers in Earth's penthouses very well indeed, but now they saw the foreshadow of a world in which it would no longer work.

From what Machiavellian mind there first crawled the idea that it was possible to improve on Nature even in this respect is unknown; its owner remains unsung, unglorified. But it is clear what he saw. Here was a new world. Into it were beginning to flow colonists from the old. They were of different nationalities, but that was beginning to matter less than it did. They were nearly all of the white race. For the most part they were tough customers more occupied with the business of living than learning; individualists, too, anxious to get on rather than combine, anxious to be lent money to buy machinery and to be put into other men's debt. That was satisfactory. But one day the ideas which were taking hold on Earth would be carried across space and begin to spread on Venus. There would be no racial bar to hold them back and little language difficulty; before long the people would rise as one. They would refuse to be exploited, to be chained down by heavy interest, to put up with low wages and poor conditions—and then the dominant moneyed class would dominate no more.

"They must not unite," said the Machiavellian mind. "They must be divided amongst themselves. And what is the greatest factor of disunion on Earth? It is race. But Nature has not seen fit to create different races of men upon Venus. Very well, then, *we will*."

Most seditiously unwritten is the history of early Venusian development. How did they set about the creation of coloured races? Did they steal children and adopt orphans? Did they distrain upon children for non-payment of debts? Did they bully or bribe? Did they drive men and women into actual slavery? Did they set up colonies in remote places? No one knows. No one is ever likely to know, for it was a secret well kept and now deeply buried.

It is only known that strange men and women, Green, Magenta-Red and Black, began to be seen about. According to rumour they were the offspring of Whites and natives to be found in some secluded parts of Venus. No one had seen these natives, but each had a friend who had. It seemed natural, if scarcely commendable.

Simultaneously began a reduction in the quota of immigration from Earth. The supply of new White blood decreased, but the numbers of coloured people appeared to increase. Whites began to marry Green, Red or Black partners, and always the child was the colour of its coloured parent. It was odd. There was considerable talk about genes, but to little purpose. It seemed that the terrestrial laws and heredity did not hold on Venus.

Later the immigration laws were relaxed to some extent and careful attention paid to the balance of the sexes. It began to become uncustomary to marry with the colours. Later it became not only illegal, but unethical.

By that time, David explained, the four "races" were firmly established.

"But how was it ever allowed to happen?" Leonie wanted to know. "There must have been people who knew, why didn't the doctors stop it?"

"For a very simple reason. Who do you think owned and ran the hospitals? A man could only be a doctor if he kept in with the authorities—and the same is true now. All doctors and hospital attendants are, as you may have noticed, of the White, the ruling, class. Oddly enough they despise the coloured for being coloured even though they are responsible for it. Even I, if I am honest with myself, do not feel that I am quite the same as a Red or a Green. That's the pressure of mass opinion, of course; against all I know, and against all reason it is there. That's where the truly diabolical nature of the thing lies. Once it was under weigh it had to go on. And what could or can we doctors do? Protest and be struck off the register or perhaps imprisoned for subversive activities? Protest that we will not give a Green woman the Green baby she expects? We cannot even protest that the colouration does any physical harm. It doesn't."

"Except to bring bloodshed and murder."

"That's not supposed to be in the doctor's province."

"But suppose you united and called a strike. Refused to do it any more."

"Well, to begin with, one would probably disappear or be struck off in the attempt to get unity. But even apart from that this thing has gone on so long now that I don't think you would get unity at all. You see, there's another side to it too.

"Try to imagine yourself a Red woman. You have always been Red, so have your family, your friends, your schoolmates. You have married a Red man. All your life you have expected and looked forward to have a Red baby. What is going to happen if someone suddenly shows you a White baby after it is all over and says: 'This is yours'? You are going to disbelieve it, of course. It is somebody else's baby, not yours. No amount of argument is going to kill the doubt in your mind. And what about your husband? He, too, has expected a Red baby. How is he going to take a White one—and what is he going to think? I told you what happened to a Green woman with a White baby. Even if you, a Red woman, were told it all as I have told it to you now and if you did believe it, you would still demand your Red baby, you would be ashamed, afraid to face the world with a White one."

"God, don't you see what we've done? We've built a lie too colossal to be disbelieved."

"And it must go on and on?"

"As long as each colour thinks itself the superior of the others—and the Government sees that it does—it must go on. There's only one way that I can see in which it might be stopped and that's by the elimination of streptococci and other infections. That would make it safe for women to have babies in their own homes, and the whole thing would come down with a run. But until then…"

Leonie sat silent, a slight frown on her forehead, her eyes staring unseen into the misty distance.

"How is it done, David, this colouring?"

"Oh, that's not very difficult. After the baby has been washed it is taken along to a special room. There it is smeared all over with a particular grease. Depending on the colour of its mother there is a colouring agent, Red, Green or Black latent in the grease. It is then placed under a projector which looks something like an X-ray tube, and is turned very carefully so that every inch of its body comes under the direct rays. They are short waves and carry the colour from the grease. They penetrate the skin and beyond, and their action is rather that of burning the special colouring agent right into and through the skin at low temperature. It sounds a little painful put that way, but actually it isn't. The child feels nothing whatever. After that it is ready to be washed again and taken back to its mother. The whole thing takes less than five minutes."

"And the colour is there for the rest of its life?"

"Yes. Though as I expect you've noticed, the colouring is rather more vivid in children than in adults."

"David. I can hardly believe it now. All these Red, Green and Black men and women…?"

"Every one of them, Leonie!"

"Was there ever a lie so big?" Leonie turned suddenly and grasped his arm.

"David," she said, desperately, "David, this mustn't, this shan't go on. It's got to be broken. Somehow there must be a way of breaking it. We've got to find it."

## IV

"HULLO, REYNICK. COME along in. Have a drink."

The Chief of the Tallor Police, secret and uniformed branches, did as he was bid. He sat down in a comfortable chair half-facing his host and raised his glass.

# THE LIVING LIES

"Always a harbinger of trouble," said Mr. Wilfred Baisham, amiably. "What is it now?"

Reynick sipped at his drink.

"It's not so much a matter of what is now," he said, "More a case of what may be soon. It's really guidance for the future I'm after. I don't think anything like this has ever shown up before."

"All right, no need to beat about. Guidance on what?"

"On Mr. Ward's daughter."

"What about her?"

"Subversive activities."

"Oh, that. They're all like that, they grow out of it. Most of 'em get interested in some young man and forget about it. She must soon see that Earth ideas aren't wanted here."

"This one seems to be growing into it."

"Give her time."

"I'm inclined to think it's more serious. In the last few months I've been hearing more and more about her. She's been working around a lot among the coloured women, telling them they're as good as the Whites, and she seems to have a way with her for I'm told they've been listening a bit." He paused to light a cigar and went on:

"Mind you, I don't say they take her very seriously, and she's certainly not got anything that could be called a following. All the same, one can't pretend that that kind of thing is good. It might conceivably catch on a bit if there were to be a wave of unrest. Another thing, anybody else who feels like that—and there are quite a few of them—and sees her getting away with it feels encouraged to have a shot at it, too. To my mind it's the kind of thing that it pays to nip right in the bud."

"Well, what am I supposed to do about it? After all, nipping things is your job," Mr. Baisham pointed out.

"Certainly, and if it had been anyone else I'd have done it by now. But this isn't easy. After all, Mr. Ward's daughter…"

"Yes, I see that."

"And it's not only that. If we touch her, either taking her up in court, or—er—less officially, we advertise the whole thing and make it much more important. Of course, we could tip off the news strips to keep it quiet, but these things get round. Besides, what's old man Ward going to say—and do? I can't see him taking it quietly.

"It's darned awkward. She's not like the usual run of Milota charity women—they'll take a hint, she won't."

Mr. Baisham leant forward and poured himself another drink.

"What you're really getting at, Reynick, is that you want me to have a go at Ward. Show him the error of his daughter's ways?"

"Well, he would take it better from you than from me."

"All right. I'll try if you like. But to be candid, I don't hold out much hope. It'll worry him a bit, but it's done that already. Between you and me, Reynick, the girl just doesn't pay any attention to him now. Ungrateful little bit, after all he's done for her and spent on her. Poor chap takes it hard. He's been looking forward to having her home for years now and she treats him like the furniture. However, as I said, I'll mention it. But if I were you, I'd think up a second line."

"Such as?"

"Well, if I were in your place I'd let her go on, but keep a careful eye on her. You might even let it be known you're keeping an eye on her. Meanwhile, you could let a little rumour circulate that she's been trying to rouse trouble between, say, the Greens and the Blacks. That may make her draw in a bit, I hope it does. But if she goes on, sometime or other she'll overstep the mark, then your men will have to see to it she disappears. If it's done neatly everybody will think it's the Greens or Blacks who did it—and they can fight that out among themselves. I'd hate you to have to do it for her father's sake as well as her own, she's a live girl and she's got pluck, but all the same, if she shows signs of getting dangerous, she's got to be stopped, no matter who she is."

"Palliam?" asked Reynick.

Wilfred Baisham frowned. Palliam, the penal island, the place of lifelong sentences never remitted. For the daughter of a good friend. It was not nice. But he shook his head regretfully.

"I'm afraid so. There's nowhere else as safe. But try everything else first."

THERE WAS A frown on Leonie's face as she shut the front door of a small Chellan house behind her and turned to walk to the spot where she had left her car in the main road. The street she must traverse to reach it was narrow and badly lit, one into which few, if any, of the other dwellers on Milota would have ventured alone by night. But Leonie had little nervousness of Chellan now. Francis Clouster had, she fancied, passed a word around on her behalf, but, more important, she had become a known figure there. It was understood by the Greens that though her ideas might be odd, she meant well.

Meant well... There lay the reason for her frown. That was their faintly damning opinion of her. Try as she would, shape her tactics as she might, she seemed unable to make progress. David had convinced her that her ambition to shout the truth about themselves to the coloured peoples would mean not only danger to herself, but disaster to her cause. They would not be told, realisation if it could come at all must not be thrust upon them so that they could resist it; it must come or appear to come from inside themselves. By hints, by becoming aware of discrepancies, by linking this and that together they must be led on to question their own state, to ponder its anomalies and arrive at the answer for themselves. She understood now that her part, if it were to be of use at all, must be played with subtlety and the utmost caution against a careless word. She must prompt ever so gently, indetectably. Urge and deflect without arousing a breath of suspicion that she was directing.

For months now she had been pursuing this course. Listening sympathetically to gain confidence, speaking little, dropping every now and then a word which should have struck a spark of inquisitive interest, but never seemed to. As far as she could see the months had been utterly wasted. There had been no progress; no Green, Red or Black had taken even the first step which might lead to his one day questioning his Greenness, Redness or Blackness. This evening had been typical of the lack of response. To a party of Green women she had in the natural course of conversation remarked how it had surprised her to find that Greens naturally had pink finger nails and toe nails just like her own. She had even been a little obvious, but no one had been much interested or wanted to compare theirs with hers. One could only hope as one had hoped so many times that the suggestion would lie dormant to arise later. Meanwhile she must continue to watch a tongue that was forever threatening to run away in its impatience.

A trifle disturbing, too, was the realisation that if her hints failed to register in the desired quarter, they were getting home somewhere else, with the result that she herself became the recipient of hints referring for the most part to the unpleasant consequences encountered by persons who tried to stir up trouble. She was uncertain at first what value to put on them, but their frequent recurrence from the most unexpected sources had lately begun to worry her more than a little. It was understandable that while her eyes were on the ground, steering her round the worst mud patches, her mind should be preoccupied.

---

SHE WAS WITHOUT suspicion as she passed the entrance of a dark alley; taken completely by surprise when a hand from behind clapped down over her mouth and an arm simultaneously whipped round her, fastening her own arms to her sides.

She lashed backward with a heel, bringing a grunt from the man behind her, but no slackening of his grip. A second man, no more than a dark figure in the gloom, dodged forward to catch her ankles and lift her feet from the ground. Without a word the two men turned to carry her back up the alley whence they had come. For a hundred yards or more they stumbled and slid along the uneven paving. Blocking the other end where the alley gave on to a wider road, she could see the shape of a car ready balanced on its two wheels. As they drew closer she could distinguish the faint humming of its gyroscopes. She struggled ineffectively. Held as she was she could do little but bend her knees and kick out again in an attempt to loosen the men's holds. It made them stumble a bit, and the man in front swore in a grumble, but practical result there was none.

They came close beside the car. The man who held her feet released his hold with one hand and reached for the door handle. At that moment there was a thud behind her. The hand dropped from her mouth and the arm around her relaxed. She felt herself falling. Simultaneously the man in front looked round.

She had a vision of an arm which held something in its hand striking down at his head. He dropped without a murmur. A groping hand found her own arm, and pulled her to her feet.

"Quick and be quiet," breathed an urgent voice.

She was being dragged at a helter-skelter stumbling run back along the alley. Halfway down they swung into another passage-way even darker, and then round corners one after another until all sense of direction was gone, and she felt like a bewildered child in a nightmare, staggering, slipping, panting, but dragged willy-nilly onwards through an endless dark labyrinth.

There came a pause at last. She leant against a wall, gasping for breath. Her companion was a black shadow in the darkness. She could hear him fumbling in his pockets. She had only one desire; to get back to her car and drive furiously home.

"My car…" she began.

"Damn your car. It's your life you want to save," said a low voice, curtly.

He ceased to fumble. There was a sound of a key in a lock. A hand urged her forward into absolute blackness. The door shut behind them. He took her wrist again, leading her cautiously forward for a dozen yards or more. Then once more he stopped.

"Lie down here," he said. "I don't suppose anyone will come, but if they do, pull the stuff right over you and don't make a sound. Don't breathe. I'm going now to see what's happened. I'll be back in an hour or so."

Bending over, Leonie felt a pile of coarse material like jute just under her hand. She heard his footsteps moving away. By the door they paused.

"If you put any value on your life," his voice came softly, "you'll stay here, and be safe."

Leonie found her voice shaky and a little meek.

"I'll stay," she said into the darkness.

She dare not strike a light to look at her watch. If it was only an hour he was away, it was the longest hour of her life, and through it all she lay on the pile of sacking with ears strained for the faintest sound. The tone of urgency in his voice had done more to raise her apprehensions than the actual events. At the long-delayed sound of the lock she started up, sitting; one hand ready to drag the musty cloth over herself.

"It's all right," said the same voice.

She let out her held breath, and put a hand to her thumping heart. He came closer.

"Come along."

He led the way in the dark along passages, through doors and finally down a flight of steps. At the bottom he closed the last door and turned on the light. Leonie blinked and then opened her eyes to find herself facing a man whose skin was green as the patina on copper. There was something faintly familiar about him, but it was always difficult to recognise people of the colours, one had to learn to remember faces by form alone without the help of complexions.

"Who are you?" she said.

"Never mind about that. The important point at the moment is that you, Miss Ward, are in a nasty spot."

"Why?"

"I should have thought you could guess that yourself. Weren't you warned that you were heading for trouble?"

"I suppose I was, but…"

"And who do you suppose those men were who grabbed you?"

"I've no idea. It was dark, Greens? I'd just been talking to some Green women."

"You've talked to too many people. Those two were secret police."

"*Secret* police, why I…"

"Yes, secret. It would have been a nice little secret business altogether. Total and inexplicable disappearance of prominent Milota citizen's daughter."

There was a pause. Leonie's gaze wandered round the room. It had the appearance of a rough workshop. There was a bench on one side, a metal surfaced table on the other, racks of tools hung on the walls, a little pile of chips and shavings covered the floor. The only breaks in the four walls were a small ventilator and the door through which they had entered. A cellar, she supposed, taking the place in with only half her mind.

"What would have happened?" she asked.

He shrugged his shoulders.

"It means you're officially listed as dangerous. You're not to be allowed to go about trying to spread disaffection on Venus. They daren't send you to Earth for they won't want your views spread there. I should say it means either imprisonment for life on Palliam or some such place—or perhaps something more drastic."

Leonie looked at him hard. There was no doubt he meant what he said.

"But without hearing—without trial?" she said, incredulously.

"Do you think they want to give you the chance to announce your views in public?"

"Then perhaps I have to thank you for my life?"

"We might see about that later on. The important thing just now is for you to disappear—only in a different way." He laid on the bench a bag which he had been carrying slung from one shoulder. Out of it he pulled a large jar and a bundle of clothes and a dark bottle. He took up the jar and started to loosen the lid.

"The White Miss Ward has got to vanish," he said. "You'll have to become a Green."

Leonie looked up at him, horror-stricken.

"Me, a Green woman. No, oh, no. I can't, I can't look like them."

"And why not?" inquired the Green man, coldly.

"To be a Green the rest of my life, never to see myself as I really am. I couldn't."

"Of course not. There's a medium which will get this stuff off once you're safely away from here and out of reach."

"Oh, I see. For a moment I thought you meant I must be made Green like they make the babies."

The Green man stared at her. Slowly he put down the jar on the bench. His eyes never left hers.

"Who told you that?" he demanded.

"A—er—I—I must have heard it somewhere."

"It's scarcely the kind of thing one hears by accident. Now I begin to understand why they wanted you so much. Tell me, have you been spreading this about? No, of course you haven't or you wouldn't be here now. But just what were you up to?"

"I wanted to make them find it out for themselves."

Surprisingly he laughed.

"What a hope. A few hints and suggestions, I suppose. Did you think those were going to get through the mass of suggestion carefully built up all their lives? Do you know anything of crowd psychology?"

"I thought they might. There didn't seem any other way. And, anyway, it doesn't seem to surprise you. Who are you?"

"Never mind about that now. We must get on. You see the stuff in this jar." He held it so that she was able to make out a dark green substance within. "You must put this on. For a week at least it will make you indistinguishable from any other Green. In the bottle there's dye for your hair. Now get your clothes off, and go to it."

"But…"

"For God's sake. Is this a time for fooling about the proprieties?"

"All right," said Leonie, meekly.

He gathered up her clothes as she shed them and put them into the bag.

"Now put the green stuff on. Do it properly, make yourself a thorough Green woman—we don't want any silly accidents. Give it ten minutes or so to take, and then wash the rest off. There's a tap in the corner. Maybe you'd better do your hair first—and don't forget your eyebrows and eyelashes. Then get dressed in these things," he pointed to the bundle of clothes he had brought, "and wait until I come back."

The door slammed and he was gone, taking her clothes with him.

Leonie set about the business of changing her "race."

---

HE WAS GONE over two hours. When he returned he submitted her to a critical survey. Leonie withstood it awkwardly, conscious of the ill-fitting cheap clothes she wore.

"Well?" she said, after his eye had taken her in from top to toe.

"You'll do. Except for that watch. No Green woman could afford a watch like that. Better give it to me."

She handed it over without protest and he slipped it in his pocket.

"I might have done better with a mirror," she observed.

"I doubt it. You'd most likely have quit altogether."

Leonie gazed at her fantastically green arm, wondered what her face was like, and thought he was probably right.

"And now?" she asked.

"And now we are going out. You are a Green woman in the Green quarter—your home, don't forget. Miss Leonie Ward is dead—murdered, to put it crudely. Somebody who didn't like her took her out to the marshes and fed her to the saurians. Only a few bloodstained rags of her clothing to show what happened. All most regrettable and upsetting, but rather the kind of thing you might expect to happen to a girl who would mix with the coloured peoples."

Leonie paused at the door. Something clicked in her memory—"Only a few bloodstained…"

"Now I know who you are. You're Dick Clouster, who's supposed to be dead. I saw you at your father's house once."

"You did. And in one of my less cautious moments. It worried me for a bit afterwards."

"And you're not a real Green after all."

"Who is? Come along now, we must be moving."

## V

MR. WILFRED BAISHAM spoke into the telephone.

"My dear friend. They've only just told me. What a ghastly thing to have happened. So young, such a lovely girl with all her life before her. An appalling tragedy."

He listened to a few sentences in Mattington Ward's attenuated voice before he spoke again.

"I? Well, yes, I have a little influence in the Police Department, I suppose, but I shan't need to use it. This thing's made their blood boil. It's an outrage which Tallor is never going to forget. They'll get them, you can depend on that, Mattington. They'll be at it night and day until they find the men that did it. Fiends like that have got to be caught, and caught quickly."

He listened a little longer before he said goodbye and rang off. For a moment he sat and looked absent-mindedly at the misty world beyond the window. Then he picked up the telephone and dialled a number.

"Hullo, Reynick. Anything about the Ward girl yet?"

"—No? Well, it's a bit soon perhaps. By the way, her father and all Milota's quite satisfied the Greens did it. Not a doubt between them. That'll make things quite simple when you do find her."

"—Yes, I'm pretty sure. The whole thing was too convenient. Why choose just the moment when your men had got her?"

"—Yes, I know people have been put out on the marshes before, but it's always been done in hot blood, with a minor or major riot of some kind to carry it through."

"—Of course you have. You didn't expect her to try to get away in her own car, did you? Now look here, when you do find her, I'd go steady. Don't pounce the moment she's spotted. Lie low a bit. We thought she was on her own, but it's pretty clear now she's not. There may be several under cover. When you make your jump you want to bag the lot if you can. Provided she's here at all, of course. It's not quite at all unlikely that's she's been acting as an agent for a group outside Tallor altogether, in which case, she's probably in another city already. Have you been able to get a line on how much she really knows?"

"—Oh, you think that, do you? Then she's more dangerous than we fancied. Still, she can't do much now she's on the run. By the way, it might do to keep an eye on that young man… Yes, Dr. David Sherrick… Yes, let me know."

Again Wilfred Baisham sat gazing speculatively out of the window. For a quarter of an hour he was lost in thought before he reached once more for the telephone.

"West Milota Hospital? ...My name's Baisham, I want to speak to the Director if he's free."

"—Hullo, Dray. I'd like a word confidentially with you, it's rather urgent. Mind if I come round right away? ...Good, I'll be there in ten minutes."

———

LEONIE STARED LONG and miserably into the mirror, studying every detail of the face which stared back. A face with a complexion soft as velvet, but green as grass. The lips, after the manner of most Green women, were painted a brilliant red, they matched the small rings in her ears. There was a faint shading of dusky powder on her eyelids which was also a fashion among Green women. When she opened her mouth her teeth gleamed a startling white: she opened it as little as possible. Her dark hair was now shorter and dressed differently from the way it had been when it was fair. Still she could scarcely believe in its reality. She put a hand up to touch it, to feel that it was her own face—a green hand with finger nails painted red as her lips.

This was herself. The thing in the mirror. This for ever more, if David failed.

She hid her face in her green hands and wept.

It had been inescapable. Two days after the attack in the alley Dick Clouster had come up to the little room he had found for her. He was carrying a black case which he set down carefully on the table.

"I'm afraid I've bad news for you. There's a comb-out going on in Chellan."

"The Police?" she asked, anxiously.

He nodded.

"Do you think they know I'm here?"

"I don't know. I don't think so. It's quite probably someone else. You're not the only White masquerading as a coloured. But that doesn't make it any less serious."

"But they'll never recognise me like this. I can stand questions. I've learnt that family history you gave me off by heart. I'm Doris Glandon, my father was..."

"I know, but they've got cute little dodges. I told you there was a medium which gets the green stuff off. Well, a little touch from a pad damped with that, and it's all up. They get real Greens to mingle in the street and touch as many hands with it as possible. Or they put it on handles of doors, anything which a lot of people may touch, and set a watch. I've even known them spray it over a crowd in the hope somebody will look spotty. The real Greens don't mind. It doesn't matter to them."

"Well," she said with a half apprehension of what was coming.

"I'm sorry, Leonie. It means you'll have to stop playing at being a Green, and really become one."

"No—no!"

"There's no other safe way. I wish there were. If you don't, they'll spot you sooner or later. For all I know they may be starting on a house-to-house test right now."

"But—oh, God, I can't do that. I can't."

"Look, I've brought a projector. It's rough, but it works—I know, because I've had to use it on myself. We can get it done in ten minutes."

"And for the rest of my life—oh, no."

"Listen. I had to do it. Do you think I liked it? But if I hadn't I should have been caught half a dozen times before this."

"You're not a woman."

"Oh, for heaven's sake! Won't you realise that it is this or your life? Your life! A live Green woman—or a nice pink and white corpse. You choose."

"Don't."

It had taken him the best part of two hours to ram it home to her, to batter down and demolish her stubborn opposition until she was left weakly and tearfully consenting.

She scarcely recalled its actual accomplishment. Vague memories of being smeared with something, of being turned this way and that beneath a tube which glared and hummed and gradually obliterated the girl who had been Leonie Ward to put Doris Glandon in her place, and of her mind still feebly protesting while her body consented.

Within twenty-four hours the necessity had been proved, and by a more direct method than she expected. There was a barrier across one of the main streets and a party of Green police at its only gap. There was no going back, everyone was ordered to pass through, to press his or her hand on a damp pad and brush it lightly across a sheet of white paper.

"Why do you take so much trouble with me?" she asked Dick Clouster the following evening. "When I look at this," she held out her green hand—"I'm not even grateful. I'm not worth your trouble."

"My father and mother tell me differently," he said, "besides, I think you are in love with David. He was one of my best friends, you know."

"Was! He would be now if he knew you were alive. And I *was* in love with him."

"You're not now?"

"I can't let myself be now—like this."

Dick Clouster made no reply to that. He had sat for some minutes in silence. When he spoke it was to ask:

"It was David who told you about the colouring of the babies, wasn't it?"

She nodded.

"Why?" he asked. "He broke his professional word. He must have had some good reason."

"Because he knew how I felt about this—this slavery of the colours. He knew that I meant to go on working against it though he warned me—he told me what happened to you, or, rather, what he thought happened to you, as a warning. And I would not take that warning."

"Do you wish you had?"

"I don't think I could have done. I should have gone on feeling as I did, and it would have shown sooner or later. Anyway, when I didn't, he knew that I should be bound to have to know about the babies sooner or later, so he told me."

"And David himself. How does he see it?"

"He says he's ready to use his life to stop it. But that any course he can see would lead only to his wasting his life without stopping it. And I understand that now," she added, bitterly.

Dick got up and began to pace the room. Her gaze followed him back and forth. Suddenly he turned on her.

"Will you swear this? Swear by everything most sacred to you that this is how he really feels?"

"I'd put my life on it."

His eyes held hers, intense and penetrating. He nodded. "I believe you." He sat down again. In a calmer tone he went on. "Then there may be a chance. Now listen, I'm going to tell you something which very few people know.

"Very many years ago an accident happened up at one of the Milota hospitals. By some mistake a child of a White woman there was taken to the colouring room. He emerged Black, indelibly Black.

"It was a disaster for the family. Their only son, and there were reasons why they would expect no more children. The mother nearly went out of her mind, the father was distracted, the child was taken home and hidden away out of sight. The father was an exceedingly rich man. If anything could be done about it, he determined to do it—at any cost. In the face of tremendous Governmental opposition he built a research laboratory, equipped it, financed it and brought experts to work in it. The prize he offered to the man who could perfect a system of harmless decolouring was fabulous.

"For over ten years he poured money into what appeared to be a hopeless quest, and then, suddenly, it was found.

"The boy was treated and emerged a normal White.

"The Government swooped like lightning and seized the machine, but neither the father nor the inventor minded that much: the one had his son; the other, a fortune.

"The fate of the machine hung in the balance a while. A considerable body of officials was for its complete destruction; another body felt that a mistake which could happen once could happen again. In the end six machines were made, again in the face of strong opposition. They were deposited in the charge of the directors of the six largest hospitals on Venus, for use only in the gravest emergencies.

"One of them is in the West Milota Hospital."

"Where David is," murmured Leonie.

"For years," Dick went on, "I've been haunted by the thought of that machine locked uselessly away. I've never seen it, but I've been told about it.

It's a projector, not unlike the one which does the staining to look at, but it almost exactly reverses the process. A jelly is applied to the skin, the rays of the projector pass through it and the skin and break down the pigments into their components, and by some ductile effect of the special jelly they are drawn out and held. It may take three or even four applications and treatments to clear every trace of the pigmentation, but it does it.

"Yes, for years I've wondered how one could get hold of that machine. I've been a Green long enough to know some other Greens who would undergo the experiment if I had the machine. But there had to be someone at the other end, someone whom I knew I could trust to risk his life for it."

"David's been there a long time. Couldn't you have…"

"Yes, I know. But he was younger when I knew him. I thought of him more than once, but I could never make up my mind to get into touch with him. You see, one's got to be certain, certain beyond all shadow of doubt. And it must be successful. It's not just our lives, yours, mine and his, that hang on it. It's the fate of all the coloured people. I was afraid to make a move because I'm as sure as I am of anything that at a bungled attempt the Government would fly into a panic and destroy all six machines at once; they'd take no second chance.

"Now, I'm going to risk it at last. I'm going to stake everything on David. I can tell him where it is and how it is protected; the rest will be up to him. If he'll do it."

"I think he'll do it. I know he will."

"We must get into touch with him. That'll have to be done carefully. Unless they're perfectly satisfied about you they'll be watching him. Probably they will anyway, because he was associated with a subversive person such as you. Yes, he'll have to be warned about that right at the beginning…"

―

HOPE REVIVED IN Leonie, but it was a much tempered hope. There would be so much risk, so many things to go wrong, so much strife to be faced later on. And would the coloured people believe even the evidence of their own eyes? Wouldn't they even then be likely to think that they had been changed by a trick into Whites, rather than see that they had been restored to their natural state? But perhaps that did not matter overmuch. They would learn in time. Success would mean something like civil war, more fighting and bloodshed. Treatment of a few of each colour done secretly would convince their friends and relatives. The desire to be a White, one of the ruling class, would spread like fire. But the power of the Government must be overthrown before they could settle down undisturbed to liberating the thousands, herself among them, from the bondage of their colours.

If David were to fail—well, thousands would never know. But she would. For the rest of her life a green face would look back at her from her mirror.

And David had come. Circuitously and, he believed, unobserved. He had been watched the last few days, he knew that, and he had taken elaborately particular pains to see that his followers were thrown off.

She had been at the meeting place, a mean cottage on the outskirts of Chellan when he had arrived. He had walked into the room, his eyes had rested on her a second remotely, uninterestedly.

She had to step forward and say:

"David!"

There had been a moment's distaste in his eyes. A fraction of a second before his ear recognised her voice. She saw the realisation come home to him, surprise, concern and something less pleasant than concern passing across his face.

"Leonie! Leonie, darling."

He opened his arms to her. She went to them and they closed around her.

"Leonie, dear."

Everything should have been the same…

Then Dick had come in to talk, advise and explain half through the night. And David had agreed as she had never doubted he would. Between the three of them they had plotted and planned down to the last detail. They had parted tired out, but buoyed up with a new hope. If it could be done at all, Leonie felt, David would do it.

But, oh, that look for a Green woman.

And so, Leonie wept.

## VI

DICK CLOUSTER WAS on his feet expounding and exhorting. Leonie looked at the faces before him. They reminded her of a crowd listening to the patter of a quack medicine man. Hope, frank disbelief, satirical amusement, they were all there. Occasionally their eyes shifted to the apparatus which David was erecting on a table in the corner, and then came back to the speaker's face. They listened, but without conviction.

There were over thirty of them in the room, men and a few women, all Greens. There had been an argument over that, but Leonie's view that there ought to be representatives of all three colours had been borne down by the two men. For one thing there were few contacts with the Reds and Blacks: it would not be easy to approach any and persuade them to come; and if they did come Dick and David were apprehensive of the results. It was notoriously difficult to handle successfully any meeting, even a small one, where the colours were mixed. Finally it was decided to introduce the machine to each group in turn, and to the Greens first because it was simplest for Dick, as a Green, to collect a group of them.

Leonie looked across at David. His face wore a serious intent expression as he bent over his work, assembling, adjusting and connecting. It was a month since the night he had come to Chellan. She had not seen him since then, it had been safer for him to seem to go on as usual and only to communicate with them if it were vitally necessary. During that time he had had to work on his own. To make certain the machine was still kept where Dick said it was; to put out of action the locks and alarms which secured it; to get it away; and finally, to cover every trace of his tampering.

She lifted her hand and looked at its green back. Soon that would be green no more. Once the organisation of the Whites was overthrown and the peril of their police removed, she would be free to put herself under the machine and become white once more.

David turned and beckoned her. She crossed over to help him erect and screw down the plated pillar which would suspend the machine over the table. In a few minutes now there would be a form lying on that table, losing for ever the affliction of its colour. It made the sight of her green hands working close to David's white ones easier to bear.

Dick was coming to his peroration now. Showing his audience what it meant. Not just change of colour for a few individuals, but revolution; the liberation of all the colours. For a moment that sentiment did not seem to appeal. Clearly there was a section which felt that if it could be done it should only apply to themselves, the Greens. How would it be possible to avoid contamination by the vicious Reds and the sordid Blacks if they were indistinguishable from other people? Wisely Dick sensed the feeling and dropped that aspect. For some minutes he concentrated on the injustices suffered by the Greens themselves; the contrast between their way of living and that of the Whites on Milota.

Finally he asked:

"Which one of you is going to be the first to regain his birthright colour? I could show you on myself how it can be done, but you might think I had tricked you. I want one of those whose family is known, whose parents and grandparents are known to everyone as Greens. Who?"

There was a pause, a dead silence. Then one of the women moved uncertainly forward. A dozen voices muttered a name, it was evident that she was known. She came slowly down the room breathing a little fast between brilliant red lips, red earrings aswing beside a face gravely beautiful in its lines, non-human in its colour.

Dick looked swiftly round the rest, his expression challenging an objection. There was none. He took her by the hand and led her towards the table.

"Your arm first," he said. "That will be enough proof."

He rolled up her sleeve and began to apply a jelly-like stuff to her hand and forearm. David connected up his apparatus and snapped a switch on and off to assure himself it was in working order. Leonie stepped back, watching the woman's face, wondering how she felt, and remembering her own experience of the reverse process. Over the whole watching room was drawn a tension that could be felt, as if at long last they had begun to understand what it meant.

Dick put the woman's arm in position beneath the projector.

"You must turn it over, very slowly, when I tell you," he instructed.

She did not seem to hear. She was looking down at it. Long, slim, green fingers, beautifully shaped red nails. Leonie, the whole room, felt her hesitate and then finally make up her mind.

Dick stepped back. David put one hand up to steady the projector, his other on the switch.

"And now to smash this lie for ever," he murmured.

The switch clicked in a breathless silence.

For a second nothing moved. Then with a scream of agony the Green woman tore her arm from beneath the projector.

Simultaneously the door across the room cracked and broke inwards.

---

THE TELEPHONE BELL rang. Mr. Wilfred Baisham turned over in bed and lifted the receiver.

"Oh, hullo Reynick. I've been expecting to hear from you. What happened? Was I right?"

The Police Chief's voice sounded thin and distant at his ear.

"You were. We had a Green there as an observer. As it happens I'm glad I took your advice to let it go through. But it was cutting it pretty fine, you know, they actually started the machine working."

"My dear Reynick, don't be absurd. It *looked* like the machine, I grant you—it was meant to. Well, what happened then?"

"Oh, I see now. That's why you advised taking no action unless absolutely necessary. You might have told me before and saved me a nasty few minutes."

"It seemed best to tell only the essential people. And it's always best to let a thing like this break itself up without outside interference. Have you pulled in those three? They're the only important ones."

"No, we—"

"They went for them, did they, when they found it didn't work? I thought they might."

"No. As a matter of fact they didn't. We were in the next room waiting for a signal from our observer—he, incidentally, doesn't believe a word of what

Clouster said. He thinks it was going to be some complicated kind of racket and so do the rest of the Greens who were there, at least those who got out do. Well, as I said, we were waiting and wondering and then suddenly there was a God-awful scream from a woman and a riot broke out."

"I thought you said—"

"I did. It wasn't the Greens. It was a gang of Reds. They'd got wind of the business somehow. As they saw it, the Greens had got hold of a dodge for making themselves look like Whites, and the Reds didn't intend to let them have a monopoly—in fact, were out to grab it for themselves. In about three minutes there was a full-sized race riot spreading half over the district."

"Tactically that was handy."

"It was. We appeared only as restorers of the peace. I— By the way, you didn't tip off those Reds, did you?" Reynick sounded suspicious.

"No, I'm afraid that was a subtlety which never occurred to me. What happened to the leaders?"

"Clouster and Sherrick got knifed, both of them—and fifteen or sixteen others, too."

"And Leonie Ward?"

"Lynched—poor kid."

Wilfred Baisham paused.

"Nasty. Was it quick?"

"I think so."

Mr. Baisham considered for a moment.

"Perhaps it was better so. A little sooner, that's all. She was too dangerous, that girl. Why must a girl with nerve like that get on the wrong side?"

"To her it was the right side, I suppose."

"I suppose so. All the same, I'm sorry."

And, indeed, it was sorrow Mr. Baisham felt as he put down the receiver. But that did not prevent him sleeping more peacefully than he had slept for some nights past.

# THE ETERNAL EVE

—

THE MAN CAME clear of the trees, showing as a small light dot against a background of dark trunks. Amanda got the glasses on to him. His clothing was in a worse state than her own: the pants had picturesque rents, and there was not a lot left of the shirt. Something unorthodox had happened to his hair and beard, too. He could have got it that way if he had let it grow until it bothered him and then impatiently hacked off a bunch here and there with a knife. At his back he carried a pack. A rifle hung by its sling from the left shoulder. When Amanda recognised him her lips pressed a little more closely together, and she reached for her own rifle.

A few yards out into the open he stopped, scanning the hillside before him. At his back the pale pennant trees streamed like weeds in a brook, tall feather-tops swung to the light breeze, the fronds of the tree-ferns rippled so that waves of motion seemed to wash across the whole plain. For a minute or two he stood quite still. His gaze passed over and beyond the spot where she lay, without a pause. Then he hitched his pack, and began to plod upwards.

Behind her tuft of scrubby bushes Amanda waited, watching him detachedly, dispassionately. Presently, with slow, careful movements, she pushed her rifle gently forward, and set the telescopic sights. Her right hand slid back to the small, her finger on to the trigger. Then she paused. She let him come on another hundred yards, making a little to her left, and then reset the sights...

When she fired, he stopped, looking round wildly. He had no cover to drop to. She fired again…

After he fell he did not move any more. She put down the rifle, and took up the glasses to make sure.

All day long he lay there, with the pale, grass-like growth beneath him reddened by his blood. Towards evening she went down the hillside, carrying a rope. With it she dragged him laboriously to the edge of the cliffs. There she carefully unfastened the rope before she pushed the body over.

Then she went back to the cave.

Amanda lay on a blanket in the cave mouth. She rested on her elbows, her face cupped in her hands. In front the ground sloped steeply down to the cliffedge. Beyond, growing dark now, was the sea—a fearsome, mysterious sea on which no ship had ever sailed.

At home, in such a setting, there would have been grey and white gulls wheeling plaintively, but here on Venus the birds were dark, businesslike creatures, with no graceful leisure in their flight. The sea, by daylight, was a pale green, and slightly milky so that one could not look down into the water. A great deal of life went on in it—more, it seemed, in these latitudes than on the land. Birds, diving to catch fish in it, were not likely to reappear. Far out, large, unidentifiable shapes would break the water and stay visible for a few minutes. Sometimes huge, squidlike creatures swam slowly past. Now and then a kind of starfish, twenty or thirty feet across and looking like red coral, would cruise past inshore, keeping just awash. Most characteristic of all were the weed banks which came up on the northern current like floating islands with a life of their own, carrying colonies of small birds that pecked and fished in their pools as they drifted.

Amanda, looking out across the unhorizoned sea, saw nothing of it. Her lips moved as she thought aloud, for she had been a long time alone.

"No!" she said. "It was *not* wrong. I've a *right* to protect myself—a *right*… He had no rights over me. No one else has rights over me. I'm my own… He need not have come—he would have been all right if he had left me alone…

"It wasn't wrong—it was horrible, but it wasn't *wrong*… If another of them comes I shall do it again…until they don't come any more.

# THE ETERNAL EVE

"They shouldn't make me do it. They've no right… It's horrible… horrible…!"

She moved back into the cave, and lit a little clay lamp for company. Its tiny flame kept the darkness just at bay.

"It *wasn't* wrong…," she said, again. "He had no right… I'm a human being, not an animal. I want love and kindness—tenderness…"

She jumped to her feet, stood with arms raised, both fists clenched, as though she hammered at something above her.

"Oh, God," cried Amanda. "Why me? Why me? Why out of all of them must it be *me*? I *won't*… I *won't*… I refuse it. Do you hear? I *refuse*…"

She sank down again. Her lips trembled. The flame of the little lamp sparkled and then blurred as she let the tears come…

―

WHEN AMANDA VARK had first landed at the Melos settlement on Venus—and that was a time that now seemed infinitely further away than its measurement on the calendar—it had been in the expectation of an interesting, but uneventful assignment. In her concentration on the nature of the job itself, it had scarcely occurred to her that for eighteen months she would have to live as one of the residents of a pioneer settlement. But the fact that the place did have a life and mind of its own was made clear to her by the reserve with which the colony received them. The arrival of three men and two women who had nothing to do with prospecting, exploration or commerce, roused immediate suspicion. The fact that they introduced themselves as an anthropological expedition and were accredited as such, scarcely helped at all. For one thing, few of the residents had any idea what anthropology was, did, or might do, while those who believed that it somehow concerned the study of natives and said so could only, in view of the nonexistence of any human natives upon Venus, be disbelieved. The assumption, therefore, had quickly grown that they were some sort of inefficiently disguised government inquiry probably portending interference—and if there was one thing the colony felt solidly about, from the Administrator down to the visiting spacehand, it was interference.

Uncle Joe, as the eminent Dr. Thorer was known to his expedition's company, set himself patiently to disperse this cloud of misunderstanding. True, he agreed, there were no human natives, but there were the griffas. From the scientific point of view these timid, silvery-furred little creatures were believed to be interesting. They were known to be intelligent and to live by some kind of social system, and it was thought likely that but for man's arrival they would in time have risen to be the masters of Venus. The expectation was, therefore, that they would provide valuable material for the study of primitive sociology.

He made slow headway. The only colonial value placed on griffas resided in their silver pelts. It was not readily comprehensible that anyone should spend good money on an expedition just to find out how they lived. Nevertheless, as it became obvious that the party's interests did actually, if perplexingly, lie in these matters, suspicion began slowly to recede.

Gradually the men of the group came to be accepted, though still with reservation, but the position of the women was more difficult. The existence of two surnameless girls who had already established themselves in the colony did not make it any easier.

Maisie and Dorrie were a pair of those good-looking, well-built girls who inevitably turn up on frontiers. You could have found them with the forty-niners, or, at the right times, in Dawson City, Kimberley, or Coolgardie. It was Maisie's fancy to move with a feline languor in shiny, inappropriate, but indisputably popular frocks. Her genuine blonde hair she wore dressed to a masterly height. When she became vocal it was to thrum deeply rather than to speak, and to convey with it the impression of a Southern accent. Dorrie's line was vivacity. Her brown eyes gleamed in a lively face framed by dark curls. Her nose tilted up a little, and her mouth was red as a new wound. She chattered volubly, introducing, except in moments of stress, sounds that were vaguely continental.

The colonists knew where they were with them: with Alice Felson and Amanda Vark they did not, so they waited to see.

In the matter of Alice it was not necessary to wait very long. At the age of twenty-nine she had already acquired two distinct reputations—one of them scholarly. To her work and to matters which interested her she brought an acutely analytical mind; when she was not working, she rested it thoroughly.

# THE ETERNAL EVE

The brilliance which exacted respect in academic circles moved right into the back seat. What took over would have been remarkable even in an uninhibited, poorly balanced seventeen-year-old; it seemed to know of no control but the accelerator. She lost practically no time in surrounding herself with an array of incipient crises very wearing to the nerves of a closed community.

But Amanda had remained problematical. There was a rumour that she was engaged to be married to someone back home on Earth. It was not true, but when she heard it, she felt it to have its uses, and refrained from denying it, so that the slight aloofness remained.

A month after her arrival she had scarcely spoken to either of the other girls. She was aware of them, and watched them with a naïve admiration for their self-confidence. They made her feel terribly inexperienced and mousy by contrast in her plain shirt and trousers. Nor, could she see, were they unconscious of Alice and herself. They watched, too, and they noted, but out of a fund of experience they made no approach.

Things settled down like that. Amanda had plenty of work on her hands. She was by far the youngest of the party, and, as such, the natural recipient of much of the donkey work. But she was interested. It had not been easy at first to make sympathetic contact with the griffas. Their naturally shy disposition had been greatly increased by the frontier tendency to shoot first and think afterwards—if at all. It took patience, perseverance, and numerous bars of chocolate to offset that result. Nevertheless, it was done, and she enjoyed helping to do it. She found them amusing and lovable little creatures, with an intelligence so avid that the task became eminently worth while. Thus the party settled down to an assignment which seemed likely to prove for her, whatever it might be for Alice, unexciting. A matter of eighteen months (in Earth reckoning) of conscientious observation and notetaking, then the return home. No dream, no presentiment ever suggested to her that a time would come when she would still be alive on Venus living alone in a cave which she called her home—because there was no other home to go to...

Amanda's better acquaintance with Maisie and Dorrie arose from an incident which revealed that the life of the colony, even outside Alice's aura, was not always placid.

Markham Renarty had been seeing her back to her hut after the customary evening's relaxation at the Clubhouse. Markham had his points—there was no need of defensive tactics with him as there was likely to be with David Brire, who was the youngest male member of the party—or as there certainly would have been with other self-suggested escorts. Markham was a family man. He was, indeed, well launched on one of his interminable and pointless anecdotes about his singularly boring wife and family back home on Earth, when a piercing scream brought them up standing.

As they realised which hut it must have come from, they began to run. They set foot on the verandah just as the scream came again. The scene inside the hut required no explaining words. Dorrie, whose hut it was, stood pressed against the further wall. Blood from a wound in her shoulder was trickling down one naked arm, and on the black satin bosom of her dress. Her visitor stood in the middle of the floor. He had a stained knife in his hand, and at the moment appeared to be trying to collect enough steadiness to approach her again. Amanda left him for Markham to deal with, and ran across to the girl. She was just in time to catch her as she folded up.

When Markham looked around from throwing out the drunk, she was trying to staunch the wound with her handkerchief.

"Better get the doctor quickly. She's losing a lot," Amanda told him.

"The doc passed out cold an hour ago," he reminded her.

"Oh, God!" said Amanda. "Well, get the first-aid satchel from my hut, then—and hurry."

Dorrie opened her eyes. "Is it bad?" she asked.

"It looks nastier and messier than it is. You'll be all right," Amanda said, hoping that she sounded convincing.

"Pretty dim of me," Dorrie said. "Must be losing my touch. I can usually handle 'em okay." And she fainted again.

Markham came back with the first-aid case and began to fill a bowl with water.

"Do you know anything about this sort of job?" Amanda asked. "It's worse than I thought."

He shook his head. "Not a thing, I'm afraid."

Amanda compressed her lips, and began to open the kit.

"Nor do I—but somebody's got to do something," she said, and set to work. "You'd better fetch her friend—if you can find her," she told him.

Maisie put in her appearance some ten minutes later. She said nothing, but sat down beside Amanda, watching, and handling things as necessary. When it was finished, they put Dorrie to bed.

Maisie looked at Amanda. She found a glass, and poured a stiff drink into it. Coming back, she put her arm round her.

"Good girl," she said. "Here, take a shot of this. You need it."

Amanda drank obediently. She choked a little on it—partly the strength of the spirit, but partly reactions.

"Sorry," she said. "I'm not the kind—I don't usually—" Then she burst soothingly into tears.

A look of gloomy purpose came into Maisie's eyes as her arm tightened round Amanda's shoulders.

"You just watch me blast the pants off that doc tomorrow," she said. "I'll get him so that he jitters at the sight of a bottle—even a Coke."

From the next day the colony had seemed to shift up and make room for Amanda. The two girls adopted an attitude towards her which varied between awe at her scholarship—which they appeared to regard as a cleverly developed though rather impractical form of higher guesswork—and a sense of responsibility towards her inexperience. Maisie particularly seemed to take this to heart. There were remarks which would make her frown.

"What troubles me, honey," she said once, "is your darned innocence. This ain't no location for it. Maybe you do genuinely forget that you're one quarter of the female population here—but others don't. In a dump like this you gotta watch your step. Honest you have, all of the time. We *know*, don't we, Dorrie?"

"Sure," agreed Dorrie. "Kinda like juggling. You know those guys that keep a dozen balls in the air at once while they ride a bicycle on a wire? Well, that's it."

"I don't see—" Amanda began.

"That's just what's bitin' me. You don't see—but you will," Maisie told her. "Trouble is you've spent your life learning things, and there's a hell of a lot of difference between the things you learn and the things you just kinda get to know. But when you do see trouble beginning to come your way from some of the big irresistibles around here, then let us know. We can handle 'em."

Dorrie backed that up. With a confidence quite unimpaired by her recent lapse of skill, she added:

"Sure. You just tell us. We can fix 'em."

Amanda did not see a great deal of them, for their lives were busiest at times when hers was not, but she was glad to have earned their good will. It was a comforting thought, even if there appeared to be no likelihood of her having to call on them for aid. It needed the coming of the unbelievable disaster to draw them closer together for mutual support.

In whatever way the first news of the disaster had reached the Melos colony, their faith in all they knew would have stopped them believing it for a time. Some never did believe: a few minds refused to take it, and pitifully broke down. In the event, the news came in installments, building up to the incredible climax.

When first the radio men could raise no reply from Earth, it was simply inconvenient, and they were blamed for poor maintenance of their gear. When the apparatus was found to be okay, the trouble was attributed to a radiation blanket which would pass in a while. When contact was made with the ship *Celestes* and her operator admitted that he too was unable to raise any of the Earth stations, it began to look more serious. But it was not until the *Astarte* which had put out from Venus a couple of weeks before reported that she would attempt to put about and return if possible—for lack of anywhere else to go— that it began to be unbelievable.

From that moment nobody talked of anything else—but they still did not really believe it. Even after the incoming *Diana* had grounded and her crew had told their story, one still hoped at heart that there had been some mistake, and a crowd still besieged the radio hut while, inside, the operators went on frenziedly trying to make contact with the Lunar Station, with the Port Gillington settlement on Mars, with ships in space, with anywhere that might answer with solid, reassuring news.

According to those on the *Diana* it had happened that there was a telescope turned back on Earth so that several of them had been able to watch the whole thing on the screen. One moment the Earth had been hanging in space, looking, as always, like a pearl with a cool, cloudy green shimmer; the next it resembled an over-ripe fruit that had split its skin, and the juice that had burst from it was flame that stabbed thousands of miles into the darkness. There had been a few dazzling, awesome moments, and then it had begun to break into pieces. So rapid had been the disintegration that half an hour later the telescopes were unable to find more than a few measurable fragments. The *Diana*'s crew could tell no more than that...

Everyone's recollection of the next few days was hazy. Most of them were dazed and absentminded. Some cursed steadily; others fell hopefully to praying for the first time in their lives. The majority chose the shortest road to illusion via the bar where they drank themselves comfortably stupid or into baseless but passionate arguments as to whether the disaster had been a natural phenomenon, a new weapon of war that had overreached itself, or the product of some atomic carelessness. To the rest, the actual cause seemed a matter of utterly unprofitable speculation. Whatever it had been, it could not possibly help anyone to know any more about it now...

A few more ships came in. Some corroborated the *Diana*'s report. Others, looking out for a routine check of bearings, had found that where the Earth should have been there was nothing. The only additional information was that the moon was heading away into space and the planetary orbits were re-balancing themselves...

On the night after the *Diana* grounded, Amanda had gone out alone, still numbly incredulous. Looking up at the clouds eternally covering the Venusian sky, she kept on telling herself that it could not be true. Whatever they were saying, the Earth must be somewhere up there still. Such a colossal catastrophe *could not* really happen...

---

THE ADMINISTRATOR MADE some attempt to pull things together, but not with success. His authority had been behind him, not in him, and now he lacked weight. His efforts did little but set malcontents recalling earlier grudges, but he persisted.

Amanda spent hours of these unreal days in the company of Maisie and Dorrie, consuming endless cups of coffee and innumerable cigarettes. For some reason—possibly because there had never been any stable background to their lives—they seemed less affected than the rest, and their companionship steadied her.

As Maisie said: "It's the guys with the biggest plans that get knocked silliest. Dorrie and me have always gambled anyway, so what? While you're still breathin' life's gotta go on—they'll get round to that in a while."

Most other people Amanda avoided. She did not flock to the landing field with the rest when the few ships that had managed to make successful diversions came in to their final groundings. She was not even there when the last of all, the U.S.S. *Annabelle Lee*, made sanctuary on her last few pounds of fuel bringing, among her crew, a young man named Michael Parbert…

—

ON THE AFTERNOON of the day that somebody knifed the Administrator, Maisie drifted into Amanda's hut. Amanda was working on some papers, but she pushed them aside and threw over a cigarette.

"What's the idea?" Maisie asked, as she lighted it. "That kind of stuff's no use to nobody no more."

"Uncle Joe's idea," Amanda explained. "He says that for all we know we're the only ones left anywhere, so it's up to us to make a record of all we know between us. Sort of encyclopaedia."

"Uh-huh. And who for?" Maisie wanted to know.

"Well, there *may* be others—and failing everything else he says the griffas will be up to learning it one day. We've come a long way in five thousand years or so, he says, but we're only at the beginning really, so we ought to save what we can to help them along."

"Ought we?" said Maisie. "Looking at the funny way we've come, I'd say give the griffas or anything else a clean start—but then, I wouldn't know."

"Nor me," admitted Amanda, "—but it makes something to do." She changed the subject. "Who did it?—The Administrator, I mean."

Maisie inhaled, and blew the smoke out. She shook her head.

"I wouldn't know that, either. I might make a near guess, but what the hell?—If it wasn't one, it'd have been another. He had it coming, anyway. Thing is, it kinda writes off the old setup."

She sent another cloud of blue smoke thoughtfully across the room.

"Meaning—?" inquired Amanda.

Maisie leaned forward, and regarded her.

"Honey, I got a feeling things are going to break open around here. In a dump like this you gotta have a boss of some kind. A stuffed one was okay—with a government in back of him—but when the government's gone, and some guy's let out the rest of the stuffing—well, then you just naturally find some other guys getting big ideas. And the climate's likely to get kinda lively while they're deciding whose idea is the biggest."

"How lively?" Amanda asked.

Maisie shook her head.

"I'd like to know that, too. What isn't funny is having a lot of dopes around that are just crazy on account of what's happened back home. I know the poor devils can't help it—but that don't make it any healthier."

"I see," said Amanda.

Maisie looked doubtful.

"Maybe you do see: maybe you don't—quite. Trouble with educated gals is they keep seeing in one pocket, and understanding in another." She paused. Then she added: "You had a boy back home? One that you were set to marry, I mean—not just the kind a gal's gotta have for self-respect?"

Amanda hesitated.

"There *was* one...," she said slowly. "But he didn't... Well, he was the only one I ever wanted—and when he chose somebody else, I wasn't interested in those things any more. So I got this job and came here."

Nevertheless, the next few days passed with less overt trouble than Maisie had led one to expect. No rival would-be leaders stood up to shoot it out, nor did any gang thrust an unsuitable chief into authority. The sensation of going to pieces continued quietly with an air of all round loosening up which it was no one's appointed business to check. Almost a whole week more passed before

Amanda had her first personal encounter with trouble. It came one evening just as she was on the point of going to bed. The latch of her hut door rattled.

"Who's there?" she called.

A thick voice she could not place answered unintelligibly.

"Go away," she said. "This is the wrong hut."

But the man did not go away. She heard his feet shuffle, then something thudded against the door so that it bulged. There was a second thud, and it flew open as a bolt socket tore out. The man who stood in the doorway was tall, burly, red-headed, and unsteady. She recognized him as one of the maintenance-shop crew.

"Get out of here, Badger," she said, firmly.

He swayed, and steadied himself by the doorpost.

"Now, now, 'Manda. 'S'not the way to speak to a visitor."

"Go on, Badger. Beat it," said Amanda.

"'S'not ladylike—'beat it'!" Badger reproved. He groped behind him for the door, and shut it. "Listen, 'Manda. You're a nishe girl, you unnerstan' things. I got nothing now, all gone, nothing to live for any more, I wanna lose m'self."

"You'll have to go lose yourself some place else," Amanda told him, unfeelingly. "Get along now."

He stood approximately still, looking at her. Then his eyes narrowed, and there was a displeasing grin on his lips.

"No, b'God! Why sh'd I go? C'm here."

Amanda did not move. She faced him steadily.

"Get out!" she said, again.

His grin widened.

"So you don't wanna play. Scared of me, huh." He began to advance, slowly and not very straightly.

Amanda was rather surprised to find herself very little scared of him. She stood her ground, carefully calculating the distance. When he was near enough, she let fly with all her strength, using her foot.

It was an unexpected, and, in Badger's view, highly dastardly form of attack. It was also successful. For the first time since his entrance she felt it safe to turn her back while she got her pistol. Then, to the groaning figure doubled up on the floor she said: "Now will you get out! Go on!"

The answer was a moaned string of curses.

Amanda pressed the trigger and sent a bullet through the floorboards close beside his head.

"Go on. Beat it, quick," she repeated.

The sound of the shot sent a gleam of sense through Badger's befuddled discomfort. He dragged himself up and hobbled to the door. He paused with his hand on the post, as if considering some Parthian line, but the sight of the pistol discouraged it. He turned away into the dark, and his picturesque mutterings faded out, to leave Amanda contemplating with some awe her own efficiency in the matter.

IT SEEMED AS if that had been the sign for more things to move. The very next day Alice's present, a husky young engineer, was neatly drilled through the head by, presumably, one of her pasts. It was a privation which rendered her inconsolable for two whole days. A night or two later an enterprising spaceman looting the general storehouse was shot by somebody else with the same idea. The following evening a ridiculous but bloody knife fight broke out in the saloon over a sentimental record agreeable to some but intolerably nostalgic to others. A couple of nights after that, Amanda, kept awake by an unusually turbulent fracas, or maybe party, in Dorrie's hut, saw the silhouette of a man at work upon her window. She gave no warning, but reached under the pillow for the pistol. She did not know whether either of her shots hit the arm she aimed at, but, anyway, he left. Hurriedly. The following evening a ridiculous attempt was made by Markham to put some bars across the windows. That evening a shot whizzed close to his head as he returned from seeing her home. The next morning she went to see Maisie about it.

"Okay. I'll get my grapevine humming," Maisie promised.

Three hours later she came around to Amanda's hut.

"It's that red-headed dope, Badger," she said. "You've got him kind of sore at you, honey. He's been telling his buddies you're gonna be his girl. The idea seems to be if he scares everyone else off, you'll just take kindly to him sooner or later, out of lonesomeness."

"Oh, is it?" said Amanda. "Well, what do I do about that?"

Maisie considered.

"That Badger's one-tracked—and just kinda naturally stupid. Trouble is he's got quite a pull over that gang of his—so I guess they must be a grade more stupid. If I was you I'd let it ride awhile till things settle down. It could be it'll just work off."

And Amanda, with no better suggestion of her own, agreed reluctantly.

It was about that time that she began to be aware that Michael Parbert, of the *Annabelle Lee*, seemed to be a member of every group she sat with in the Clubhouse. Sedulously she took no more notice of him than of any of the others. It was impossible not to know that he was a personable young man—but so were a number of others. She began to understand Dorrie's words on juggling and tightwires. There was a feeling that everyone was just waiting for her to fumble or slip. It needed some immense concentration to show no suggestion of partiality. It even drove her to staying away from the Clubhouse some evenings, to ease the strain by sitting in her hut in resentful solitude.

Some three uneasy weeks later Maisie came around to Amanda's hut again.

"Big fight last night," she observed, as she lit her cigarette.

"Oh," said Amanda. She was not greatly interested. There seemed to be fights big or small most nights lately.

"Yeh. That Badger got beaten up," Maisie added.

Amanda looked up from the shirt she was mending.

"Badger! Who was it?"

"Michael. He had Badger out cold at the end, they tell me." She paused. Amanda said nothing. She went on: "You wouldn't want to know what it was all about?"

"No," said Amanda.

Maisie flicked her ash thoughtfully on the floor.

"Listen, honey. You gotta face it. What're you gonna do?"

It was no good pretending not to understand Maisie. Amanda had learned that. She said:

"Nothing. Why should I?"

Maisie shook her head.

"You gotta do something."

"I don't see why."

"Now, don't act dumb with me, honey. You gotta pick yourself a boy-friend."

Maisie looked at her. "Say, who do you think you are? There's all these guys lined up—all the men that are left now—all you gotta do is point at one an' say 'I'll have that dope there,' an' he'll come runnin'. Sakes alive, what more do you want? It's all on a dish—and you don't even have to find a local Reno if he pans out bad."

"No," said Amanda. "I told you I only ever wanted one guy—I mean, man."

"But listen. Things are all different. From now on you gotta *live* here—we all have. That's not the same as you just stayin' awhile—an' it's no good foolin' yourself that it is. You gotta quit playing the old act before it flops hard. You can't go on being the little mascot any more. An' if you keep on trying it, you'll be causing more trouble around here than that Alice. Maybe it's nice for you to sit there like a pretty little honey-pot with the lid tight on—I wouldn't know; I never been that way—but it's just hell and temptation for a lot of these guys. An' you can't blame 'em for that; it's human nature."

"Human nature?" said Amanda, scornfully.

"Sure. What else? You gotta make up your mind. You gotta team up, so's they can see the way things are. Just so long as you keep dangling around like a forbidden fruit we ain't goin' to have no kind of peace in this dump—an' that's a fact. Now what about this Michael, honey?"

"No," said Amanda.

"Now, listen, honey—"

"No, no, no!" said Amanda, violently. "*No!* Do you hear? I won't be the purse in a sluggers' prize fight. And I'm certainly not going to run to the big strong victor for protection. It's disgusting to be fought over as I were a—a—a she-buffalo, or something. No!"

But Maisie was patient and persistent. "Things are getting kinda primitive here," she said. "You ought to know the sort of thing that means, seein' it's your own subject. In a set-up that's goin' that way a girl's got two lines open: either she plays 'em along, the way Dorrie an' I do—an' I reckon you just ain't got the temperament—or she takes up with a guy who can put the fear of God into the rest of 'em. You think it over, honey, an' you'll see. You can get yourself a good guy to look after you, an' have cute babies, an' all that… It could be swell…"

"If you're so fond of babies—" Amanda began, and then stopped suddenly. "I'm sorry, Maisie."

"That's all right, 'Manda, dear. That's the way life is, an' I gotta take it… But *you* haven't, honeylamb. So just think it over…"

"No!" said Amanda, and shook her head.

Nevertheless she did spend a considerable part of her time thinking it over. There was no dodging it any more. She became increasingly aware of the tension around her as she sat in the Clubhouse, the way men looked at her—and at one another. There were more fights, sometimes between surprisingly unexpected persons. She grew nervous and self-conscious, unable to speak naturally to any of them for fear of what a careless word might provoke.

Even Uncle Joe felt himself moved to give her advice—and though its form was more classical, it was to much the same effect as Maisie's.

The feeling of pressure building up made Amanda restless and edgy, but it also increased her obstinacy.

"No!" she repeated to herself. "I *won't*… I won't be driven at one of them. I'm me; my own self. They won't make me *belong* to one of them. Never… never… Damn them, all of them."

But resistance did not diminish the pressures. The climax came when she wakened to hear a shot just outside her hut. Exactly what happened she never found out. To her ears it sounded like a private fight which the intervention of other parties turned into a brisk skirmish. In the course of it at least two bullets slammed in through the hut's wooden wall, and out the other side. Amanda stayed in bed, having her mind made up for her. When the sounds of battle died away, she had reached her decision.

The next day she managed to slip off unnoticed into the forest to make contact with the griffas. The little creatures welcomed her. Since the disaster they had been neglected, for the classes to which they had come so eagerly, both for instruction and candy, had been discontinued.

It was difficult to know how much they grasped of the situation, but they seemed clear enough on two essentials—secrecy, and willingness to act as porters for payment in chocolate. They were able to come and go without causing comment, and for a week they did so, carrying away into the forest parcels suitable for their size.

On the final day Maisie came in again. She put up all the old arguments, and ended:

"Honey, I know this isn't your kind of life. The way I see you is in an old cottage somewhere in your England—a place with a garden an' you in a print frock, an' a big hat, an' so on—but hell, kid, it just ain't there any more. You gotta face it…"

"No!" said Amanda.

It had been hard not to say goodbye to Maisie, but she resisted the temptation. With tears in her eyes she watched the tall figure in its ridiculous shiny dress sway lazily away.

In the evening she wrote a note for Maisie. Then she strapped up her pack, fixed the holster on her belt, and put the rifle to hand. After she had turned out the light, she sat waiting, watching the uncurtained window.

The fuse took longer than she had calculated. Then, just as she was deciding that something must have gone wrong there came a felty thump, and in a few seconds flames burst from the windows of an empty hut a hundred and fifty yards away. There were shouts and sounds of running feet. Against the flames she could see dark figures dodging excitedly about. When she was satisfied that the blaze had attracted the attention of all who chanced not to be paralytically drunk, she opened her door and slipped quietly away through the darkness towards the forest.

The thing that saved both Amanda's resolution and her reason was that the griffas did not abandon her during her months in the cave. Even when all the chocolate was gone, their insatiable curiosity still brought them up from the forest to examine, observe, and ask endless questions until she found herself holding classes again. Long ago she had ceased to use even the little she had been able to learn of their language, and now they, too, seemed to be in the process of dropping it. Frequently she would hear them talking between themselves in their odd, fluty form of English—the more curious for its being learned from the *Works of William Shakespeare* and the *Oxford Book of English Verse*, which were Amanda's only books.

Nor was it a one-sided arrangement. By way of payment they kept her supplied with fruits, vegetables and edible roots, teaching her to live off the land in a way she could never have taught herself.

Nearly six months passed before she had any news of the settlement, then one of the griffas surprised her by producing a packet of papers tied round with a string. She opened it to find a number of sheets written in a large, unpracticed hand, with the signature 'Maisie' at the end.

From them she learned that the colony, after passing through a crisis, had now become more orderly. At the worst time Badger had acquired a following which threatened to dominate the whole place unless it were suppressed. Accordingly, it had been suppressed, and Uncle Joe had been elected president, chief, or whatever you liked to call it. After that Badger had disappeared. The radio operator had picked up distorted sounds on the Mars wavelength to show that at least somebody there was still alive. Alice had disappeared, and alone. This was so improbable, that everyone feared the worst. She had been moody for a couple of days, and then vanished. No one had seen her go, she seemed to have taken nothing with her, and after two months there was still no sign of her. Dorrie had been dangerously ill, but was now almost recovered. She was bitterly disappointed though; apparently she had always wanted a baby, though nobody had guessed it, and now there was no more chance of it. Finally, what about Amanda coming back?

The implication was not lost on Amanda. She was now the very last hope. It was another bit of pressure to nag at her.

"No!" said Amanda. "I won't—I *won't*. They can't force me." She wrote a brief reply on the back of one of the sheets, used the rest for lighting her fire, and decided to forget it.

—

FOR A DAY before he arrived Amanda had known from the griffas that there was a man coming her way. It did not greatly surprise her. Sooner or later someone would be bound to find out where she was. She had not known that it was

Badger until she saw him through the glasses. Nor did she know how he found her. She suspected he must have caught and tortured a griffa till it told him. If so, he had got what he deserved. He'd torture no more griffas now.

After a day or two the shooting worried her less. If a soldier could claim a clear conscience in defending his country and his womenfolk, how could hers be the worse for defending herself?

Her life went on as before, for if one thing was certain, it was that Badger would not have passed on the details of his ill-gotten bit of information.

Yet, a few weeks later, the griffas brought her news of another man working that way.

Once more she took the rifle and concealed herself in the same spot. As before she watched a distant figure come out of the trees. Through the glasses she saw that it was Michael Parbert—the 'good guy' that Maisie had wanted her to choose. She lowered the glasses, with a frown. The situation would have been easier had it been one of Badger's gang. She hesitated a moment, and then called to one of the griffas. A few minutes later she watched the little creature make a detour and then go scuttling down the hillside. As it got nearer to the man it raised its arms, and she knew that it was calling to him. Through the glasses, she watched them meet. She could see it giving him her warning, and telling him to go back, but he made no move to do so. For a moment he appeared to dispute. The griffa reached up and took hold of his pants, dragging back the way he had come. He did not move, but stood looking up at the hill. Then with an impatient movement he shook the griffa off and started to climb.

Amanda's frown returned.

"Very well, then," she said grimly. And she reached for her rifle...

Later on, she slung the coil of rope over her shoulder, and set off down the slope with a purposeful step. What she had done before, she was prepared to do again. But when she got there, he was not dead. He lay on the pale, matted grassy stuff, with the blood slowly oozing and caking round his two wounds. He was light-headed, and crying like a child. She had never seen a man cry before. Her heart turned over, and she went down on her knees beside him.

"Oh, God," said Amanda, with tears in her own eyes. "What have I done...? What have I done...?"

For several days it remained anybody's guess what Amanda had done, but then, though he was very weak, he began unmistakably to get better.

Amanda, with a dozen or so griffas assisting, had carried him up to the cave. She had made him the most comfortable she could contrive with a mattress of springy twigs. And there he lay, delirious at first, then resting most of the time with his eyes shut. He made no complaints when she moved him to dress his wounds, and at first he was too exhausted to talk much. Occasionally she would see that his eyes were open, and that he had been watching her as she moved about the cave. Once he asked:

"Somebody shot me?"

"Yes," Amanda told him.

"Was it you?"

"Yes," she said, again.

"You're a bad shot. Why didn't you leave me there?"

"I don't know."

"Going to shoot me again when you've patched me up?"

"Go to sleep now, and stop asking silly questions," Amanda told him.

"I've got a letter for you. In my jacket—right hand pocket."

She found it, and pulled it out. It was queer to see an envelope again, and with 'Miss Amanda Vark' neatly written on it.

"Uncle Joe?" she asked.

He nodded. She tore it open. There were several sheets, and they started somewhat heavily. Dr. Thorer was prone to be a little pompous on paper:

*My Dear Amanda,*

*This letter will not be easy for me to write, nor, perhaps, for you to read, yet I beg you to read it carefully and to consider its contents with the honesty which you would give to any social problem in your work...*

Amanda read steadily on, with an expression which revealed none of her feelings to Michael as he watched her. When she had finished it, she went to the cave mouth. She sat there for some minutes, unmoving, and gazing out across the sea. Then she picked up the letter, and read the last few lines again:

# THE ETERNAL EVE

*...It may be that elsewhere in the system some of us will survive, but we do not* know *that, nor are we likely ever to know. What we do know is that* here *it is* you, *my dear, who hold the keys of life and death. Why it should be to you that this wonderful and terrible thing has happened we shall also never know. But there is the chance that you might have daughters... You, and you alone, are* vas vitae, *the vessel of our life. Are you content that this shall be the end of it all? Can you carry such a burden on your mind? For you, Amanda, here, at least, are—*Eve.

When she looked up, she saw that Michael was still watching her.

"Do you know what this is?" she asked.

He nodded. "You did, too, even before you opened it," he said.

Amanda turned and looked over the sea again. Her fists were clenched.

"Why me...? Why me...? Am I an animal—a brood mare? I won't, I tell you! My life is *mine*—it doesn't belong to any of you. I *won't*...!"

She crumpled up the letter and threw it into the small fire before the cave. It curled, singed, and then caught.

"See! You can tell him. You can tell all of them when you go back."

And she ran away out of the cave.

---

CONVALESCENCE WAS SLOW. To begin with he tired quickly. In the evening the feebleness of the clay lamps left them with nothing to do but talk. He could, she found, do plenty of that, and she herself had some months of arrears to make up. Their conversations rambled in every direction, skirting only the present situation—though it was not always easy to do that. It was difficult when they spoke of laughter, crowds, children, not to stop short suddenly, remembering that these things would never be again...

But it was natural that most of the talk should be retrospective, and it could often be so without being altogether saddening. Talking of places made them live again—for a time. Amanda found herself growing familiar with Massachusetts Avenue, and the Common, with Brattle Street, and the Halls and elms of Harvard. She had all the best shops in Boston marked down, and could have found her way to Aunt Mary's house in Back Bay, if necessary. In return she toured him around the colleges of Oxford, took him for a summer evening punt on the river, and showed him sunrise from Magdalen College tower...

The griffas continued to come for lessons, and as Michael grew stronger he, too, became a teacher. He made types of simple tools for them to copy; he showed them how to fish with both net and rod; made them a potter's wheel, and a simple loom. It amused Amanda to look across and see him working with a serious expression, while the little creatures clustered about him no less intently, rather like—children. She knew that he was enjoying it, and for some reason it pleased her to see that he got on better with them than had the less practical men of her own party...

When he first began to get about again, she had formed the habit of keeping her pistol handy at night. It occurred to her that he had not once treated her as he might not have treated a younger brother, nor did he show the least sign of changing that attitude. In fact it would have seemed more normal if... But, anyway, you never could tell. She did not know that he had noticed the pistol until one night she turned round from tucking it into its place, and saw him looking at her. He was smiling. It was not an attractive kind of smile, because it turned the corners of his mouth down instead of up. He shook his head.

"You needn't bother with that thing. You're perfectly safe, you know. I'm kind of particular—allergic, you might say, to girls that shoot me from cover. Sort of funny that way: just naturally got no interest in homicides, I guess."

"Oh," said Amanda, flatly. It didn't seem like the kind of thing you could follow up.

On a day which had begun like any other day he laid aside his breakfast bowl, and told her without warning:

"I'm okay now, near enough, so I'll be moving along."

Something hurt quite suddenly and unexpectedly in Amanda's chest.

"You—you don't mean you're going?" she said.

"Yes. I can make it now—easy stages."

"But not today?"

"Looks a perfectly good day to me."

"But—"

"But what?"

"I—I don't know… Are you sure you're well enough yet?"

"Near ninety percent, anyway. If I get stuck, one of the griffas can fetch someone to pick me up."

"Yes, only—well, it's so unexpected, that's all."

"Why? What *did* you expect?"

Amanda looked at him confusedly. She had been to some trouble to prevent herself forming definite expectations of any kind.

"I—I don't know… I suppose it's goodbye, then?"

"That's it. Goodbye—and thank you for changing your mind."

"Changing—? But if you know I've—" she began. Then she stopped. "What do you mean?" she asked awkwardly.

"About killing me. What else?"

"Oh," said Amanda. "Oh that."

As if in a dream she watched him put on his pack, still with the hole where one of her bullets had torn it. Her knuckles were white. As he picked up his rifle, she made an uncertain movement, then checked it.

"Goodbye," he said again.

"Goodbye," said Amanda, and damned her voice for sounding queer.

He went out of the cave. Half a minute later she followed round the shoulder of the hill to a point where she could watch him go. A party of griffas emerged from the trees to join him, and he strode on into the forest amongst them. He did not give one backward glance…

The whole landscape blurred before Amanda's eyes.

After he had gone, the cave should have reverted to what it was before he came. Logically, when one had got rid of the loom and all the other innovations by parking them in a smaller cave nearby, one was back to normal—only there was evidently something wrong with logic. Things did not automatically return to their former placid order. Amanda found herself restless. Conversation with none but the griffas irked her. She grew short-tempered with them, to their dismay and bewilderment, and then was contrite over her burst of impatience, only to find herself behaving in the same way again five minutes later.

More than ever she was aware of the alienness of the things about her. When one was alone they seemed to press more closely. She became aware of that loneliness and the quiet as she had never been before. The days lacked purpose. She seemed incapable of getting back into the old routine by day, and by night the cave was too quiet. If she woke in the darkness, she missed the reassuring sound of his slow, steady breathing. Instead, the only thing to be heard was the distant scrape and stir of the crabs down on the shore...

For the first time she began to have misgivings about her own strength. It was no longer simple to be detached. In her more honest moments she knew that something was happening to her resolution—but it was happening too late. Some weeks ago she could have heeded Uncle Joe's letter. She could have returned to the settlement and made her choice, with her pride saved by his appeal. But now—how could she go back now? After he had walked away from her—without once looking back...

She swayed between moods of loneliness and determination, misery, and bitter resolve. Yet she knew that the resolve was weakening. She would never again have the confidence which had coldly trained the rifle on the approaching Badger. She wondered what steps she would take when the griffas next warned her of someone's approach...and then left it to be decided at the time.

In the event, it was a decision she did not have to make, for there was no warning. Early on a day about a month after Michael had left, she heard the griffas arriving as usual for their lesson, but among the pattering of their feet she detected another step. She pulled the pistol from her belt, and pointed it at the entrance. A figure, huge among its little escort, came to a stop in the cave mouth. Amanda's heart leaped once, and then sank. Against the light she could not see who it was; but she knew who it was not...the figure stood still a moment, then it said slowly, on a reproving note:

"Would you mind putting that thing down, honeylamb. It looks kinda nervous to me."

Amanda lowered the pistol, and stared at Maisie as she came in. Something seemed to give way and pour up inside her. She ran forward and clung. Maisie put up both arms and held her.

"There, there, honey," she soothed her. It was all either of them said for quite a little time.

"How did you get here?" Amanda asked.

She had recovered, and hospitably brought out baskets of sweet shoots, and flat-cakes made from root flour.

"It wasn't so much the getting as the getting to get," Maisie explained. "I'd have been here long before, but if there's one thing those griffas have a thorough hold on, it's the meaning of the word 'secret.' I've been trying for months to persuade or bribe 'em. But it's kinda difficult with griffas, you know: now if it had been men— Anyway, here I am—and three days of steady going it's taken me."

Amanda regarded her with admiring gratitude. Forest travel was not an activity one associated with Maisie, any more than one associated her with the practical suit she now wore. She said:

"Why have you come, Maisie?"

"Well, honey, I wanted to see you. An', for another thing, I reckoned that anyone else who came would likely get shot. It's said to be sort of rough in these parts."

"Then—then he did get back all right?"

"Yeh," said Maisie. She did not amplify, but began a hunt in the pockets of her jacket and trouser. "I got a message for you some place."

"Yes…?" Amanda leaned forward, eagerly.

"Sure. Now where the hell would I have put it? This ain't my kind of outfit, you know," she complained. "Oh, here it is." She smoothed out the envelope. "From Uncle Joe," she added, handing it over.

"Oh…" said Amanda, flatly.

She took it. She opened it with reluctance, for she was sure what it would say. She was perfectly right.

"No!" she said again, crumpling it up. "No!" But the negative lacked something of its old force—and there was another quality about it, too.

"That's all?" she asked.

"What else would there be?"

"I wondered… I don't know…"

Suddenly Amanda was crying.

Maisie took her hand.

"Now, honey, you don't want to get that way. You've been too long alone here. Snap out of it now, and come along back with me."

"But—but I can't—not now," sobbed Amanda. "He doesn't want me. He—he never looked back. He s-said he h-hated girls that shoot from cover."

"Nonsense," Maisie told her, briskly. "Every smart girl always shoots from cover. So you've fallen for this guy, have you?"

"Y-yes," wept Amanda.

"Huh," said Maisie, "then I reckon that fixes it."

She got up and went to the entrance.

A minute later another step outside the cave made Amanda look up suddenly.

"It's—it's— Oh, Maisie, you've been cheating!"

"Me, honey? Never on your life. It's just what they call a forcing bid, maybe," Maisie said, and she drifted out of the cave as Michael walked in.

An hour later she returned, with a heavy footfall.

"Long enough, you two," she said.

Amanda, sitting close behind Michael, looked up.

"Not yet," she said, "we're going to have a—a kind of honeymoon first."

"I'll see about fixing a hut ready for you. *And* I'll tell Uncle Joe you've decided to take his advice—he'll be kinda tickled."

"No!" said Amanda, with all her old decision. "I'm *not* taking his advice. *This* hasn't got anything at all to do with duty to community, or to posterity, or to history, or to moral obligations, or to the racial urge to survive—or with anything but *me*. I'm doing it because I *want* to do it."

"Uh-huh," said Maisie, peaceably. "Well, it's your affair, so you should know, honey. Still, it wouldn't surprise me one little bit to hear that the other Eve once said that self-same thing..."

# PAWLEY'S PEEPHOLES

—

WHEN I CALLED round at Sally's I showed her the paragraph in the *Westwich Evening News*.

"What do you think of that?" I asked her.

She read it, standing, and with an impatient frown on her pretty face.

"I don't believe it," she said, finally.

Sally's principles of belief and disbelief are a thing I've never got quite lined up. How a girl can dismiss a pack of solid evidence as though it were kettle steam, and then go and fall for some advertisement that's phoney from the first word as though it were holy writ, I just don't... Oh, well, it keeps on happening, anyway.

This paragraph read:

**MUSIC WITH A KICK**

*Patrons of the concert at the Adams Hall last night were astonished to see a pair of legs dangling knee-deep from the ceiling during one of the items. The whole audience saw them, and all reports agree that they were bare legs, with some kind of sandals on the feet. They remained visible for some three or four minutes, during which time they several times moved back and forth across the ceiling. Finally, after making a kicking movement, they disappeared upwards, and were seen no more. Examination of the roof shows no traces, and the owners of the Hall are at a loss to account for the phenomenon.*

"It's just one more thing," I said.

"What does it prove, anyway?" said Sally, apparently forgetful that she was not believing it.

"I don't know that—yet," I admitted.

"Well, there you are, then," she said.

Sometimes I get the feeling that Sally has no real respect for logic.

However, most people were thinking the way Sally was, more or less, because most people like things to stay nice and normal. But it had already begun to look to me as if there were things happening that ought to be added together and make something.

The first man to bump up against it—the first I can find on record, that is—was one Constable Walsh. It may be that others before him saw things, and just put them down as a new kind of pink elephant; but Constable Walsh's idea of a top-notch celebration was a mug of strong tea with a lot of sugar, so when he came across a head sitting up on the pavement on what there was of its neck, he stopped to look at it pretty hard. The thing that really upset him, according to the report he turned in when he had run half a mile back to the station and stopped gibbering, was that it had looked back at him.

Well, it isn't good to find a head on a pavement at any time, and 2 a.m. does somehow make it worse, but as for the rest, well, you can get what looks like a reproachful glance from a cod on a slab if your mind happens to be on something else. Constable Walsh did not stop there, however. *He* reported that the thing opened its mouth 'as if it was trying to say something.' If it did, he should not have mentioned it; it just naturally brought the pink elephants to mind. However, he stuck to it, so after they had examined him and taken disappointing sniffs at his breath, they sent him back with another man to show just where he had found the thing. Of course, there wasn't any head, nor blood, nor signs of cleaning up. And that's about all there was to the incident—save, doubtless, a few curt remarks on a conduct-sheet to dog Constable Walsh's future career.

BUT THE CONSTABLE hadn't a big lead. Two evenings later a block of flats was curdled by searing shrieks from a Mrs. Rourke in No. 35, and simultaneously from a Miss Farrell who lived above her. When the neighbours arrived, Mrs. Rourke was hysterical about a pair of legs that had been dangling from her bedroom ceiling, and Miss Farrell the same about an arm and shoulder that had stretched out from under her bed. But there was nothing to be seen on the ceiling, and nothing more than a discreditable amount of dust to be found under Miss Farrell's bed.

And there were a number of other incidents, too.

It was Jimmy Lindlen who works, if that isn't too strong a word for it, in the office next to mine who drew my attention to them in the first place. Jimmy collects facts. His definition of a fact is anything that gets printed in a newspaper—poor fellow. He doesn't mind a lot what subjects his facts cover as long as they look queer. I suspect that he once heard that the truth is never simple, and deduced from that that everything that's not simple must be true.

I was used to him coming into my room, full of inspiration, and didn't take much account of it, so when he brought in his first batch of cuttings about Constable Walsh and the rest I didn't ignite much.

But a few days later he was back with some more. I was a bit surprised by his playing the same kind of phenomena twice running, so I gave it a little more attention than usual.

"You see. Arms, heads, legs, torsos, all over the place. It's an epidemic. There's something behind it. *Something's happening!*" he said, as near as one can vocalize italics.

When I had read a few of them I had to admit that this time he had got hold of something where the vein of queerness was pretty constant.

A bus driver had seen the upper half of a body set up vertically in the road before him—but a bit too late. When he stopped and climbed out, sweating, to examine the mess, there was nothing there. A woman hanging out of a window, watching the street, saw another head below her doing the same, but this one was projecting out of the solid brickwork. Then there was a pair of arms that had risen out of the floor of a butcher's shop and seemed to grope for something; after a minute or two they had withdrawn into the solid cement without trace—unless one were to count some detriment to the butcher's trade. There was the man on a building job who had become aware of a strangely dressed figure standing close to him, but supported by empty air—after which he had to be helped down and sent home. Another figure was noticed between the rails in the path of a heavy goods train, but was found to have vanished without trace when the train had passed.

---

WHILE I SKIMMED through these and some others, Jimmy stood waiting, like a soda siphon. I didn't have to say more than, "Huh!"

"You see," he said. "Something *is* happening."

"Supposing it is," I conceded cautiously, "then what is it?"

"The manifestation zone is limited," Jimmy told me impressively, and produced a town plan. "If you look where I've marked the incidents you'll see that they're grouped. Somewhere in that circle is 'the focus of disturbance'." This time he managed to vocalize the inverted commas, and waited for me to register amazement.

"So?" I said. "Disturbance of just what?"

He dodged that one.

"I've a pretty good idea now of the cause," he told me weightily.

That was normal, though it might be a different idea an hour later.

"I'll buy it," I offered.

"Teleportation!" he announced. "That's what it is. Bound to come sooner or later. Now someone's on to it."

"H'm," I said.

"But it *must* be." He leaned forward earnestly. "How else'd you account for it?"

"Well, if there could be teleportation, or teleportage, or whatever it is, surely there would have to be a transmitter and some sort of reassembly station," I pointed out. "You couldn't expect a person or object to be kind of broadcast and then come together again in any old place."

"But you don't *know* that," he said. "Besides, that's part of what I was meaning by 'focus'. The transmitter is somewhere else, but focused on that area."

"If it is," I said, "he seems to have got his levels and positions all to hell. I wonder just what happens to a fellow who gets himself reassembled half in and half out of a brick wall?"

It's details like that that get Jimmy impatient.

"Obviously it's early stages. Experimental," he said.

It still seemed to me uncomfortable for the subject, early stages or not, but I didn't press it.

―

THAT EVENING WAS the first time I mentioned it to Sally, and, on the whole, it was a mistake. After making it quite clear that she didn't believe it, she went on to say that if it was true it was probably just another invention.

"What do you mean, 'just another invention'? Why, it'd be revolutionary!" I told her.

"The wrong kind of revolution, the way we'd use it."

"Meaning?" I asked.

Sally was in one of her withering moods. She turned on her disillusioned voice:

"We've got two ways of using inventions," she said. "One is to kill more people more easily: the other is to enable quick-turnover spivs to make easy money out of suckers. Maybe there are a few exceptions like X-rays, but not many. Inventions! What we do with the product of genius is first of all ram it down to the lowest common denominator and then multiply it by the vulgarest possible fraction. What a century! What a world! When I think what other centuries are going to say about ours it makes me go hot all over."

"I shouldn't worry. You won't be hearing them," I said.

The withering eye was on me.

"I should have known. That is a remark well up to the twentieth-century standard."

"You're a funny girl," I told her. "I mean, the way you think may be crazy, but you do do it, in your own way. Now most girls' futures are all cloud-cuckoo beyond next season's hat or next year's baby. Outside of that it might be going to snow split atoms for all they care—they've got a comforting feeling deep down that nothing's ever changed much, or ever will."

"A lot you know about what most girls think," said Sally.

"That's what I was meaning. How could I?" I said.

She seemed to have set her mind so firmly against the whole business that I dropped it for the evening.

A couple of days later Jimmy looked into my room again.

"He's laid off," he said.

"Who's laid off what?"

"This teleporting fellow. Not a report later than Tuesday. Maybe he knows somebody's on to him."

"Meaning you?" I asked.

"Maybe."

"Well, are you?"

He frowned. "I've started. I took the bearings on the map of all the incidents, and the fix came on All Saints' Church. I had a look all over the place, but I didn't find anything. Still, I must be close—why else'd he stop?"

I couldn't tell him that. Nor could anyone else. But that very evening there was a paragraph about an arm and a leg that some woman had watched travel along her kitchen wall. I showed it to Sally.

"I expect it will turn out to be some new kind of advertisement," she said.

"A kind of secret advertising?" I suggested. Then, seeing the withering look working up again: "How about going to a picture?" I suggested.

It was overcast when we went in; when we came out it was raining hard. Seeing that there was less than a mile to her place, and all the taxis in the town were apparently busy, we decided to walk it. Sally pulled on the hood of her mackintosh, put her arm through mine, and we set out through the rain. For a bit we didn't talk, then:

"Darling," I said, "I know that I can be regarded as a frivolous person with low ethical standards, but has it ever occurred to you what a field there is there for reform?"

"Yes," she said, decisively, but not in the right tone.

"What I mean is," I told her patiently, "if you happened to be looking for a good work to devote your life to, what could be better than a reclamation job on such a character. The scope is tremendous, just—"

"Is this a proposal of some kind?" Sally inquired.

"*Some* kind! I'd have you know— Good God!" I broke off.

---

WE WERE IN Tyler Street. A short street, rainswept now, and empty, except for ourselves. What stopped me was the sudden appearance of some kind of vehicle, further along. I couldn't make it out very clearly on account of the rain, but I had the impression of a small, low-built lorry with several figures in light clothes on it driving across Tyler Street quite quickly, and vanishing. That wouldn't have been so bad if there were any street crossing Tyler Street, but there isn't; it had just come out of one side and gone into the other.

"Did you see what I saw?" I asked.

"But how on earth—?" she began

We walked a little further until we came to the place where the thing had crossed, and looked at the solid brick wall on one side and the housefronts on the other.

"You must have been mistaken," said Sally.

"Well, for— *I* must have been mistaken!"

"But it just couldn't have happened, could it?"

"Now, listen, darling—" I began.

But at that moment a girl stepped out from the solid brick about ten feet ahead of us. We stopped, and gaped at her.

I don't know whether her hair would be her own, art and science together can do so much for a girl, but the way she was wearing it, it was like a great golden chrysanthemum a good foot and a half across, and with a red flower set in it a little left of centre. It looked sort of top-heavy. She was wearing some kind of brief pink tunic, silk perhaps, and more appropriate to one of those elderly gentleman floor-shows than Tyler Street on a filthy wet night. What made it a real shocker was the things that had been achieved by embroidery. I never would have believed that any girl could—oh, well, anyway, there she stood, and there we stood.

When I say 'she stood', she certainly did, but somehow she did it about six inches above ground level. She looked at us both, then she stared back at Sally just as hard as Sally was staring at her. It must have been some seconds before any of us moved. The girl opened her mouth as if she were speaking, but no sound came. Then she shook her head, made a forget-it gesture, and turned and walked back into the wall.

Sally didn't move. With the rain shining on her mackintosh she looked like a black statue. When she turned so that I could see her face under the hood it had an expression I had never seen there before. I put my arm round her, and found that she was trembling.

"I'm scared, Jerry," she said.

"No need for that, Sal. There's bound to be a simple explanation of some kind," I said, falsely.

"But it's more than that, Jerry. Didn't you see her face? She was exactly like me!"

"She was pretty much like—" I conceded.

"Jerry, she was *exactly* like— I'm—I'm scared."

"Must have been some trick of the light. Anyway, she's gone now," I said.

All the same, Sally was right. That girl was the image of herself. I've wondered about that quite a bit since…

Jimmy brought a copy of the morning paper into my room next day. It carried a brief, facetious leader on the number of local citizens who had been seeing things lately.

"They're beginning to take notice, at last," he proclaimed.

"How's your own line going?" I asked.

He frowned. "I'm afraid it can't be quite the way I thought. I reckon it *is* still in the experimental stage, all right, but the transmitter may not be in these parts at all. It could be that this is just the area he has trained it on for tests."

"But why here?"

"How would I know? It has to be somewhere—and the transmitter itself could be anywhere." He paused, struck by a portentous thought. "It might be really serious. Suppose the Russians had a transmitter which could project people—or bombs—here by teleportation…?"

"Why here?" I said again. "I should have thought that Harwell or a Royal Arsenal—"

"Experimental, so far," he reminded me.

"Oh," I said, abashed. I went on to tell him what Sally and I had seen the previous night. "She sort of didn't look much like the way I think of Russians," I added.

Jimmy shook his head. "Might be camouflage. After all, behind that curtain they have to get their idea of the way our girls look mostly from magazines and picture papers," he pointed out.

---

THE NEXT DAY, after about seventy-five per cent of its readers had written in to tell about the funny things they had been seeing, the *News* dropped the facetious angle. In two days more, the thing had become factional, dividing sharply into what you might call the Classical and Modern camps. In the latter, schismatic groups argued the claims of teleportage against three-dimensional projection, or some theory of spontaneous molecular assembly: in the former, opinions could be sorted as beliefs in a ghostly invasion, a suddenly acquired visibility of habitually wandering spirits, or the imminence of Judgement Day. In the heat of debate it was rapidly becoming difficult to tell who had seen how much of what, and who was enthusiastically bent on improving his case at some expense of fact.

On Saturday Sally and I met for lunch. Afterwards, we started off in the car for a little place in the hills which seemed to me an ideal spot for a proposal. But at the main crossing in the High Street the man in front jumped on his brakes. So did I, and the man behind me. The one behind him didn't quite. There was an interesting crunch of metal going on on the other side of the crossing, too. I stood up to see what it was all about, and then pulled Sally up beside me.

"Here we go again," I said. "Look!"

Slap in the middle of the crossing was—well, you could scarcely call it a vehicle—it was more like a flat trolley or platform, about a foot off the ground. And when I say off the ground, I mean just that. No wheels, or legs. It kind of hung there, from nothing. Standing on it, dressed in coloured things like long shirts or smocks, were half a dozen men looking interestedly around them. Along the edge of the platform was lettered: PAWLEY'S PEEPHOLES. One of the men was pointing out All Saints' Church to another; the rest were paying more attention to the cars and the people. The policeman on duty was hanging a goggling face over the edge of his traffic-control box. Then he pulled himself together. He shouted, he blew his whistle, then he shouted again. The men on the platform took no notice at all. The policeman got out of his box and went across the road looking like a volcano that had seen a nice place to erupt.

"Hey!" he shouted to them.

It didn't worry them, but when he got within a yard or two of them they noticed him, and they nudged one another, and grinned. The policeman's face was purplish, he spoke to them luridly, but they just went on watching him with amused interest. He reached a truncheon out of his back pocket, and went closer. He grabbed at a fellow in a yellow shirt—and his arm went right through him.

The policeman stepped back. You could see his nostrils sort of spread, the way a horse's do. Then he took a firmer hold of his truncheon and made a fine circular sweep at the lot of them. They kept on grinning back at him as the stick went through them.

―

I TAKE OFF my hat to that policeman. He didn't run. He stared at them for a moment with a very queer expression on his face, then he turned, and walked deliberately back to his box; just as deliberately he signalled the north–south traffic across. The man ahead of me was ready for it. He drove right at, and through, the platform. It began to move, but I'd have nicked it myself, had it been nickable. Sally, looking back, said that it slid away on a curve and disappeared through the front of the Penny Savings Bank.

When we got to the spot I'd had in mind the weather had come over bad to make the place look dreary and unpropitious, so we drove about a bit, and then back to a nice quiet roadside restaurant just outside Westwich. I was getting the conversation round to the mood where I wanted it when who should come across to our table but Jimmy.

"Fancy meeting you two!" he said. "Did you hear what happened at the Crossing this afternoon, Jerry?"

"We were there," I told him.

"You know, Jerry, this is something bigger than we thought—a whole lot bigger. That platform thing. These people are way ahead of us technically. Do you know what I reckon they are?"

"Martians?" I suggested.

He stared at me, taken aback. "Now, how on earth did *you* guess that?" he said, amazedly.

"I sort of saw it had to come," I admitted. "But," I added, "I do have a kind of feeling that Martians wouldn't be labelled 'Pawley's Peepholes'."

"Oh, were they? Nobody told me that," said Jimmy.

He went away sadly, but even by breaking in at all he had wrecked the mood I'd been building up.

---

ON MONDAY MORNING our typist, Anna, arrived even more scattered than commonly.

"The most terrible thing happened to me," she told us as soon as she was inside the door. "Oh, dear. And did I blush all over!"

"*All* over?" inquired Jimmy interestedly.

She scorned him.

"There I was in my bath, and when I happened to look up there was a man in a green shirt, standing watching me. Of course, I screamed, at once."

"Of course," agreed Jimmy. "Very proper. And what happened then, or shouldn't we—"

"He just stood there," said Anna. "Then he sniggered, and walked away *through the wall*. Was I mortified!"

"Very mortifying thing, a snigger," Jimmy agreed.

Anna explained that it was not entirely the snigger that had mortified her. "What I mean is," she said, "things like that oughtn't to be allowed. If a man is going to be able to walk through a girl's bathroom wall, where is he going to stop?"

Which seemed a pretty fair question.

The boss arrived just then. I followed him into his room. He wasn't looking happy.

"What the hell's going on in this damned town, Jerry?" he demanded. "Wife comes home yesterday. Finds two incredible girls in the sitting-room. Thinks it's something to do with me. First bust-up in twenty years. In the middle of it girls vanish," he said succinctly.

One couldn't do more than make a few sympathetic sounds.

That evening when I went to see Sally I found her sitting on the steps of the house, in the drizzle.

"What on earth—?" I began.

She gave me a bleak look.

"Two of them came into my room. A man and a girl. They wouldn't go. They just laughed at me. Then they started to behave just as though I weren't there. It got—well, I just couldn't stay, Jerry."

She went on looking miserable, and then suddenly burst into tears.

—

FROM THEN ON it was stepped up. There was a brisk, if one-sided, engagement in the High Street next morning. Miss Dotherby, who comes of one of Westwich's most respected families, was outraged in every lifelong principle by the appearance of four mop-headed girls who stood giggling on the corner of Northgate. Once she had retracted her eyes and got her breath back, she knew her duty. She gripped her umbrella as if it had been her grandfather's sword, and advanced. She sailed through them, smiting right and left—and when she turned round they were laughing at her. She swiped wildly through them again, and they kept on laughing. Then she started babbling, so someone called an ambulance to take her away.

By the end of the day the town was full of mothers crying shame and men looking staggered, and the Town Clerk and the police were snowed under with demands for somebody to do something about it.

The trouble seemed to come thickest in the district that Jimmy had originally marked out. You *could* meet them elsewhere, but in that area you couldn't help encountering gangs of them, the men in coloured shirts, the girls with their amazing hair-dos and even more amazing decorations on their shirts, sauntering arm-in-arm out of walls, and wandering indifferently through cars and people alike. They'd pause anywhere to point things out to one another and go off into helpless roars of silent laughter. What tickled them most was when people got angry with them. They'd make signs and faces at the stuffier sort until they got them tearing mad—and the madder, the funnier. They ambled as the spirit took them, through shops and banks, and offices, and homes, without a care for the raging occupants. Everybody started putting up 'Keep Out' signs; that amused them a lot, too.

It didn't seem as if you could be free of them anywhere in the central area, though they appeared to be operating on levels that weren't always the same as ours. In some places they did have the look of walking on the ground or floor, but elsewhere they'd be inches above it, and then in some places you would encounter them moving along as though they were wading through the solid surface. It was very soon clear that they could no more hear us than we could hear them, so that there was no use appealing to them or threatening them in that way, and none of the notices that people put up seemed to do anything but whet their curiosity.

After three days of it there was chaos. In the worst affected parts there just wasn't any privacy any more. At the most intimate moments they were liable to wander through, visibly sniggering or guffawing. It was all very well for the police to announce that there was no danger, that the visitors appeared unable actually to *do* anything, so the best way was to ignore them. There are times and places when giggling bunches of youth and maidens demand more ignore-power than the average person has got. It could send even a placid fellow like me wild at times, while the women's leagues of this-and-that, and the watch-committee-minded were living in a constant state of blown tops.

The news had begun to get about, and that didn't help, either, News collectors of all kinds came streaming in. They overflowed the place. The streets were snaked with leads to movie cameras, television cameras, and microphones, while the press-photographers were having the snappy-picture time of their lives, and, being solid, they were almost as much of a nuisance as the visitors themselves.

But we hadn't reached the peak of it yet. Jimmy and I happened to be present at the inception of the next stage. We were on our way to lunch, doing our best to ignore visitors, as instructed, by walking through them. Jimmy was subdued. He had had to give up theories because the facts had largely submerged him. Just short of the café we noticed that there was some commotion further up the High Street, and seemingly it was coming our way, so we waited for it. After a bit it emerged through a tangle of halted cars further down, and approached at a rate of some six or seven miles an hour. Essentially it was a platform like the one that Sally and I had seen at the crossroads the previous Saturday, but this was a deluxe model. There were sides to it, glistening with new paint, red, yellow, and blue, enclosing seats set four abreast. Most of the passengers were young, though there was a sprinkling of middle-aged men and women dressed in a soberer version of the same fashions. Behind the first platform followed half a dozen others. We read the lettering on their sides and backs as they went by:

> *Pawley's Peepholes on the Past—Greatest Invention of the Age*
> *History Without Tears—for £1*
> *See How Great Great Grandma Lived*
> *Ye Quainte Olde 20th Century Expresse*
> *See Living History in Comfort—Quaint Dresses, Old Customs*
> *Educational! Learn Primitive Folkways—Living Conditions*

# PAWLEY'S PEEPHOLES

*Visit Romantic 20th Century—Safety Guaranteed*
*Know Your History—Get Culture—£1 Trip*
*Big Money Prize if you Identify Own Granddad/Ma*

Most of the people on the vehicles were turning their heads this way and that in gog-eyed wonder interspersed with spasms of giggles. Some of the young men waved their arms at us and produced silent witticisms which sent their companions into inaudible shrieks of laughter. Others leaned back comfortably, bit into large, yellow fruits, and munched. They cast occasional glances at the scene, but reserved most of their attention for the ladies whose waists they clasped. On the back of the next-to-last car we read:

*Was Great Great Grandma as Good as she Made Out? See the Things Your Family History Never Told You*

and on the final one:

*Spot the Famous before they got Careful—The Real Inside Dope may win you a Big Prize!*

As the procession moved away, it left the rest of us looking at one another kind of stunned. Nobody seemed to have much left to say just then.

The show must have been something in the nature of a grand premiere, I fancy, for after that you were liable anywhere in the town to come across a platform labelled something like:

*History is Culture—Broaden Your Mind Today for only £1!*

or:

*Know the Answers About Your Ancestors*

with full, good-time loads aboard, but I never heard of another regular procession.

IN THE COUNCIL Offices they were tearing what was left of their hair, and putting up notices left, right, and centre about what was not allowed to the "tourists"—and giving them more good laughs—but all the while the thing got more embarrassing. Those "tourists" who were on foot took to coming close up and peering into your face, and comparing it with some book or piece of paper they were carrying—after which they looked disappointed and annoyed with you, and moved on to someone else. I came to the conclusion there was no prize at all for finding me.

Well, work has to go on: we couldn't think of any way of dealing with it, so we had to put up with it. Quite a number of families moved out of the town for privacy and to stop their daughters from catching the new ideas about dress, and so on, but most of us just had to keep along as best we could. Pretty nearly everyone one met those days looked either dazed or scowling—except, of course, the 'tourist.'

I called for Sally one evening about a fortnight after the platform procession. When we came out of the house there was a ding-dong going on further down the road. A couple of girls with heads that looked like globes of gilded basket-work were scratching the daylights out of one another. One of the fellows standing by was looking proud of himself, the rest of the party was whooping things on. We went the other way.

"It just isn't like our town any more," said Sally. "Even our homes aren't ours any more. Why can't they all go away and leave us in peace? Oh, damn them, all of them! I hate them!"

But just outside the park we came upon one little chrysanthemum-head sitting on apparently nothing at all, and crying her heart out. Sally softened a little.

"Perhaps they are human, some of them. But what right have they to turn our town into a horrible fun-fair?"

We found a bench and sat on it, looking at the sunset. I wanted to get her away out of the place.

"It'd be grand away in the hills now," I said.

"It'd be lovely to be there, Jerry," she sighed.

I took her hand, and she didn't pull it away.

"Sally, darling—" I began.

And then, before I could get any further, two tourists, a man and a girl, had to come along and anchor themselves in front of us. That time I was angry. You might see the platforms almost anywhere, but you did reckon to be free of the walking tourists in the park where there was nothing to interest them, anyway—or should not have been. These two, however, had found something. It was Sally, and they stood staring at her, unabashed. She took her hand out of mine. They conferred. The man opened a folder he was carrying, and took a piece of paper out of it. They looked at the paper, then at Sally, then back to the paper. It was too much to ignore. I got up and walked through them to see what the paper was. There I had a surprise. It was a piece of the *Westwich Evening News,* obviously taken from a very ancient copy indeed. It was badly browned and tattered, and to keep it from falling to bits entirely it had been mounted inside some thin, transparent plastic. I wish I had noticed the date, but naturally enough I looked where they were looking—and Sally's face looked back at me from a smiling photograph. She had her arms spread wide, and a baby in the crook of each. I had just time to see the headline: 'Twins for Town Councillor's Wife', when they folded up the paper, and made off along the path, running. I reckoned they would be hot on the trail of one of their damned prizes—and I hoped it would turn round and bite them.

---

I WENT BACK and sat down again beside Sally. That picture certainly had spoilt things—'Councillor's Wife'! Naturally she wanted to know what I'd seen on the paper, and I had to sharpen up a few lies to cut my way out of that one.

We sat on awhile, feeling gloomy, saying nothing.

A platform went by, labelled:

*Trouble-free Culture—Get Educated in Modern Comfort*

We watched it glide away through the railings and into the traffic.

"Maybe it's time we moved," I suggested.

"Yes," agreed Sally, dully.

We walked back towards her place, me still wishing that I had been able to see the date on that paper.

"You wouldn't," I asked her casually, "you wouldn't happen to know any Councillors?"

She looked surprised.

"Well—there's Mr. Falmer," she said, rather doubtfully.

"He'd be a—a youngish man?" I inquired, off-handedly.

"Why, no. He's ever so old—as a matter of fact, it's really his wife I know."

"Ah!" I said. "You don't know any of the younger ones?"

"I'm afraid not. Why?"

I put over a line about a situation like this needing young men of ideas.

"Young men of ideas don't have to be councillors," she remarked, looking at me.

Maybe, as I said, she doesn't go much on logic, but she has her own ways of making a fellow feel better. I'd have felt better still if I had had some ideas, though.

—

THE NEXT DAY found public indignation right up the scale again. It seems there had been an evening service going on in All Saints' Church. The vicar had ascended his pulpit and was just drawing breath for a brief sermon when a platform labelled:

*Was Gt Gt Granddad one of the Boys?—Our £1 Trip may Show you*

floated in through the north wall and slid to a stop in front of the lectern. The vicar stared at it for some seconds in silence, then he crashed his fist down on his reading desk.

"This," he boomed. "This is *intolerable*! We shall wait until this *object* is removed."

He remained motionless, glaring at it. The congregation glared with him.

The tourists on the platform had an air of waiting for the show to begin. When nothing happened they started passing round bottles and fruit to while away the time. The vicar maintained his stony glare. When still nothing happened the tourists began to get bored. The young men tickled the girls, and the girls giggled them on. Several of them began to urge the man at the front end of their craft. After a bit he nodded, and the platform slid away through the south wall.

It was the first point our side had ever scored. The vicar mopped his brow, cleared his throat, and then extemporized the address of his life, on the subject of 'The Cities of the Plain'.

---

BUT NO MATTER how influential the tops that were blowing, there was still nothing getting done about it. There were schemes, of course. Jimmy had one of them: it concerned either ultra-high or infra-low frequencies that were going to shudder the projections of the tourists to bits. Perhaps something along those lines might have been worked out sometime, but it was a quicker kind of cure that we were needing; and it is damned difficult to know what you can do about something which is virtually no more than a three-dimensional movie portrait unless you can think up some way of fouling its transmission. All its functions are going on not where you see it, but in some unknown place where the origin is—so how do you get at it? What you are actually seeing doesn't feel, doesn't eat, doesn't breathe, doesn't sleep… It was while I was considering what it actually does do that I had my idea. It struck me all of a heap—so simple. I grabbed my hat and took off for the Town Hall.

By this time the daily processions of sizzling citizens, threateners, and cranks had made them pretty cautious about callers there, but I worked through at last to a man who got interested, though doubtful.

"No one's going to like that much," he said.

"No one's meant to like it. But it couldn't be much worse than this—*and it's likely to do local trade a bit of good, too*," I pointed out.

He brightened a bit at that. I pressed on:

"After all, the Mayor has his restaurants, and the pubs'll be all for it, too."

"You've got a point there," he admitted. "Very well, we'll put it to them. Come along."

———

FOR THE WHOLE of three days we worked hard on it. On the fourth we went into action. Soon after daylight there were gangs out on all the roads fixing barriers at the municipal limits, and when they'd done that they put up big white boards lettered in red:

WESTWICH

THE CITY THAT LOOKS AHEAD

COME AND SEE

IT'S BEYOND THE MINUTE—NEWER THAN TOMORROW

SEE

THE WONDER CITY OF THE AGE

TOLL (Non-Residents) 2/6

The same morning the television permission was revoked, and the national papers carried large display advertisements:

COLOSSAL!—UNIQUE!—EDUCATIONAL!

WESTWICH

presents the only authentic

FUTURAMATIC SPECTACLE

WANT TO KNOW:

*What Your Great Great Granddaughter will Wear?*

*How Your Great Great Grandson will Look?*

*Next Century's Styles?*

*How Customs will Change?*

# PAWLEY'S PEEPHOLES

> COME TO WESTWICH AND SEE FOR YOURSELF
> THE OFFER OF THE AGES
> THE FUTURE FOR 2/6

We reckoned that with the publicity there had been already there'd be no need for more detail than that—though we ran some more specialized advertisements in the picture dailies:

> WESTWICH
> GIRLS! GIRLS!! GIRLS!!!
> THE SHAPES TO COME
> SAUCY FASHIONS—CUTE WAYS
> ASTONISHING—AUTHENTIC—UNCENSORED
> GLAMOUR GALORE FOR 2/6

and so on. We bought enough space to get it mentioned in the news columns in order to help those who like to think they are doing things for sociological, psychological, and other intellectual reasons.

And they came.

There had been quite a few looking in to see the sights before, but now they learned that it was something worth charging money for the figures jumped right up—and the more they went up, the gloomier the Council Treasurer got because we hadn't made it five shillings, or even ten.

After a couple of days we had to take over all vacant lots, and some fields further out, for car parks, and people were parking far enough out to need a special bus service to bring them in. The streets became so full of crowds stooging around greeting any of Pawley's platforms or tourists with whistles, jeers, and catcalls, that local citizens simply stayed indoors and did their smouldering there.

The Treasurer began to worry now over whether we'd be liable for Entertainment Tax. The list of protests to the Mayor grew longer each day, but he was so busy arranging special convoys of food and beer for his restaurants that he had little time to worry about them. Nevertheless, after a few days of it I started to wonder whether Pawley wasn't going to see us out, after all. The tourists didn't care for it much, one could see, and it must have interfered a lot with their prize-hunts, but it hadn't cured them of wandering about all over the place, and now we had the addition of thousands of trippers whooping it up with pandemonium for most of the night. Tempers all round were getting short enough for real trouble to break out.

Then, on the sixth night, when several of us were just beginning to wonder whether it might not be wiser to clear out of Westwich for a bit, the first crack showed—a man at the Town Hall rang me up to say he had seen several platforms with empty seats on them.

The next night I went down to one of their regular routes to see for myself. I found a large, well-lubricated crowd already there, exchanging cracks and jostling and shoving, but we hadn't long to wait. A platform slid out on a slant through the front of the Coronation Café, and the label on it read:

CHARM & ROMANCE OF 20TH CENTURY—15/-

and there were half a dozen empty seats, at that.

---

THE ARRIVAL OF the platform brought a well-supported Bronx cheer, and a shrilling of whistles. The driver remained indifferent as he steered straight through the crowds. His passengers looked less certain of themselves. Some of them did their best to play up; they giggled, made motions of returning slap for slap and grimace for grimace with the crowd to start with. Possibly it was as well that the tourist girls couldn't hear the things the crowd was shouting to them, but some of the gestures were clear enough. It couldn't have been a lot of fun gliding straight into the men who were making them. By the time the platform was clear of the crowd and disappearing through the front of the Bon Marché pretty well all the tourists had given up pretending that it was; some of them were looking a little sick. By the expression on several of the faces I reckoned that Pawley might be going to have a tough time explaining the culture aspect of it to a deputation somewhere.

The next night there were more empty seats than full ones, and someone reported that the price had come down to 10s.

The night after that they did not show up at all, and we all had a busy time with the job of returning the half-crowns, and refusing claims for wasted petrol.

And the next night they didn't come, either; or the one after that; so then all we had to do was to pitch into the job of cleaning up Westwich, and the affair was practically over—apart from the longer-term business of living down the reputation the place had been getting lately.

At least, we say it's over. Jimmy, however, maintains that that is probably only the way it looks from here. According to him, all they had to do was to modify out the visibility factor that was causing the trouble, so it's possible that they are still touring around here—and other places.

Well, I suppose he could be right. Perhaps that fellow Pawley, whoever he is, or will be, has a chain of his funfairs operating all round the world and all through history at this very moment. But we don't know—and, as long as he keeps them out of sight, I don't know that we care a lot, either.

Pawley has been dealt with as far as we are concerned. He was a case for desperate measures; even the vicar of All Saints' appreciated that; and undoubtedly he had a point to make when he began his address of thanksgiving with: "Paradoxical, my friends, paradoxical can be the workings of vulgarity…"

---

ONCE IT WAS settled I was able to make time to go round and see Sally again. I found her looking brighter than she'd been for weeks, and lovelier on account of it. She seemed pleased to see me, too.

"Hullo, Jerry," she said. "I've just been reading in the paper how you organized the plan for getting rid of them. I think it was just wonderful of you."

A little time ago I'd probably have taken that for a cue, but it was no trigger now. I sort of kept on seeing her with her arms full of twins, and wondering in a dead-inside way how they got there.

"There wasn't a lot to it, darling," I told her modestly. "Anyone else might have hit on the idea."

"That's as maybe—but a whole lot of people don't think so. And I'll tell you another thing I heard today. They're going to ask you to stand for the Council, Jerry."

"Me on the Council. That'd be a big laugh—" I began. Then I stopped suddenly. "If—I mean, would that mean I'd be called 'Councillor'?" I asked her.

"Why—well, yes, I suppose so," she said, looking puzzled.

Things shimmered a bit.

"Er—Sally, darling—er, sweetheart, there's—er—something I've been trying to get round to saying to you for quite a time…" I began.

# THE WHEEL

—

THE OLD MAN sat on his stool and leaned back against the whitened wall. He had upholstered the stool elegantly with a hare skin because there didn't seem to be much between his own skin and bones these days. It was exclusively his stool, and recognized in the farmstead as such. The strands of a whip that he was supposed to be plaiting drooped between his bent fingers, but, because the stool was comfortable and the sun was warm, his fingers had stopped moving, and his head was nodding.

The yard was empty save for a few hens that pecked more inquisitively than hopefully in the dust, but there were sounds that told of others who had not the old man's leisure for siesta. From round the corner of the house came the occasional plonk of an empty bucket as it hit the water, and its scrape on the sides of the well as it came up full. In the shack across the yard a dull pounding went on rhythmically and soporifically. The old man's head fell further forward as he drowsed.

Presently, from beyond the rough, enclosing wall there came another sound, slowly approaching. A rumbling and a rattling, with an intermittent squeaking. The old man's ears were no longer sharp, and for some minutes it failed to disturb him. Then he opened his eyes and, locating the sound, sat staring incredulously towards the gateway. The sound drew closer and a boy's head showed above the wall. He grinned at the old man, an expression of excitement in his eyes. He did not call out, but moved a little faster until he came to the gate. There he turned into the yard proudly towing behind him a box mounted on four wooden wheels.

The old man got up suddenly from his seat, alarm in every line. He waved both arms at the boy as though he would push him back. The boy stopped. His expression of gleeful pride faded into astonishment. He stared at the old man who was waving him away so urgently. While he still hesitated the old man continued to shoo him off with one hand while he placed the other on his own lips, and started to walk towards him. Reluctantly and bewilderedly the boy turned, but too late. The pounding in the shed stopped. A middle-aged woman appeared in the doorway. Her mouth was open to call, but the words did not come. Her jaw dropped slackly, her eyes seemed to bulge, then she crossed herself, and screamed...

The sound split the afternoon peace. Behind the house the bucket fell with a clatter, and a young woman's head showed round the corner. Her eyes widened. She crammed the back of one hand across her mouth, and crossed herself with the other. A young man appeared in the stable doorway, and stood there transfixed. Another girl came pelting out of the house with a little girl behind her. She stopped as suddenly as if she had run into something. The little girl stopped too, vaguely alarmed by the tableau, and clinging to her skirt.

The boy stood quite still with all their gaze upon him. His bewilderment began to give way to fright at the expression in their eyes. He looked from one horrified face to another until his gaze met the old man's. What he saw there seemed to reassure him a little—or to frighten him less. He swallowed. Tears were not far away as he spoke:

"Gran, what's the matter? What are they all looking at me like that for?"

As if the sound of his voice had released a spell the middle-aged woman came to life. She reached for a hayfork which leaned against the shack wall. Raising its points towards the boy she walked slowly in between him and the gate. In a hard voice she said:

"Go on! Get in the shed!"

"But, Ma—" the boy began.

"Don't you dare call me that now," she told him.

# THE WHEEL

In the tense lines of her face the boy could see something that was almost hatred. His own face screwed up, and he began to cry.

"Go on," she repeated harshly. "Get in there."

The boy backed away, a picture of bewildered misery. Then, suddenly, he turned and ran into the shed. She shut the door on him, and fastened it with a peg. She looked round at the rest as though defying them to speak. The young man withdrew silently into the gloom of the stable. The two young women crept away, taking the little girl with them. The woman and the old man were left alone.

Neither of them spoke. The old man stood motionless, regarding the box where it stood on its wheels. The woman suddenly put her hands up to her face. She made little moaning noises as she swayed, and the tears came trickling out between her fingers. The old man turned. His face was devoid of all expression. Presently she recovered herself a little.

"I never would have believed it. My own little David…!" she said.

"If you'd not screamed, nobody need have known," said the old man.

His words took some seconds to sink in. When they did, her expression hardened again.

"Did you show him how?" she asked, suspiciously.

He shook his head.

"I'm old, but I'm not crazy," he told her. "And I'm fond of Davie," he added.

"You're wicked, though. That was a wicked thing you just said."

"It was true."

"I'm a god-fearing woman. I'll not have evil in my house—whatever shape it comes in. And when I see it I know my duty."

The old man drew breath for a reply, but checked it. He shook his head. He turned, and went back to his stool, looking, somehow, older than before.

—

THERE WAS A tap on the door. A whispered "Sh!" For a moment Davie saw a square of night sky with a dark shape against it. Then the door closed again.

"You had your supper, Davie?" a voice asked.

"No, Gran. Nobody's been."

The old man grunted.

"Thought not. Scared of you, all of 'em. Here, take this. Cold chicken, it is."

Davie's hand sought and found what the other held out to him. He gnawed on a leg while the other man moved about in the dark, searching for somewhere to sit. He found it, and let himself down with a sigh.

"This is a bad business, Davie, boy. They've sent for the priest. He'll be along to-morrow."

"But I don't understand, Gran. Why do they all act like I've done something wrong?"

"Oh, Davie!" said his grandfather, reproachfully.

"Honest, I don't, Gran."

"Come now, Davie. Every Sunday you go to church, and every time you go, you pray. What do you pray?"

The boy gabbled a prayer. After a few moments the old man stopped him.

"There," he said. "That last bit."

"Preserve us from the Wheel?" Davie repeated, wonderingly. "What *is* the Wheel, Gran? It must be something terrible bad, I know, 'cos when I ask them they just say it's wicked, and not to talk of it. But they don't say what it is."

The old man paused before he replied, then he said:

"That box you got out there. Who told you to fix it that way?"

"Why, nobody, Gran. I just reckoned it'd move easier that way. It does, too."

"Listen, Davie. Those things you put on the side of it—they're *wheels*."

It was some time before the boy's voice came back out of the darkness. When it did, it sounded bewildered.

"What, those round bits of wood? But they can't be, Gran. That's all they are—just round bits of wood. But the Wheel—that's something awful, terrible, something everybody's holy scared of."

"All the same, that's what they are." The old man ruminated awhile. "I'll tell you what's going to happen to-morrow, Davie. In the morning the priest will come here and see your box. It'll be still there because nobody dares to touch it. He'll sprinkle some water on it and say a prayer just to make it safe to handle. Then they'll take it into the field and make a fire under it, and they'll stand round singing hymns while it burns.

# THE WHEEL

"Then they'll come back, and take you down to the village, and ask you questions. They'll ask you what the Devil looked like when he came to you, and what he offered to give you if you'd use the Wheel."

"But there wasn't any Devil, Gran."

"That don't matter. If they think there was, then sooner or later you'll be telling them there was, *and* just how he looked when you saw him. They've got ways... Now what you got to do is act innocent. You got to say you found that box just the way it is now. You didn't know what it was, but you just brought it along on account of it would make good firewood. That's your story, and you've got to stick to it. 'F you stick to it, no matter what they do, *maybe* you'll get through okay."

"But Gran, what is there that's so bad about the Wheel? I just can't understand."

The old man paused more lengthily than before.

"Well, it's a long story, Davie—and it all began a long, long while ago. Seems like in those days the Devil came along and met a man and told him that he could give him something to make him as strong as a hundred men, an' make him to run faster than the wind, an' fly higher than the birds. Well, the man said that'd be mighty fine, an' what did the Devil want for it? And the Devil said he didn't want a thing—not just then. And so he gave the man the Wheel.

"By and by, after the man had played around with the Wheel awhile he found out a whole lot of things about it; how it would make other Wheels, and still more Wheels, and do all the things the Devil had said, with a whole heap more."

"What, it'd fly, 'n everything?" said the boy.

"Sure. It did all those things. And it began to kill people, too—one way and another. Folks put more and more Wheels together the way the Devil told them, and they found they could do a whole lot bigger things, and kill more people, too. And they couldn't stop using the Wheel then on account of they would have starved if they had.

"Well, that was just what the Devil wanted. He'd got 'em cinched, you see. Pretty near everything in the world was depending on Wheels, and things got worse and worse, and the old Devil just lay back an' laughed to see what his Wheel was doing. Then things got terrible bad. I don't know quite the way it happened, but things got so terrible worse that there wasn't scarcely anybody left alive—only just a few, like it had been after the Flood. An' they was near finished."

"And all that was on account of the Wheel?"

"Uh-huh— Leastways, it couldn't have happened without it. Still, somehow they made out. They built shacks, an' planted corn, and by an' by the Devil met a man, and started talking about his Wheel again. Now this man was very old and very wise and very godfearing, so he said to the Devil: "No. You go right back to Hell," and then he went all around warning everybody about the Devil and his Wheel, and got 'em all plumb scared.

"But the old Devil don't give up that easy. He's mighty tricky, too—there's times when a man gets an idea that turns out to be pretty nearly a Wheel—maybe like rollers, or screws, or somethin'—but it'll just pass so long as it ain't fixed in the middle. Yes, he keeps along trying, an' now and then he does tempt a man into making a Wheel. Then the priest comes and they burn the Wheel. And they take the man away. And to stop him making any more Wheels, and to discourage any other folk, they burn him, too."

"They b-burn him?" stammered the boy.

"That's what they do. So you see why you got to say you *found* it, and stick to that."

"Maybe if I promised never to make another—?"

"That wouldn't be no good, Davie. They're all scared of the Wheel, and when men are scared they get angry and cruel. No, you gotta keep to it."

The boy thought for some moments, then he said:

"What about Ma? She'll know. I had that box off her yesterday. Does it matter?"

The old man grunted. He said, heavily:

"Yes, it does matter. Women do a lot of pretending to be scared—but once they do scare, they scare more horribly than men. And your Ma's dead scared."

There was a long silence in the darkness of the shed. When the old man spoke again, it was in a calm, quiet voice:

"Listen, Davie, lad. I'm going to tell you something. And you're going to keep it to yourself—not tell a soul till maybe you're an old man like me?"

# THE WHEEL

"Sure. Gran, 'f you say."

"I'm tellin' you because you found out about the Wheel for yourself. There'll always be boys like you who do. There've got to be. You can't kill an idea the way they try to. You can keep it down awhile, but sooner or later it'll come out. Now what you've got to understand is that the Wheel's *not* evil. Never mind what the scared men all tell you. No discovery is good or evil until men make it that way. Think about that, Davie, boy. One day they'll start to use the Wheel again. I hoped it would be in my time, but—well, maybe it'll be in yours. When it does come, don't you be one of the scared ones; be one of the ones that's going to show 'em how to use it better than they did last time. It's not the Wheel—it's fear that's evil, Davie. Remember that."

He stirred in the darkness. His feet clumped on the hard earth floor.

"Reckon it's time I was gettin' along. Where are you, boy?"

His groping hand found Davie's shoulder, and then rested a moment on his head.

"God bless you, Davie. And don't worry any more. It's goin' to be all right. You trust me?"

"Yes, Gran."

"There you go to sleep. There's some hay in the corner, there."

The glimpse of dark sky showed briefly again. Then the sound of the old man's feet shuffled across the yard into silence.

---

WHEN THE PRIEST arrived he found a horror-stricken knot of people collected in the yard. They were gazing at an old man who worked away with a mallet and pegs on a wooden box. The priest stood, scandalized.

"Stop!" he cried. "In the name of God, stop!"

The old man turned his head towards him. There was a grin of crafty senility on his face.

"Yesterday," he said, "I was a fool. I only made four wheels for it. To-day I am a wise man—I am making two more wheels so that it will run half as easily again."

—

THEY BURNT THE box, as he said they would. Then they took him away.

In the afternoon a small boy whom everyone had forgotten turned his eyes from a column of smoke that rose in the direction of the village, and hid his face in his hands.

"I'll remember, Gran. I'll remember. It's only fear that's evil," he said, and his voice choked in his tears.

# SURVIVAL

—

AS THE SPACEPORT bus trundled unhurriedly over the mile or more of open field that separated the terminal buildings from the embarkation hoist, Mrs. Feltham stared intently forward across the receding row of shoulders in front of her. The ship stood up on the plain like an isolated silver spire. Near its bow she could see the intense blue light which proclaimed it all but ready to take off. Among and around the great tailfins, dwarf vehicles and little dots of men moved in a fuss of final preparations. Mrs. Feltham glared at the scene, at this moment loathing it and all the inventions of men, with a hard, hopeless hatred.

Presently she withdrew her gaze from the distance and focused it on the back of her son-in-law's head, a yard in front of her. She hated him, too.

She turned, darting a swift glance at the face of her daughter in the seat beside her. Alice looked pale; her lips were firmly set, her eyes fixed straight ahead.

Mrs. Feltham hesitated. Her glance returned to the spaceship. She decided on one last effort. Under cover of the bus noise she said:

"Alice, darling, it's not too late, even now, you know."

The girl did not look at her. There was no sign that she had heard, save that her lips compressed a little more firmly. Then they parted.

"Mother, please!" she said.

But Mrs. Feltham, once started, had to go on.

"It's for your own sake, darling. All you have to do is to say you've changed your mind."

The girl held a protesting silence.

"Nobody would blame you," Mrs. Feltham persisted. "They'd not think a bit worse of you. After all, everybody knows that Mars is no place for—"

"Mother, please stop it," interrupted the girl. The sharpness of her tone took Mrs. Feltham aback for a moment. She hesitated. But time was growing too short to allow herself the luxury of offended dignity. She went on:

"You're not used to the sort of life you'll have to live there, darling. Absolutely primitive. No kind of life for any woman. After all, dear, it is only a five-year appointment for David. I'm sure if he really loves you he'd rather know that you *are* safe here and waiting—"

The girl said, harshly:

"We've been over all this before, Mother. I tell you it's no good. I'm not a child. I've thought it out, and I've made up my mind."

—

MRS. FELTHAM SAT silent for some moments. The bus swayed on across the field, and the rocketship seemed to tower further into the sky.

"If you had a child of your own—" she said, half to herself. "—Well, I expect some day you will. Then you will begin to understand…"

"I think it's you who don't understand," Alice said. "This is hard enough, anyway. You're only making it harder for me."

"My darling, I love you. I gave birth to you. I've watched over you always and I *know* you. I *know* this can't be the kind of life for you. If you were a hard, hoydenish kind of girl, well, perhaps—but you aren't, darling. You know quite well you aren't."

"Perhaps you don't know me quite as well as you imagine you do, Mother."

Mrs. Feltham shook her head. She kept her eyes averted, boring jealousy into the back of her son-in-law's head.

"He's taken you right away from me," she said dully.

"That's not true, Mother. It's—well, I'm no longer a child. I'm a woman with a life of my own to live."

"'Whither thou goest, I will go...'" said Mrs. Feltham reflectively. "But that doesn't really hold now, you know. It was all right for a tribe of nomads, but nowadays the wives of soldiers, sailors, pilots, spacemen—"

"It's more than that, Mother. You don't understand. I must become adult and real to myself..."

The bus rolled to a stop, puny and toylike beside the ship that seemed too large ever to lift. The passengers got out and stood staring upwards along the shining side. Mr. Feltham put his arms round his daughter. Alice clung to him, tears in her eyes. In an unsteady voice he murmured:

"Good-bye, my dear. And all the luck there is."

He released her, and shook hands with his son-in-law.

"Keep her safe, David. She's everything—"

"I know. I will. Don't you worry."

Mrs. Feltham kissed her daughter farewell, and forced herself to shake hands with her son-in-law.

A voice from the hoist called: "All passengers aboard, please!"

The doors of the hoist closed. Mr. Feltham avoided his wife's eyes. He put his arm round her waist, and led her back to the bus in silence.

As they made their way, in company with a dozen other vehicles, back to the shelter of the terminal, Mrs. Feltham alternately dabbed her eyes with a wisp of white handkerchief and cast glances back at the spaceship standing tall, inert, and apparently deserted now. Her hand slid into her husband's.

"I can't believe it even now," she said. "It's so utterly unlike her. Would you ever have thought that our little Alice...? Oh, why did she have to marry him...?" Her voice trailed to a whimper.

Her husband pressed her fingers, without speaking.

"It wouldn't be so surprising with some girls," she went on. "But Alice was always so quiet. I used to worry because she was so quiet—I mean in case she might become one of those timid bores. Do you remember how the other children used to call her Mouse?

"And now this! Five years in that dreadful place! Oh, she'll never stand it, Henry. I know she won't, she's not the type. Why didn't you put your foot down, Henry? They'd have listened to you. You could have stopped it."

Her husband sighed. "There are times when one can give advice, Miriam, though it's scarcely ever popular, but what one must not do is to try to live other people's lives for them. Alice is a woman now, with her own rights. Who am I to say what's best for her?"

"But you could have stopped her going."

"Perhaps—but I didn't care for the price."

She was silent for some seconds, then her fingers tightened on his hand.

"Henry—Henry, I don't think we shall ever see them again. I feel it."

"Come, come, dear. They'll be back safe and sound, you'll see."

"You don't really believe that, Henry. You're just trying to cheer me up. Oh, why, why must she go to that horrible place? She's so young. She could have waited five years. Why is she so stubborn, so hard—not like my little Mouse at all?"

Her husband patted her hand reassuringly.

"You must try to stop thinking of her as a child, Miriam. She's not; she's a woman now and if all our women were mice, it would be a poor outlook for our survival…"

—

THE NAVIGATING OFFICER of the s/r *Falcon* approached his captain.

"The deviation, sir."

Captain Winters took the piece of paper held out to him.

"One point three six five degrees," he read out. "H'm. Not bad. Not at all bad, considering. South-east sector again. Why are nearly all deviations in the S.E. sector, I wonder, Mr. Carter?"

"Maybe they'll find out when we've been at the game a bit longer, sir. Right now it's just one of those things."

"Odd, all the same. Well, we'd better correct it before it gets any bigger."

The Captain loosened the expanding book-rack in front of him and pulled out a set of tables. He consulted them and scribbled down the result.

# SURVIVAL

"Check, Mr. Carter."

The navigator compared the figures with the table, and approved.

"Good. How's she lying?" asked the Captain.

"Almost broadside, with a very slow roll, sir."

"You can handle it. I'll observe visually. Align her and stabilize. Ten seconds on starboard laterals at force two. She should take about thirty minutes, twenty seconds to swing over, but we'll watch that. Then neutralize with the port laterals at force two. Okay?"

"Very good, sir." The Navigating Officer sat down in the control chair, and fastened the belt. He looked over the keys and switches carefully.

"I'd better warn 'em. May be a bit of a jolt," said the Captain. He switched on the address system, and pulled the microphone bracket to him.

"Attention all! Attention all! We are about to correct course. There will be several impulses. None of them will be violent, but all fragile objects should be secured, and you are advised to seat yourselves and use the safety-belts. The operation will take approximately half an hour and will start in five minutes from now. I shall inform you when it has been completed. That is all." He switched off.

"Some fool always thinks the ship's been holed by a meteor if you don't spoon it out," he added. "Have that woman in hysterics, most likely. Doesn't do any good." He pondered idly. "I wonder what the devil she thinks she's doing out here, anyway. A quiet little thing like that; what she ought to be doing is sitting in some village back home, knitting."

"She knits here," observed the Navigating Officer.

"I know—and think what it implies! What's the idea of that kind going to Mars? She'll be as homesick as hell, and hate every foot of the place on sight. That husband of hers ought to have had more sense. Comes damn near cruelty to children."

"It mightn't be his fault, sir. I mean, some of those quiet ones can be amazingly stubborn."

The captain eyed his officer speculatively.

"Well, I'm not a man of wide experience, but I know what I'd say to my wife if she thought of coming along."

"But you can't have a proper ding-dong with those quiet ones, sir. They kind of featherbed the whole thing, and then get their own way in the end."

"I'll overlook the implication of the first part of that remark, Mr. Carter, but out of this extensive knowledge of women can you suggest to me why the devil she is here if he didn't drag her along? It isn't as if Mars were domestically hazardous, like a convention."

"Well, sir—she strikes me as the devoted type. Scared of her own shadow ordinarily, but with an awful amount of determination when the right string's pulled. It's sort of—well, you've heard of ewes facing lions in defence of their cubs, haven't you?"

"Assuming that you mean lambs," said the Captain, "the answers would be, A: I've always doubted it; and, B: she doesn't have any."

"I was just trying to indicate the type, sir."

The Captain scratched his cheek with his forefinger.

"You may be right, but I know if I were going to take a wife to Mars, which heaven forbid, I'd feel a tough, gun-toting Momma was less of a liability. What's his job there?"

"Taking charge of a mining company office, I think."

"Office hours, huh? Well, maybe it'll work out some way, but I still say the poor little thing ought to be in her own kitchen. She'll spend half the time scared to death, and the rest of it pining for home comforts." He glanced at the clock. "They've had enough time to batten down the chamber-pots now. Let's get busy."

He fastened his own safety-belt, swung the screen in front of him on its pivot, switching it on as he did so, and leaned back watching the panorama of stars move slowly across it.

"All set, Mr. Carter?"

The Navigating Officer switched on a fuel line, and poised his right hand above a key.

"All set, sir."

"Okay. Straighten her up."

The Navigating Officer glued his attention to the pointers before him. He tapped the key beneath his fingers experimentally. Nothing happened. A slight

# SURVIVAL

double furrow appeared between his brows. He tapped again. Still there was no response.

"Get on with it, man," said the Captain irritably.

The Navigating Officer decided to try twisting her the other way. He tapped one of the keys under his left hand. This time there was response without delay. The whole ship jumped violently sideways and trembled. A crash jangled back and forth through the metal members around them like a diminishing echo.

Only the safety-belt kept the Navigating Officer in his seat. He stared stupidly at the gyrating pointers before him. On the screen the stars were streaking across like a shower of fireworks. The Captain watched the display in ominous silence for a moment, then he said coldly:

"Perhaps when you have had your fun, Mr. Carter, you will kindly straighten her up."

The navigator pulled himself together. He chose a key, and pressed it. Nothing happened. He tried another. Still the needles on the dials revolved smoothly. A slight sweat broke out on his forehead. He switched to another fuel line, and tried again.

The Captain lay back in his chair, watching the heavens stream across his screen.

"Well?" he demanded curtly.

"There's—no response, sir."

Captain Winters unfastened his safety-belt and clacked across the floor on his magnetic soles. He jerked his head for the other to get out of his seat, and took his place. He checked the fuel line switches. He pressed a key. There was no impulse: the pointers continued to turn without a check. He tried other keys, fruitlessly. He looked up and met the navigator's eyes. After a long moment he moved back to his own desk, and flipped a switch. A voice broke into the room:

"—would I know? All I know is that the old can's just bowling along head over elbow, and that ain't no kind of way to run a bloody spaceship. If you ask me—"

"Jevons," snapped the Captain.

The voice broke off abruptly.

"Yes, sir?" it said, in a different tone.

"The laterals aren't firing."

"No, sir," the voice agreed.

"Wake up, man. I mean they *won't* fire. They've packed up."

"What—all of 'em, sir?'

"The only ones that have responded are the port laterals—and they shouldn't have kicked the way they did. Better send someone outside to look at 'em. I didn't like that kick."

"Very good, sir."

The Captain flipped the communicator switch back, and pulled over the announcement mike.

"Attention, please. You may release all safety-belts and proceed as normal. Correction of course has been postponed. You will be warned before it is resumed. That is all."

Captain and navigator looked at one another again. Their faces were grave, and their eyes troubled…

---

CAPTAIN WINTERS STUDIED his audience. It comprised everyone aboard the *Falcon*. Fourteen men and one woman. Six of the men were his crew; the rest passengers. He watched them as they found themselves places in the ship's small living-room. He would have been happier if his cargo had consisted of more freight and fewer passengers. Passengers, having nothing to occupy them, were always making mischief one way and another. Moreover, it was not a quiet, subservient type of man who recommended himself for a job as a miner, prospector, or general adventurer on Mars.

The woman could have caused a great deal of trouble aboard had she been so minded. Luckily she was diffident, self-effacing. But even though at times she was irritatingly without spirit, he thanked his luck that she had not turned out to be some incendiary blonde who would only add to his troubles.

All the same, he reminded himself, regarding her as she sat beside her husband, she could not be quite as meek as she looked. Carter must have been

# SURVIVAL

right when he spoke of a stiffening motive somewhere—without that she could never have started on the journey at all, and she would certainly not be coming through steadfast and uncomplaining so far. He glanced at the woman's husband. Queer creatures, women. Morgan was all right, but there was nothing about him, one would have said, to lead a woman on a trip like this...

He waited until they had finished shuffling around and fitting themselves in. Silence fell. He let his gaze dwell on each face in turn. His own expression was serious.

"Mrs. Morgan and gentlemen," he began. "I have called you here together because it seemed best to me that each of you should have a clear understanding of our present position.

"It is this. Our lateral tubes have failed. They are, for reasons which we have not yet been able to ascertain, useless. In the case of the port laterals they are burnt out, and irreplaceable.

"In case some of you do not know what that implies, I should tell you that it is upon the laterals that the navigation of the ship depends. The main drive tubes give us the initial impetus for take-off. After that they are shut off, leaving us in free fall. Any deviations from the course plotted are corrected by suitable bursts from the laterals.

"But it is not only for steering that we use them. In landing, which is an infinitely more complex job than take-off, they are essential. We brake by reversing the ship and using the main drive to check our speed. But I think you can scarcely fail to realize that it is an operation of the greatest delicacy to keep the huge mass of such a ship as this perfectly balanced upon the thrust of her drive as she descends. It is the laterals which make such balance possible. Without them it cannot be done."

A dead silence held the room for some seconds. Then a voice asked, drawling:

"What you're saying, Captain, is, the way things are, we can neither steer nor land—is that it?"

Captain Winters looked at the speaker. He was a big man. Without exerting himself, and, apparently, without intention, he seemed to possess a natural domination over the rest.

"That is exactly what I mean," he replied.

A tenseness came over the room. There was the sound of a quickly drawn breath here and there.

The man with the slow voice nodded, fatalistically. Someone else asked:

"Does that mean that we might crash on Mars?"

"No," said the Captain. "If we go on travelling as we are now, slightly off course, we shall miss Mars altogether."

"And so go on out to play tag with the asteroids," another voice suggested.

"That is what would happen if we did nothing about it. But there is a way we can stop that, if we can manage it." The Captain paused, aware that he had their absorbed attention. He continued:

"You must all be well aware from the peculiar behaviour of space as seen from our ports that we are now tumbling along all as—er—head over heels. This is due to the explosion of the port laterals. It is a highly unorthodox method of travelling, but it does mean that by an impulse from our main tubes given at exactly the critical moment we should be able to alter our course approximately as we require."

"And how much good is that going to do us if we can't land?" somebody wanted to know. The Captain ignored the interruption. He continued:

"I have been in touch by radio with both home and Mars, and have reported our state. I have also informed them that I intend to attempt the one possible course open to me. That is of using the main drive in an attempt to throw the ship into an orbit about Mars.

"If that is successful we shall avoid two dangers—that of shooting on towards the outer parts of the system, and of crashing on Mars. I think we have a good chance of bringing it off."

When he stopped speaking he saw alarm in several faces, thoughtful concentration in others. He noticed Mrs. Morgan holding tightly to her husband's hand, her face a little paler than usual. It was the man with the drawl who broke the silence.

"You *think* there is a good chance?" he repeated questioningly.

"I do. I also think it is the only chance. But I'm not going to try to fool you by pretending complete confidence. It's too serious for that."

"And if we do get into this orbit?"

"They will try to keep a radar fix on us, and send help as soon as possible."

"H'm," said the questioner. "And what do you personally think about that, Captain?"

"I—well, it isn't going to be easy. But we're all in this together, so I'll tell you just what they told me. At the very best we can't expect them to reach us for some months. The ship will have to come from Earth. The two planets are well past conjunction now. I'm afraid it's going to mean quite a wait."

"Can we hold out long enough, Captain?"

"According to my calculations we should be able to hold out for about seventeen or eighteen weeks."

"And that will be long enough?"

"It'll have to be."

He broke the thoughtful pause that followed by continuing in a brisker manner.

"This is not going to be comfortable, or pleasant. But, if we all play our parts, and keep strictly to the necessary measures, it can be done. Now, there are three essentials: air to breathe—well, luckily we shan't have to worry about that. The regeneration plant and stock of spare cylinders, and cylinders in cargo will look after that for a long time. Water will be rationed. Two pints each every twenty-four hours, for *everything*. Luckily we shall be able to draw water from the fuel tanks, or it would be a great deal less than that. The thing that is going to be our most serious worry is food."

He explained his proposals further, with patient clarity. At the end he added: "And now I expect you have some questions?"

A small, wiry man with a weather-beaten face asked:

"Is there no hope at all of getting the lateral tubes to work again?"

Captain Winters shook his head.

"Negligible. The impellent section of a ship is not constructed to be accessible in space. We shall keep on trying, of course, but even if the others could be made to fire, we should still be unable to repair the port laterals."

He did his best to answer the few more questions that followed in ways that held a balance between easy confidence and despondency. The prospect was by no means good. Before help could possibly reach them they were all going to need all the nerve and resolution they had—and out of sixteen persons some must be weaker than others.

His gaze rested again on Alice Morgan and her husband beside her. Her presence was certainly a possible source of trouble. When it came to the pinch the man would have more strain on account of her—and, most likely, fewer scruples.

Since the woman was here, she must share the consequences equally with the rest. There could be no privilege. In a sharp emergency one could afford a heroic gesture, but preferential treatment of any one person in the long ordeal which they must face would create an impossible situation. Make any allowances for her, and you would be called on to make allowances for others on health or other grounds—with heaven knew what complications to follow.

A fair chance with the rest was the best he could do for her—not, he felt, looking at her as she clutched her husband's hand and looked at him from wide eyes in a pale face, not a very good best.

He hoped she would not be the first to go under. It would be better for morale if she were not the very first…

—

SHE WAS NOT the first to go. For nearly three months nobody went.

The *Falcon,* by means of skilfully timed bursts on the main tubes, had succeeded in nudging herself into an orbital relationship with Mars. After that, there was little that the crew could do for her. At the distance of equilibrium she had become a very minor satellite, rolling and tumbling on her circular course, destined, so far as anyone could see, to continue this untidy progress until help reached them, or perhaps for ever…

Inboard, the complexity of her twisting somersaults was not perceptible unless one deliberately uncovered a port. If one did, the crazy cavortings of the universe outside produced such a sense of bewilderment that one gladly shut the cover again to preserve the illusion of stability within. Even Captain Winters and the Navigating Officer took their observations as swiftly as possible and were relieved when they had shut the whizzing constellations off the screen, and could take refuge in relativity.

# SURVIVAL

For all her occupants the *Falcon* had become a small, independent world, very sharply finite in space, and scarcely less so in time.

It was, moreover, a world with a very low standard of living; a community with short tempers, weakening distempers, aching bellies, and ragged nerves. It was a group in which each man watched on a trigger of suspicion for a hairsbreadth difference in the next man's ration, and where the little he ate so avidly was not enough to quiet the rumblings of his stomach. He was ravenous when he went to sleep; more ravenous when he woke from dreams of food.

Men who had started from Earth full-bodied were now gaunt and lean, their faces had hardened from curved contours into angled planes and changed their healthy colours for a grey pallor in which their eyes glittered unnaturally. They had all grown weaker. The weakest lay on their couches torpidly. The more fortunate looked at them from time to time with a question in their eyes. It was not difficult to read the question: "Why do we go on wasting good food on this guy? Looks like he's booked, anyway." But as yet no one had taken up that booking.

The situation was worse than Captain Winters had foreseen. There had been bad stowage. The cans in several cases of meat had collapsed under the terrific pressure of other cans above them during take-off. The resulting mess was now describing an orbit of its own around the ship. He had had to throw it out secretly. If the men had known of it, they would have eaten it gladly, maggots and all. Another case shown on his inventory had disappeared. He still did not know how. The ship had been searched for it without trace. Much of the emergency stores consisted of dehydrated foods for which he dared not spare sufficient water, so that though edible they were painfully unattractive. They had been intended simply as a supplement in case the estimated time was overrun, and were not extensive. Little in the cargo was edible, and that mostly small cans of luxuries. As a result, he had had to reduce the rations expected to stretch meagrely over seventeen weeks. And even so, they would not last that long.

The first who did go owed it neither to sickness nor malnutrition, but to accident.

—

JEVONS, THE CHIEF engineer, maintained that the only way to locate and correct the trouble with the laterals was to effect an entry into the propellent section of the ship. Owing to the tanks which backed up against the bulkhead separating the sections this could not be achieved from within the ship herself.

It had proved impossible with the tools available to cut a slice out of the hull; the temperature of space and the conductivity of the hull caused all their heat to run away and dissipate itself without making the least impression on the tough skin. The one way he could see of getting in was to cut away round the burnt-out tubes of the port laterals. It was debatable whether this was worth while since the other laterals would still be unbalanced on the port side, but where he found opposition solidly against him was in the matter of using precious oxygen to operate his cutters. He had to accept that ban, but he refused to relinquish his plan altogether.

"Very well," he said, grimly. "We're like rats in a trap, but Bowman and I aim to do more than just keep the trap going, and we're going to try, even if we have to cut our way into the damned ship by hand."

Captain Winters had okayed that; not that he believed that anything useful would come of it, but it would keep Jevons quiet, and do no one else any harm. So for weeks Jevons and Bowman had got into their spacesuits and worked their shifts. Oblivious after a time of the wheeling heavens about them, they kept doggedly on with their sawing and filing. Their progress, pitifully slow at best, had grown even slower as they became weaker.

Just what Bowman was attempting when he met his end still remained a mystery. He had not confided in Jevons. All that anyone knew about it was the sudden lurch of the ship and the clang of reverberations running up and down the hull. Possibly it was an accident. More likely he had become impatient and laid a small charge to blast an opening.

For the first time for weeks ports were uncovered and faces looked out giddily at the wheeling stars. Bowman came into sight. He was drifting inertly, a dozen yards or more outboard. His suit was deflated, and a large gash showed in the material of the left sleeve.

# SURVIVAL

The consciousness of a corpse floating round and round you like a minor moon is no improver of already lowered morale. Push it away, and it still circles, though at a greater distance. Some day a proper ceremony for the situation would be invented—perhaps a small rocket would launch the poor remains upon their last, infinite voyage. Meanwhile, lacking a precedent, Captain Winters decided to pay the body the decent respect of having it brought inboard. The refrigeration plant had to be kept going to preserve the small remaining stocks of food, but several sections of it were empty...

A day and a night by the clock had passed since the provisional interment of Bowman when a modest knock came on the control-room door. The Captain laid blotting-paper carefully over his latest entry in the log, and closed the book.

"Come in," he said.

The door opened just widely enough to admit Alice Morgan. She slipped in, and shut it behind her. He was somewhat surprised to see her. She had kept sedulously in the background, putting the few requests she had made through the intermediation of her husband. He noticed the changes in her. She was haggard now as they all were, and her eyes anxious. She was also nervous. The fingers of her thin hands sought one another and interlocked themselves for confidence. Clearly she was having to push herself to raise whatever was in her mind. He smiled in order to encourage her.

"Come and sit down, Mrs. Morgan," he invited, amiably.

She crossed the room with a slight clicking from her magnetic soles, and took the chair he indicated. She seated herself uneasily, and on the forward edge.

It had been sheer cruelty to bring her on this voyage, he reflected again. She had been at least a pretty little thing, now she was no longer that. Why couldn't that fool husband of hers have left her in her proper setting—a nice quiet suburb, a gentle routine, a life where she would be protected from exaction and alarm alike. It surprised him again that she had had the resolution and the stamina to survive conditions on the *Falcon* as long as this. Fate would probably have been kinder to her if it had disallowed that.

He spoke to her quietly, for she perched rather than sat, making him think of a bird ready to take off at any sudden movement.

"And what can I do for you, Mrs. Morgan?"

Alice's fingers twined and intertwined. She watched them doing it. She looked up, opened her mouth to speak, closed it again.

"It isn't very easy," she murmured apologetically.

Trying to help her, he said:

"No need to be nervous, Mrs. Morgan. Just tell me what's on your mind. Has one of them been—bothering you?"

She shook her head.

"Oh, no, Captain Winters. It's nothing like that at all."

"What is it, then?"

"It's—it's the rations, Captain. I'm not getting enough food."

The kindly concern froze out of his face.

"None of us is," he told her, shortly.

"I know," she said, hurriedly. "I know, but—"

"But what?" he inquired in a chill tone.

She drew a breath.

"There's the man who died yesterday. Bowman. I thought if I could have his rations—"

The sentence trailed away as she saw the expression on the Captain's face.

He was not acting. He was feeling just as shocked as he looked. Of all the impudent suggestions that ever had come his way, none had astounded him more. He gazed dumbfounded at the source of the outrageous proposition. Her eyes met his, but, oddly, with less timidity than before. There was no sign of shame in them.

"I've *got* to have more food," she said, intensely.

Captain Winters's anger mounted.

"So you thought you'd just snatch a dead man's share as well as your own! I'd better not tell you in words just where I class that suggestion, young woman. But you can understand this: we share, and we share equally. What Bowman's death means to us is that we can keep on having the same ration for a little longer—that, and only that. And now I think you had better go."

But Alice Morgan made no move to go. She sat there with her lips pressed together, her eyes a little narrowed, quite still save that her hands trembled.

# SURVIVAL

Even through his indignation the Captain felt surprise, as though he had watched a hearth cat suddenly become a hunter. She said stubbornly:

"I haven't asked for any privilege until now, Captain. I wouldn't ask you now if it weren't absolutely necessary. But that man's death gives us a margin now. And I *must* have more food."

The Captain controlled himself with an effort.

"Bowman's death has *not* given us a margin, or a windfall—all it has done is to extend by a day or two the chance of our survival. Do you think that every one of us doesn't ache just as much as you do for more food? In all my considerable experience of effrontery—"

She raised her thin hand to stop him. The hardness of her eyes made him wonder why he had ever thought her timid.

"Captain. Look at me!" she said, in a harsh tone.

He looked. Presently his expression of anger faded into shocked astonishment. A faint tinge of pink stole into her pale cheeks.

"Yes," she said. "You see, you've *got* to give me more food. My baby *must* have the chance to live."

The Captain continued to stare at her as if mesmerized. Presently he shut his eyes, and passed his hand over his brow.

"God in heaven. This is terrible," he murmured.

Alice Morgan said seriously, as if she had already considered that very point:

"No. It isn't terrible—not if my baby lives." He looked at her helplessly, without speaking. She went on:

"It wouldn't be robbing anyone, you see. Bowman doesn't need his rations any more—but my baby does. It's quite simple, really." She looked questioningly at the Captain. He had no comment ready. She continued: "So you couldn't call it unfair. After all, I'm two people now, really, aren't I? I *need* more food. If you don't let me have it you will be murdering my baby. So you *must*... *must*... My baby has *got* to live—he's got to..."

---

WHEN SHE HAD gone Captain Winters mopped his forehead, unlocked his private drawer, and took out one of his carefully hoarded bottles of whisky. He had the self-restraint to take only a small pull on the drinking-tube and then put it back. It revived him a little, but his eyes were still shocked and worried.

Would it not have been kinder in the end to tell the woman that her baby had no chance at all of being born? That would have been honest; but he doubted whether the coiner of the phrase about honesty being the best policy had known a great deal about group-morale. Had he told her that, it would have been impossible to avoid telling her why, and once she knew why it would have been impossible for her not to confide it, if only to her husband. And then it would be too late.

The Captain opened the top drawer, and regarded the pistol within. There was always that. He was tempted to take hold of it now and use it. There wasn't much use in playing the silly game out. Sooner or later it would have to come to that, anyway.

He frowned at it, hesitating. Then he put out his right hand and gave the thing a flip with his finger, sending it floating to the back of the drawer, out of sight. He closed the drawer. Not yet...

But perhaps he had better begin to carry it soon. So far, his authority had held. There had been nothing worse than safety-valve grumbling. But a time would come when he was going to need the pistol either for them or for himself.

If they should begin to suspect that the encouraging bulletins that he pinned up on the board from time to time were fakes: if they should somehow find out that the rescue ship which they believed to be hurtling through space towards them had not, in fact, even yet been able to take off from Earth—that was when hell would start breaking loose.

It might be safer if there were to be an accident with the radio equipment before long...

—

"TAKEN YOUR TIME, haven't you?" Captain Winters asked. He spoke shortly because he was irritable, not because it mattered in the least how long anyone took over anything now.

The Navigating Officer made no reply. His boots clicked across the floor. A key and an identity bracelet drifted towards the Captain, an inch or so above the surface of his desk. He put out a hand to check them.

"I—" he began. Then he caught sight of the other's face. "Good God, man, what's the matter with you?"

He felt some compunction. He wanted Bowman's identity bracelet for the record, but there had been no real need to send Carter for it. A man who had died Bowman's death would be a piteous sight. That was why they had left him still in his spacesuit instead of undressing him. All the same, he had thought that Carter was tougher stuff. He brought out a bottle. The last bottle.

"Better have a shot of this," he said.

The navigator did, and put his head in his hands. The Captain carefully rescued the bottle from its mid-air drift, and put it away. Presently the Navigating Officer said, without looking up:

"I'm sorry, sir."

"That's okay, Carter. Nasty job. Should have done it myself."

The other shuddered slightly. A minute passed in silence while he got a grip on himself. Then he looked up and met the Captain's eyes.

"It—it wasn't just that, sir."

The Captain looked puzzled.

"How do you mean?" he asked.

The officer's lips trembled. He did not form his words properly, and he stammered.

"Pull yourself together. What are you trying to say?" The Captain spoke sharply to stiffen him.

Carter jerked his head slightly. His lips stopped trembling.

"He—he—" he floundered; then he tried again, in a rush. "He—hasn't any legs, sir."

"Who? What *is* this? You mean Bowman hasn't any legs?"

"Y—yes, sir."

"Nonsense, man. I was there when he was brought in. So were you. He had legs, all right."

"Yes, sir. He did have legs then—but he hasn't now!"

The Captain sat very still. For some seconds there was no sound in the control-room but the clicking of the chronometer. Then he spoke with difficulty, getting no further than two words:

"You mean—?"

"What else could it be, sir?"

*"God in heaven!"* gasped the Captain.

He sat staring with eyes that had taken on the horror that lay in the other man's...

—

TWO MEN MOVED silently, with socks over their magnetic soles. They stopped opposite the door of one of the refrigeration compartments. One of them produced a slender key. He slipped it into the lock, felt delicately with it among the wards for a moment, and then turned it with a click. As the door swung open a pistol fired twice from within the refrigerator. The man who was pulling the door sagged at the knees, and hung in mid-air.

The other man was still behind the half-opened door. He snatched a pistol from his pocket and slid it swiftly round the corner of the door, pointing into the refrigerator. He pulled the trigger twice.

A figure in a spacesuit launched itself out of the refrigerator, sailing uncannily across the room. The other man shot at it as it swept past him. The spacesuited figure collided with the opposite wall, recoiled slightly, and hung there. Before it could turn and use the pistol in its hand, the other man fired again. The figure jerked, and floated back against the wall. The man kept his pistol trained, but the spacesuit swayed there, flaccid and inert.

The door by which the men had entered opened with a sudden clang. The Navigating Officer on the threshold did not hesitate. He fired slightly after the other, but he kept on firing...

When his pistol was empty the man in front of him swayed queerly, anchored by his boots; there was no other movement in him. The Navigating Officer put out a hand and steadied himself by the doorframe. Then, slowly and painfully, he made his way across to the figure in the spacesuit. There were gashes in the suit. He managed to unlock the helmet and pull it away.

The Captain's face looked somewhat greyer than undernourishment had made it. His eyes opened slowly. He said in a whisper:

"Your job now, Carter. Good luck!"

The Navigating Officer tried to answer, but there were no words, only a bubbling of blood in his throat. His hands relaxed. There was a dark stain still spreading on his uniform. Presently his body hung listlessly swaying beside his Captain's.

---

"I FIGURED THEY were going to last a lot longer than this," said the small man with the sandy moustache.

The man with the drawl looked at him steadily.

"Oh, you did, did you? And do you reckon your figuring's reliable?"

The smaller man shifted awkwardly. He ran the tip of his tongue along his lips.

"Well, there was Bowman. Then those four. Then the two that died. That's seven."

"Sure. That's seven. Well?' inquired the big man softly. He was not as big as he had been, but he still had a large frame. Under his intent regard the emaciated small man seemed to shrivel a little more.

"Er—nothing. Maybe my figuring was kind of hopeful," he said.

"Maybe. My advice to you is to quit figuring and keep on hoping. Huh?"

The small man wilted. "Er—yes. I guess so."

The big man looked round the living-room, counting heads.

"Okay. Let's start," he said.

A silence fell on the rest. They gazed at him with uneasy fascination. They fidgeted. One or two nibbled at their fingernails. The big man leaned forward. He put a space-helmet, inverted, on the table. In his customary leisurely fashion he said:

"We shall draw for it. Each of us will take a paper and hold it up unopened until I give the word. *Un*opened. Got that?"

They nodded. Every eye was fixed intently upon his face.

"Good. Now one of those pieces of paper in the helmet is marked with a cross. Ray, I want you to count the pieces there and make sure that there are nine—"

"Eight!" said Alice Morgan's voice sharply.

All the heads turned towards her as if pulled by strings. The faces looked startled, as though the owners might have heard a turtle-dove roar. Alice sat embarrassed under the combined gaze, but she held herself steady and her mouth was set in a straight line. The man in charge of the proceedings studied her.

"Well, well," he drawled. "So you don't want to take a hand in our little game!"

"No," said Alice.

"You've shared equally with us so far—but now we have reached this regrettable stage you don't want to?"

"No," agreed Alice again.

He raised his eyebrows.

"You are appealing to our chivalry, perhaps?"

"No," said Alice once more. "I'm denying the equity of what you call your game. The one who draws the cross dies—isn't that the plan?"

"*Pro bono publico*," said the big man. "Deplorable, of course, but unfortunately necessary."

"But if *I* draw it, two must die. Do you call that equitable?" Alice asked.

The group looked taken aback. Alice waited.

The big man fumbled it. For once he was at a loss.

"Well," said Alice, "isn't that so?"

One of the others broke the silence to observe: "The question of the exact stage when the personality, the soul of the individual, takes form is still highly debatable. Some have held that until there is separate existence—"

The drawling voice of the big man cut him short. "I think we can leave that point to the theologians, Sam. This is more in the Wisdom of Solomon class. The point would seem to be that Mrs. Morgan claims exemption on account of her condition."

"My baby has a right to live," Alice said doggedly.

"We all have a right to live. We all want to live," someone put in.

"Why should you—?" another began; but the drawling voice dominated again.

"Very well, gentlemen. Let us be formal. Let us be democratic. We will vote on it. The question is put: do you consider Mrs. Morgan's claim to be valid—or should she take her chance with the rest of us? Those in—"

"Just a minute," said Alice, in a firmer voice than any of them had heard her use. "Before you start voting on that you'd better listen to me a bit." She looked round, making sure she had the attention of all of them. She had; and their astonishment as well.

"Now the first thing is that I am a lot more important than any of you," she told them simply. "No, you needn't smile. I am—and I'll tell you why.

"Before the radio broke down—"

"Before the Captain wrecked it, you mean," someone corrected her.

"Well, before it became useless," she compromised. "Captain Winters was in regular touch with home. He gave them news of us. The news that the Press wanted most was about me. Women, particularly women in unusual situations, are always news. He told me I was in the headlines: GIRL-WIFE IN DOOM ROCKET, WOMAN'S SPACE WRECK ORDEAL, that sort of thing. And if you haven't forgotten how newspapers look, you can imagine the leads, too: 'Trapped in their living space tomb, a girl and fifteen men now wheel helplessly around the planet Mars...'

"All of you are just men—hulks, like the ship, I am a woman, therefore my position is romantic, so I am young, glamorous, beautiful..." Her thin face showed for a moment the trace of a wry smile. "I am a heroine..."

She paused, letting the idea sink in. Then she went on:

"I was a heroine even before Captain Winters told them that I was pregnant. But after that I became a phenomenon. There were demands for interviews, I wrote one, and Captain Winters transmitted it for me. There have been interviews with my parents and my friends, anyone who knew me. And now an enormous number of people know a great deal about me. They are intensely interested in me. They are even more interested in my baby—which is likely to be the first baby ever born in a spaceship...

"Now do you begin to see? You have a fine tale ready. Bowman, my husband, Captain Winters, and the rest were heroically struggling to repair the port laterals. There was an explosion. It blew them all away out into space.

"You may get away with that. But if there is no trace of me and my baby—or of our bodies—*then* what are you going to say? How will you explain that?"

She looked round the faces again.

"Well, what *are* you going to say? That I, too, was outside repairing the port laterals? That I committed suicide by shooting myself out into space with a rocket?

"Just think it over. The whole world's press is wanting to know about me—with all the details. It'll have to be a mighty good story to stand up to that. And if it doesn't stand up—well, the rescue won't have done you much good.

"You'll not have a chance in hell. You'll hang, or you'll fry, every one of you—unless it happens they lynch you first..."

There was silence in the room as she finished speaking. Most of the faces showed the astonishment of men ferociously attacked by a Pekinese, and at a loss for suitable comment.

The big man sat sunk in reflection for a minute or more. Then he looked up, rubbing the stubble on his sharp-boned chin thoughtfully. He glanced round the others and then let his eyes rest on Alice. For a moment there was a twitch at the corner of his mouth.

"Madam," he drawled, "you are probably a great loss to the legal profession." He turned away. "We shall have to reconsider this matter before our next meeting. But, for the present, Ray, *eight* pieces of paper as the lady said..."

—

"IT'S HER." SAID the Second, over the Skipper's shoulder.

The Skipper moved irritably. "Of course it's her. What else'd you expect to find whirling through space like a sozzled owl?" He studied the screen for a moment. "Not a sign. Every port covered."

"Do you think there's a chance, Skipper?"

"What, after all this time! No, Tommy, not a ghost of it. We're—just the morticians, I guess."

"How'll we get aboard her, Skip?"

The Skipper watched the gyrations of the *Falcon* with a calculating eye.

"Well, there aren't any rules, but I reckon if we can get a cable on her we *might* be able to play her gently, like a big fish. It'll be tricky, though."

Tricky, it was. Five times the magnet projected from the rescue ship failed to make contact. The sixth attempt was better judged. When the magnet drifted close to the *Falcon* the current was switched on for a moment. It changed course, and floated nearer to the ship. When it was almost in contact the switch went over again. It darted forward, and glued itself limpet-like to the hull.

Then followed the long game of playing the *Falcon;* of keeping tension on the cable between the two ships, but not too much tension, and of holding the rescue ship from being herself thrown into a roll by the pull. Three times the cable parted, but at last, after weary hours of adroit manoeuvre by the rescue ship the derelict's motion had been reduced to a slow twist. There was still no trace of life aboard. The rescue ship closed a little.

The Captain, the Third Officer, and the doctor fastened on their spacesuits and went outboard. They made their way forward to the winch. The Captain looped a short length of line over the cable, and fastened both ends of it to his belt. He laid hold of the cable with both hands, and with a heave sent himself skimming into space. The others followed him along the guiding cable.

They gathered beside the *Falcon*'s entrance port. The Third Officer took a crank from his satchel. He inserted it in an opening, and began to turn until he was satisfied that the inner door of the airlock was closed. When it would turn no more, he withdrew it, and fitted it into the next opening; that should set the motors pumping air out of the lock—if there were air, and if there were still current to work the motors. The Captain held a microphone against the hull, and listened. He caught a humming.

"Okay. They're running," he said.

He waited until the humming stopped.

"Right. Open her up," he directed.

The Third Officer inserted his crank again, and wound it. The main port opened inwards, leaving a dark gap in the shining hull. The three looked at the opening sombrely for some seconds. With a grim quietness the Captain's voice said: "Well. Here we go!"

They moved carefully and slowly into the blackness, listening.
The Third Officer's voice murmured:

*"The silence that is in the starry sky,*
*The sleep that is among the lonely hills..."*

Presently the Captain's voice asked:
"How's the air, Doc?"
The doctor looked at his gauges.
"It's okay," he said, in some surprise. "Pressure's about six ounces down, that's all." He began to unfasten his helmet. The others copied him. The Captain made a face as he took his off.
"The place stinks," he said, uneasily. "Let's—get on with it."
He led the way towards the lounge. They entered it apprehensively.
The scene was uncanny and bewildering. Though the gyrations of the *Falcon* had been reduced, every loose object in her continued to circle until it met a solid obstruction and bounced off it upon a new course. The result was a medley of wayward items churning slowly hither and thither.
"Nobody here, anyway," said the Captain, practically. "Doc, do you think—?"
He broke off at the sight of the doctor's strange expression. He followed the line of the other's gaze. The doctor was looking at the drifting flotsam of the place. Among the flow of books, cans, playing-cards, boots, and miscellaneous rubbish, his attention was riveted upon a bone. It was large and clean and had been cracked open.
The Captain nudged him. "What's the matter, Doc?"
The doctor turned unseeing eyes upon him for a moment, and then looked back at the drifting bone.
"That"—he said in an unsteady voice—"that, Skipper, is a human femur."
In the long moment that followed while they stared at the grisly relic the silence which had lain over the *Falcon* was broken. The sound of a voice rose, thin, uncertain, but perfectly clear. The three looked incredulously at one another as they listened:

# SURVIVAL

*"Rock-a-bye baby*
*On the tree top*
*When the wind blows*
*The cradle will rock…"*

Alice sat on the side of her bunk, swaying a little, and holding her baby to her. It smiled, and reached up one miniature hand to pat her cheek as she sang:

*"…When the bough breaks*
*The cradle will fall.*
*Down will—"*

Her song cut off suddenly at the click of the opening door. For a moment she stared as blankly at the three figures in the opening as they at her. Her face was a mask with harsh lines drawn from the points where the skin was stretched tightly over the bones. Then a trace of expression came over it. Her eyes brightened. Her lips curved in a travesty of a smile.

She loosed her arms from about the baby, and it hung there in mid-air, chuckling a little to itself. She slid her right hand under the pillow of the bunk, and drew it out again, holding a pistol.

The black shape of the pistol looked enormous in her transparently thin hand as she pointed it at the men who stood transfixed in the doorway.

"Look, baby," she said. "Look there! Food! Lovely food…"

# CHINESE PUZZLE

—

THE PARCEL, WAITING provocatively on the dresser, was the first thing that Hwyl noticed when he got in from work.

"From Dai, is it?" he inquired of his wife.

"Yes, indeed. Japanese the stamps are," she told him.

He went across to examine it: it was the shape a small hatbox might be, about ten inches each way, perhaps. The address: Mr. & Mrs. Hwyl Hughes, Ty Derwen, Llynllawn, Llangolwgcoch, Brecknockshire, S. Wales, was lettered carefully, for the clear understanding of foreigners. The other label, also hand-lettered, but in red, was quite clear, too. It said: Eggs—fragile—With great care.

"There is funny to send eggs so far," Hwyl said. "Plenty of eggs we are having. Might be chocolate eggs, I think?"

"Come you to your tea, man," Bronwen told him. "All day I have been looking at that old parcel, and a little longer it can wait now."

Hwyl sat down at the table and began his meal. From time to time, however, his eyes strayed again to the parcel.

"If it is real eggs they are, careful you should be," he remarked. "Reading in a book I was once how in China they keep eggs for years. Bury them in the earth, they do, for a delicacy. There is strange for you, now. Queer they are in China, and not like Wales, at all."

303

Bronwen contented herself with saying that perhaps Japan was not like China, either.

When the meal had been finished and cleared, the parcel was transferred to the table. Hwyl snipped the string and pulled off the brown paper. Within was a tin box which, when the sticky tape holding its lid had been removed, proved to be full to the brim with sawdust. Mrs. Hughes fetched a sheet of newspaper, and prudently covered the table-top. Hwyl dug his fingers into the sawdust.

"Something there, there is," he announced.

"There is stupid you are. Of course there is something there," Bronwen said, slapping his hand out of the way.

She trickled some of the sawdust out on to the newspaper, and then felt inside the box herself. Whatever it was, it felt much too large for an egg. She poured out more sawdust and felt again. This time, her fingers encountered a piece of paper. She pulled it out and laid it on the table; a letter in Dafydd's handwriting. Then she put in her hand once more, got her fingers under the object, and lifted it gently out.

"Well, indeed! Look at that now! Did you ever?" she exclaimed. "Eggs, he was saying, is it?"

They both regarded it with astonishment for some moments.

"So big it is. Queer, too," said Hwyl, at last.

"What kind of bird to lay such an egg?" said Bronwen.

"Ostrich, perhaps?" suggested Hwyl.

But Bronwen shook her head. She had once seen an ostrich's egg in a museum, and remembered it well enough to know that it had little in common with this. The ostrich's egg had been a little smaller, with a dull, sallow-looking, slightly-dimpled surface. This was smooth and shiny, and by no means had the same dead look: it had a lustre to it, a nacreous kind of beauty.

"A pearl, could it be?" she said, in an awed voice.

"There is silly you are," said her husband. "From an oyster as big as Llangolwgcoch Town Hall, you are thinking?"

He burrowed into the tin again, but "Eggs," it seemed, had been a manner of speaking: there was no other, nor room for one.

Bronwen put some of the sawdust into one of her best vegetable-dishes, and bedded the egg carefully on top of it. Then they sat down to read their son's letter:

*S.S. Tudor Maid,*
*Kobe.*

*Dear Mam and Dad,*
   *I expect you will be surprised about the enclosed I was too. It is a funny looking thing I expect they have funny birds in China after all they have Pandas so why not. We found a small sampan about a hundred miles off the China coast that had bust its mast and should never have tried and all except two of them were dead they are all dead now. But one of them that wasn't dead then was holding this egg-thing all wrapped up in a padded coat like it was a baby only I didn't know it was an egg then not till later. One of them died coming aboard but this other one lasted two days longer in spite of all I could do for him which was my best. I was sorry nobody here can speak Chinese because he was a nice little chap and lonely and knew he was a goner but there it is. And when he saw it was nearly all up he gave me this egg and talked very faint but I'd not have understood anyway. All I could do was take it and hold it careful the way he had and tell him I'd look after it which he couldn't understand either. Then he said something else and looked very worried and died poor chap.*
   *So here it is. I know it is an egg because I took him a boiled egg once he pointed to both of them to show me but nobody on board knows what kind of egg. But seeing I promised him I'd keep it safe I am sending it to you to keep for me as this ship is no place to keep anything safe anyway and hope it doesn't get cracked on the way too.*
   *Hoping this finds you as it leaves me and love to all and you special.*
                                                                                                    *Dai.*

"Well, there is strange for you, now," said Mrs. Hughes, as she finished reading. "And *looking* like an egg it is, indeed—the shape of it," she conceded.

"But the colours are not. There is pretty they are. Like you see when oil is on the road in the rain. But never an egg like that have I seen in my life. Flat the colour is on eggs, and not to shine."

Hwyl went on looking at it thoughtfully.

"Yes. There is beautiful," he agreed, "but what use?"

"Use, is it, indeed!" said his wife. "A trust, it is, and sacred, too. Dying the poor man was, and our Dai gave him his word. I am thinking of how we will keep it safe for him till he will be back, now."

They both contemplated the egg awhile.

"Very far away, China is," Bronwen remarked, obscurely.

—

SEVERAL DAYS PASSED, however, before the egg was removed from display on the dresser. Word quickly went round the valley about it, and the callers would have felt slighted had they been unable to see it. Bronwen felt that continually getting it out and putting it away again would be more hazardous than leaving it on exhibition.

Almost everyone found the sight of it rewarding. Idris Bowen who lived three houses away was practically alone in his divergent view.

"The shape of an egg, it has," he allowed. "But careful you should be, Mrs. Hughes. A fertility symbol it is, I am thinking, and stolen, too, likely."

"Mr. Bowen—" began Bronwen, indignantly.

"Oh, by the men in that boat, Mrs. Hughes. Refugees from China they would be, see. Traitors to the Chinese people. And running away with all they could carry, before the glorious army of the workers and peasants could catch them, too. Always the same, it is, as you will be seeing when the revolution comes to Wales."

"Oh, dear, dear! There is funny you are, Mr. Bowen. Propaganda you will make out of an old boot, I think," said Bronwen.

Idris Bowen frowned.

"Funny, I am not, Mrs. Hughes. And propaganda there is in an honest boot, too," he told her as he left with dignity.

By the end of a week practically everyone in the village had seen the egg and been told no, Mrs. Hughes did not know what kind of a creature had laid it, and the time seemed to have come to store it away safely against Dafydd's return. There were not many places in the house where she could feel sure that it would rest undisturbed, but, on consideration, the airing-cupboard seemed as likely as any, so she put it back on what sawdust was left in the tin, and stowed it in there.

It remained there for a month, out of sight, and pretty much out of mind until a day when Hwyl returning from work discovered his wife sitting at the table with a disconsolate expression on her face, and a bandage on her finger. She looked relieved to see him.

"Hatched, it is," she observed.

The blankness of Hwyl's expression was irritating to one who had had a single subject on her mind all day.

"Dai's egg," she explained. "Hatched out, it is, I am telling you."

"Well, there is a thing for you, now!" said Hwyl. "A nice little chicken, is it?"

"A chicken it is not, at all. A monster, indeed, and biting me it is, too." She held out her bandaged finger.

She explained that this morning she had gone to the airing-cupboard to take out a clean towel, and as she put her hand in, something had nipped her finger, painfully. At first she had thought that it might be a rat that had somehow got in from the yard, but then she had noticed that the lid was off the tin, and the shell of the egg there was all broken to pieces.

"How is it to see?" Hwyl asked.

Bronwen admitted that she had not seen it well. She had had a glimpse of a long, greeny-blue tail protruding from behind a pile of sheets, and then it had looked at her over the top of them, glaring at her from red eyes. On that, it had seemed to her more the kind of a job a man should deal with, so she had slammed the door, and gone to bandage her finger.

"Still there, then, is it?" said Hwyl.

She nodded.

"Right now. Have a look at it, we will, now then," he said, decisively.

He started to leave the room, but on second thoughts turned back to collect a pair of heavy working-gloves. Bronwen did not offer to accompany him.

Presently there was a scuffle of his feet, an exclamation or two, then his tread descending the stairs. He came in, shutting the door behind him with his foot. He set the creature he was carrying down on the table, and for some seconds it crouched there, blinking, but otherwise unmoving.

"Scared, he was, I think," Hwyl remarked.

In the body, the creature bore some resemblance to a lizard—a large lizard, over a foot long. The scales of its skin, however, were much bigger, and some of them curled up and stood out here and there, in a fin-like manner. And the head was quite unlike a lizard's, being much rounder, with a wide mouth, broad nostrils, and, overall, a slightly pushed-in effect, in which were set a pair of goggling red eyes. About the neck, and also making a kind of mane, were curious, streamer-like attachments with the suggestion of locks of hair which had permanently cohered. The colour was mainly green, shot with blue, and having a metallic shine to it, but there were brilliant red markings about the head and in the lower parts of the locks. There were touches of red, too, where the legs joined the body, and on the feet, where the toes finished in sharp yellow claws. Altogether, a surprisingly vivid and exotic creature.

It eyed Bronwen Hughes for a moment, turned a baleful look on Hwyl, and then started to run about the table-top, looking for a way off. The Hugheses watched it for a moment or two, and then regarded one another.

"Well, there is nasty for you, indeed," observed Bronwen.

"Nasty it may be. But beautiful it is, too, look," said Hwyl.

"Ugly old face to have," Bronwen remarked.

"Yes, indeed. But fine colours, too, see. Glorious, they are, like technicolor, I am thinking," Hwyl said.

The creature appeared to have half a mind to leap from the table. Hwyl leaned forward and caught hold of it. It wriggled, and tried to get its head round to bite him, but discovered he was holding it too near the neck for that. It paused in its struggles. Then, suddenly, it snorted. Hwyl dropped it abruptly, partly from alarm, but more from surprise. Bronwen gave a squeal, and climbed hastily on to her chair.

The creature itself seemed a trifle astonished. For a few seconds it stood turning its head and waving the sinuous tail that was quite as long as its body. Then it scuttled across to the hearthrug, and curled itself up in front of the fire.

"By dammo! There was a thing for you!" Hwyl exclaimed, regarding it a trifle nervously. "Fire there was with it, I think. I will like to understand that, now."

"Fire indeed, and smoke, too," Bronwen agreed. "There is shocking it was, and not natural, at all."

She looked uncertainly at the creature. It had so obviously settled itself for a nap that she risked stepping down from the chair, but she kept on watching it, ready to jump again if it should move. Then:

"Never did I think I will see one of those. And not sure it is right to have in the house, either," she said.

"What is it you are meaning, now?" Hwyl asked, puzzled.

"Why, a dragon, indeed," Bronwen told him.

Hwyl stared at her.

"Dragon!" he exclaimed. "There is foolish—" Then he stopped. He looked at it again, and then down at the place where the flame had scorched his glove. "No, by dammo!" he said. "Right, you. A dragon it is, I believe."

They both regarded it with some apprehension.

"Glad, I am, not to live in China," observed Bronwen.

―

THOSE WHO WERE privileged to see the creature during the next day or two supported almost to a man the theory that it was a dragon. This, they established by poking sticks through the wire-netting of the hutch that Hwyl had made for it until it obliged with a resentful huff of flame. Even Mr. Jones, the Chapel, did not doubt its authenticity, though on the propriety of its presence in his community he preferred to reserve judgement for the present.

After a short time, however, Bronwen Hughes put an end to the practice of poking it. For one thing, she felt responsible to Dai for its well-being; for another, it was beginning to develop an irritable disposition, and a liability to emit flame without cause; for yet another, and although Mr. Jones's decision on whether it could be considered as one of God's creatures or not was still pending, she felt that in the meantime it deserved equal rights with other dumb animals. So she put a card on the hutch saying: PLEASE NOT TO TEASE, and most of the time was there to see that it was heeded.

Almost all Llynllawn, and quite a few people from Llangolwgcoch, too, came to see it. Sometimes they would stand for an hour or more, hoping to see it huff. If it did, they went off satisfied that it was a dragon; but if it maintained a contented, non-fire-breathing mood, they went and told their friends that it was really no more than a little old lizard, though big, mind you.

Idris Bowen was an exception to both categories. It was not until his third visit that he was privileged to see it snort, but even then he remained unconvinced.

"Unusual, it is, yes," he admitted. "But a dragon it is not. Look you at the dragon of Wales, or the dragon of St. George, now. To huff fire is something, I grant you, but wings, too, a dragon must be having, or a dragon he is not."

But that was the kind of cavilling that could be expected from Idris, and disregarded.

After ten days or so of crowded evenings, however, interest slackened. Once one had seen the dragon and exclaimed over the brilliance of its colouring, there was little to add, beyond being glad that it was in the Hugheses house rather than one's own, and wondering how big it would eventually grow. For, really, it did not do much but sit and blink, and perhaps give a little huff of flame if you were lucky. So, presently, the Hugheses home became more their own again.

And, no longer pestered by visitors, the dragon showed an equable disposition. It never huffed at Bronwen, and seldom at Hwyl. Bronwen's first feeling of antagonism passed quickly, and she found herself growing attached to it. She fed it, and looked after it, and found that on a diet consisting chiefly of minced horseflesh and dog-biscuits it grew with astonishing speed. Most of the time, she let it run free in the room. To quieten the misgivings of callers she would explain:

"Friendly, he is, and pretty ways he has with him, if there is not teasing. Sorry for him, I am, too, for bad it is to be an only child, and an orphan worse still. And less than an orphan, he is, see. Nothing of his own sort he is knowing, nor likely, either. So very lonely he is being, poor thing, I think."

But, inevitably, there came an evening when Hwyl, looking thoughtfully at the dragon, remarked:

# CHINESE PUZZLE

"Outside you, son. There is too big for the house you are getting, see."

Bronwen was surprised to find how unwilling she felt about that.

"Very good and quiet, he is," she said, "There is clever he is to tuck his tail away not to trip people, too. And clean with the house he is, also, and no trouble. Always out to the yard at proper times. Right as clockwork."

"Behaving well, he is, indeed," Hwyl agreed. "But growing so fast, now. More room he will be needing, see. A fine hutch for him in the yard, and with a run to it, I think."

The advisability of that was demonstrated a week later when Bronwen came down one morning to find the end of the wooden hutch charred away, the carpet and rug smouldering, and the dragon comfortably curled up in Hwyl's easy chair.

"Settled, it is, and lucky indeed not to burn in our bed. Out you," Hwyl told the dragon. "A fine thing to burn a man's house for him, and not grateful, either. For shame, I am telling you."

The insurance man who came to inspect the damage thought similarly.

"Notified, you should have," he told Bronwen. "A fire-risk, he is, you see."

Bronwen protested that the policy made no mention of dragons.

"No, indeed," the man admitted, "but a normal hazard he is not, either. Inquire, I will, from Head Office how it is, see. But better to turn him out before more trouble, and thankful, too."

So, a couple of days later, the dragon was occupying a larger hutch, constructed of asbestos sheets, in the yard. There was a wire-netted run in front of it, but most of the time Bronwen locked the gate, and left the back-door of the house open so that he could come and go as he liked. In the morning he would trot in, and help Bronwen by huffing the kitchen fire into a blaze, but apart from that he had learnt not to huff in the house. The only times he was any bother to anyone were the occasions when he set his straw on fire in the night so that the neighbours got up to see if the house was burning, and were somewhat short about it the next day.

Hwyl kept a careful account of the cost of feeding him, and hoped that it was not running into more than Dai would be willing to pay. Otherwise, his only worries were his failure to find a cheap, non-inflammable bedding-stuff, and speculation on how big the dragon was likely to grow before Dai should return to take him off his hands. Very likely all would have gone smoothly until that happened, but for the unpleasantness with Idris Bowen.

The trouble which blew up unexpectedly one evening was really of Idris's own finding. Hwyl had finished his meal, and was peacefully enjoying the last of the day beside his door, when Idris happened along, leading his whippet on a string.

"Oh, hullo you, Idris," Hwyl greeted him, amiably.

"Hullo you, Hwyl," said Idris. "And how is that phoney dragon of yours, now then?"

"Phoney, is it, you are saying?" repeated Hwyl indignantly.

"Wings, a dragon is wanting, to be a dragon," Idris insisted, firmly.

"Wings to hell, man! Come you and look at him now then, and please to tell me what he is if he is no dragon."

He waved Idris into the house, and led him through into the yard. The dragon, reclining in its wired run, opened an eye at them, and closed it again.

Idris had not seen it since it was lately out of the egg. Its growth impressed him.

"There is big he is now," he conceded. "Fine the colours of him, and fancy, too. But still no wings to him; so a dragon he is not."

"What then is it he is?" demanded Hwyl. "Tell me that."

How Idris would have replied to this difficult question was never to be known, for at that moment the whippet jerked its string free from his fingers, and dashed, barking, at the wire-netting. The dragon was startled out of its snooze. It sat up suddenly, and snorted with surprise. There was a yelp from the whippet which bounded into the air, and then set off round and round the yard, howling. At last Idris managed to corner it and pick it up. All down the right side its hair had been scorched off, making it look very peculiar. Idris's eyebrows lowered.

"Trouble you want, is it? And trouble you will be having, by God!" he said.

He put the whippet down again, and began to take off his coat.

It was not clear whether he had addressed, and meant to fight, Hwyl or the dragon, but either intention was forestalled by Mrs. Hughes coming to investigate the yelping.

"Oh! Teasing the dragon, is it!" she said. "There is shameful, indeed. A lamb the dragon is, as people know well. But not to tease. It is wicked you are, Idris Bowen, and to fight does not make right, either. Go you from here, now then."

Idris began to protest, but Bronwen shook her head and set her mouth.

"Not listening to you, I am, see. A fine brave man, to tease a helpless dragon. Not for weeks now has the dragon huffed. So you go, and quick."

Idris glowered. He hesitated, and pulled on his jacket again. He collected his whippet, and held it in his arms. After a final disparaging glance at the dragon, he turned.

"Law I will have of you," he announced ominously, as he left.

---

NOTHING MORE, HOWEVER, was heard of legal action. It seemed as if Idris had either changed his mind or been advised against it, and that the whole thing would blow over. But three weeks later was the night of the Union Branch Meeting.

It had been a dull meeting, devoted chiefly to passing a number of resolutions suggested to it by its headquarters, as a matter of course. Then, just at the end, when there did not seem to be any other business, Idris Bowen rose.

"Stay you!" said the chairman to those who were preparing to leave, and he invited Idris to speak.

Idris waited for persons who were half-in and half-out of their overcoats to subside, then:

"Comrades—" he began.

There was immediate uproar. Through the mingled approbation and cries of "Order" and "Withdraw" the chairman smote energetically with his gavel until quiet was restored.

"Tendentious, that is," he reproved Idris. "Please to speak half-way, and in good order."

Idris began again:

"Fellow-workers. Sorry indeed, I am, to have to tell you of a discovery I am making. A matter of disloyalty, I am telling you: grave disloyalty to good friends and com—and fellow workers, see." He paused, and went on:

"Now, every one of you is knowing of Hwyl Hughes's dragon, is it? Seen him for yourselves you have likely, too. Seen him myself, I have, and saying he was no dragon. But now then, I am telling you, wrong I was, wrong, indeed. A dragon he is, and not to doubt, though no wings.

"I am reading in the Encyclopædia in Merthyr Public Library about two kinds of dragons, see. Wings the European dragon has, indeed. But wings the Oriental dragon has not. So apologizing now to Mr. Hughes, I am, and sorry."

A certain restiveness becoming apparent in the audience was quelled by a change in his tone.

"*But*—" he went on, "but another thing, too, I am reading there, and troubled inside myself with it, I am. I will tell you. Have you looked at the feet of this dragon, is it? Claws there is, yes, and nasty, too. But how many, I am asking you? And five, I am telling you. Five with each foot." He paused dramatically, and shook his head. "Bad, is that, bad, indeed. For, look you, Chinese a five-toed dragon is, yes—but five-toed is not a Republican dragon, five-toed is not a People's dragon; five-toed is an *Imperial* dragon, see. A symbol, it is, of the oppression of Chinese workers and peasants. And shocking to think that in our village we are keeping such an emblem. What is it that the free people of China will be saying of Llynllawn when they will hear of this, I am asking? What is it Mao Tse Tung, a glorious leader of the heroic Chinese people in their magnificent fight for peace, will be thinking of South Wales and this imperialist dragon—?" he was continuing, when difference of view in the audience submerged his voice.

Again the chairman called the meeting to order. He offered Hwyl the opportunity to reply, and after the situation had been briefly explained, the dragon was, on a show of hands, acquitted of political implication by all but Idris's doctrinaire faction, and the meeting broke up.

Hwyl told Bronwen about it when he got home.

"No surprise there," she said. "Jones the Post is telling me, telegraphing Idris has been."

"Telegraphing?" inquired Hwyl.

"Yes, indeed. Asking the *Daily Worker,* in London, how is the party-line on Imperialist dragons, he was. But no answer yet, though."

# CHINESE PUZZLE

A FEW MORNINGS later the Hugheses were awakened by a hammering on their door. Hwyl went to the window and found Idris below. He asked what the matter was.

"Come you down here, and I will show you," Idris told him.

After some argument, Hwyl descended. Idris led the way round to the back of his own house, and pointed.

"Look you there, now," he said.

The door of Idris's henhouse was hanging by one hinge. The remains of two chickens lay close by. A large quantity of feathers was blowing about the yard.

Hwyl looked at the henhouse more closely. Several deep-raked scores stood out white on the creosoted wood. In other places there were darker smears where the wood seemed to have been scorched. Silently Idris pointed to the ground. There were marks of sharp claws, but no imprint of a whole foot.

"There is bad. Foxes is it?" inquired Hwyl.

Idris choked slightly.

"Foxes, you are saying. Foxes, indeed! What will it be but your dragon? And the police to know it, too."

Hwyl shook his head.

"No," he said.

"Oh," said Idris. "A liar, I am, is it? I will have the guts from you, Hwyl Hughes, smoking hot, too, and glad to do it."

"You talk too easy, man," Hwyl told him. "Only how the dragon is still fast in his hutch, I am saying. Come you now, and see."

They went back to Hwyl's house. The dragon was in the hutch, sure enough, and the door of it was fastened with a peg. Furthermore, as Hwyl pointed out, even if he had left it during the night, he could not have reached Idris's yard without leaving scratches and traces on the way, and there were none to be found.

They finally parted in a state of armistice. Idris was by no means convinced, but he was unable to get round the facts, and not at all impressed with

Hwyl's suggestion that a practical joker could have produced the effect on the henhouse with a strong nail and a blow-torch.

Hwyl went again upstairs to finish dressing.

"There is funny it is, all the same," he observed to Bronwen. "Not seeing, that Idris was, but scorched the peg is, on the *outside* of the hutch. And how should that be, I wonder?"

"Huffed four times in the night the dragon has, five, perhaps," Bronwen said. "Growing, he is, too, and banging that old hutch about. Never have I heard him like that before."

"There is queer," Hwyl said, frowning. "But never out of his hutch, and that to swear to."

Two nights later Hwyl was awakened by Bronwen shaking his shoulder.

"Listen, now then," she told him.

"Huffing, he is, see," said Bronwen, unnecessarily.

There was a crash of something thrown with force, and the sound of a neighbour's voice cursing. Hwyl reluctantly decided that he had better get up and investigate.

Everything in the yard looked as usual, except for the presence of a large tin-can which was clearly the object thrown. There was, however, a strong smell of burning, and a thudding noise, recognizable as the sound of the dragon tramping round and round in his hutch to stamp out the bedding caught alight again. Hwyl went across and opened the door. He raked out the smouldering straw, fetched some fresh, and threw it in.

"Quiet, you," he told the dragon. "More of this, and the hide I will have off you, slow and painful, too. Bed, now then, and sleep."

He went back to bed himself, but it seemed as if he had only just laid his head on the pillow when it was daylight, and there was Idris Bowen hammering on the front door again.

Idris was more than a little incoherent, but Hwyl gathered that something further had taken place at his house, so he slipped on jacket and trousers, and went down. Idris led the way down beside his own house, and threw open the yard door with the air of a conjuror. Hwyl stared for some moments without speaking.

In front of Idris's henhouse stood a kind of trap, roughly contrived of angle-iron and wire-netting. In it, surrounded by chicken feathers, and glaring at them from eyes like live topazes, sat a creature, blood-red all over.

"Now, there is a dragon for you, indeed," Idris said. "Not to have colours like you see on a merry-go-round at a circus, either. A serious dragon, that one, and proper—wings, too, see?"

Hwyl went on looking at the dragon without a word. The wings were folded at present, and the cage did not give room to stretch them. The red, he saw now, was darker on the back, and brighter beneath, giving it the rather ominous effect of being lit from below by a blast-furnace. It certainly had a more practical aspect than his own dragon, and a fiercer look about it, altogether. He stepped forward to examine it more closely.

"Careful, man," Idris warned him, laying a hand on his arm.

The dragon curled back its lips, and snorted. Twin flames a yard long shot out of its nostrils. It was a far better huff than the other dragon had ever achieved. The air was filled with a strong smell of burnt feathers.

"A fine dragon, that is," Idris said again. "A real Welsh dragon for you. Angry he is, see, and no wonder. A shocking thing for an imperialist dragon to be in his country. Come to throw him out, he has, and mincemeat he will be making of your namby-pamby, best-parlour dragon, too."

"Better for him not to try," said Hwyl, stouter in word than in heart.

"And another thing, too. Red this dragon is, and so a real people's dragon, see."

"Now then. Now then. Propaganda with dragons again, is it? Red the Welsh dragon has been two thousand years, and a fighter, too, I grant you. But a fighter for Wales, look; not just a loud-mouth talker of fighting for peace, see. If it is a good red Welsh dragon he is, then out of some kind of egg laid by your Uncle Joe, he is not; and thankful, too, I think," Hwyl told him. "And look you," he added as an afterthought, "this one it is who is stealing your chickens, not mine, at all."

"Oh, let him have the old chickens, and glad," Idris said. "Here he is come to chase a foreign imperialist dragon out of his rightful territory, and a proper thing it is, too. None of your D.P. dragons are we wanting round Llynllawn, or South Wales, either."

"Get you to hell, man," Hwyl told him. "Sweet dispositioned my dragon is, no bother to anyone, and no robber of henhouses, either. If there is trouble at all, the law I will be having of you and your dragon for disturbing the peace, see. So I am telling you. And goodbye, now."

He exchanged another glance with the angry-looking, topaz eyes of the red dragon, and then stalked away, back to his own house.

—

THAT EVENING. JUST as Hwyl was sitting down to his meal, there was a knock at the front door. Bronwen went to answer it, and came back.

"Ivor Thomas and Dafydd Ellis wanting you. Something about the Union," she told him.

He went to see them. They had a long and involved story about dues that seemed not to have been fully paid. Hwyl was certain that he was paid-up to date, but they remained unconvinced. The argument went on for some time before, with head-shaking and reluctance, they consented to leave. Hwyl returned to the kitchen. Bronwen was waiting, standing by the table.

"Taken the dragon off, they have," she said, flatly.

Hwyl stared at her. The reason why he had been kept at the front door in pointless argument suddenly came to him. He crossed to the window, and looked out. The back fence had been pushed flat, and a crowd of men carrying the dragon's hutch on their shoulders was already a hundred yards beyond it. Turning round, he saw Bronwen standing resolutely against the back door.

"Stealing, it is, and you not calling," he said accusingly.

"Knocked you down, they would, and got the dragon just the same," she said. "Idris Bowen and his lot, it is."

Hwyl looked out of the window again.

"What to do with him, now then?" he asked.

"Dragon fight, it is," she told him. "Betting, they were. Five to one on the Welsh dragon, and sounding very sure, too."

Hwyl shook his head.

"Not to wonder, either. There is not fair, at all. Wings, that Welsh dragon had, so air attacks he can make. Unsporting, there is, and shameful indeed."

He looked out of the window again. More men were joining the party as it marched its burden across the waste-ground, towards the slag-heap. He sighed.

"There is sorry I am for our dragon. Murder it will be, I think. But go and see it, I will. So no tricks from that Idris to make a dirty fight dirtier."

Bronwen hesitated.

"No fighting for you? You promise me?" she said.

"Is it a fool I am, girl, to be fighting fifty men, and more. Please to grant me some brains, now."

She moved doubtfully out of his way, and let him open the door. Then she snatched up a scarf, and ran after him, tying it over her head as she went.

The crowd that was gathering on a piece of flat ground near the foot of the slag-heap already consisted of something more like a hundred men than fifty, and there were more hurrying to join it. Several self-constituted stewards were herding people back to clear an oval space. At one end of it was the cage in which the red dragon crouched huddled, with a bad-tempered look. At the other, the asbestos hutch was set down, and its bearers withdrew. Idris noticed Hwyl and Bronwen as they came up.

"And how much is it you are putting on your dragon?" he inquired, with a grin.

Bronwen said, before Hwyl could reply:

"Wicked, it is, and shamed you should be, Idris Bowen. Clip your dragon's wings to fight fair, and we will see. But betting against a horseshoe in the glove, we are not." And she dragged Hwyl away.

All about the oval the laying of bets went on, with the Welsh dragon gaining favour all the time. Presently, Idris stepped out into the open, and held up his hands for quiet.

"Sport it is for you tonight. Super colossal attractions, as they are saying on the movies, and never again, likely. So put you your money, now. When the English law is hearing of this, no more dragon-fighting, it will be—like no more to cockfight." A boo went up, mingled with the laughter of those who knew a thing or two about cockfighting that the English law did not. Idris went on: "So now the dragon championship, I am giving you. On my sight, the Red Dragon of Wales, on his home ground. A people's dragon, see. For more than a coincidence, it is, that the colour of the Welsh dragon—" His voice was lost for some moments in controversial shouts. It re-emerged, saying: "—left, the decadent dragon of the imperialist exploiters of the suffering Chinese people who, in their glorious fight for peace under the heroic leadership—" But the rest of his introduction was also lost among the catcalls and cheers that were still continuing when he beckoned forward attendants from the ends of the oval, and withdrew.

At one end, two men reached up with a hooked pole, pulled over the contraption that enclosed the red dragon, and ran back hurriedly. At the far end, a man knocked the peg from the asbestos door, pulled it open, scuttled round behind the hutch, and no less speedily out of harm's way.

The red dragon looked round, uncertainly. It tentatively tried unfurling its wings. Finding that possible, it reared up on its hind legs, supporting itself on its tail, and flapped them energetically, as though to dispel the creases.

The other dragon ambled out of its hutch, advanced a few feet, and stood blinking. Against the background of the waste-ground and the slag-heap it looked more than usually exotic. It yawned largely, with a fine display of fangs, rolled its eyes hither and thither, and then caught sight of the red dragon.

Simultaneously, the red dragon noticed the other. It stopped flapping, and dropped to all four feet. The two regarded one another. A hush came over the crowd. Both dragons remained motionless, except for a slight waving of the last foot or so of their tails.

The oriental dragon turned its head a little on one side. It snorted slightly, and shrivelled up a patch of weeds.

The red dragon stiffened. It suddenly adopted a pose gardant, one forefoot uplifted with claws extended, wings raised. It huffed with vigour, vapourized a puddle, and disappeared momentarily in a cloud of steam. There was an anticipatory murmur from the crowd.

The red dragon began to pace round, circling the other, giving a slight flap of its wings now and then.

# CHINESE PUZZLE

The crowd watched it intently. So did the other dragon. It did not move from its position, but turned as the red dragon circled, keeping its head and gaze steadily toward it.

With the circle almost completed, the red dragon halted. It extended its wings widely, and gave a full-throated roar. Simultaneously, it gushed two streams of fire, and belched a small cloud of black smoke. The part of the crowd nearest to it moved back, apprehensively.

At this tense moment Bronwen Hughes began suddenly to laugh. Hwyl shook her by the arm.

"Hush, you! There is not funny, at all," he said, but she did not stop at once.

The oriental dragon did nothing for a moment. It appeared to be thinking the matter over. Then it turned swiftly round, and began to run. The crowd behind it raised a jeer, those in front waved their arms to shoo it back. But the dragon was unimpressed by arm-waving. It came on, with now and then a short spurt of flame from its nostrils. The people wavered, and then scattered out of its way. Half a dozen men started to chase after it with sticks, but soon gave up. It was travelling at twice the pace they could run.

With a roar, the red dragon leapt into the air, and came across the field, spitting flames like a strafing aircraft. The crowd scattered still more swiftly, tumbling over itself as it cleared a way.

The running dragon disappeared round the foot of the slag-heap, with the other hovering above it. Shouts of disappointment rose from the crowd, and a good part of it started to follow, to be in at the death.

But in a minute or two the running dragon came into view again. It was making a fine pace up the mountainside, with the red dragon still flying a little behind it. Everybody stood watching it wind its way up and up until, finally, it disappeared over the shoulder. For a moment the flying dragon still showed as a black silhouette above the skyline, then, with a final whiff of flame, it, too, disappeared—and the arguments about paying up began.

Idris left the wrangling to come across to the Hugheses.

"So there is a coward your imperialist dragon is, then. And not one good huff, or a bite to him, either," he said.

Bronwen looked at him, and smiled.

"So foolish, you are, Idris Bowen, with your head full of propaganda and fighting. Other things than to fight, there is, even for dragons. Such a brave show your red dragon was making, such a fine show, oh, yes—and very like a peacock, I am thinking. Very like the boys in their Sunday suits in Llangolwgcoch High Street, too—all dressed up to kill, but not to fight."

Idris stared at her.

"And our dragon," she went on. "Well, there is not a very new trick, either. Done a bit of it before now, I have, myself." She cast a sidelong glance at Hwyl.

Light began to dawn on Idris.

"But—but it is *he* you were always calling your dragon," he protested.

Bronwen shrugged.

"Oh, yes, indeed. But how to tell with dragons?" she asked.

She turned to look up the mountain.

"There is lonely, lonely the red dragon must have been these two thousand years—so not much bothering with your politics, he is, just now. More single with his mind, see. And interesting it will be, indeed, to be having a lot of baby dragons in Wales before long, I am thinking."

# PERFORCE TO DREAM

—

"**B**UT, MY DEAR Miss Kursey," said the man behind the desk, speaking with patient clarity, "it is not that we have changed our minds about the quality of your book. Our readers were enthusiastic. We stand by our opinion that it is a charming light romance. But you must see that we are now in an impossible position. We simply cannot publish two books that are almost identical—and now that we know that two exist, we can't even publish one of them. Very understandably either you or the other author would feel like making trouble. Equally understandably we don't want trouble of that kind."

Jane looked at him steadily, with hurt reproach.

"But mine was first," she objected.

"By three days," he pointed out.

She dropped her eyes, and sat playing with the silver bracelet on her wrist. He watched her uncomfortably. He was not a man who enjoyed saying no to personable young women at any time; also, he was afraid she was going to cry.

"I'm terribly sorry," he said earnestly.

Jane sighed. "I suppose it was just too good to be true— I might have known." Then she looked up. "Who wrote the other one?" she added.

He hesitated. "I don't know that we can—" he began.

Jane broke in: "Oh, but you must! It wouldn't be fair not to tell me. You simply must give me—us—a chance to clear this up."

His instinct was to steer safely out of the whole thing. If he had had the least doubt about her sincerity he would have done so. As it was, his sense of justice won. She did have a right to know, and the chance to sort the whole thing out; if she could.

"Her name is Leila Mortridge," he admitted.

"That's her real name?"

"I believe so."

Jane shook her head. "I've never heard it. It's so queer," she went on. "Nobody can have seen my manuscript. I don't believe anyone knew I was writing it. I just can't understand it at all."

The publisher had no comment to make on that. Coincidences, he knew, do occur. It seems sometimes as though an idea were afloat in the ether and settles in two independent minds simultaneously. But this was something beyond that. Save for the last two chapters, Miss Kursey's *Amaryllis in Arcady* had not only the same story as Miss Mortridge's *Strephon Take My Heart,* but the settings, as well as much of the conversation, were identical. There could not be any question of chance about it.

Curiously, he asked:

"Where did it come from? How did you get the idea of it in the first place, I mean?"

Jane saw that he was looking at her with a peculiar intensity. She looked back at him uncertainly, miserably aware of tears not far behind her eyes.

"I—I dreamt it—at least, I think I dreamt it," she told him.

She was not able to see the puzzled astonishment that came over his face, for suddenly, and to her intense exasperation, tears from a source deeper than mere disappointment about the book overwhelmed her.

He groaned inwardly, and sat regarding her with helpless embarrassment.

Out in the street again, conscious of looking far from her best although considerably recovered, Jane made her way to a café in a mood of deep self-disgust. The exhibition she had put on was the kind of thing she heartily despised: a thing, in fact, that she would have thought herself quite incapable of a year ago.

But the truth of the matter, which she scarcely admitted to herself, was that she was no longer the same person as she had been a year ago. Though a careful observer might have said that her manner was a little altered, her assurance more individual, yet superficially she was the same Jane Kursey doing the same job in the same way. Only she knew how much more tedious the job had gradually become.

It is galling for a young woman of literary leanings to keep on day after day for what seems several lifetimes writing with a kind of standardized verve and coded excitement about such subjects as diagonal tucks, slashed necklines, swing backs, and double peplums; frustrating for her to have to season her work with the adjectives heavenly, tiny, captivating, enchanting, divine, delicious, marching round and round like an operatic army when she yearns to put her soul on paper. When, in fact, something has happened to her so that she feels that a spirit such as hers should be mounting skylark-like to the empyrean, that her heart is no less tender than that of Elaine the Lovable, that, should the occasion arise, she would be found not incompetent among the hetaerae.

The publisher's letter, therefore, had, despite her attempts to retain a level sensibleness, given her a choky, heart-thumping excitement. It did more than disclose the first rungs of a new and greatly preferable career for which many of her associates also struggled: it petted and pleased her secret self. The publisher had spoken of literary merit as if drawing a line between her and those others who worked with three-quarters of their attention on the film-rights.

Her novel, he told her frankly, he found charming. An idyllic romance which could not fail to delight a large number of readers. There were, perhaps, a few passages where the feeling was a little Elizabethan for these prudish times, but they could be toned down with scarcely perceptible loss...

The only qualification of her delight was a faint suspicion of her own undeserving—but, after all, was a dream any more of a gift than a talent? It was just a matter of the way your mind worked really, and if hers happened to work better when she slept than when she was awake, what of it? Nobody had ever been heard to think the worse of Coleridge for dreaming Kubla Khan rather than thinking it up. And anyway, she would not be taken literally even though she admitted frankly to dreaming it...

And now there came this blow. Something so like her own story that the publisher would not touch it! She did not see how that could possibly have happened. She had not told anyone anything about it, not even that she was working on a book…

She gazed moodily into her coffee. Then, as she raised the cup, she became aware of the other person who had come to her table almost unnoticed. The woman was looking her over with careful speculation. Jane paused with her cup a few inches from her mouth, returning the scrutiny. She was about her own age, quietly dressed, but wearing a fur coat that was beyond Jane's means, and a becoming small fur cap on her fair hair. But for the difference in dress she was not unlike Jane herself; the same build and size, the same colouring, hair, too, that was a similar shade, though differently worn. Jane lowered her cup. As she put it down she noticed a wedding-ring on the other woman's hand. The woman spoke first:

"You are Jane Kursey," she said, in a tone that was more statement than question.

Jane had a curious sense of tenseness.

"Yes," she admitted.

"My name," said the woman, "is Leila Mortridge."

"Oh," said Jane. She could not find anything to add to that at the moment.

The other woman sipped her coffee, with Jane's eyes following every movement. She set her cup very precisely in the saucer, and looked up again.

"It seemed likely that they would be wanting to see you, too," she said. "So I waited outside the publisher's to see." She paused. "There is something here that requires an explanation," she added.

"Yes," Jane agreed again.

For some seconds they regarded one another levelly without speaking.

"Nobody knew I was writing it," the woman observed.

"Nobody knew *I* was writing it," said Jane.

She looked back at the woman, unhappily, resentfully, bitterly. Even if it had been only a dream—and it was hard to believe it was only that, for she had never heard of a dream that went on in instalments night by night so vividly that one seemed to be living two alternating lives—but, even if it were, it was *her* dream, her *private* dream, save for such parts of it as she had chosen to write down—and even those parts should remain private until they were published.

"I don't see—" she began, and then broke off, feeling none too certain of herself.

The other woman's self-control was none too good, either; the corners of her mouth were unsteady. Jane went on:

"We can't talk in this place. My flat's quite near."

They walked the few hundred yards there immersed in thought. Not until they were in Jane's small sitting-room did the woman speak again. When she did she looked at Jane as though she were hating her.

"How did you find out?" she demanded.

"Find out what?" Jane countered.

"What I was writing."

Jane regarded her coldly.

"Attack is sometimes the best form of defence, but not in this case. The first I knew of your existence was in the publisher's office about one hour ago. I gather that you found out about me in the same way, just a little earlier. That makes us practically even. I *know* you can't have read my manuscript. I know I've not read yours. It's a waste of time starting with accusations. What we have to find out is what has really happened. I—I—" But there she floundered to a stop without any idea how she had intended to continue.

"Perhaps you have a copy of your manuscript here?" suggested Mrs. Mortridge.

Jade hesitated, then without a word she went to her desk, unlocked a lower drawer, and took out a pile of carbon copy. Still without speaking, she handed it over. The other took it without hesitation. She read a page, and stared at it for a little, then she turned on and started to read another page. Jane went into her bedroom, and stood there awhile, staring listlessly out of the window. When she went back the pile of pages was lying on the floor, and Leila Mortridge was hunched forward, crying uncontrollably into a scrap of a handkerchief.

Jane sat down, looking moodily at the script and the weeping girl. For the moment she was feeling cold and dead inside, as if with a numbness which would turn to pain as it passed. Her dream was being killed, and now she was terribly afraid of life without it...

The dream had begun about a year ago. When and where it was placed she neither knew, nor cared to know. A never, never land perhaps, for it seemed always to be spring or early summer there in a sweet, unwithering Arcady. She was lying on a bank where the grass grew close like green velvet. It ran down to a small stream of clear water chuckling over smooth white stones. Her bare feet were dabbling in the fresh coolness. The sunshine was warm on her bare arms. Her dress was a simple white cotton frock patterned with small flowers and little amorets.

There were small flowers set among the grass, too: she could not name them, but she could describe them minutely. A bird no larger than a blue-tit came down close to her, and drank. It turned a sparkling eye on her, drank again, and then flew away, unafraid. A light breeze rustled the taller grasses beside her and shimmered the trees beyond. Her whole body drank in the warmth of the sunshine as though it were an elixir.

Dimly she could remember another kind of life full of work and bustle, but it did not interest her: *it* was the dream, and this the reality. She could feel the ripples against her feet, the grass under her finger-tips, the glow of the sun. She was intensely aware of the colours, the sounds, the scents in the air; aware as she had never been before, not merely of being alive, but of being part of the whole flow of life.

She had a glimpse of a figure approaching in the distance. A quickening excitement ran through every vein, and her heart sang. But she did not move. She lay with her head turned to one side on her arm. A tress of hair rested on her other cheek, heavy and soft as a silk tassel. She let her eyes close, but more than ever she was aware of the world about her.

She heard the soft approaching footsteps and felt the faint tremor of them in the ground. Something light and cool rested on her breast and the scent of flowers filled her nostrils. Still she did not move. She opened her eyes. A head with short dark curls was just above her own. Brown eyes were watching her from a sun-tanned face. Lips smiling slightly. She reached up with both arms, and clasped them round his neck...

That was how it had begun. The sentimental dream of a schoolgirl, but preciously sweet for all that, and with a bright might-have-been quality which dulled still further the following dull day. She could remember waking with a radiance which was gradually drained away by the dimness of ordinary things and people. She was left, too, with a sense of loss, of having been robbed of what she should have been, and should have felt. It was as though in the dream she had been her rightful, essential self while by day she was forced to carry out a drab mechanical part, an animated lay figure—something at any rate that was not properly alive in a world that was not properly alive.

The following night the dream came again. It did not repeat; it continued. She had never heard of a dream that did that, but there it was. It was the same countryside, the same people, the same particular person, and herself. A world in which she felt quite familiar, and with people whom she seemed always to have known. There was a cottage which she could describe to the smallest detail, where she seemed to have spent all her life, in a village where she knew everyone. There was her work at which her fingers flickered surely among innumerable bobbins and produced exquisite lace upon a black pillow. The neighbours she talked to, the girls she had grown up with, the young men who smiled at her, were all of them quite real. They became even more real than the world of offices, dress-shows, and editors demanding copy. In her waking world she came gradually to feel a drab among drabs; in her village world she was alive, perceptive—and in love...

For the first week or two she had opened her eyes on the workaday world with painful reluctance, afraid that the dream would slip from her. But it was not finished. It went on, becoming all the time less elusive and more solid, until tentatively she allowed herself the hope that it had come to stay. She scarcely dared to believe that at first for fear of the blankness that would follow if it should stop when she had allowed herself really to live in it. Yet as the weeks went on she could only admit it fully, and cherish it more. Once she had allowed that, it began curiously to illuminate her daily life and pierce the dullness with unexpected glimpses. She found pleasure in noticing details which she had never observed before. Things and people changed in value and importance. She had more sense of detachment, and less of struggle. It came to her one day with a shock to find how her interests had altered and her impatience had declined.

The dream had caused that. Now that she had begun to feel that there was not the likelihood of it fading away any moment she could risk feeling happy in it—and the more tolerant of things outside it. The world looked altogether a different place when you knew that you had only to close your eyes at night to come alive as your true self in Arcady.

And why, she wondered, could real life not be like that? Or, perhaps, for some people, it was—sometimes, in glimpses…

There had been that wonderful night when they had gone along the green path which led up the little hill to the pavilion. She had been excited, happy, a little tremulous. They had lain on cushions, looking out between the square oak pillars while the sun sank smoky red, and the thin bank of cloud lost its tinge to become dark lines across a sky that had turned almost green. All the sounds had been soft. A faint susurring of insects, the constant whisper of leaves, and, far away, a nightingale singing… His muscles were firm and brave; she was soft as a sun-warmed peach. Does a rose, she had wondered, feel like this when it is about to open…?

And then she had rested content, looking up at the stars, listening to the nightingale still singing, and to all nature gently breathing…

In the morning when her eyes were open to her familiar small room and her ears to the sound of traffic in the street below, she had lain for a while in happy lassitude. It was then that she had decided to write the book—not, at first, for others to read, but for herself, so that she would never forget.

Unashamedly it was a sentimental book—one such as she had never thought herself capable of writing. But she enjoyed writing it, and reliving in it. And then it had occurred to her that perhaps she was not the only person who was tired of carrying a tough, unsentimental carapace. So she had produced a second version of the book, somewhat pruned—though not quite enough, apparently, for the publisher's taste—and added an ending of her own invention.

And here, now, was the inexplicable result…

---

THE FIRST PRESSURE of Leila Mortridge's flood of tears subsided. She dabbed at her eyes, giving little sniffs.

With the air of one accepting the necessity of somebody being practical, Jane said:

"It seems to me it's quite clear that one of two things has happened: either there is some kind of telepathy between us—and I don't see that that fits very well—or we are both having the same dream."

Mrs. Mortridge sniffed again.

"That's impossible," she said, decidedly.

"The whole situation's impossible," Jane told her shortly, "but it's happened—and we have to find the least impossible explanation. Anyway, is two people having the same dream so much more unlikely than anybody having a dream which goes on and on, like a serial?"

Mrs. Mortridge dabbed again, and regarded her thoughtfully.

"I don't see," she said, a trifle primly, "how an unmarried girl like you could be having a dream like that at all."

Jane stared.

"Come off it," she advised, briefly. "Besides," she added, after a moment's reflection, "it seems to me every bit as unsuitable for a respectably married woman."

Mrs. Mortridge looked forlorn.

"It's ruined my marriage," she said, a little plaintively.

Jane nodded understandingly.

"I was engaged—and it wrecked that," she told her. "How could one? I mean, after—" She let the sentence trail away.

"Quite," said Mrs. Mortridge.

They fell into abstract contemplation for some moments; Mrs. Mortridge broke the silence to say:

"And now *you're* spoiling *it,* too."

"Spoiling your marriage?" said Jane amazedly.

"No, spoiling the dream."

Jane said firmly:

"Now, don't let's be silly about this. We're both in the same boat. Do you think I want you muscling in on my dream?"

"*My* dream."

Jane disregarded that, and thought for a while. At last:

"Perhaps it won't make any difference," she suggested. "After all, if we were both dreaming we were her, and didn't know anything about one another then, why shouldn't we go on without knowing anything about one another?"

"But we do."

"No, when we are *there,* I mean. If that's so, it won't really matter, will it? At least, perhaps it won't."

Mrs. Mortridge looked unconsoled.

"It'll m-matter when I wake up and know you've b-been sharing—" she mumbled, tearfully.

"Do you think I like the idea of that any more than you do?" Jane said, coldly.

It took her a further twenty minutes to get rid of her visitor. Only then did she feel at liberty to sit down and have a good cry about it all.

—

THE DREAM DID not stop, as Jane had half-feared it might. Neither was it spoiled. Only for a few succeeding mornings was Jane troubled on waking by the thought that Leila Mortridge must be aware of every detail of the night's experience—and though there should have been some compensation to be found in the fact that she was equally aware of what had happened to Leila Mortridge, it did not, for some reason, seem to work quite that way.

That the girl in the dream was in no way affected for either of them by their knowledge of one another they established over the telephone the following morning with a thankfulness which was almost amiability. That settled, the besetting fear lost something of its edge, and antagonism began to dwindle. Indeed, so thoroughly did it decline, that the end of the month saw it replaced by a certain air of sorority, expressed largely in telephone calls that were almost schoolgirlish in manner, if not in content. For after all, Jane said to herself, if a secret had to be shared, why not make the best of the sharing...?

—

IT WAS ON an evening some three months after their first meeting that Leila Mortridge came through on the telephone with an unusual, almost panicky note in her voice.

"My dear," she demanded, "have you seen this evening's *Gazette*?"

Jane said that she had just glanced at it.

"If you have it there, look at page four. It's in *Theatre Chat*. The thing in the second column, headed "Dual Role"—no, don't ring off..."

Jane laid down the receiver. She found the newspaper, and the paragraph:

DUAL ROLE

*The production due to open shortly at the Countess Theatre is described as a romantic play with music. In it Miss Rosalie Marbank will have the unique distinction of being both the Leading Lady and the Authoress. This work, which is her first venture into authorship, is, she explains, neither a musical comedy, nor a miniature opera, but a play with music, that has been specially composed by Alan Cleat. It is the rustic love-story of a girl lacemaker...*

Jane read on to the end of the paragraph and sat quite still, clutching the paper. A tinny chattering from the neglected telephone recalled her. She picked it up.

"You've read it?" Leila Mortridge's voice inquired.

"Yes," said Jane, slowly. "Yes...I— You don't happen to know her, do you?"

"I don't remember ever hearing of her. But it looks well, I mean, what else can it be...?"

"It *must* be." Jane thought for a moment, then: "All right. We'll find out," she said, decisively. "I'll get on to our critic and push him into wangling us a couple of seats for the first night. Will you be free?"

"I'm certainly going to be."

---

THE DREAM WENT on. That night there was some kind of fair in the village. Her little stall looked lovely. Her lace was as delicate as if large snowflake patterns had been spun from the finest spider-thread. It was true that nobody was buying, but that did not seem to matter. When he came he found her sitting on the ground beside the stall telling stories to two adorable, wide-eyed children. Later on, they closed up the stall. She hung her hat over her arm by its ribbons, and they danced. When the moon came up they drifted away from the crowd. On a little rise they turned and looked back at the bonfire and the flares and the people still dancing. Then they went away along a path through the woods, and forgot all about everything and everybody but each other.

———

ONE OF THE reasons why Jane was able to get her tickets with no great difficulty was the clash of the opening night of *Idyll* with that of a better publicized and more ambitious production. As a result, few of the regular first-night ornaments were to be seen, and the critics were second-flight. Nevertheless, the house was full.

She and Leila Mortridge found their seats a few minutes before the lights were lowered. The orchestra began an overture of some light, pretty music, but she could pay little attention to it for her empty, sick feeling of excitement. She put out an unsteady hand. Leila's grasped it, and she could feel that it, too, was trembling. She found herself wishing very much that she had not come, and guessed that Leila was feeling the same, but they had *had* to come: it would have been still worse not to...

The orchestra wove its way from one simple, happy tune to another, and finished. There were five seconds of expectancy, and then the curtain rose. A sound that was half-sigh and half-gasp rustled through the theatre and shrank into a velvet silence.

A girl lay on a green bank set with star-like flowers. She wore a simple dress of white, patterned with small flowers and amorets. Her bare feet dabbled in the edge of a pool.

Somewhere in the audience a woman gave a giggling sob, and was hushed.

The girl on the bank stirred in lazy bliss. She raised her head and looked beyond the bank. She smiled, and then lowered her head, lying as if asleep, with a tress of hair across her cheek.

From the audience there was no sound. It seemed not to breathe. A clarinet in the orchestra began a plaintive little theme. Every eye in the house left the girl, and dwelt upon the o.p. side of the stage.

A man in a green shirt and russet trousers came out of the bushes. He was carrying a bunch of flowers, and treading softly.

At the sight of him a sigh, as of huge, composite relief breathed through the house. Jane's hand relaxed its unconscious pressure upon Leila's. He was not *the* man.

He approached the girl on the bank, bent over, looking down at her for a moment, then gently laid the flowers on her breast. He sat down beside her, leaning over on one elbow to gaze into her face...

It was at that moment that something impelled Jane to take her attention from the stage. She turned her head slowly, as if drawn invisibly. Then she froze. Her heart gave a jump that was physically painful. She clutched Leila's arm.

"Look!" she whispered. "In that box up there!"

There could not be a moment's doubt. She knew the face better than she knew her own: every curl of his hair, every plane of his features, every lash around the brown eyes. She knew the tender smile with which he was leaning forward to watch the stage so well that she ached. She knew—everything about him...

Then, suddenly, she was aware that the eyes of almost every woman in the audience had left the stage and turned the same way as her own. The expressions on the rows of faces made her shiver and hold more tightly to Leila's arm.

For some minutes the man continued to watch, appearing oblivious of anything but the lighted scene. Then something, perhaps the intense stillness of the audience, caused him to turn his head.

Before the hundreds of eyes that were watching, his smile faded.

Abruptly the silence was broken by hysterics in half a dozen parts of the house at once.

He stood up uncertainly, his expression became tinged with alarm. Then, decisively, he turned towards the back of the box. What happened there was invisible from the floor, but in a moment Jane was aware that he had not left. He came into view again, backing away from the door towards the rail of the box. Beyond him the heads of several women came into sight. The look on their faces caused Jane to shudder. When the man turned she could see that he was afraid. He was cornered, and the women came on towards him like outraged furies.

With a merely momentary hesitation he swung one leg over the rail of the box, and clambered outside. Quite evidently he intended to escape by climbing to the neighbouring box. With a foot on one of the light brackets, he reached for its edge. Simultaneously two of the women in the box he was leaving clutched at his other arm. They broke his hold upon the rail. For a fearful, prolonged moment he teetered there, arms waving to regain his balance. Then he went, turning as he fell backwards, and crashed headfirst into the aisle below...

Jane clutched Leila to her, and bit her lip to keep from screaming. She need not have made the effort: practically everyone else screamed...

---

BACK IN HER own room, Jane sat looking at the telephone for a long time before she could bring herself to use it. At last she lifted the receiver, and got through to the office. She gave a desk number, then:

"Oh Don. It's about that—man at the Countess Theatre to-night. Do you know anything?" she asked, in a voice flatly unlike her own.

"Sure. Just doing the obit now," said a cheerful voice. "What do you want to know?"

"Just—" she said, unsteadily. "Oh, just who he was—and things."

"Fellow called Desmond Haley. Age thirty-five. Quite a show of letters after his name, medical mostly. Practised as a psychiatrist. Seems to have written quite a flock of things. Best known is a standard work: *Crowd Psychology and the Communication of Hysteria*. Latest listed publication is a paper which appears to be generally considered pretty high-flown bunk called *The Inducement of Collective Hallucination*. He lived at—hullo there, what's wrong?"

"Nothing," Jane told him, levelling her voice with an effort.

"Thought you sounded— I say, you didn't know him or anything, did you?"

"No," said Jane, as steadily as she could. "No, I didn't know him."

Very precisely she returned the telephone to its rest. Very carefully she walked into the next room. Very deliberately and sadly she drooped on her bed, and let the tears flow as they would.

—

AND WHO SHALL say how many tears flowed upon how many pillows for the dream that did not come that night, nor never again…?

# NEVER ON MARS

—

THE ODDS ARE that they won't actually hang Jeremy Chambet. After all, the jury has to be satisfied beyond all doubt that murder was committed. And I don't see how, in spite of the newspapers and the radio and all the talk, some of them can fail to have a doubt or two.

And all the evidence is circumstantial—or expert. Juries feel a bit uneasy when it's entirely circumstantial. Nor are they very fond of expert witnesses. They're impressed in a way, but antagonistic, too. In the course of their lives they've all at some time or other had expert advice that turned out to be wrong.

All the same, Jeremy is in a spot. Public fickleness must be hell. First they put you on top of the world, then, given a whiff of righteous motive for an excuse, the whole lot will turn right round and jump on your neck with a jealous, sadistic satisfaction. Nearly everybody's delighted to find himself holier than a hero in some way.

And, in court, Jeremy's story hasn't sounded too good. Still, even truth isn't dressed all non-crushable—and after she's been mauled around the way they do it she doesn't look quite flavour-sealed-in either. When Jeremy told me the story in his own way soon after he got back it sounded fantastic, of course—any story told by the first man back from Mars was bound to sound fantastic—but that isn't to say that it sounded untrue, not necessarily, anyway. It wasn't till the prosecution got to pounding it that it began to look like hash.

Just to refresh your memory.

Not even the defence claims that Jeremy was the first man to reach Mars. The contention is that he's the first one to come back—and the source of his trouble is that he's the *only* one to come back.

There were, you will remember, a crew of three to the General Rockets' Ship, *Uniac 5*. Christopher Deeley was captain—an excellent navigator with wide experience in rocketry, theoretical and practical, fine physique, dependable personality, altogether a first-class choice for the job. There was Jeremy Chambet, a physicist of considerable reputation, no laboratory hermit, going along to observe and record technical data. And Peter Quorridge who, after a roving career chasing up troubles in all corners of the Earth as a special correspondent, had got the job of representing the eyes and ears of the world on the trip.

The take-off was noted, but not played-up in the press. It was about the tenth or twelfth shot—or maybe it would have been a higher number than that if the Russians didn't regard secrecy and misinformation as prime national virtues—and since nothing had ever been heard of the others since they passed the radio-reflecting layers, news value, and expectation, had dwindled. Moreover, Jeremy's statement on what they expected to find could only have made the ordinary reader wonder why anyone was fool enough to even start. Those who did read it just wrote off another expensive ship and three more nuts.

But this time they were wrong. Several months later *Uniac 5*'s automatic radio signals were picked up. Then came Jeremy's voice calling. He was circling and reducing speed, he said. He was alone. He'd not a hope of landing the ship safely, so he proposed to drop her in the sea. His intention was to slow to a stop, check fall, shut off power, and bail out before velocity mounted again. He'd leave the automatic going for stations to keep a fix on him.

The last wasn't entirely necessary. The *Uniac 5* not only assaulted the ears of the inhabitants of San Salvador Island in the Bahamas by thundering round their sky, but treated them to unusual glimpses of a celestial firecracker gone crazy.

Jeremy explained afterwards that he could not get the balance of the thing right to keep it sitting on its jets. Every time he used the lateral stabilisers they over-corrected, first one way and then the other until the thing had swung over and whizzed off at an angle, so then he'd have to fight for height in order to have another try. The wonder of it was, seeing that he'd never tried to handle a rocket before, that he didn't destroy it and himself at the first attempt. Finally, however, this cavorting had to come to an end because his fuel ran out, so then he had to jump for it anyway. The *Uniac 5* came down at high speed and blew up like a geyser—maybe she didn't have any fuel, but his haywire antics up there had run her tubes mighty hot. Jeremy himself dripped into the drink twenty miles away and floated around firing smoke signals at intervals until a helicopter came and dangled a ladder to him.

Well, it's not likely you've forgotten the hoo-ha that followed. The contracts for advertising, radio, movies, and the rest of it came raining in. Jeremy was sitting pretty with mountains of dollars growing up on all sides. But Jeremy isn't a mean man. As far as we know, no close relative of Peter Quorridge exists. But Chris Deeley had left a widow, Monica, and two children. Jeremy made over to them one half of the receipts arising. It was generous. When his friends pointed out: 'It was *you* that took the risk. One-third would be fair enough,' he replied: 'Well, it was Chris who got us there—and landed us safely.'

The prize-money was what began the trouble. The New York *Epoch* had offered the largest—one million dollars to the first crew to make the two-way journey, but there were a number of others, not negligible by any means. The *Epoch* is not one of the ornaments of journalism. Maybe it betted there'd never be a call for the cash. When the call came it thought it over and then informed Jeremy that since only one-third of the crew had made the double journey, it had decided to only award one-third of the prize. That seemed a good idea to one or two offerers unexpectedly brought to face the results of carefree gestures.

Jeremy didn't worry. More dollars than he had ever thought of were rolling towards him anyway, more than he knew how to use. But Monica Deeley was a tougher proposition. 'Enough' was a word that she kept shut up in the dictionary. The moment she got the sharing agreement with Jeremy signed up she put in a claim against the *Epoch* and its similar-minded friends for payment in full.

The sympathy was all with her and Jeremy to begin with, but then rumours got going—from a guessable source. After all, there was only Jeremy's word for what had happened on the expedition. The *Uniac 5* with such records as there might be lay scattered in bits at the bottom of the sea. It occurred to someone to turn Jeremy's own generosity against him—after all he had no need to give Monica Deeley more than a third share, no compulsion to do even that. So was there something behind it? Conscience money…? A very distant relative of Quorridge showed up and put in a claim on the ground of Peter's intestacy, and as good as accused Jeremy of murdering both of his companions for the sake of the prize-money. A few newspapers remained staunch, but a number of the more sensational moved over to the side of the *Epoch* which by this time had the characters of both Jeremy and Monica in shreds.

The *Epoch* lost its case, and appealed. In addition, the libel writs had begun to fly. In the middle of it all Monica Deeley sprang a mine by going to the police and alleging that Jeremy had confessed to murdering her husband in order that he could marry her. It was by no means a likely story, but a lot of people pounced on it as an explanation of his generosity—that he intended to have the lot in the end, even if he had to marry to get it. And once the information had been sworn, the police were unable to ignore it.

Monica Deeley is a fool—and a dangerous fool. If she'd let the whole thing alone, and just sat back taking the dollars as they came along, they'd both have all they could do with. Whoever it was suggested to her that if Jeremy were put out of the way she would rake it all in has a lot to answer for. Now she stands to lose badly whatever happens.

Meanwhile Jeremy has to sit there in court and hear everything he says ripped to bits. They've gleefully tripped him in a slip or two such as anyone's memory might make—but he's made no contradictions of his main story, and he's sticking to it.

By this time we have all become so confused with the comments of the newspapers, and those of learned counsel, that what Jeremy actually said in the first place is becoming obscure. So let me give you the story as he told it to me soon after he had come back, well before the row began and all this forensic talent pitched into him.

# NEVER ON MARS

THE NEXT TIME they send anyone to Mars (said Jeremy) they might let a social psychologist in on the selection of the crew. Technical qualifications come first, of course, but the people who hold them are going to have to live together for a number of weeks. And by far the most troublesome thing to control when you're shut into a small metal shell out there in Space is yourself.

Your sense of proportion goes all to bits. Fiddling little things that you would never even notice anywhere else can drive you to distraction when they are thrust under your nose day after day and you can't get away from them. Small habits, mannerisms, tricks of speech—they can get on your nerves in a way that would seem fantastic in ordinary life. Each man has to watch himself all the time to keep from showing how intolerable he finds another man's way of clearing his throat, hesitating for a word, eating his food, and that becomes quite a strain by itself.

Roughly speaking we were the man of action, the reasoner, the observer. We had been chosen *because* we had been trained to think in different patterns. It may be good coverage, but it doesn't make for easy association.

I am a scientist—that is to say that when I have assembled all the proved facts I draw a deduction which includes them *all* as logically as human frailty permits. Chris Deeley was the man of action, but as a modern, educated man of action, he was also a considerable technician. This gave us at least some ground in common. But Peter Quorridge! Well, frankly, I don't understand the type. Maybe I could find it amusing for an hour or so in a bar—but the *Uniac 5* was no bar, and it was a matter of solid weeks.

It's all right being revolutionary and sceptical about everything at twenty—most of the best are. But you expect a man to grow out of it. Maybe it's the job of making a sensation out of everything that did it with Peter. The way he watched you when you were speaking; you could almost see his mind picking out bits here and there and building up conclusions which left out all the rest. When, in exasperation, I said that it was more than ordinary perversity in him, and something more like downright anti-rationality, he grinned.

"—And you're not even constructive," I added.

He shrugged. "The construction's your job—not mine. And, my God, what you fellows do construct!"

"But you'd rather be a demolition expert?"

He put his head on one side, and considered. "I'd not call myself that," he said. "As I see my job, I'm more like the Standards Bureau. I test. If the breaking strain is low, the thing gives. —And when I think of all the aethers, elements, and crackpot theories you fellows have put up in your time I reckon I represent a pretty necessary safety device."

That'll give you some idea of his angle. He'd challenge pretty nearly every theory ever made, and quite a little of that was enough to be intensely exasperating. After all, if you don't have some axioms how do you start going any place at all?

To begin with, it wasn't too bad. Once we had got over the start, which is a physically distressing business, we settled in. We arranged a rota for meals and sleeping based on Earth time. It's the best you can do—it'd be a lot better if one could sleep most of the twenty-four hours instead of a smaller proportion than usual from lack of exercise. There's a good opening there for a non-habit-forming hypnotic, by the way. When things began to pall Peter was better off than we were. Chris's periodical course-checks and my observations left us with a lot of time unoccupied, but Peter had brought along a stack of notes he was in the process of working up into a book. We got more bored with reading than he did with writing.

To help pass the time Chris taught me something of Space-navigation. I found it fascinating—it also turned out to be useful: without it I'd not be here now. But that didn't take up all our time. Among other things, we discussed quite a bit what we were likely to find on Mars—if we made it. My own expectations were far from sensational. From all I knew I envisaged an almost arid planet. There would be little, if any, atmosphere. Rigorous cold by night, a day temperature of anything from thirty to eighty degrees at the equator, depending on the season. Polar caps of frozen methane or carbon-dioxide. Possibly, just possibly, a little vegetation of a primitive kind still surviving. Perhaps the thing that I looked forward to the most was clearing up, once and for all, the matter of those markings to which the astronomer Schiaparelli, had given the name, in my opinion then, so unfortunate, of *canali*.

Chris, of course, hoped for more. I could see that though he did not press it, he had been affected as most people have by the views of the irresponsible Lowell and others who have taken what seemed to the informed, a childishly geomorphic view of the planets. It was while I was pointing out to him what a quantity of romantic mischief had originated in Flagstaff, Arizona, that I became aware that Peter had stopped writing and was listening, with his eyebrows slightly raised.

"You honestly believe that's all we're going to find? Just red deserts—" he put in.

"Orange deserts—there's a refractional effect," I told him.

"All right, orange deserts then, split up by natural cleavages, and with the odd patch of lichen here and there?"

"Yes—that's about it," I agreed.

"Then what in heck are we doing here?"

"Well, for one thing, we're verifying theory—adding to knowledge."

Peter put away his pen.

"What are you expecting? Mr. Burroughs's Barsoom?" I suggested.

"My idea is to find out. If I knew, I wouldn't be here. You see, not being a scientist, I don't make my approach stuffed with prejudices."

That was the perverse kind of remark I had learned to expect from him. This time I did not rise to it.

"You must have some views," I said, mildly.

"Well, I certainly have a number of questions. I want to know, for instance, why your despised *canali* markings take, unlike anything else in nature, the shortest path between two points. Also why the junctions are situated, as a rule, just where you might expect an engineer to put them. Why some astronomers speak of obscuration by cloud when others say there's no atmosphere. Oh, there are a whole lot of things I *want* to know—and intend to know. Only, not being a scientist, I don't explain them to everyone before I *do* know."

"That," I said, "is not only frivolous, it's a contradiction in terms. The word 'scientist' by its very derivations means one who knows."

"In practice," he replied gently, "a scientist will often hotly defend a theory, with scientific proofs to show that it is fact. Now, how can a fact need defence? It just *is*. So what the scientist is really trying to do is to prove his own beliefs—which puts him along with the rest of us, though on a slightly less intelligible level."

What are you to do with a man who talks that way?

"At least," I said to him another time, "science builds theories. If your attitude of mind were general, nothing would ever get built at all."

"True," he admitted. "But let's just think where we'd be if there weren't people like me to challenge your scientific theories—and proofs. Off-hand I can recall that it was proved on paper that iron ships would not float, and, when they, disconcertingly for the experts, did—then it was steel ships that wouldn't be seaworthy. It was shown with figures that a steamship could not carry enough coal to get her across the Atlantic. Evidence was adduced that no human constitution could withstand the speed of sixty miles per hour. At the number of times it was proved that heavier than air craft could never fly the imagination positively boggles. In 1927 a father of a friend of mine gave up an aircraft designing job because it was proved to him that the limit of the size of land-based planes had been reached. It was shown that the idea of the internal combustion turbine was comparable on visionary grounds with that of perpetual motion. You will yourself remember a lot of the things that were said authoritatively about nuclear fission. As for the possibility of rocket flight…! And dozens more. But luckily there is always a class of people who don't believe the scientists' conclusions.

"But does that prevent scientists from continuing to prove that the next thing is just as impossible? Not a bit of it."

I'm afraid I used to get more than a little heated with him after a time, so that Chris felt it necessary tactfully to intervene. But people ought to have some respect for the opinions of experts in fields where they themselves know nothing. And Peter seemed to have none. You can't argue unless you have common ground. I told him quite flatly that he was nothing better than an ignoramus in my subjects. He took it quite cheerfully.

"An African witch-doctor told me almost the self-same thing once—and a Voodoo priest, too. It must be a professional tenet," he said.

How would you like to have to put up for week after week after week of close association with a man who talked such stuff? You see what I mean when I said he was anti-rational? He would, for instance, address me as 'Father.' When I objected he raised his eyebrows.

"My dear fellow, would you deny your calling? You are a priest of this century's mystique. The educated accept you as an authority on the mysteries of nature, the uneducated think you're crazy, but a bit dangerous maybe, so they respect you superficially, too. You can't explain your mysteries to the laity—yes, you often use the actual word—and you call anyone who attempts to do so a vulgariser. It's a cult, old man. All the characteristics of a priesthood—including profound faith in your own words."

"What a lot of nonsense you do put over," I told him. "You know as well as I do that the difference between the scientific method and the religious is that we deduce from proved facts."

"That's what amazes me. I can remember as a kid coming across a series of diagrams in an old magazine; they showed the build-up of resistance, and thus proved scientifically that no airplane could fly faster than the speed of sound. How come—on your showing?"

"Faulty reasoning, of course."

"I see. Nothing wrong with the system. Only the incompetent servant. Just the same way that unfortunate woman, Joan of Arc, happened to get burnt."

"If you can't see—oh, go to hell," I told him.

But he just grinned.

―

ADDED TO THE close-quarters living, lack of exercise, and sheer boredom was the uncertainty. You forget that afterwards, but at the time it tells. Then you don't *know* that you are going to make it. The chances are very much against you, and what you *do* know is that all the others who tried before you did *not* make it. And you're very much aware, too, that you don't know why they failed, so you can't take any precautions against whatever it was that made them fail. It's not at all good. While you lie there trying to sleep, some pretty nasty pictures get into your mind—rockets floating on through Space for ever, with just a load of human bones aboard—rockets sliced wide open by wandering asteroids—a rocket which has turned into just a patch of metal fragments in the Martian desert. Things like that are difficult to fence out of your mind. The crew of the

*Santa Maria*'s chief worry was whether they would sail over the edge: on the *Uniac 5* we had a lot more possibilities. Maybe death, seeing that it catches up with everyone, isn't so important as we like to think—but it can come in a hell of a lot of nasty ways... And you kind of get to thinking about them...

Nearer the end of the trip, when it began to look as if we really might make it, our mood changed. It's the long term waiting that gets you down. For a definite operation such as a landing you can brace yourself up. And we did. The thing depended on Chris now, and we'd a high level of trust in him. Peter Quorridge and I tactfully agreed to forget that we'd not been speaking to one another for a couple of weeks, and dropped the armed neutrality.

We began to spend more and more time at the telescope or bending over the projection table. We were fascinated right out of our previous boredom. In spite of myself I began to be converted to the belief that the *canali* were artifacts of some kind, and possibly that they had even been real canals at one time. As they became clearer there seemed to be no other explanation. Over dark patches such as Syrtis Major and others to which romanticists have definitely given the title of 'Sea' I was still puzzled. So much water was highly unlikely, and there was an indefinite quality about the edges. I found myself siding with those who claimed them to be areas of vegetation.

It had been for me to decide the position of our landing, subject to Chris's practical considerations, and I had for some time made up my mind that it should be in the area of the *Ismenius Lacus*. At this great junction of *canali* we should be able to settle the question for good and all, and here, if anywhere at all, we should be able to find traces of civilisation.

I'm not going to be technical. I'll just say that Chris did set us down to a perfect landing somewhere in the north-west quadrant. Around the *Ismenius Lacus* itself the ground was dark and broken for many miles and, in Chris's opinion, likely to be swamp so he took us some distance to the west along the line of the large channel called the *Deuteronilus*.

The first thing I saw when we got the cover off a port was that the sand *was* orange red. I mention that now because in that, if nothing else, my predictions were right. You'll be able to read all the details in my book when it comes out, so now I'll keep as much as possible to what happened.

# NEVER ON MARS

To my amazement the atmosphere showed sufficient oxygen content to sustain us—rarefied, of course, so that it might have caused us a little distress on Earth, but there it required little output of energy to move our bodies. So, with the temperature showing at over forty, we risked going out without spacesuits.

Peter Quorridge took a deep breath, and looked round.

"H'm. No bug-eyed monsters anyway—yet," he remarked.

I regret that such a frivolous remark should be the first recorded utterance of a human being upon Mars, but I am merely reporting.

Chris insisted that our first task should be to set the rocket up in the starting position.

"Just a matter of making it possible to leave in a hurry if we should want to," he explained.

The contingency seemed improbable, but we helped him drive an anchor post and fix the trim. The little engine chugged, with its air-intake wide open, and through a fantastic reduction gear got on with the job of pulling the ship up on to her tail fins.

There wasn't a lot to see, but to me most of it was improbable. The sandy, rockset plain I had expected, but not the scrawny bushes that dotted it. They were poor, gnarled things with just a few coppery leaves. To the south they grew closer together, to the north they became rapidly fewer. In all directions the land was flat, save to the south-east where a tumulus of rocks broke the monotony.

Once the rocket was up, and the living compartment high in the air we had an extended view. It was Peter who took the first look through the south-facing port. He picked up his glasses, then he grunted, and handed them to me.

"Lowell winning on points," he said.

Beyond the bushes which thickened into a dark band I saw a gleam.

"Well?" asked Peter. "Now tell me it could be a saltpan."

"It *could*," I agreed, "but maybe it *is* water."

We went there the next day. It was a canal all right. And well-filled, at that. The edges were fringed with plants not unlike small terrestrial rushes, and where the water began there was plentiful submarine vegetation. Our position gave us a close, watery horizon, and we could not tell what the width of the canal might be. To either side of us the bank ran away in a geometrically straight line—so straight in fact that I was surprised. One would have thought that even light wind erosion which was probably all the wear it ever got would have indented the edges here and there in time.

We withdrew through the fringe of more sturdy bushes which would have made walking along the actual bank a tiresome business, and took an eastward course parallel with the canal, headed in the direction of the rocky pile. The nearer we approached to it, the closer became our interest. The stones which formed it lay in a jumble upon one another, but while we were still some distance away we lost all idea that unaided nature had produced them. The sharp edges of the stones had been worn smooth, but the blocks themselves had been squared. We had no doubt they were the ruins—of something.

But even when we reached them, we could make tantalisingly little of them. It seemed tolerably clear that they could not lie as they did by a process of mere collapse. We all agreed that some immensely destructive force must at some time have hurled them about.

Another thing struck us. You would have expected any building or group of buildings close to the canal to front right upon it, but this pile stood some three hundred yards back from the bank, and on that side was chopped off short in a reasonably straight line. It looked at first as if the canal must have been narrowed at some time and the line represented the original waterfrontage. But Chris, climbing up on to one of the stones, disposed of that idea. He called us to follow him, and when we did, we were able to see that the bare space between the pile and the canal showed traces of foundations in several places.

"Somebody, sometime has been doing a bit of clearance work around here," said Peter. "By the look of it they took the stones and shipped them down the canal.—But quite a while ago."

Chris hesitated over that. He pointed to some of the lower stones in the straight face of the pile. Their edges, unlike those above, were sharp.

"These haven't been exposed anything like as long as the rest," he said.

"Only a few hundred thousand years, maybe," said Peter. "—Or are we on Barsoom after all? Beware of the bug-eyes, and all that?"

"So far," I pointed out, "we've not seen the smallest vestige of animal life of any kind."

"Maybe that's what makes it feel the way it does—even a few desert rats would give it a homey touch," Peter murmured.

We spent the rest of the day taking photographs and collecting specimens. When we got back to the rocket Peter said:

"Well, maybe you weren't quite right in the details, Father, but your general slant was okay. If there's anything duller than a worn out planet, I don't want to hear about it."

I spent the first part of the following day labelling specimens and writing up notes. Chris had insinuated himself into the non-habitable part of the ship and was inspecting things there. Peter, after hanging about pensively, went off somewhere on his own. He came back just as we were finishing our midday meal. He didn't say anything until he had eaten his share and lit a cigarette, then:

"I've found out where the stones went to," he told us.

"Where?" asked Chris. Peter grinned.

"Into the canal," he said.

We both looked at him. You never knew with Peter.

"Who'd want to lug them into the canal?" Chris asked.

"Exactly," Peter agreed. "But that's where they are."

I knew enough of him by now to be sure that he'd not finished. "How do you know that?" I asked.

"I've seen 'em. During the night I seemed to remember that the bank there isn't quite straight like the rest; it's been worn into a bit of a bow. At first I thought that it would have been worn away by the ships or barges or whatever they were using. Then it occurred to me that the stones themselves would have gradually worn away the edge if they'd been pushed into the water."

"That's possible," I agreed. "If anyone had reason for doing it."

"That's what I wanted to see about.—So I took along one of the inflatable mattresses, and floated out a bit on it. It gets deep fairly rapidly, but sixty yards or so out you can still see the bottom well. And that's where the stones are."

"But that's crazy. —Or—you mean the bottom of the canal is paved with them?"

Peter drew on his cigarette.

"No, I don't. You see, what they apparently were wanted for was—building."

---

SOMEWHERE IN THE middle of the following night the rocket fell over—and an exceedingly lucky thing it was for all of us that our couches were free in their gimbals. Since one of their main purposes was to take up shock, none of us suffered more than an abrupt awakening. Chris sat up and turned on the light. A few loose articles had been thrown into a heap, but no damage was done inside. Peter's voice said, comatosely:

"Let the damn thing stay. It can't fall any further."

It seemed sound advice to me. If the ship was damaged, it would still be just as much damaged when daylight came. But that wasn't Chris's way. He wanted to be reassured at once. He got out and sorted his clothes from the heap into which they'd all been flung. It was unfortunate for him that he happened to be balanced on one leg in the act of negotiating his pants when the rocket started to roll. He took several staggering hops before he managed to clutch his couch and haul himself aboard, half clad. At that moment the ship came down with a thud, and we bounced on our springs.

"What the —— —— goes on?" Chris demanded, as the ship continued to roll.

It was very odd indeed. The *Uniac 5* wasn't a perfect cylinder as you know. The three atmospheric stabilising fins projected somewhat beyond her greatest girth. They should have made it quite impossible for her to roll. But they didn't. She rose slightly as she turned, then *thud* again as we bounced once more. There was a secondary thump as the one port cover that was free bumped down on to its gasket on the turn. Peter lit a cigarette.

"There are two possible explanations," he observed. "Either the damn planet's got tilted up someway, or else something's shoving. Hell!" he added, as we thudded over again.

Chris glared at him.

"Put that thing out. We might fracture a fuel line or something any minute."

Peter obliged, and lay back. We swung in the gimbals while the place turned round us and thudded over again.

"And something with a mighty powerful shove, too," he added.

Chris was reaching for a locker door. By the time he had got it open we had turned further so that the entire contents of the cupboard fell out on him, but he succeeded in grabbing the thing he wanted, a flashlight. When the port cover swung free, he turned the beam on the port itself. It was quite useless. The fused quartz surface just reflected the light, making the darkness outside seem yet denser. Chris cursed. We continued to turn with regular thuds. The port cover looked like buckling its hinges. The next time it thudded shut he jumped to secure it, and managed to get back just before we went over again. He sat there considering for some moments. Then, choosing the time carefully, he climbed to the pilot seat and set it free to swing in its gimbals. He considered the instrument board thoughtfully for a minute, then he depressed one key, and held it down. He waited until we had thudded again, then he gave a light touch on another key. A tremor ran through the ship, and the turning stopped.

"Fine," said Peter. "Rout of bug-eyed monster."

I was irritated.

"That kind of fooling doesn't help. This may be serious," I said.

He turned an amused eye on me.

"You've got a scientific theory," he said. "But me, I take things as they come—not as I think they ought to come."

At that moment we began to turn again, and thudded down on to the next fin. Chris played his piece on the lateral firing keys once more. We stopped again.

"I was premature," said Peter, in the following pause. "The bug-eye has patience, and imperviousness to heat—hey! Here we go again!"

We did. It was not until Chris had repeated his treatment five or six times that the pause lengthened out so that we began to feel it was permanent.

"That would seem to have fixed them," he said, with satisfaction.

"If it is 'them,'" Peter said. "We might take a look if we didn't happen to be lying on the entrance-port side."

NEXT MORNING, AFTER Chris had rolled us with a lateral blast, we went out to inspect. We now rested something over a hundred yards to the south of our original position. The sand over which the ship had travelled showed not only the indentations made by the fins, but a number of shallow furrows—the kind of mark that might be left by a full sack being dragged along. We could make nothing of them. They extended all around the ship as she now lay, and stretched away on the other side in a broad trail to the south.

Chris inspected the vessel with increasing relief.

"Okay, I think," he said at length. "We've the local gravity to thank for that. Those fins would never have stood it with her Earth weight."

He debated whether to set her up again, and then decided against it until we should know more. It would not do her any good simply to be toppled over once more.

We decided to follow the trail to the south and see what we could find.

"There's only one place that can lead," said Peter, and he went into the ship to emerge shortly carrying a deflated mattress.

He was right. The marks kept on in an approximately straight line. The bushes on its way had been flattened as though by a heavy weight. At the canal it ended. We examined the bank carefully for signs of a craft that had been moored. There weren't any.

"There's one answer to that," Peter said, looking at me, with raised eyebrows.

When we had inflated the mattress we took it in turns to float a little way out on it and look down into the water. I went second, after Chris.

I don't mind saying that I had doubted Peter. It wasn't that I thought he was putting up a spoof, but that I half expected to see something fortuitous though maybe bearing a close resemblance to what he fancied. I was wrong. Hanging my head over the edges of the mattress and shielding off reflections as best I could with my hands, I found myself looking down on no jumble of stones, but an orderly collection of buildings.

The designs and plans of them were, of course, strange, yet, with an effort of the imagination, one could almost fancy himself looking down from the air upon a foreign city. One which was built on a hillside and sloped away until it dimmed out of sight in the depths. I stared down at it long and incredulously.

It presented so many degrees of improbability beyond the plain fact that it was there at all, that I was utterly bewildered. But there was no hallucination about it. I could quite clearly see individual buildings with flat roofs and lane-like streets between them. I strained my eyes to catch some sign of life or movement down there, but I saw none save a few small, fish-like creatures idling along or nosing inquisitively into crevices. Then I noticed something more. It was that in one or two of the upper buildings that I could see most clearly roof-slabs had fallen in, and had not been replaced. And on considering a 'street' which lay directly beneath me I observed that it was carpeted with weed that stirred as if in a slight current. Its untouched appearance in conjunction with the rest made me feel that I was looking down upon a deserted place.

After a lengthy inspection which told me no more, I paddled back to the others on the bank. Peter looked interrogative without speaking.

"I don't understand it. I don't understand it at all," I admitted. "They can't be houses that have been submerged. Yet they are simply a dry land type under water. If we grant for a moment the possibility of an intelligent swimming creature—then we must admit that that is simply not the kind of structure it would build. The design just wouldn't suit its nature or needs. To assume that a creature able to move up and down as easily as sideways would adopt the same general forms that we find convenient would be arrant nonsense."

Peter nodded. "For once we agree. And that leaves us with a choice of two possibilities, doesn't it? Either the places *were* built by some approximately human types and later submerged—which, as you say, doesn't look likely. Or whatever built them does not swim."

"Some bottom-dwelling form—like a crab, for instance," Chris suggested.

"Maybe—or maybe something not a bit like a crab. Someway I don't see any crustacean evolving a high I.Q.," Peter replied.

"If there is anything there now," I said, "it looks as if it had abandoned the shallower parts for the deeps."

"Of course there's something there," Peter put in. "Our rocket didn't roll itself."

We paused, contemplating the possibilities for a moment.

"Well, there's one way of finding out—and that's to go and have a look," Chris said.

The rest of the day he spent tinkering around with one of our hitherto unused spacesuits.

"I don't see why it shouldn't make a perfectly good diving-suit," he explained. "I know the pressure will be inverted, but it won't be great here even if the depth is considerable—which doesn't seem likely. The trouble will be to keep down. Everything weighs so damn little."

—

THAT NIGHT I was awakened from a dream of touring Mars along the bottoms of endless canals by a familiar bump.

"Good old bug-eyes back again," muttered Peter.

Chris grunted, and swung himself into his chair. He repeated his counter-measures, but this time they were less effective in dealing with whatever was outside. Sometimes the motion was checked briefly, sometimes not at all. With a gesture of irritation he changed his tactics and let off a blast on the other side. The ship suddenly reversed her roll, and thudded back. That seemed more effective. Half-an-hour passed. But then we began to tilt again. Chris held his hand until we were in top-centre of the supporting fin, and then let the foreside laterals have it again. We dropped back. Then a kind of see-saw contest went on for a while. He began to look a little worried.

"We've got a good fuel margin," he said, "all the same, we won't be able to keep this up indefinitely."

However, the same appeared to apply to whatever was doing the pushing. After a bit more back and forth it—or they—apparently decided to call it off for the night.

By daylight we saw that the night's work had been poorer from their point of view. All the same the rocket now lay some thirty yards further in the direction of the canal.

—

# NEVER ON MARS

CHRIS CLIMBED INTO the spacesuit on the bank. Before he closed the helmet he strapped on a belt hung with such weighty and portable objects as he could find, and we fixed a spare air-bottle in place on his back.

It had been arranged that Peter should float above him and observe for as long as he was able, while I watched from the bank. I would have liked a running commentary on Chris's discoveries, but the built-in radio was not practicable for use under water.

Chris closed the helmet, and tested, then he waved his hand to me, and began to walk carefully into the water. Peter, lying face down on the mattress, paddled it out slowly with his hands. After little more than a dozen paces Chris's head disappeared beneath the surface. I sat down and lit a cigarette, watching Peter paddling gently out, pausing now and then, and all the time looking steadily down into the water.

About an hour passed. I had got cold sitting there, and was walking up and down the bank for exercise. Peter was a hundred and fifty yards or more away. I could see him cupping his hands round his eyes as he peered down.

Suddenly he jerked up his head, rocking the mattress violently. His voice came to me in a shout. A moment later there was a splash near him, and Chris shot up, rising more than half out of the water. He struck out for the mattress at once. Peter was reaching out a hand to him. Then out of the water close behind him something rose dripping. I can't say what it was, a sort of grab, perhaps— or a kind of claw... It moved so quickly, I couldn't say. It swung over, and fell upon Chris and Peter with a mighty splash... When the spray dropped there was nothing there...

I stood there frozen while the ripples spread out and came lapping to my feet. Then I fancy I ran back and forth along the water's edge crazily wringing my hands... I can't be sure... I was distraught...

You see, there was something worse than losing my friends, worse than the horror of whatever dwelt in the canal—I was suddenly alone, utterly alone, alone as a man has never been alone before... And all at once I was terribly afraid. Afraid of the unbroken silence all round me. Deadly afraid of fear itself...

You know how fear can tread close on your heels when you are alone on a dark night...? This was something worse than that. Far, far worse—and in full sunlight... I was a mote, a tiny speck of life, the only thing that moved on the face of all that dreadful land... The only human soul in millions of miles of Space...

I felt that I must burrow. I was a frightened, shell-less creature that must dig itself in somewhere and hide... Agoraphobia they call that... It's so easy to pin a long name on what you have never felt...

There was only one place I could hide. How I forced myself along that journey to the rocket I don't know. But once I was inside I slammed the port behind me, and screwed it shut. I was shaking like a man with a fever. The sweat and tears ran down my face together... I don't understand it... I'm not a lot afraid of death—if I were I'd never have been there... I guess fear's a lot more frightening than death, somehow...

—

BY THE TIME night fell I'd recovered quite a bit. Safe in a hiding hole I'd been able to calm off gradually. I'd even made myself eat. But sleep, of course, was out of the question. I sat there in the silence straining my ears for some sound to tell me the creatures from the canal were coming again. I didn't hear it, but they came all right...

Sitting in Chris's seat, I felt the ship begin to roll. I did my best to imitate the movements he had made, but my knowledge of the controls was picked up from watching him, and I hadn't his touch. I wasn't clear what I was supposed to be doing, and I had made a mess of it. Once or twice, by luck, I did something which gave the creature—or creatures—outside reason to pause, and I did jerk the ship around a bit, but mostly it was ineffective. Then, remembering Chris's concern, I got into a panic at the thought of the good fuel I was wasting. It was a choice of evils, but at least the thing outside was making pretty slow work of it. I made myself climb over to my berth, and kept myself swinging there while the place continued to turn around me in jerks—thud—thud—thud...

The early light showed me that the night's stint had shifted me further among the scrawny bushes and a full three hundred yards nearer to the canal. Two more nights at that rate would see the *Uniac 5* pretty close to the water's edge, I reckoned. The choice was clear enough: either she and I went down into the canal together, or I risked trying to take her off... Well, you could scarcely call that a choice; it was just a chance, and a poor one, I thought.

It took all my resolution to get me outside again, but I did it. And I had the luck to find an outcrop of rock to which I could hitch the raising gear and save myself the labour of driving an anchor. While the engine was bringing her slowly up I studied Chris's tables.

Take-off time there worked out just an hour or so after sunset. That was plain easy figuring—but I wasn't risking it. I put the time forward a couple of hours and worked out the allowances—not such plain figuring, but well worth the trouble.

I had my heart in my mouth when I did start. But it turns out there's not a lot to shooting them off—any fool could do it with the tables, especially against Mars gravity. It's bringing them down that needs the skill—and I didn't have any...

―

WELL, THAT'S THE way Jeremy told it to me. And when he'd finished I said:

"But these things in the canal—you must have some idea what they were like?"

"No," he said. "We never saw them."

That's just one of the questions a lot of people have asked him since then.

The prosecution, having obtained a ruling that a ship in Space beyond the limits of Earth's atmosphere shall be considered a part of that territory where it was registered, has set out to prove that a double murder has taken place in Space, and that in fact Mars has not been reached. If this can be established, all claims to prizes will, of course, be conveniently invalidated. For the purpose they have been calling a great deal of expert talent to the witness's stand. Men with famous names have stood there to give scientific proof that Jeremy Chambet is lying. They have shown on scientific grounds that Mars cannot have a breathable atmosphere, that the *canali* are not canals, that whatever they are there cannot be any appreciable quantity of water in them, that the chances against any form of life familiar to us (and certainly any intelligence of the human type) having ever developed there are so great as to make the whole idea sheer moonshine, that Jeremy cannot describe his creatures from the canals because there could not be any such—nor could any form that his imagination could create make their existence credible even to his own reason. That, in fact, every word of his story is a fabrication and a fraud.

Bitterest of all, they bring up against him his own scientifically deduced opinions of the conditions that must logically prevail on Mars written, some of them, years before the *Uniac 5* took off.

Maybe the shade of Peter Quorridge is having a quiet laugh some place.

"But you yourself advanced this as scientific finding," they say to Jeremy.

"I know," he admits miserably. "But I think I was wrong."

"Colleagues of yours have checked the deductions, and support them."

"I know," he says again. "But they are wrong."

"You deny the validity of scientific findings then?"

"I—" He raises his eyes. He gazes helplessly round the courtroom meeting the looks of men whose scientific integrity he has always revered, men of his own circle. He looks down at the floor. "I—I don't know—now," he murmurs.

And there he sits, looking a little more shrunken and grey each day as the logic of scientific conclusion piles up against him. A very bewildered man, for how can the findings of science be wrong?

And, you know, when he told his story to me I didn't feel that he was inventing any of it. So I can't believe they'll actually hang him—at least, I hope not…

# COMPASSION CIRCUIT

—

BY THE TIME Janet had been five days in hospital she had become converted to the idea of a domestic robot. It had taken her two days to discover that Nurse James *was* a robot, one day to get over the surprise, and two more to realize what a comfort an attendant robot could be.

The conversion was a relief. Practically every house she visited had a domestic robot; it was the family's second or third most valuable possession—the women tended to rate it slightly higher than the car; the men, slightly lower. Janet had been perfectly well aware for some time that her friends regarded her as a nitwit or worse for wearing herself out with looking after a house which a robot would be able to keep spick and span with a few hours' work a day. She had also known that it irritated George to come home each evening to a wife who had tired herself out by unnecessary work. But the prejudice had been firmly set. It was not the diehard attitude of people who refused to be served by robot waiters, or driven by robot drivers (who, incidentally, were much safer), led by robot shop-guides, or see dresses modelled by robot mannequins. It was simply an uneasiness about them, and being left alone with one—and a disinclination to feel such an uneasiness in her own home.

She herself attributed the feeling largely to the conservatism of her own home which had used no house-robots. Other people, who had been brought up in homes run by robots, even the primitive types available a generation before, never seemed to have such a feeling at all. It irritated her to know that her husband thought she was *afraid* of them in a childish way. That, she had explained to George a number of times, was not so, and was not the point, either: what she did dislike was the idea of one intruding upon her personal, domestic life, which was what a house-robot was bound to do.

The robot who was called Nurse James was, then, the first with which she had ever been in close personal contact and she, or it, came as a revelation.

Janet told the doctor of her enlightenment, and he looked relieved. She also told George when he looked in in the afternoon: he was delighted. The two of them conferred before he left the hospital. "Excellent," said the doctor. "To tell you the truth I was afraid we were up against a real neurosis there—and very inconveniently, too. Your wife can never have been strong, and in the last few years she's worn herself out running the house."

"I know," George agreed. "I tried hard to persuade her during the first two years we were married, but it only led to trouble so I had to drop it. This is really a culmination—she was rather shaken when she found that the reason she'd have to come here was partly because there was no robot at home to look after her."

"Well, there's one thing certain, she can't go on as she has been doing. If she tries to she'll be back here inside a couple of months," the doctor told him.

"She won't now. She's really changed her mind," George assured him. "Part of the trouble was that she's never come across a really modern one, except in a superficial way. The newest that any of our friends has is ten years old at least, and most of them are older than that. She'd never contemplated the idea of anything as advanced as Nurse James. The question now is what pattern?"

The doctor thought a moment.

"Frankly, Mr. Shand, your wife is going to need a lot of rest and looking after, I'm afraid. What I'd really recommend for her is the type they have here. It's something pretty new this Nurse James model. A specially developed high-sensibility job with a quite novel contra-balanced compassion-protection circuit—a very tricky bit of work that—any direct order which a normal robot would obey at once is evaluated by the circuit, it is weighed against the benefit or harm to the patient, and unless it is beneficial, or at least harmless, to the patient, it is not

obeyed. They've proved to be wonderful for nursing and looking after children—but there is a big demand for them, and I'm afraid they're pretty expensive."

"How much?" asked George.

The doctor's round-figure price made him frown for a moment. Then he said:

"It'll make a hole, but, after all, it's mostly Janet's economies and simple-living that's built up the savings. Where do I get one?"

"You don't. Not just like that," the doctor told him. "I shall have to throw a bit of weight about for a priority, but in the circumstances I shall get it, all right. Now, you go and fix up the details of appearance and so on with your wife. Let me know how she wants it, and I'll get busy."

---

"A PROPER ONE." said Janet. "One that'll look right in a house, I mean. I couldn't do with one of those levers-and-plastic box things that stare at you with lenses. As it's got to look after the house, let's have it looking like a housemaid."

"Or a houseman, if you like?"

She shook her head. "No. It's going to have to look after me, too, so I think I'd rather it was a housemaid. It can have a black silk dress and a frilly white apron and a cap. And I'd like it blonde—a sort of darkish blonde—and about five feet ten, and nice to look at, but not *too* beautiful. I don't want to be jealous of it…"

---

THE DOCTOR KEPT Janet ten days more in the hospital while the matter was settled. There had been luck in coming in for a cancelled order, but inevitably some delay while it was adapted to Janet's specification—also it had required the addition of standard domestic pseudo-memory patterns to suit it for housework.

It was delivered the day after she got back. Two severely functional robots carried the case up the front path, and inquired whether they should unpack it. Janet thought not, and told them to leave it in the outhouse.

When George got back he wanted to open it at once, but Janet shook her head.

"Supper first," she decided. "A robot doesn't mind waiting."

Nevertheless it was a brief meal. When it was over, George carried the dishes out and stacked them in the sink.

"No more washing-up," he said, with satisfaction.

He went out to borrow the next-door robot to help him carry the case in. Then he found his end of it more than he could lift, and had to borrow the robot from the house opposite, too. Presently the pair of them carried it in and laid it on the kitchen floor as if it were a featherweight, and went away again.

George got out the screwdriver and drew the six large screws that held the lid down. Inside there was a mass of shavings. He shoved them out, on to the floor.

Janet protested.

"What's the matter? *We* shan't have to clear up," he said, happily.

There was an inner case of wood pulp, with a snowy layer of wadding under its lid. George rolled it up and pushed it out of the way, and there, ready dressed in black frock and white apron, lay the robot.

They regarded it for some seconds without speaking.

It was remarkably lifelike. For some reason it made Janet feel a little queer to realize that it was *her* robot—a trifle nervous, and, obscurely, a trifle guilty...

"Sleeping beauty," remarked George, reaching for the instruction book on its chest.

In point of fact the robot was not a beauty. Janet's preference had been observed. It was pleasant and nice-looking without being striking, but the details were good. The deep gold hair was quite enviable—although one knew that it was probably threads of plastic with waves that would never come out. The skin—another kind of plastic covering the carefully built-up contours—was distinguishable from real skin only by its perfection.

Janet knelt down beside the box, and ventured a forefinger to touch the flawless complexion. It was quite, quite cold.

She sat back on her heels, looking at it. Just a big doll, she told herself; a contraption, a very wonderful contraption of metal, plastics and electronic circuits, but still a contraption, and made to look as it did simply because people, including herself, would find it harsh or grotesque if it should look any other way... And yet, to have it looking as it did was a bit disturbing, too. For one thing, you couldn't go on thinking of it as "it" any more; whether you liked it or not, your mind thought of it as "her". As "her" it would have to have a name; and, with a name, it would become still more of a person.

"'A battery-driven model,'" George read out, "'will normally require to be fitted with a new battery every four days. Other models, however, are designed to conduct their own regeneration from the mains as and when necessary.' Let's have her out."

He put his hands under the robot's shoulders, and tried to lift it.

"Phew!" he said. "Must be about three times my weight." He had another try. "Hell," he said, and referred to the book again.

"'The control switches are situated at the back, slightly above the waistline.' All right, maybe we can roll her over."

With an effort he succeeded in getting the figure on to its side and began to undo the buttons at the back of her dress. Janet suddenly felt that to be an indelicacy.

"I'll do it," she said.

Her husband glanced at her.

"All right. It's yours," he told her.

"She can't be just 'it.' I'm going to call her Hester."

"All right, again," he agreed.

Janet undid the buttons and fumbled about inside the dress.

"I can't find a knob, or anything," she said.

"Apparently there's a small panel that opens," he told her.

"Oh, no!" she said, in a slightly shocked tone.

He regarded her again.

"Darling, she's just a robot; a mechanism."

"I know," said Janet, shortly. She felt about again, discovered the panel, and opened it.

"You give the upper knob a half-turn to the right and then close the panel to complete the circuit," instructed George, from the book.

Janet did so, and then sat swiftly back on her heels again, watching.

The robot stirred and turned. It sat up, then it got to its feet. It stood before them, looking the very pattern of a stage parlourmaid.

"Good day, madam," it said. "Good day, sir. I shall be happy to serve you."

—

"THANK YOU, HESTER." Janet said, as she leaned back against the cushion placed behind her. Not that it was necessary to thank a robot, but she had a theory that if you did not practise politeness with robots you soon forgot it with other people.

And, anyway, Hester was no ordinary robot. She was not even dressed as a parlourmaid any more. In four months she had become a friend, a tireless, attentive friend. From the first Janet had found it difficult to believe that she was only a mechanism, and as the days passed she had become more and more of a person. The fact that she consumed electricity instead of food came to seem little more than a foible. The time she couldn't stop walking in a circle, and the other time when something went wrong with her vision so that she did everything a foot to the right of where she ought to have been doing it, these things were just indispositions such as anyone might have, and the robot-mechanic who came to adjust her paid his call much like any other doctor. Hester was not only a person; she was preferable company to many.

"I suppose," said Janet, settling back in her chair, "that you must think me a poor, weak thing?"

What one must not expect from Hester was euphemism.

"Yes," she said, directly. But then she added: "I think all humans are poor, weak things. It is the way they are made. One must be sorry for them."

Janet had long ago given up thinking things like: "That'll be the compassion-circuit speaking," or trying to imagine the computing, selecting, associating, and shunting that must be going on to produce such a remark. She took it as she might from—well, say, a foreigner. She said:

"Compared with robots we must seem so, I suppose. You are so strong and untiring, Hester. If you knew how I envy you that…"

Hester said, matter of factly:

"We were designed: you were just accidental. It is your misfortune, not your fault."

"You'd rather be you than me?" asked Janet.

"Certainly," Hester told her. "We are stronger. We don't have to have frequent sleep to recuperate. We don't have to carry an unreliable chemical factory inside us. We don't have to grow old and deteriorate. Human beings are so clumsy and fragile and so often unwell because something is not working properly. If anything goes wrong with us, or is broken, it doesn't hurt and is easily replaced. And you have all kinds of words like pain, and suffering, and unhappiness, and weariness that we have to be taught to understand, and they don't seem to us to be useful things to have. I feel very sorry that you must have these things and be so uncertain and so fragile. It disturbs my compassion-circuit."

"Uncertain and fragile," Janet repeated. "Yes, that's how I feel."

"Humans have to live so precariously," Hester went on. "If my arm or leg should be crushed I can have a new one in a few minutes, but a human would have agony for a long time, and not even a new limb at the end of it—just a faulty one, if he is lucky. That isn't as bad as it used to be because in designing us you learned how to make good arms and legs, much stronger and better than the old ones. People would be much more sensible to have a weak arm or leg replaced at once, but they don't seem to want to if they can possibly keep the old ones."

"You mean they can be grafted on? I didn't know that," Janet said. "I wish it were only arms or legs that's wrong with me. I don't think I would hesitate…" She sighed. "The doctor wasn't encouraging this morning, Hester. You heard what he said? I've been losing ground: must rest more. I don't believe he does expect me to get any stronger. He was just trying to cheer me up before… He had a funny sort of look after he'd examined me… But all he said was rest. What's the good of being alive if it's only rest—rest—rest…? And there's poor George. What sort of a life is it for him, and he's so patient with me, so sweet… I'd rather anything than go on feebly like this. I'd sooner die…"

Janet went on talking, more to herself than to the patient Hester standing by. She talked herself into tears. Then, presently, she looked up.

"Oh, Hester, if you were human I couldn't bear it; I think I'd hate you for being so strong and so well—but I don't, Hester. You're so kind and so patient when I'm silly, like this. I believe you'd cry with me to keep me company if you could."

"I would if I could," the robot agreed. "My compassion-circuit—"

"Oh, *no!*" Janet protested. "It can't be just that. You've a heart somewhere, Hester. You must have."

"I expect it is more reliable than a heart," said Hester.

She stepped a little closer, stooped down, and lifted Janet up as if she weighed nothing at all.

"You've tired yourself out, Janet, dear," she told her. "I'll take you upstairs; you'll be able to sleep a little before he gets back."

Janet could feel the robot's arms cold through her dress, but the coldness did not trouble her any more, she was aware only that they were strong, protecting arms around her. She said:

"Oh, Hester, you are such a comfort, you *know* what I ought to do." She paused, then she added miserably: "I know what he thinks—the doctor, I mean. I could see it. He just thinks I'm going to go on getting weaker and weaker until one day I'll fade away and die… I said I'd sooner die…but I wouldn't, Hester. I don't want to die…"

The robot rocked her a little, as if she were a child.

"There, there, dear. It's not as bad as that—nothing like," she told her. "You mustn't think about dying. And you mustn't cry any more, it's not good for you, you know. Besides, you don't want him to see you've been crying."

"I'll try not to," agreed Janet obediently, as Hester carried her out of the room and up the stairs.

—

THE HOSPITAL RECEPTION-ROBOT looked up from the desk.

"My wife," George said, "I rang you up about an hour ago."

The robot's face took on an impeccable expression of professional sympathy.

"Yes, Mr. Shand. I'm afraid it has been a shock for you, but as I told you, your house-robot did quite the right thing to send her here at once."

"I've tried to get on to her own doctor, but he's away," George told her.

"You don't need to worry about that, Mr. Shand. She has been examined, and we have had all her records sent over from the hospital she was in before. The operation has been provisionally fixed for tomorrow, but of course we shall need your consent."

George hesitated. "May I see the doctor in charge of her?"

"He isn't in the hospital at the moment, I'm afraid."

"Is it—absolutely necessary?" George asked after a pause.

The robot looked at him steadily, and nodded.

"She must have been growing steadily weaker for some months now," she said. George nodded.

"The only alternative is that she will grow weaker still, and have more pain before the end," she told him.

George stared at the wall blankly for some seconds.

"I see," he said bleakly.

He picked up a pen in a shaky hand and signed the form that she put before him. He gazed at it awhile without seeing it.

"She'll—she'll have—a good chance?" he asked.

"Yes," the robot told him. "There is never complete absence of risk, of course, but she has a better than seventy-per-cent likelihood of complete success."

George sighed, and nodded.

"I'd like to see her," he said.

The robot pressed a bell-push.

"You may *see* her," she said. "But I must ask you not to disturb her. She's asleep now, and it's better for her not to be woken."

George had to be satisfied with that, but he left the hospital feeling a little better for the sight of the quiet smile on Janet's lips as she slept.

—

THE HOSPITAL CALLED him at the office the following afternoon. They were reassuring. The operation appeared to have been a complete success. Everyone was quite confident of the outcome. There was no need to worry. The doctors were perfectly satisfied. No, it would not be wise to allow any visitors for a few days yet. But there was nothing to worry about. Nothing at all.

George rang up each day just before he left, in the hope that he would be allowed a visit. The hospital was kindly and heartening, but adamant about visits. And then, on the fifth day, they suddenly told him she had left on her way home. George was staggered: he had been prepared to find it a matter of weeks. He dashed out, bought a bunch of roses, and left half a dozen traffic regulations in fragments behind him.

"Where is she?" he demanded of Hester as she opened the door.

"She's in bed. I thought it might be better if—" Hester began, but he lost the rest of the sentence as he bounded up the stairs.

Janet was lying in the bed. Only her head was visible, cut off by the line of the sheet and a bandage round her neck. George put the flowers down on the bedside table. He stooped over Janet and kissed her gently. She looked up at him from anxious eyes.

"Oh, George dear. Has she told you?"

"Has who told me what?" he asked, sitting down on the side of the bed.

"Hester. She said she would. Oh, George, I didn't mean it, at least I don't think I meant it… She sent me, George. I was so weak and wretched. I wanted to be strong. I don't think I really understood. Hester said—"

"Take it easy, darling. Take it easy," George suggested with a smile. "What on earth's all this about?"

He felt under the bedclothes and found her hand.

"But, George—" she began. He interrupted her.

"I say, darling, your hand's dreadfully cold. It's almost like—" His fingers slid further up her arm. His eyes widened at her, incredulously. He jumped up suddenly from the bed and flung back the covers. He put his hand on the thin nightdress, over her heart—and then snatched it away as if he had been stung.

"God!— *NO!*—" he said, staring at her.

"But George. George, darling—" said Janet's head on the pillows.

"NO!— *NO!*" cried George, almost in a shriek.

He turned and ran blindly from the room.

In the darkness on the landing he missed the top step of the stairs, and went headlong down the whole flight.

# COMPASSION CIRCUIT

—

HESTER FOUND HIM lying in a huddle in the hall. She bent down and gently explored the damage. The extent of it, and the fragility of the frame that had suffered it disturbed her compassion-circuit very greatly. She did not try to move him, but went to the telephone and dialled.

"Emergency?" she asked, and gave the name and address. "Yes, at once," she told them. "There may not be a lot of time. Several compound fractures, and I think his back is broken, poor man. No. There appears to be no damage to his head. Yes, much better. He'd be crippled for life, even if he did get over it... Yes, better send the form of consent with the ambulance so that it can be signed at once... Oh, yes, that'll be quite all right. His wife will sign it."

# BRIEF TO COUNSEL

—

"**A**ND THAT," INSISTED the clerk of the Court, "is the verdict of you all?"

"Yes," said the foreman of the jury. Then, as if he felt a monosyllable to be inadequate to the solemnity of the occasion, he added, "It is."

The clerk of the Court let his eyes rest upon the members of the jury for a moment, then he turned towards the dock.

"Prisoner at the bar," he said, "you stand convicted of capital murder. Have you anything to say as to why the Court should not proceed to judgment according to law?"

The prisoner regarded his own hands gripping the rail. He looked up. "Yes," he said, and turned towards the Judge. "My lord, I do not understand why the evidence of my witnesses, which is vital to me, has been disregarded."

The Judge leaned forward a little.

"If you consider that an irregularity has taken place at this trial, your remedy lies in an Appeal on those grounds," he explained. "The purpose of this allocutus is to permit you to draw the Court's attention to any irregularity you consider to exist on the face of the record."

"Am I to understand, my lord, that the law completely denies the existence of the power of second sight?" the prisoner inquired.

"Any person professing to tell fortunes is considered in law to be a rogue and a vagabond, and so becomes liable to prosecution under the Vagrancy Act of 1824. Does that answer your question?" asked his lordship.

The prisoner considered. "Not entirely, my lord. Does professing mean *falsely* professing?"

"It means what it says: it means one who claims to be able to tell fortunes. And I take the profession of a power of second sight to be such a claim."

"But, my lord, I cannot see why I was not given an opportunity to show whether my claim was, in certain circumstances, true—any more than I can see why my witnesses' evidence that I have such an ability was ruled to be inadmissible."

"For the latter, as I have said, your remedy may lie on Appeal." The prisoner and the Judge regarded one another steadily for a moment.

"And now, if—" began the Judge.

"But, my lord—" said the prisoner, simultaneously.

The Judge, mindful that justice should not only be done, but should be seen to be done, checked himself.

The prisoner continued earnestly, "My lord, I am a Midlander, but my parents were not. They came from the Outer Isles. The power of the sight is well recognised there; it was in both their families, and I have it, too. Not always, but sometimes, and with some men, I can see it and feel it—as though the angel of death were hovering near them.

"When I was young I let several of my friends know about it, they are my witnesses; but when I grew older I found that was unwise, so I did not talk of it.

"On the evening my friend was shot I called at his house. That is why my footprints were there; that is why my fingerprints were found in his sitting-room. I had meant to spend the evening with him, but then, while I was sitting there, I suddenly had the sight. I could see death close, close behind him, reaching out for him, dreadfully near. It is a terrible thing, my lord. I could not tell him, but I could not stay there with him—I could not.

"So I left him, and I went into the inn. I drank because I was distressed for my friend. I drank too much. I'd have said nothing if I had been sober. But I told them he was dead. And although I was drunk I must have impressed them, for two men went off to see what had happened—and they found him dead. But nobody has believed me. Everybody has said, 'You must have been there at the time, or you could not have known...' But I did, my lord. I saw it close upon him.

"All the rest is circumstantial. The footprints, the fingerprints, I have never denied them. The pistol, as I have told you, had been missing for more than a week before it happened; I did not report that because I had no licence for it. His ring—would I put his ring in my desk for anyone to find, if I had done it? The ring was put there to provide evidence against me; and the money, too. He was my friend, my lord. I had nothing to do with it, except that I saw death so close to him, and knew that it must come very soon. I did not know how. All I ask, my lord, is the chance to prove what I claim..."

The Judge shook his head slightly. "The Court has already heard all this. The jury have considered it, and delivered their verdict. If you have nothing further to add, I shall proceed. Well, have you something to add?"

"I have, my lord. I do not wish to do it, but I am left with no alternative."

His eyes left the bench and turned towards the body of the Court where they encountered those of the prosecuting counsel. He hesitated, then he raised his right hand, his finger pointing at counsel.

"That man," he said, "has about twelve minutes to live, God help him."

The Judge frowned.

"That is a thoroughly improper remark," he observed.

A growing murmur in the Court was sharply called to order and hushed.

The Judge, looking at the prisoner, remarked, "I cannot imagine what you hope to gain by such impertinence, but if I am right in assuming it to be some form of threat of revenge, you must learn that the course of justice in Her Majesty's Courts is not to be diverted by threats. I shall now proceed in judgment. The sentence of the Court upon you is that you suffer death in the manner authorised by law."

Silence hung over the Court.

It was broken by a curious sound from one of the benches. All eyes turned in time to see the counsel for the prosecution loll inertly to one side, and slip from the bench to the floor.

For a moment no one moved, then two barristers jumped forward, and went down on their knees beside the black-gowned figure of their colleague.

Slowly the Judge's head turned back until his eyes met those of the prisoner still standing in the dock. For an instant the two regarded one another.

"Your lordship has about two months," said the prisoner.

Then, as his escort tapped him on the arm, he bowed very slightly to the Judge.

# ODD

—

WHEN, ON A day in the late December of 1958, Mr. Reginald Aster called upon the legal firm of Cropthorne, Daggit, and Howe, of Bedford Row, at their invitation, he found himself received by a Mr. Fratton, an amiable young man, barely out of his twenties, but now head of the firm in succession to the defunct Messrs. C, D & H.

And when Mr. Aster was informed by Mr. Fratton that under the terms of the late Sir Andrew Vincell's will he was a beneficiary to the extent of six thousand Ordinary Shares in British Vinvinyl, Ltd., Mr. Aster appeared, as Mr. Fratton expressed it to a colleague later, to miss for a while on several plugs.

The relevant clause added that the bequest was made "in recognition of a most valuable service which he once rendered me". The nature of this service was not specified, nor was it any of Mr. Fratton's business to inquire into it, but the veil over his curiosity was scarcely opaque.

The windfall, standing just then at 83s. 6d. per share, came at a fortunate moment in Mr. Aster's affairs. Realization of a small part of the shares enabled him to settle one or two pressing problems, and in the course of this re-ordering, the two men met several times. At length there came a time when Mr. Fratton, urged on by curiosity, stepped slightly closer to the edge of professional discretion than he usually permitted himself, to remark in a tentative fashion:

"You did not know Sir Andrew very well, did you?"

It was the kind of advance that Mr. Aster could easily have discouraged had he wished to, but, in fact, he made no attempt at parry. Instead, he looked thoughtful, and eyed Mr. Fratton with speculation.

"I met Sir Andrew once," he said. "For perhaps an hour and a half."

"That is rather what I thought," said Mr. Fratton, allowing his perplexity to become a little more evident. "Some time last June, wasn't it?"

"The twenty-fifth of June," Mr. Aster agreed.

"But never before that?"

"No—nor since."

Mr. Fratton shook his head uncomprehendingly.

After a pause Mr. Aster said:

"You know, there's something pretty rum about this."

Mr. Fratton nodded, but made no comment. Aster went on:

"I'd rather like to—well, look here, are you free for dinner tomorrow?"

Mr. Fratton was, and when the dinner was finished they retired to a quiet corner of the club lounge with coffee and cigars. After a few moments of consideration Aster said:

"I must admit I'd feel happier if this Vincell business was a bit clearer. I don't see—well, there's something altogether off-beat about it. I might as well tell you the whole thing. Here's what happened."

—

THE TWENTY-FIFTH OF June was a pleasant evening in an unpleasant summer. I was just strolling home enjoying it. In no hurry at all, and just wondering whether I would turn in for a drink somewhere when I saw this old man. He was standing on the pavement in Thanet Street, holding on to the railings with one hand, and looking about him in a dazed, glassy-eyed way.

Well, in our part of London, as you know, there are plenty of strangers from all over the world, particularly in the summer, and quite a few of them look a bit lost. But this old man—well on in the seventies, I judged—was not that sort. Certainly no tourist. In fact, elegant was the word that occurred to me when I saw him. He had a grey, pointed beard, carefully trimmed, a black felt hat meticulously brushed; a dark suit of excellent cloth and cut; his shoes were expensive; so was his discreetly beautiful silk tie. Gentlemen of this type are not altogether unknown to us in our parts, but they are likely to be off their usual beat; and alone, and in a glassy-eyed condition in public, they are quite rare. One or two people walking ahead of me glanced at him briefly, had the reflex thought about his condition, and passed on. I did not; he did not appear to me to be ordinarily fuddled—more, indeed, as if he were frightened... So I paused beside him.

"Are you unwell?" I asked him. "Would you like me to call a taxi?"

He turned to look at me. His eyes were bewildered, but it was an intelligent face, slightly ascetic, and made to look the thinner by bushy white eyebrows. He seemed to bring me into focus only slowly; his response came more slowly still, and with an effort.

"No," he said, uncertainly, "no, thank you. I—I am not unwell."

It did not appear to be the full truth, but neither was it a definite dismissal, and, having made the approach, I did not care to leave him like that.

"You have had a shock," I told him.

His eyes were on the traffic in the street. He nodded, but said nothing.

"There is a hospital just a couple of streets away—" I began. But he shook his head.

"No," he said again. "I shall be all right in a minute or two."

He still did not tell me to go away, and I had a feeling that he did not want me to. His eyes turned this way and that, and then down at himself. At that, he became quite still and tense, staring down at his clothes with an astonishment that could not be anything but real. He let go of the railings, lifted his arm to look at his sleeve, then he noticed his hand—a shapely, well-kept hand, but thin with age, knuckles withered, blue veins prominent. It wore a gold signet ring on the little finger...

Well, we have all read of eyes bulging, but that is the only time I have seen it happen. They looked ready to pop out, and the extended hand began to shake distressingly. He tried to speak, but nothing came. I began to fear that he might be in for a heart attack.

"The hospital—" I began again, but once more he shook his head.

I did not know quite what to do, but I thought he ought to sit down; and brandy often helps, too. He said neither yes nor no to my suggestion, but came with me acquiescently across the street and into the Wilburn Hotel. I steered him to a table in the bar there, and sent for double brandies for both of us. When I turned back from the waiter, the old man was staring across the room with an expression of horror. I looked over there quickly. It was himself he was staring at, in a mirror.

He watched himself intently as he took off his hat and put it down on a chair beside him; then he put up his hand, still trembling, to touch first his beard, and then his handsome silver hair. After that, he sat quite still, staring.

I was relieved when the drinks came. So, evidently, was he. He took just a little soda with his, and then drank the lot. Presently his hand grew steadier, a little colour came into his cheeks, but he continued to stare ahead. Then with a sudden air of resolution he got up.

"Excuse me a moment," he said, politely.

He crossed the room. For fully two minutes he stood studying himself at short range in the glass. Then he turned and came back. Though not assured, he had an air of more decision, and he signed to the waiter, pointing to our glasses. Looking at me curiously, he said as he sat down again:

"I owe you an apology. You have been extremely kind."

"Not at all," I assured him. "I'm glad to be of any help. Obviously you must have had a nasty shock of some sort."

"Er—several shocks," he admitted, and added: "It is curious how real the figments of a dream can seem when one is taken unaware by them."

There did not seem to be any useful response to that, so I attempted none.

"Quite unnerving at first," he added, with a kind of forced brightness.

"What happened?" I asked, feeling still at sea.

"My own fault, entirely my own fault—but I was in a hurry," he explained. "I started to cross the road behind a tram, then I saw the one coming in the opposite direction, almost on top of me. I can only think it must have hit me."

"Oh," I said, "er—oh, indeed. Er—where did this happen?"

"Just outside here, in Thanet Street," he told me.

"You—you don't seem to be hurt," I remarked.

"Not exactly," he agreed, doubtfully. "No, I don't seem to be hurt."

He did not, nor even ruffled. His clothing was, as I have said, immaculate—besides, they tore up the tram rails in Thanet Street about twenty-five years ago. I wondered if I should tell him that, and decided to postpone it. The waiter brought our glasses. The old man felt in his waistcoat pocket, and then looked down in consternation.

"My sovereign-case! My watch…!" he exclaimed.

I dealt with the waiter by handing him a one-pound note. The old man watched intently. When the waiter had given me my change and left:

"If you will excuse me," I said, "I think this shock must have caused you a lapse of memory. You do—er—you do remember who you are?"

With his finger still in his waistcoat pocket, and a trace of suspicion in his eyes, he looked at me hard.

"Who I am? Of course I do. I am Andrew Vincell. I live quite close here, in Hart Street."

I hesitated, then I said:

"There *was* a Hart Street near here. But they changed the name—in the thirties I think; before the war, anyway."

The superficial confidence which he had summoned up deserted him, and he sat quite still for some moments. Then he felt in the inside pocket of his jacket, and pulled out a wallet. It was made of fine leather, had gold corners, and was stamped with the initials A.V. He eyed it curiously as he laid it on the table. Then he opened it. From the left side he pulled a one-pound note, and frowned at it in a puzzled way; then a five-pound note, which seemed to puzzle him still more.

Without comment he felt in the pocket again, and brought out a slender book clearly intended to pair with the wallet. It, too, bore the initials A.V. in the lower right-hand corner, and in the upper it was stamped simply: "Diary—1958." He held it in his hand, looking at it for quite some time before he lifted his eyes to mine.

"Nineteen-fifty-eight?" he said, unsteadily.

"Yes," I told him.

There was a long pause, then:

"I don't understand," he said, almost like a child. "My life! What has happened to my life?"

His face had a pathetic, crumpled look. I pushed the glass towards him, and he drank a little of the brandy. Opening the diary, he looked at the calendar inside.

"Oh, God!" he said. "This is too real. What—what has happened to me?"

I said, sympathetically:

"A partial loss of memory isn't unusual after a shock, you know—in a little time it comes back quite all right as a rule. I suggest you look in there"—I pointed to the wallet—"very likely there will be something to remind you."

He hesitated, but then felt in the right-hand side of it. The first thing he pulled out was a colour-print of a snapshot; obviously a family group. The central figure was himself, five or six years younger, in a tweed suit; another man, about forty-five, bore a family resemblance, and there were two slightly younger women, and two girls and two boys in their early teens. In the background part of an eighteenth-century house was visible across a well-kept lawn.

"I don't think you need to worry about your life," I said. "It would appear to have been very satisfactory."

There followed three engraved cards, separated by tissues, which announced simply: "Sir Andrew Vincell", but gave no address. There was also an envelope addressed to Sir Andrew Vincell, O.B.E., British Vinvinyl Plastics, Ltd., somewhere in London EC1.

He shook his head, took another sip of the brandy, looked at the envelope again, and gave an unamused laugh. Then with a visible effort he took a grip on himself, and said, decisively:

"This is some silly kind of dream. How does one wake up?" He closed his eyes, and declared in a firm tone: "I am Andrew Vincell. I am aged twenty-three. I live at number forty-eight Hart Street. I am articled to Penberthy and Trull, chartered accountants, of one hundred and two, Bloomsbury Square. This is July the twelfth, nineteen hundred and six. This morning I was struck by a tram in Thanet Street. I must have been knocked silly, and have been suffering from hallucinations. Now!"

He re-opened his eyes, and looked genuinely surprised to find me still there. Then he glared at the envelope, and his expression grew peevish.

"*Sir* Andrew Vincell!" he exclaimed scornfully, "and Vinvinyl Plastics, Limited! What the devil is that supposed to mean?"

"Don't you think," I suggested, "that we must assume that you are a member of the firm—I would say, from appearances, one of its directors?"

"But I told you—" He broke off. "What *is* plastics?" he went on. "It doesn't suggest anything but modelling clay to me. What on earth would I be doing with modelling clay?"

I hesitated. It looked as if the shock, whatever it was, had had the effect of cutting some fifty years out of his memory. Perhaps, I thought, if we were to talk of a matter which was obviously familiar and important to him it might stir his recollection. I tapped the table top.

"Well, this, for instance, is a plastic," I told him.

He examined it, and clicked his finger-nails on it.

"I'd not call that plastic. It is very hard," he observed.

I tried to explain:

"It was plastic before it hardened. There are lots of different kinds of plastics. This ash-tray, the covering on your chair, this pen, my cheque-book cover, that woman's raincoat, her handbag, the handle of her umbrella, dozens of things all round you—even my shirt is a woven plastic."

He did not reply immediately, but sat looking from one to another of these things with growing attention. At last he turned back to me again. This time his eyes gazed into mine with great intensity. His voice shook slightly as he said once more:

"This really *is* 1958?"

"Certainly it is," I assured him. "If you don't believe your own diary, there's a calendar hanging behind the bar."

"No horses," he murmured to himself, "and the trees in the Square grown so tall…a dream is never consistent, not to that extent…" He paused, then, suddenly: "My God!" he exclaimed, "my God, if it really *is*…" He turned to me again, with an eager gleam in his eyes. "Tell me about these plastics," he demanded urgently.

I am no chemist, and I know no more about them than the next man. However, he was obviously keen, and, as I have said, I thought that a familiar subject might help to revive his memory, so I decided to try. I pointed to the ash-tray.

"Well, this is very likely Bakelite, I think. If so, it is one of the earliest of the thermosetting plastics. A man called Baekeland patented it, about 1909, I fancy. Something to do with phenol and formaldehyde."

"Thermosetting? What's that?" he inquired.

I did my best with that, and then went on to explain what little I had picked up about molecular chains and arrangements, polymerization and so on, and some of the characteristics and uses. He did not give me any feeling of trying to teach my grandmother, on the contrary, he listened with concentrated attention, occasionally repeating a word now and then as if to fix it in his mind. This hanging upon my words was quite flattering, but I could not delude myself that they were doing anything to revive his memory.

We must—at least, I must—have talked for nearly an hour, and all the time he sat earnest and tense, with his hands clenched tightly together. Then I noticed that the effect of the brandy had worn off, and he was again looking far from well.

"I really think I had better see you home," I told him. "Can you remember where you live?"

"Forty-eight Hart Street," he said.

"No. I mean where you live now," I insisted.

But he was not really listening. His face still had the expression of great concentration.

"If only I can remember—if only I can remember when I wake up," he murmured desperately, to himself rather than to me. Then he turned to look at me again.

"What is your name?" he asked.

I told him.

"I'll remember that, too, if I can," he assured me, very seriously.

I leaned over and lifted the cover of the diary. His name was on the fly-leaf, with an address in Upper Grosvenor Street. I folded the wallet and the diary together, and put them into his hand. He stowed them away in his pocket automatically, and then sat gazing with complete detachment while the porter got us a taxi.

An elderly woman, a housekeeper, I imagine, opened the door of an impressive flat. I suggested that she should ring up Sir Andrew's doctor, and stayed long enough to explain the situation to him when he arrived.

The following evening I rang up to inquire how he was. A younger woman's voice answered. She told me that he had slept well after a sedative, woken somewhat tired, but quite himself, with no sign of any lapse of memory. The doctor saw no cause for alarm. She thanked me for taking care of him, and bringing him home, and that was that.

In fact, I had practically forgotten the whole incident until I saw the announcement of his death in the paper, in December.

―

MR. FRATTON MADE no comment for some moments, then he drew at his cigar, sipped some coffee, and said, not very constructively:

"It's odd."

"So I thought—think," said Mr. Aster.

"I mean," went on Mr. Fratton, "I mean, you certainly did him a kindly service, but scarcely, if you will forgive me, a service that one would expect to find valued at six thousand one-pound shares—standing at eighty-three and sixpence, too."

"Quite," agreed Mr. Aster.

"Odder still," Mr. Fratton went on, "this meeting occurred last summer. But the will containing the bequest was drawn up and signed seven years ago." He again drew thoughtfully on his cigar. "And I cannot see that I am breaking any confidence if I tell you that it superseded an earlier will drawn up twelve years before, and in that will also, the same clause occurred." He meditated upon his companion.

"I have given it up," said Mr. Aster, "but if you are collecting oddities, you might perhaps like to make a note of this one." He produced a pocket-book, and took from it a cutting. The strip of paper was headed: "Obituary. Sir Andrew Vincell—A Pioneer in Plastics." Mr. Aster located a passage halfway down the column, and read out:

"'It is curious to note that in his youth Sir Andrew foreshadowed none of his later interests, and was indeed articled at one time to a firm of chartered accountants. At the age of twenty-three, however, in the summer of 1906, he abruptly and quite unexpectedly broke his articles, and began to devote himself to chemistry. Within a few years he had made the first of the important discoveries upon which his great company was subsequently built.'"

"H'm," said Mr. Fratton. He looked carefully at Mr. Aster. "He *was* knocked down by a tram in Thanet Street, in 1906 you know."

"Of course. He told me so," said Mr. Aster.

Mr. Fratton shook his head.

"It's all very queer," he observed.

"Very odd indeed," agreed Mr. Aster.

# THE ASTEROIDS, 2194

—

MY FIRST VISIT to New Caledonia was in the summer of 2199. At that time an exploration party under the leadership of Gilbert Troon was cautiously pushing its way up the less radio-active parts of Italy, investigating the prospects of reclamation. My firm felt there might be a popular book in it, and assigned me to put the proposition to Gilbert. When I arrived, however, it was to find that he had been delayed, and was now expected a week later. I was not at all displeased. A few days of comfortable laziness on a Pacific island, all paid for and counting as work, is the kind of perquisite I like.

New Caledonia is a fascinating spot, and well worth the trouble of getting a landing permit—if you can get one. It has more of the past—and more of the future, too, for that matter—than any other place, and somehow it manages to keep them almost separate.

At one time the island, and the group, were, in spite of the name, a French colony. But in 2044, with the eclipse of Europe in the Great Northern War, it found itself, like other ex-colonies dotted all about the world, suddenly thrown upon its own resources. While most mainland colonies hurried to make treaties with their nearest powerful neighbours, many islands such as New Caledonia had little to offer and not much to fear, and so let things drift.

For two generations the surviving nations were far too occupied by the tasks of bringing equilibrium to a half-wrecked world to take any interest in scattered islands. It was not until the Brazilians began to see Australia as a possible challenger of their supremacy that they started a policy of unobtrusive, and tactfully mercantile, expansion into the Pacific. Then, naturally, it occurred to the Australians, too, that it was time to begin to extend *their* economic influence over various island-groups.

The New Caledonians resisted infiltration. They had found independence congenial, and steadily rebuffed temptations by both parties. The year 2144, in which Space declared for independence, found them still resisting; but the pressure was now considerable. They had watched one group of islands after another succumb to trade preferences, and thereafter virtually slide back to colonial status, and they now found it difficult to doubt that before long the same would happen to themselves when, whatever the form of words, they should be annexed—most likely by the Australians in order to forestall the establishment of a Brazilian base there, within a thousand miles of the coast.

It was into this situation that Jayme Gonveia, speaking for Space, stepped in 2150 with a suggestion of his own. He offered the New Caledonians guaranteed independence of either big Power, a considerable quantity of cash and a prosperous future if they would grant Space a lease of territory which would become its Earth headquarters and main terminus.

The proposition was not altogether to the New Caledonian taste, but it was better than the alternatives. They accepted, and the construction of the Spaceyards was begun.

Since then the island has lived in a curious symbiosis. In the north are the rocket landing and dispatch stages, warehouses and engineering shops, and a way of life furnished with all modern techniques, while the other four-fifths of the island all but ignores it, and contentedly lives much as it did two and a half centuries ago. Such a state of affairs cannot be preserved by accident in this world. It is the result of careful contrivance both by the New Caledonians who like it that way, and by Space which dislikes outsiders taking too close an interest in its affairs. So, for permission to land anywhere in the group, one needs hard-won visas from both authorities. The result is no exploitation by tourists or salesmen, and a scarcity of strangers.

HOWEVER, THERE I was, with an unexpected week of leisure to put in, and no reason why I should spend it in Space-Concession territory. One of the secretaries suggested Lahua, down in the south at no great distance from Noumea, the capital, as a restful spot, so thither I went.

Lahua has picture-book charm. It is a small fishing town, half-tropical, half-French. On its wide white beach there are still canoes, working canoes, as well as modern. At one end of the curve a mole gives shelter for a small anchorage, and there the palms that fringe the rest of the shore stop to make room for a town.

Many of Lahua's houses are improved-traditional, still thatched with palm, but its heart is a cobbled rectangle surrounded by entirely untropical houses, known as the Grande Place. Here are shops, pavement cafés, stalls of fruit under bright striped awnings guarded by Gauguinesque women, a state of Bougainville, an atrociously ugly church on the east side, a *pissoir*, and even a *mairie*. The whole thing might have been imported complete from early twentieth-century France, except for the inhabitants—but even they, some in bright sarongs, some in European clothes, must have looked much the same when France ruled there.

I found it difficult to believe that they are real people living real lives. For the first day I was constantly accompanied by the feeling that an unseen director would suddenly call "Cut," and it would all come to a stop.

On the second morning I was growing more used to it. I bathed, and then with a sense that I was beginning to get the feel of the life, drifted to the *place*, in search of apéritif. I chose a café on the south side where a few trees shaded the tables, and wondered what to order. My usual drinks seemed out of key. A dusky, brightly saronged girl approached. On an impulse, and feeling like a character out of a very old novel I suggested a pernod. She took it as a matter of course.

"*Un pernod? Certainement, monsieur,*" she told me.

I sat there looking across the Square, less busy now that the *déjeuner* hour was close, wondering what Sydney and Rio, Adelaide and São Paulo had gained and lost since they had been the size of Lahua, and doubting the value of the gains...

The pernod arrived. I watched it cloud with water, and sipped it cautiously. An odd drink, scarcely calculated, I felt, to enhance the appetite. As I contemplated it a voice spoke from behind my right shoulder.

"An island product, but from the original recipe," it said. "Quite safe, in moderation, I assure you."

I turned in my chair. The speaker was seated at the next table; a well-built, compact, sandy-haired man, dressed in a spotless white suit, a panama hat with a coloured band, and wearing a neatly trimmed, pointed beard. I guess his age at about thirty-four though the grey eyes that met my own looked older, more experienced and troubled.

"A taste that I have not had the opportunity to acquire," I told him. He nodded.

"You won't find it outside. In some ways we are a museum here, but little the worse, I think, for that."

"One of the later Muses," I suggested. "The Muse of Recent History. And very fascinating, too."

I became aware that one or two men at tables within earshot were paying us—or rather me—some attention; their expressions were not unfriendly, but they showed what seemed to be traces of concern.

"It is—" my neighbour began to reply, and then broke off, cut short by a rumble in the sky.

I turned to see a slender white spire stabbing up into the blue overhead. Already, by the time the sound reached us, the rocket at its apex was too small to be visible. The man cocked an eye at it.

"Moon-shuttle," he observed.

"They all sound and look alike to me," I admitted.

"They wouldn't if you were inside. The acceleration in that shuttle would spread you all over the floor—very thinly," he said, and then went on: "We don't often see strangers in Lahua. Perhaps you would care to give me the pleasure of your company for luncheon? My name, by the way, is George."

I hesitated, and while I did I noticed over his shoulder an elderly man who moved his lips slightly as he gave me what was without doubt an encouraging nod. I decided to take a chance on it.

"That's very kind of you. My name is David—David Myford, from Sydney," I told him. But he made no amplification regarding himself, so I was left wondering whether George was his forename, or his surname.

I moved to his table, and he lifted a hand to summon the girl.

"Unless you are averse to fish you must try the bouillabaisse—*spécialité de la maison,*" he told me.

I was aware that I had gained the approval of the elderly man, and apparently of some others as well, by joining George. The waitress, too, had an approving air. I wondered vaguely what was going on, and whether I had been let in for the town bore, to protect the rest.

"From Sydney," he said reflectively. "It's a long time since I saw Sydney. I don't suppose I'd know it now."

"It keeps on growing," I admitted, "but Nature would always prevent you from confusing it with anywhere else."

We went on chatting. The bouillabaisse arrived; and excellent it was. There were hunks of first-class bread, too, cut from those long loaves you see in pictures in old European books. I began to feel, with the help of the local wine, that a lot could be said for the twentieth-century way of living.

In the course of our talk it emerged that George had been a rocket pilot, but was grounded now—not, one would judge, for reasons of health, so I did not inquire further…

—

THE SECOND COURSE was an excellent coupe of fruits I had never heard of, and, overall, iced passion-fruit juice. It was when the coffee came that he said, rather wistfully I thought:

"I had hoped you might be able to help me, Mr. Myford, but it now seems to me that you are not a man of faith."

"Surely everyone has to be very much a man of faith," I protested. "For everything a man cannot do for himself he has to have faith in others."

"True," he conceded. "I should have said "spiritual faith". You do not speak as one who is interested in the nature and destiny of his soul—or of anyone else's soul—I fear?"

I felt that I perceived what was coming next. However if he was interested in saving my soul he had at least begun the operation by looking after my bodily needs with a generously good meal.

"When I was young," I told him, "I used to worry quite a lot about my soul, but later I decided that that was largely a matter of vanity."

"There is also vanity in thinking oneself self-sufficient," he said.

"Certainly," I agreed. "It is chiefly with the conception of the soul as a separate entity that I find myself out of sympathy. For me it is a manifestation of mind which is, in its turn, a product of the brain, modified by the external environment and influenced more directly by the glands."

He looked saddened, and shook his head reprovingly.

"You are so wrong—so very wrong. Some are always conscious of their souls, others, like yourself, are unaware of them, but no one knows the true value of his soul as long as he has it. It is not until a man has lost his soul that he understands its value."

It was not an observation making for easy rejoinder, so I let the silence between us continue. Presently he looked up into the northern sky where the trail of the moon-bound shuttle had long since blown away. With embarrassment I observed two large tears flow from the inner corners of his eyes and trickle down beside his nose. He, however, showed no embarrassment; he simply pulled out a large, white, beautifully laundered handkerchief, and dealt with them.

"I hope you will never learn what a dreadful thing it is to have no soul," he told me, with a shake of his head. "It is to hold the emptiness of space in one's heart: to sit by the waters of Babylon for the rest of one's life."

Lamely I said:

"I'm afraid this is out of my range. I don't understand."

"Of course you don't. No one understands. But always one keeps on hoping that one day there will come somebody who does understand and can help."

"But the soul is a manifestation of the self," I said. "I don't see how that *can* be lost—it can be changed, perhaps, but not lost."

"Mine is," he said, still looking up into the vast blue. "Lost adrift somewhere out there. Without it I am a sham. A man who has lost a leg or an arm is still a man, but a man who has lost his soul is nothing—nothing—nothing…"

"Perhaps a psychiatrist—" I started to suggest, uncertainly. That stirred him, and checked the tears.

"Psychiatrist!" he exclaimed scornfully. "Damned frauds! Even to the word. They may know a bit about minds; but about the psyche! —why they even deny its existence…!"

There was a pause.

"I wish I could help…" I said, rather vaguely.

"There was a chance. You *might* have been one who could. There's always the chance…" he said consolingly, though whether he was consoling himself or me seemed moot. At this point the church clock struck two. My host's mood changed. He got up quite briskly.

"I have to go now," he told me. "I wish you had been the one, but it has been a pleasant encounter all the same. I hope you enjoy Lahua."

---

I WATCHED HIM make his way along the *place*. At one stall he paused, selected a peach-like fruit and bit into it. The woman beamed at him amiably, apparently unconcerned about payment.

The dusky waitress arrived by my table, and stood looking after him.

"*O le pauvre monsieur Georges,*" she said sadly. We watched him climb the church steps, throw away the remnant of his fruit, and remove his hat to enter. "*Il va faire la prière,*" she explained. "*Tous les jours* 'e make pray for 'is soul. In ze morning, in ze afternoon. *C'est si triste.*"

I noticed the bill in her hand. I fear that for a moment I misjudged George, but it had been a good lunch. I reached for my notecase. The girl noticed, and shook her head.

"*Non, non, monsieur, non. Vous êtes convive. C'est d'accord. Alors, monsier Georges* 'e sign bill tomorrow. *S'arrange. C'est okay,*" she insisted, and stuck to it.

The elderly man whom I had noticed before broke in:

"It's all right—quite in order," he assured me. Then he added: "Perhaps if you are not in a hurry you would care to take a café-cognac with me?"

There seemed to be a fine open-handedness about Lahua. I accepted, and joined him.

"I'm afraid no one can have briefed you about poor George," he said.

I admitted this was so. He shook his head in reproof of persons unknown, and added:

"Never mind. All went well. George always has hopes of a stranger, you see: sometimes one has been known to laugh. We don't like that."

"I'm sorry to hear that," I told him. "His state strikes me as very far from funny."

"It is indeed," he agreed. "But he's improving. I doubt whether he knows it himself, but he is. A year ago he would often weep quietly through the whole *déjeuner*. Rather depressing until one got used to it."

"He lived here in Lahua, then?" I asked.

"He exists. He spends more of his time in the church. For the rest he wanders round. He sleeps at that big white house up on the hill. His granddaughter's place. She sees that he's decently turned out, and pays the bills for whatever he fancies down here."

I thought I must have misheard.

"His granddaughter!" I exclaimed. "But he's a young man. He can't be much over thirty…"

He looked at me.

"You'll very likely come across him again. Just as well to know how things stand. Of course it isn't the sort of thing the family likes to publicize, but there's no secret about it."

The café-cognacs arrived. He added cream to his, and began:

About five years ago (he said), yes, it would be in 2194, young Gerald Troon was taking a ship out to one of the larger asteroids—the one that de Gasparis called Psyche when he spotted it in 1852. The ship was a space-built freighter called the *Celestis,* working from the moon-base. Her crew was five, with not bad accommodation forward. Apart from that and the motor-section these ships are not much more than one big hold which is very often empty on the outward journeys unless it is carrying gear to set up new workings. This time it was empty because the assignment was simply to pick up a load of uranium ore—Psyche is half made of high-yield ore, and all that was necessary was to set going the digging machinery already on the site, and load the stuff in. It seemed simple enough.

# THE ASTEROIDS, 2194

But the Asteroid Belt is still a very tricky area, you know. The main bodies and groups are charted, of course—but that only helps you to find them. The place is full of outfliers of all sizes that you couldn't hope to chart, but have to avoid. About the best you can do is to tackle the Belt as near to your objective as possible, reduce speed until you are little more than local orbit velocity and then edge your way in, going very canny. The trouble is the time it can take to keep on fiddling along that way for thousands—hundreds of thousands, maybe—of miles. Fellows get bored and inattentive, or sick to death of it and start to take chances. I don't know what the answer is. You can bounce radar off the big chunks and hitch that up to a course-deflector to keep you away from them. But the small stuff is just as deadly to a ship, and there's so much of it about that if you were to make the course-deflector sensitive enough to react to it you'd have your ship shying off everything the whole time, and getting nowhere. What we want is someone to come up with a kind of repulse mechanism with only a limited range of operation—say, a hundred miles—but no one does. So, as I say, it's tricky. Since they first started to tackle it back in 2150 they've lost half a dozen ships in there and had a dozen more damaged one way or another. Not a nice place at all… On the other hand, uranium is uranium…

Gerald's a good lad though. He had the authentic Troon yen for space without being much of a chancer; besides, Psyche isn't too far from the inner rim of the orbit—not nearly the approach problem Ceres is, for instance—what's more, he'd done it several times before.

Well, he got into the Belt, and jockeyed and fiddled and niggled his way until he was about three hundred miles out from Psyche and getting ready to come in. Perhaps he'd got a bit careless by then; in any case he'd not be expecting to find anything in orbit around the asteroid. But that's just what he did find—the hard way…

There was a crash which made the whole ship ring round him and his crew as if they were in an enormous bell. It's about the nastiest—and very likely to be the last—sound a spaceman can ever hear. This time, however, their luck was in. It wasn't too bad. They discovered that as they crowded to watch the indicator dials. It was soon evident that nothing vital had been hit, and they were able to release their breath.

Gerald turned over the controls to his First, and he and the engineer, Steve, pulled spacesuits out of the locker. When the airlock opened they hitched their safety-lines on to spring hooks, and slid their way aft along the hull on magnetic soles. It was soon clear that the damage was not on the airlock side, and they worked round the curve of the hull.

One can't say just what they expected to find—probably an embedded hunk of rock, or maybe just a gash in the side of the hold—anyway it was certainly not what they did find, which was half of a small spaceship projecting out of their own hull.

One thing was evident right away—that it had hit with no great force. If it had, it would have gone right through and out the other side, for the hold of a freighter is little more than a single-walled cylinder: there is no need for it to be more, it doesn't have to conserve warmth, or contain air, or resist the friction of an atmosphere, nor does it have to contend with any more gravitational pull than that of the moon; it is only in the living-quarters that there have to be the complexities necessary to sustain life.

Another thing, which was immediately clear, was that this was not the only misadventure that had befallen the small ship. Something had, at some time, sliced off most of its after part, carrying away not only the driving tubes but the mixing-chambers as well, and leaving it hopelessly disabled.

—

SHUFFLING ROUND THE wreckage to inspect it, Gerald found no entrance. It was thoroughly jammed into the hole it had made, and its airlock must lie forward, somewhere inside the freighter. He sent Steve back for a cutter and for a key that would get them into the hold. While he waited he spoke through his helmet-radio to the operator in the *Celestis*'s living-quarters, and explained the situation. He added:

"Can you raise the Moon-Station just now, Jake? I'd better make a report."

"Strong and clear, Cap'n," Jake told him.

"Good. Tell them to put me on to the Duty Officer, will you."

He heard Jake open up and call. There was a pause while the waves crossed and re-crossed the millions of miles between them, then a voice:

"Hullo, *Celestis*! Hullo *Celestis*! Moon-Station responding. Go ahead, Jake. Over!"

Gerald waited out the exchange patiently. Radio waves are some of the things that can't be hurried. In due course another voice spoke.

"Hello, *Celestis*! Moon-Station Duty Officer speaking. Give your location and go ahead."

"Hullo, Charles. This is Gerald Troon calling from *Celestis* now in orbit about Psyche. Approximately three-twenty miles altitude. I am notifying damage by collision. No harm to personnel. *Not* repeat *not* in danger. Damage appears to be confined to empty hold-section. Cause of damage…" He went on to give particulars, and concluded: "I am about to investigate. Will report further. Please keep the link open. Over!"

The engineer returned, floating a self-powered cutter with him on a short safety-cord, and holding the key which would screw back the bolts of the hold's entrance-port. Gerald took the key, placed it in the hole beside the door, and inserted his legs into the two staples that would give him the purchase to wind it.

The moon man's voice came again.

"Hullo, Ticker. Understand no immediate danger. But don't go taking any chances, boy. Can you identify the derelict?"

"Repeat no danger," Troon told him. "Plumb lucky. If she'd hit six feet farther forward we'd have had real trouble. I have now opened small door of the hold, and am going in to examine the forepart of the derelict. Will try to identify it."

The cavernous darkness of the hold made it necessary for them to switch on their helmet lights. They could now see the front part of the derelict; it took up about half the space there was. The ship had punched through the wall, turning back the tough alloy in curled petals, as though it had been tinplate. She had come to rest with her nose a bare couple of feet short of the opposite side. The two of them surveyed her for some moments. Steve pointed to a ragged hole, some five or six inches across, about halfway along the embedded section. It had a nasty significance that caused Gerald to nod sombrely.

He shuffled to the ship, and on to its curving side. He found the airlock on the top, as it lay in the *Celestis,* and tried the winding key. He pulled it out again.

"Calling you, Charles," he said. "No identifying marks on the derelict. She's not space-built—that is, she could be used in atmosphere. Oldish pattern—well, must be—she's pre the standardization of winding keys, so that takes us back a bit. Maximum external diameter, say, twelve feet. Length unknown—can't say how much after part there was before it was knocked off. She's been holed forward, too. Looks like a small meteorite, about five inches. At speed, I'd say. Just a minute... Yes, clean through and out, with a pretty small exit hole. Can't open the airlock without making a new key. Quicker to cut our way in. Over!"

He shuffled back, and played his light through the small meteor hole. His helmet prevented him getting his face close enough to see anything but a small part of the opposite wall, with a corresponding hole in it.

"Easiest way is to enlarge this, Steve," he suggested.

The engineer nodded. He brought his cutter to bear, switched it on and began to carve from the edge of the hole.

"Not much good, Ticker," came the voice from the moon. "The bit you gave could apply to any one of four ships."

"Patience, dear Charles, while Steve does his bit of fancywork with the cutter," Troon told him.

It took twenty minutes to complete the cut through the double hull. Steve switched off, gave a tug with his left hand, and the joined, inner and outer circles of metal floated away.

"*Celestis* calling moon. I am about to go into the derelict, Charles. Keep open," Troon said.

—

HE BENT DOWN, took hold of the sides of the cut, kicked his magnetic soles free of contact and gave a light pull which took him floating head-first through the hole in the manner of an underwater swimmer. Presently his voice came again, with a different tone:

"I say, Charles, there are three men in here. All in spacesuits—old-time spacesuits. Two of them are belted on to their bunks. The other one is... Oh, his leg's gone. The meteorite must have taken it off... There's a queer— Oh, God, it's his blood frozen into a solid ball...!"

After a minute or so he went on:

"I've found the log. Can't handle it in these gloves, though. I'll take it aboard, and let you have particulars. The two fellows on the bunks seem to be quite intact—their suits I mean. Their helmets have those curved strip-windows so I can't see much of their faces. Must've—that's odd... Each of them has a sort of little book attached by a wire to the suit fastener. On the cover it has: 'Danger—Perigoso' in red, and, underneath: 'Do not remove suit— Read instructions within,' repeated in Portuguese. Then: 'Hapson Survival System.' What would all that mean, Charles? Over!"

While he waited for the reply Gerald clumsily fingered one of the tag-like books and discovered that it opened concertina-wise, a series of small metal plates hinged together printed on one side in English and on the other in Portuguese. The first leaf carried little print, but what there was was striking. It ran "CAUTION! Do *NOT* open suit until you have read these instructions or you will KILL the wearer."

When he had got that far the Duty Officer's voice came in again:

"Hullo, Ticker. I've called the Doc. He says do NOT, repeat NOT, touch the two men on any account. Hang on, he's coming to talk to you. He says the Hapson system was scrapped over thirty years ago— He—oh, here he is..."

Another voice came in:

"Ticker? Laysall here. Charles tells me you've found a couple of Hapsons, undamaged. Please confirm, and give circumstances."

Troon did so. In due course the doctor came back:

"Okay. That sounds fine. Now listen carefully, Ticker. From what you say it's practically certain those two are not dead—yet. They're—well, they're in cold storage. That part of the Hapson system was good. You'll see a kind of boss mounted on the left of the chest. The thing to do in the case of extreme emergency was to slap it good and hard. When you do that it gives a multiple injection. Part of the stuff puts you out. Part of it prevents the building-up in the body of large ice crystals that would damage the tissues. Part of it—oh well, that'll do later. The point is that it works practically a hundred per cent. You get Nature's own deep-freeze in space. And if there's something to keep off direct radiation from the sun you stay like that until somebody finds you—if anyone ever does. Now I take it that these two have been in the dark of an airless ship which is now in the airless hold of your ship. Is that right?"

"That's so, Doc. There are two small meteorite holes, but they would not get direct beams from there."

"Fine. Then keep 'em just like that. Take care they don't get warmed. Don't try anything the instruction-sheet says. The point is that though the success of the Hapson freeze is almost sure, the resuscitation isn't. In fact, it's very dodgy indeed—a poorer than twenty-five-per-cent chance at best. You get lethal crystal formations building up, for one thing. What I suggest is that you try to get 'em back exactly as they are. Our apparatus here will give them the best chance they can have. Can you do that?"

Gerald Troon thought for a moment. Then he said:

"We don't want to waste this trip—and that's what'll happen if we pull the derelict out of our side to leave a hole we can't mend. But if we leave her where she is, plugging the hole, we can at least take on a half-load of ore. And if we pack that well in, it'll help to wedge the derelict in place. So suppose we leave the derelict just as she lies, and the men too, and seal her up to keep the ore out of her. Would that suit?"

"That should be as good as can be done," the doctor replied. "But have a look at the two men before you leave them. Make sure they're secure in their bunks. As long as they are kept in space conditions about the only thing likely to harm them is breaking loose under acceleration, and getting damaged."

"Very well, that's what we'll do. Anyway, we'll not be using any high acceleration the way things are. The other poor fellow shall have a space burial..."

---

AN HOUR LATER both Gerald and his companions were back in the *Celestis*'s living-quarters, and the First Officer was starting to manoeuvre for the spiral-in to Psyche. The two got out of their spacesuits. Gerald pulled the derelict's log from the outside pocket, and took it to his bunk. There he fastened the belt, and opened the book.

Five minutes later Steve looked across at him from the opposite bunk, with concern.

"Anything the matter, Cap'n? You're looking a bit queer."

"I'm feeling a bit queer, Steve... That chap we took out and consigned to space, he was Terence Rice, wasn't he?"

"That's what his disc said," Steve agreed.

"H'm." Gerald Troon paused. Then he tapped the book. "This," he said, "is the log of the *Astarte*. She sailed from the Moon-Station 3 January 2149—forty-five years ago—bound for the Asteroid Belt. There was a crew of three: Captain George Montgomery Troon, engineer Luis Gompez, radio-man Terence Rice...

"So, as the unlucky one was Terence Rice, it follows that one of those two back there must be Gompez, and the other—well, must be George Montgomery Troon, the one who made the Venus landing in 2144... And, incidentally, my grandfather..."

---

"WELL," SAID MY companion, "they got them back all right. Gompez was unlucky, though—at least I suppose you'd call it unlucky—anyway, he didn't come through the resuscitation. George did, of course...

"But there's more to resuscitation than mere revival. There's a degree of physical shock in any case, and when you've been under as long as he had there's plenty of mental shock, too.

"He went under, a youngish man with a young family; he woke up to find himself a great-grandfather; his wife a very old lady who had remarried; his friends gone, or elderly; his two companions in the *Astarte* dead.

"That was bad enough, but worse still was that he knew all about the Hapson System. He knew that when you go into a deep-freeze the whole metabolism comes quickly to a complete stop. You are, by every known definition and test, dead... Corruption cannot set in, of course, but every vital process has stopped; every single feature which we regard as evidence of life has ceased to exist...

"So you are dead...

"So if you believe, as George does, that your psyche, your soul, has independent existence, then it must have left your body when you died.

"And how do you get it back? That's what George wants to know—and that's why he's over there now, praying to be told..."

I leant back in my chair, looking across the *place* at the dark opening of the church door.

"You mean to say that that young man, that George who was here just now, is the very same George Montgomery Troon who made the first landing on Venus, half a century ago?" I said.

"He's the man," he affirmed.

I shook my head, not for disbelief, but for George's sake.

"What will happen to him?" I asked.

"God knows," said my neighbour. "He *is* getting better; he's less distressed than he was. And now he's beginning to show touches of the real Troon obsession to get into space again.

"But what then? ...You can't ship a Troon as crew. And you can't have a Captain who might take it into his head to go hunting through Space for his soul...

"Me, I think I'd rather die just once..."

# A STITCH IN TIME

—

ON THE SHELTERED side of the house the sun was hot. Just inside the open french windows Mrs. Dolderson moved her chair a few inches, so that her head would remain in the shade while the warmth could comfort the rest of her. Then she leant her head back on the cushion, looking out.

The scene was, for her, timeless.

Across the smooth lawn the cedar stood as it had always stood. Its flat spread boughs must, she supposed, reach a little further now than they had when she was a child, but it was hard to tell; the tree had seemed huge then, it seemed huge now. Farther on, the boundary hedge was just as trim and neat as it had always been. The gate into the spinney was still flanked by the two unidentifiable topiary birds, Cocky and Olly—wonderful that they should still be there, even though Olly's tail feathers had become a bit twiggy with age.

The flower-bed on the left, in front of the shrubbery, was as full of colour as ever—well, perhaps a little brighter; one had a feeling that flowers had become a trifle more strident than they used to be, but delightful nevertheless. The spinney beyond the hedge, however, had changed a little; more young trees, some of the larger ones gone. Between the branches were glimpses of pink roof where there had been no neighbours in the old days. Except for that, one could almost, for a moment, forget a whole lifetime.

The afternoon drowsing while the birds rested, the bees humming, the leaves gently stirring, the bonk-bonk from the tennis court round the corner, with an occasional voice giving the score. It might have been any sunny afternoon out of fifty or sixty summers.

Mrs. Dolderson smiled upon it, and loved it all; she had loved it when she was a girl, she loved it even more now.

In this house she had been born; she had grown up in it, married from it, come back to it after her father died, brought up her own two children in it, grown old in it... Some years after the second war she had come very near to losing it—but not quite; and here she still was...

It was Harold who had made it possible. A clever boy, and a wonderful son... When it had become quite clear that she could no longer afford to keep the house up, that it would have to be sold, it was Harold who had persuaded his firm to buy it. Their interest, he had told her, lay not in the house, but in the site—as would any buyer's. The house itself was almost without value now, but the position was convenient. As a condition of sale, four rooms on the south side had been converted into a flat which was to be hers for life. The rest of the house had become a hostel housing some twenty young people who worked in the laboratories and offices which now stood on the north side, on the site of the stables and part of the paddock. One day, she knew, the old house would come down, she had seen the plans, but for the present, for her time, both it and the garden to the south and west could remain unspoilt. Harold had assured her that they would not be required for fifteen or twenty years yet—much longer than she would know the need of them...

Nor, Mrs. Dolderson thought calmly, would she be really sorry to go. One became useless, and, now that she must have a wheelchair, a burden to others. There was the feeling, too, that she no longer belonged—that she had become a stranger in another people's world. It had all altered so much; first changing into a place that it was difficult to understand, then growing so much more complex that one gave up trying to understand. No wonder, she thought, that the old become possessive about *things;* cling to objects which link them with the world that they could understand...

Harold was a dear boy, and for his sake she did her best not to appear too stupid—but, often, it was difficult... Today, at lunch, for instance, he had been so excited about some experiment that was to take place this afternoon. He had

*had* to talk about it, even though he must know that practically nothing of what he said was comprehensible to her. Something about dimensions again—she had grasped that much, but she had only nodded, and not attempted to go further. Last time the subject had cropped up, she had observed that in her youth there had been only three, and she did not see how even all this progress in the world could have added more. This had set him off on a dissertation about the mathematician's view of the world through which it was, apparently, possible to perceive the existence of a series of dimensions. Even the moment of existence in relation to time was, it seemed, some kind of dimension. Philosophically, Harold had begun to explain—but there, and at once, she had lost him. He led straight into confusion. She felt sure that when she was young philosophy, mathematics, and metaphysics had all been quite separate studies—nowadays they seemed to have quite incomprehensibly run together. So this time she had listened quietly, making small, encouraging sounds now and then, until at the end he had smiled ruefully, and told her she was a dear to be so patient with him. Then he had come round the table and kissed her cheek gently as he put his hand over hers, and she had wished him the best of luck with the afternoon's mysterious experiment. Then Jenny had come in to clear the table, and wheel her closer to the window...

The warmth of the slumbrous afternoon carried her into a half-dream, took her back fifty years to just such an afternoon when she had sat here in this very window—though certainly with no thought of a wheelchair in those days—waiting for Arthur...waiting with an ache in her heart for Arthur...and Arthur had never come...

Strange, it was, the way things fell out. If Arthur had come that day she would almost certainly have married him. And then Harold and Cynthia would never have existed. She would have had children, of course, but they would not have been Harold and Cynthia... What a curious, haphazard thing one's existence was... Just by saying "no" to one man, and "yes" to another, a woman might bring into existence a potential murderer... How foolish they all were nowadays—trying to tidy everything up, make life secure, while behind, back in everyone's past, stretched the chance-studded line of women who had said "yes" or "no", as the fancy took them...

Curious that she should remember Arthur now. It must be years since she had thought of him...

She had been quite sure that he would propose that afternoon. It was before she had even heard of Colin Dolderson. And she would have agreed. Oh yes, she would have accepted him.

There had never been any explanation. She had never known *why* he did not come then—or any more. He had never written to her. Ten days, perhaps a fortnight later there had been a somewhat impersonal note from his mother telling her that he had been ill, and the doctor had advised sending him abroad. But after that, nothing at all—until the day she had seen his name in a newspaper, more than two years later...

She had been angry of course—a girl owed that to her pride—and hurt, too, for a time... Yet how could one know that it had not been for the best, in the end? —Would his children have been as dear to her, or as kind, and as clever as Harold and Cynthia...?

Such an infinity of chances...all those genes and things they talked about nowadays...

The thump of tennis-balls had ceased, and the players had gone; back, presumably, to their recondite work. Bees continued to hum purposefully among the flowers; half a dozen butterflies were visiting there too, though in a dilettante, unairworthy-looking way. The farther trees shimmered in the rising heat. The afternoon's drowsiness became irresistible. Mrs. Dolderson did not oppose it. She leant her head back, half aware that somewhere another humming sound, higher in pitch than the bees', had started, but it was not loud enough to be disturbing. She let her eyelids drop...

Suddenly, only a few yards away, but out of sight as she sat, there were feet on the path. The sound of them began quite abruptly, as if someone had just stepped from the grass on to the path—only she would have seen anyone crossing the grass... Simultaneously there was the sound of a baritone voice, singing cheerfully, but not loudly to itself. It, too, began quite suddenly; in the middle of a word in fact:

"'—rybody's doin' it, doin' it, do—'"

The voice cut off suddenly. The footsteps, too, came to a dead stop.

Mrs. Dolderson's eyes were open now—very wide open. Her thin hands gripped the arms of her chair. She recollected the tune: more than that, she was even certain of the voice—after all these years... A silly dream, she told herself... She had been remembering him only a few moments before she closed her eyes... How foolish...!

And yet it was curiously undreamlike... Everything was so sharp and clear, so familiarly reasonable... The arms of the chair quite solid under her fingers...

Another idea leapt into her mind. She had died. That was why it was not like an ordinary dream. Sitting here in the sun, she must have quietly died. The doctor had said it might happen quite unexpectedly... And now it had! She had a swift moment of relief—not that she had felt any great fear of death, but there had been that sense of ordeal ahead. Now it was over—and with no ordeal. As simple as falling asleep. She felt suddenly happy about it; quite exhilarated... Though it was odd that she still seemed to be tied to her chair...

The gravel crunched under shifting feet. A bewildered voice said:

"That's rum! Dashed queer! What the devil's happened?"

Mrs. Dolderson sat motionless in her chair. There was no doubt whatever about the voice.

A pause. The feet shifted, as if uncertain. Then they came on, but slowly now, hesitantly. They brought a young man into her view. —Oh, such a very young man, he looked. She felt a little catch at her heart...

He was dressed in a striped club-blazer, and white flannel trousers. There was a silk scarf round his neck, and, tilted back off his forehead, a straw hat with a coloured band. His hands were in his trousers pockets, and he carried a tennis-racket under his left arm.

She saw him first in profile, and not quite at his best, for his expression was bewildered, and his mouth slightly open as he stared towards the spinney at one of the pink roofs beyond.

"Arthur," Mrs. Dolderson said gently.

He was startled. The racket slipped, and clattered on the path. He attempted to pick it up, take off his hat, and recover his composure all at the same time;

not very successfully. When he straightened his face was pink, and its expression still confused.

He looked at the old lady in the chair, her knees hidden by a rug, her thin, delicate hands gripping the arms. His gaze went beyond her, into the room. His confusion increased, with a touch of alarm added. His eyes went back to the old lady. She was regarding him intently. He could not recall ever having seen her before, did not know who she could be—yet in her eyes there seemed to be something faintly, faintly not unfamiliar.

She dropped her gaze to her right hand. She studied it for a moment as though it puzzled her a little, then she raised her eyes again to his.

"You don't know me, Arthur?" she asked quietly.

There was a note of sadness in her voice that he took for disappointment, tinged with reproof. He did his best to pull himself together.

"I—I'm afraid not," he confessed. "You see I—er—you—er—" he stuck, and then went on desperately: "You must be Thelma's—Miss Kilder's—aunt?"

She looked at him steadily for some moments. He did not understand her expression, but then she told him:

"No. I am not Thelma's aunt."

Again his gaze went into the room behind her. This time he shook his head in bewilderment.

"It's all different—no, sort of half-different," he said, in distress. "I say, I can't have come to the wrong—?" He broke off, and turned to look at the garden again. "No, it certainly isn't that," he answered himself decisively. "But what—what *has* happened?"

His amazement was no longer simple; he was looking badly shaken. His bewildered eyes came back to her again.

"Please—I don't understand—*how* did you know me?" he asked.

His increasing distress troubled her, and made her careful.

"I recognized you, Arthur. We have met before, you know."

"Have we? I can't remember… I'm terribly sorry…"

"You're looking unwell, Arthur. Draw up that chair, and rest a little."

"Thank you, Mrs.—er—Mrs.—?"

"Dolderson," she told him.

"Thank you, Mrs. Dolderson," he said, frowning a little, trying to place the name.

She watched him pull the chair closer. Every movement, every line familiar, even to the lock of fair hair that always fell forward when he stooped. He sat down and remained silent for some moments, staring under a frown, across the garden.

Mrs. Dolderson sat still, too. She was scarcely less bewildered than he, though she did not reveal it. Clearly the thought that she was dead had been quite silly. She was just as usual, still in her chair, still aware of the ache in her back, still able to grip the arms of the chair and feel them. Yet it was not a dream—everything was too textured, too solid, too real in a way that dream things never were... Too sensible, too—that was, they would have been had the young man been any other than Arthur...?

Was it just a simple hallucination? —A trick of her mind imposing Arthur's face on an entirely different young man?

She glanced at him. No, that would not do—he had answered to Arthur's name. Indubitably he was Arthur—and wearing Arthur's blazer, too... They did not cut them that way nowadays, and it was years and years since she had seen a young man wearing a straw hat...?

A kind of ghost...? But no—he was quite solid; the chair had creaked as he sat down, his shoes had crunched on the gravel... Besides, whoever heard of a ghost in the form of a thoroughly bewildered young man, and one, moreover, who had recently nicked himself in shaving...?

He cut her thoughts short by turning his head.

"I thought Thelma would be here," he told her. "She *said* she'd be here. Please tell me, where is she?"

Like a frightened little boy, she thought. She wanted to comfort him, not to frighten him more. But she could think of nothing to say beyond:

"Thelma isn't far away."

"I must find her. She'll be able to tell me what's happened." He made to get up.

She laid a hand on his arm, and pressed down gently.

"Wait a minute," she told him. "What is it that seems to have happened? What is it that worries you so much?"

"This," he said, waving a hand to include everything about them. "It's all different—and yet the same—and yet not… I feel as if—as if I'd gone a little mad."

She looked at him steadily, and then shook her head.

"I don't think you have. Tell me, what is it that's wrong?"

"I was coming here to play tennis—well, to see Thelma really," he amended. "Everything was all right then—just as usual. I rode up the drive and leant my bike against the big fir tree where the path begins. I started to come along the path, and then, just when I reached the corner of the house, everything went funny…"

"Went funny?" Mrs. Dolderson inquired. "What—went funny?"

"Well, nearly everything. The sun seemed to jerk in the sky. The trees suddenly looked bigger, and not quite the same. The flowers in the bed over there went quite a different colour. This creeper which was all over the wall was suddenly only halfway up—and it looks like a different *kind* of creeper. And there are houses over there. I never saw them before—it's just an open field beyond the spinney. Even the gravel on the path looks more yellow than I thought. And this room… It *is* the same room. I know that desk, and the fireplace—and those two pictures. But the paper is quite different. I've never seen that before—but it isn't new, either… Please tell me where Thelma is… I want her to explain it… I *must* have gone a bit mad…"

She put her hand on his, firmly.

"No," she said decisively. "Whatever it is, I'm quite sure it's not that."

"Then what—?" He broke off abruptly, and listened, his head a little on one side. The sound grew. "What is it?" he asked, anxiously.

Mrs. Dolderson tightened her hand over his.

"It's all right," she said, as if to a child. "It's all right, Arthur."

She could feel him grow tenser as the sound increased. It passed right overhead at less than a thousand feet, jets shrieking, leaving the buffeted air behind it rumbling back and forth, shuddering gradually back to peace.

Arthur saw it. Watched it disappear. His face when he turned it back to her was white and frightened. In a queer voice he asked:

"What—what was that?"

Quietly, as if to force calm upon him, she said:

"Just an aeroplane, Arthur. Such horrid, noisy things they are."

He gazed where it had vanished, and shook his head.

"But I've *seen* an aeroplane, and *heard* it. It isn't like that. It makes a noise like a motor-bike, only louder. This was terrible! I don't understand—I don't understand what's happened…" His voice was pathetic.

Mrs. Dolderson made as if to reply, and then checked at a thought, a sudden sharp recollection of Harold talking about dimensions, of shifting them into different planes, speaking of time as though it were simply another dimension… With a kind of shock of intuition she understood—no, understood was too firm a word—she perceived. But, perceiving, she found herself at a loss. She looked again at the young man. He was still tense, trembling slightly. He was wondering whether he was going out of his mind. She must stop that. There was no kind way—but how to be least unkind?

"Arthur," she said, abruptly.

He turned a dazed look on her.

Deliberately she made her voice brisk.

"You'll find a bottle of brandy in that cupboard. Please fetch it—and two glasses," she ordered.

With a kind of sleep-walking movement he obeyed. She filled a third of a tumbler with brandy for him, and poured a little for herself.

"Drink that," she told him. He hesitated. "Go on," she commanded. "You've had a shock. It will do you good. I want to talk to you, and I can't talk to you while you're knocked half-silly."

He drank, coughed a little, and sat down again.

"Finish it," she told him firmly. He finished it. Presently she inquired:

"Feeling better now?"

He nodded, but said nothing. She made up her mind, and drew breath carefully. Dropping the brisk tone altogether, she asked:

"Arthur. Tell me, what day is it today?"

"Day?" he said, in surprise, "Why, it's Friday. It's the—er—twenty-seventh of June."

"But the year, Arthur. What year?"

He turned his face fully towards her.

"I'm not *really* mad, you know. I know who I am, and where I am—I think… It's *things* that have gone wrong, not me. I can tell you—"

"What I want you to tell me, Arthur, is the year." The peremptory note was back in her voice again.

He kept his eyes steadily on hers as he spoke.

"Nineteen-thirteen, of course," he said.

Mrs. Dolderson's gaze went back to the lawn and the flowers. She nodded gently. That was the year—and it had been a Friday; odd that she should remember that. It might well have been the twenty-seventh of June… But certainly a Friday in the summer of nineteen-thirteen was the day he had not come… All so long, long ago…

His voice recalled her. It was unsteady with anxiety.

"Why—why do you ask me that—about the year, I mean?"

His brow was so creased, his eyes so anxious. He was very young. Her heart ached for him. She put her thin fragile hand on his strong one again.

"I—I think I know," he said shakily. "It's—I don't see how, but you wouldn't have asked that unless… That's the queer thing that's happened, isn't it? Somehow it isn't nineteen-thirteen any longer—that's what you mean? The way the trees grew…that aeroplane…" He stopped, staring at her with wide eyes. "You must tell me… Please, please… What's happened to me? —Where am I now? —Where is this…?"

"My poor boy…" she murmured.

"Oh, please…"

*The Times,* with the crossword partly done, was pushed down into the chair beside her. She pulled it out half-reluctantly. Then she folded it over and held it towards him. His hand shook as he took it.

"London, Monday, the first of July," he read. And then, in an incredulous whisper: *"Nineteen-sixty-three!"*

He lowered the page, looked at her imploringly.

She nodded twice, slowly.

They sat staring at one another without a word. Gradually, his expression changed. His brows came together, as though with pain. He looked round jerkily, his eyes darting here and there as if for an escape. Then they came back to her. He screwed them shut for a moment. Then opened them again, full of hurt—and fear.

"Oh, no—no…! No…! You're not… You can't be… You—you told me… You're Mrs. Dolderson, aren't you…? You said you were… You can't—you can't be—Thelma…?"

Mrs. Dolderson said nothing. They gazed at one another. His face creased up like a small child's.

"Oh, God! Oh—oh—oh…!" he cried, and hid his face in his hands.

Mrs. Dolderson's eyes closed for a moment. When they opened she had control of herself again. Sadly she looked on the shaking shoulders. Her thin, blue-veined left hand reached out towards the bowed head, and stroked the fair hair, gently.

Her right hand found the bell-push on the table beside her. She pressed it, and kept her finger upon it…

AT THE SOUND of movement her eyes opened. The venetian blind shaded the room but let in light enough for her to see Harold standing beside her bed.

"I didn't mean to wake you, Mother," he said.

"You didn't wake me, Harold. I was dreaming, but I was not asleep. Sit down, my dear. I want to talk to you."

"You mustn't tire yourself, Mother. You've had a bit of a relapse, you know."

"I dare say, but I find it more tiring to wonder than to know. I shan't keep you long."

"Very well, Mother." He pulled a chair close to the bedside and sat down, taking her hand in his. She looked at his face in the dimness.

"It was you who did it, wasn't it, Harold? It was that experiment of yours that brought poor Arthur here?"

"It was an accident, Mother."

"Tell me."

"We were trying it out. Just a preliminary test. We knew it was theoretically possible. We had shown that if we could—oh, dear, it's so difficult to explain in words—if we could, well, twist a dimension, kind of fold it back on itself, then two points that are normally apart must coincide… I'm afraid that's not very clear…"

"Never mind, dear. Go on."

"Well, when we had our field-distortion-generator fixed up we set it to bring together two points that are normally fifty years apart. Think of folding over a long strip of paper that has two marks on it, so that the marks are brought together."

"Yes?"

"It was quite arbitrary. We might have chosen ten years, or a hundred, but we just picked on fifty. And we got astonishingly close, too, Mother, quite remarkably close. Only a four-day calendar error in fifty years. It's staggered us. The thing we've got to do now is to find out that source of error, but if you'd asked any of us to bet—"

"Yes, dear, I'm sure it was quite wonderful. But what *happened*?"

"Oh, sorry. Well, as I said, it was an accident. We only had the thing switched on for three or four seconds—and he must have walked slap into the field of coincidence right then. An outside—a millions-to-one chance. I wish it had not happened, but we couldn't possibly know…"

She turned her head on the pillow.

"No. You couldn't know," she agreed. "And then?"

"Nothing, really. We didn't know until Jenny answered your bell to find you in a faint, and this chap, Arthur, all gone to pieces, and sent for me.

"One of the girls helped to get you to bed. Doctor Sole arrived, and took a look at you. Then he pumped some kind of tranquillizer into this Arthur. The poor fellow needed it, too—one hell of a thing to happen when all you were expecting was a game of tennis with your best girl.

"When he'd quietened down a bit he told us who he was, and where he'd come from. Well, there was a thing for you! Accidental living proof at the first shot.

"But all *he* wanted, poor devil, was to get back just as soon as he could. He was very distressed—quite a painful business. Doctor Sole wanted to put him right under to stop him cracking altogether. It looked that way, too—and it didn't look as if he'd be any better when he came round again, either.

"We didn't know if we *could* send him back. Transference "forward", to put it crudely, can be regarded as an infinite acceleration of a natural progression, but the idea of transference "back" is full of the most disconcerting implications once you start thinking about it. There was quite a bit of argument, but Doctor Sole clinched it. If there was a fair chance, he said, the chap had a right to try, and we had an obligation to try to undo what we'd done to him. Apart from that, if we did not try we should certainly have to explain to someone how we came to have a raving loony on our hands, and fifty years off course, so to speak.

"We tried to make it clear to this Arthur that we couldn't be sure that it would work in reverse—and that, anyway, there was this four-day calendar error, so at best it wouldn't be exact. I don't think he really grasped that. The poor fellow was in a wretched state; all he wanted was just a chance—any kind of chance—to get out of here. He was simply one-track.

"So we decided to take the risk—after all, if it turned out not to be possible he'd—well, he'd know nothing about it—or nothing would happen at all…

"The generator was still on the same setting. We put one fellow on to that, took this Arthur back to the path by your room, and got him lined up there.

"'Now walk forward,' we told him. 'Just as you were walking when it happened.' And we gave the switch-on signal. What with the doctor's dope and one thing and another he was pretty groggy, but he did his best to pull himself together. He went forward at a kind of stagger. Literal-minded fellow; he was half-crying, but in a queer sort of voice he was trying to sing: 'Everybody's doin' it, do—'

"And then he disappeared—just vanished completely." He paused, and added regretfully: "All the evidence we have now is not very convincing—one tennis-racket, practically new, but vintage, and one straw-hat, ditto."

Mrs. Dolderson lay without speaking. He said:

"We did our best, Mother. We could only try."

"Of course you did, dear. And you succeeded. It wasn't your fault that you couldn't undo what you'd done… No, I was just wondering what would have happened if it had been a few minutes earlier—or later, that you had switched your machine on. But I don't suppose that *could* have happened… You wouldn't have been here at all if it had…"

He regarded her a little uneasily.

"What *do* you mean, Mother?"

"Never mind, dear. It was, as you said, an accident. —At least, I suppose it was—though so many important things seem to be accidents that one does sometimes wonder if they aren't really *written* somewhere…"

Harold looked at her, trying to make something of that, then he decided to ask:

"But what makes you think that we did succeed in getting him back, Mother?"

"Oh, I *know* you did, dear. For one thing I can very clearly remember the day I read in the paper that Lieutenant Arthur Waring Batley had been awarded a D.S.O.—some time in November nineteen-fifteen, I think it was.

"And, for another, I have just had a letter from your sister."

"From Cynthia? How on earth does she come into it?"

"She wants to come and see us. She is thinking of getting married again, and she'd like to bring the young man—well, not such a very *young* man, I suppose—down here to show him."

"That's all right, but I don't see—"

"She thinks you might find him interesting. He's a physicist."

"But—"

Mrs. Dolderson took no notice of the interruption. She went on:

"Cynthia tells me his name is Batley—and he's the son of a Colonel Arthur Waring Batley, D.S.O., of Nairobi, Kenya."

"You mean, he's the son of—?"

"So it would seem, dear. Strange, isn't it?" She reflected a moment, and added: "I must say that if these things *are* written, they do sometimes seem to be written in a very queerly distorted way, don't you think…?"

## COPYRIGHT INFORMATION

"Introduction" Copyright © 2024 by Michael Marshall Smith. First appeared in this volume.

"The Lost Machine" Copyright © 1932 by The Estate of John Wyndham. First appeared in *Amazing Stories*, April 1932, edited by T. O'Conor Sloane, Ph.D.

"Spheres of Hell" Copyright © 1933 by The Estate of John Wyndham. First appeared in *Wonder Stories*, October 1933, edited by Hugo Gernsback.

"The Man from Beyond" Copyright © 1934 by The Estate of John Wyndham. First appeared in *Wonder Stories*, September 1934, edited by Hugo Gernsback.

"Beyond the Screen" Copyright © 1938 by The Estate of John Wyndham. First appeared in *Fantasy, Number 1*, edited by T. Stanhope Sprigg.

"Child of Power" Copyright © 1939 by The Estate of John Wyndham. First appeared in *Fantasy, Number 3*, edited by T. Stanhope Sprigg.

"The Living Lies" Copyright © 1946 by The Estate of John Wyndham. First appeared in *New Worlds*, October 1946, edited by John Carnell.

"The Eternal Eve" Copyright © 1950 by The Estate of John Wyndham. First appeared in *Amazing Stories*, September 1950, edited by Howard Browne.

"Pawley's Peepholes" Copyright © 1951 by The Estate of John Wyndham. First appeared in *Science-Fantasy*, Winter 1951, edited by John Carnell.

"The Wheel" Copyright © 1952 by The Estate of John Wyndham. First appeared in *Startling Stories*, January 1952, edited by Samuel Mines.

"Survival" Copyright © 1952 by The Estate of John Wyndham. First appeared in *Thrilling Wonder Stories*, February 1952, edited by Samuel Mines.

"Chinese Puzzle" Copyright © 1953 by The Estate of John Wyndham. First appeared in *Argosy* (UK), February 1953, edited by Editors of Argosy (UK).

"Perforce to Dream" Copyright © 1954 by The Estate of John Wyndham. First appeared in *Beyond Fantasy Fiction*, January 1954, edited by H. L. Gold.

"Never on Mars" Copyright © 1954 by The Estate of John Wyndham. First appeared in *Fantastic Universe*, January 1954, edited by Beatrice Jones.

"Compassion Circuit" Copyright © 1954 by The Estate of John Wyndham. First appeared in *Fantastic Universe*, December 1954, edited by Leo Margulies.

"Brief to Counsel" Copyright © 1959 by The Estate of John Wyndham. First appeared in *Argosy* (UK), February 1959, edited by Editors of Argosy (UK).

"Odd" Copyright © 1961 by The Estate of John Wyndham. First appeared in *Consider Her Ways and Others*.

"The Asteroids, 2194" Copyright © 1960 by The Estate of John Wyndham. First appeared in *New Worlds Science Fiction*, #100 November, edited by John Carnell.

"A Stitch in Time" Copyright © 1961 by The Estate of John Wyndham. First appeared in *The Magazine of Fantasy and Science Fiction*, March 1961, edited by Robert P. Mills.